# Linda Lael Miller

## EMMA AND THE OUTLAW

POCKET BOOKS

New York  London  Toronto  Sydney  New Delhi

Pocket Books
A Division of Simon & Schuster, Inc.
1230 Avenue of the Americas
New York, NY 10020

This book is a work of fiction. Any references to historical events, real people, or real places are used fictitiously. Other names, characters, places, and events are products of the author's imagination, and any resemblance to actual events or places or persons, living or dead, is entirely coincidental.

This Pocket Books paperback edition September 2014

POCKET and colophon are registered trademarks of Simon & Schuster, Inc.

For information about special discounts for bulk purchases, please contact Simon & Schuster Special Sales at 1-866-506-1949 or business@simonandschuster.com.

The Simon & Schuster Speakers Bureau can bring authors to your live event. For more information or to book an event, contact the Simon & Schuster Speakers Bureau at 1-866-248-3049 or visit our website at www.simonspeakers.com.

Cover illustration by Aleta Rafton

Manufactured in the United States of America

30   29   28   27   26   25   24   23   22   21   20

ISBN 978-0-671-67637-7
ISBN 978-1-4516-5536-0 (ebook)

# Books by Linda Lael Miller

Available from Pocket Books

For Vicki Webster.

*Life is a dance,*
*and she knows the Steps.*

# EMMA AND THE
# OUTLAW

# ❧ *Prologue* ❧

Beaver Crossing, Nebraska
*December 10, 1865*

*E*mma Chalmers stood rooted to the railroad platform, braced like the other orphans, against the biting
chill of a prairie winter and the prospect of being
separated from Lily. The child, at six a year younger than
Emma, clung to her sister's skirts, her brown eyes huge
with alarm. Caroline, their eldest sister, had been
adopted back in Lincoln, and Lily was all Emma had left,
except for the small photograph of them all tucked into
the pocket of her pinafore.

The tiny, wiry woman facing her studied Emma from
the top of her head to the toes of her too-small, pinchy
shoes. She made a tsk-tsk sound, then announced to the
conductor, "I'll take this red-haired one here."

It was a moment before Emma could speak. Her arm
tightened around Lily's thin little shoulders. "Take my
sister, too," she pleaded. "Please, ma'am—don't make
me leave Lily."

The woman grunted derisively. "I'm lucky to get one
girl to help out around the place," she said. "If I brung
home two, Mr. Carver would black my eyes."

Just then the conductor scooped Lily up and carried her, fighting and twisting, away from Emma and back to the train. The parting was so cruel that, for a moment, Emma could not move. Lily was hardly more than a baby. Who would take care of her? Who would protect her from the orphan boys who delighted in teasing her?

Emma didn't move; she just stood on the platform, breathing hard, tears of helplessness and despair brimming in her dark blue eyes, the snow falling like a lace mantilla on her strawberry-blonde hair. She wanted to scream, just throw back her head and *scream,* but she sensed that the Carver woman would slap her if she did.

"Come along, now. Mr. Carver's down at the saloon, and it ain't a good idea to leave him waitin'," said Emma's adoptive mother. She wore a colorless calico dress, a tattered bonnet, and a cloak that looked as though it might have come from the rummage pile. "Mind you don't rile him, now, 'cause Ben's got him a fierce temper."

The train whistle moaned, and steam hissed from the train's engine, rising in clouds around its wheels. Glancing back over one shoulder, Emma looked for Lily in the window of the passenger car, but there was no sign of her.

She followed Mrs. Carver down the slippery, snow-laden steps of the rough board platform. The cold clawed at her through her thin dress and coat, but Emma was numb to that. All she could feel was the slow splintering of her heart. The pain of it nearly took her breath away.

"Adopted yourself a girl, did you, Molly?"

Emma looked around Mrs. Carver's thin frame to see a beautiful woman dressed in a green velvet cloak with a feathered hat to match.

"What if I did, Chloe Reese?" Molly demanded, stiffening like a wall in front of Emma.

The fancy woman reached out to touch Emma's snow-dampened hair. "Mighty pretty little thing."

Molly was still bristling. "She looks fit to work."

The train whistle shrilled again, and the sound went through Emma like a bayonet. Her small shoulders stooped slightly, and once more she glanced back at the window. Lily was there, pale face pressed to the sooty glass, searching the crowd of farmers and returning travelers for Emma.

"You must have used up that poor little Alice you got last time," Miss Reese remarked, opening her fine handbag. Molly Carver said nothing to that, but Emma noticed that her hands clenched into fists at her sides. "Don't take her home, Molly," Chloe went on presently. "You know what Benjamin will do to her."

Emma felt a shiver creep up her spine and then down again. For some reason, she thought of Mama's soldier, and how he'd always wanted to hold her on his lap when there was no one else around. She bit down on her lower lip, sensing that something important was happening between these two strangers, one so very different from the other.

Emma's eyes widened when she saw Miss Reese's gloved hand produce a sizable bill from the gold-tasseled handbag. "Here, Molly. You take this, and you tell your man there weren't any good orphans to be had this time."

Molly's brown hand trembled as she reached for the bribe. "You gonna make her into a whore?"

Emma's breath caught. She'd heard men call her mother by that word, though they'd all seemed to like pretty Kathleen well enough. She knew the word meant something bad.

Chloe Reese's emerald green eyes moved over Emma in a gentle assessment, and humor curved her painted lips. "I think not," she said quietly. "Truth is, I've always wanted a little girl of my very own."

Molly's cracked shoes made a crunching sound in the snow as she walked away without looking back, taking Chloe's money with her.

"Come along, now," Chloe said in a kindly voice. "We'll get you some food and something decent to wear. You must be a real looker when that hair of yours is brushed."

Behind them the train was grinding into motion.

Emma turned, her heart in her throat and her vision blurred, to wave at her sister. Lily, having found her at last, waved back.

"Was that your friend?" Chloe asked as she led Emma away to a fine buggy waiting on the other side of the tiny depot.

Emma couldn't speak, she was so overcome by the magnitude of her loss. First Caroline, and now Lily. And already Lily probably needed to go—she had a dreadful way of always having to use the pot when it was most inconvenient for everyone—and those terrible boys at the back of the car would tease her.

"There, now," Chloe said, her clothes and skin giving off a pleasant, flowery scent on that snowy December day. "You'll have other friends, once we get settled out in Whitneyville. That's in Idaho, honey."

Emma sat, shivering and confused, in the buggy seat beside her benefactress, praying that someone, somewhere, would look after Lily. She was so little, and she'd never been alone before.

"Don't say much, do you?" Chloe smacked the horse with the reins and it leaped forward through the snow, bells jingling on its brown leather harness.

Emma thought with bleak irony of all the times Mama had slapped her across the mouth for talking too much. "No, ma'am," she said, her voice small and raw from tears shed and unshed, "Gramma used to say I could make a scarecrow get restless."

Chloe laughed at that, and the sound was a bit too hearty to be ladylike. But then, Emma had already guessed that Chloe wasn't exactly a lady. "So you had a grandma, did you? How did you end up on an orphan train, if you have folks?"

The question stung her, made her stiffen her back and run her coat sleeve across her eyes and nose in an effort to regain her dignity. "Gramma died last winter. Then Mama took up with a soldier, and he didn't want us. He said she had to put us on the orphan train, so she did."

The pity in Chloe's eyes was carefully veiled, and

Emma liked her for that. "Us? How many of you were there?"

"Three," Emma answered in utter despondency. "Caroline got adopted yesterday, in Lincoln. Lily's still on the train."

"Is she older than you, this Lily?"

Emma shook her head. "Lily's only six, and I'm seven." Fidgeting, she found the paper the woman at the orphanage in Chicago had pinned to her coat. It had a thirty-two written on it in firm, neat numerals. She tore it off and threw it, crumpled, into the muddy snow alongside the road.

"Dear Lord," Chloe muttered, and it seemed she was speaking more to herself than Emma. "What kind of people send babies west, all on their own, to be fair game to men like Benjamin Carver?"

Since she knew no answer was expected—indeed, she didn't have one—Emma said nothing at all. Besides, she could hear the train rattling off into the distance, and she felt like screaming again.

The store fronts of the bustling prairie town stood on either side of the single, muddy road that led through Beaver Crossing. Emma looked at the gowns and hats in the dressmaker's window, seeing through them to a very little girl, with fair hair and wide, haunted eyes, all alone on a train headed west.

"She'll be all right," Chloe said, holding the reins in one hand so she could pat Emma on the shoulder with the other. "The good Lord, He looks after the young ones. Didn't He watch over you by having me be at the station to see one of my girls off when you came in?"

Emma could follow neither Chloe's logic nor the Lord's, but she looked at her with wary interest. "You have other girls besides me?"

Chloe smiled as she brought the buggy to a stop in front of a large building. Emma couldn't read the big gilded sign over the door, but she was a city girl, and she guessed accurately that the place was a hotel. "Yes, I have other girls. But they're not daughters. You're going to be my own child from now on." She paused to laugh disbelievingly. "Lord have mercy, I don't even know your name."

"It's Emma," the girl said politely. "Emma Chalmers."

Chloe put out a strong gloved hand. "Good to meet you, Emma Chalmers. My name's Chloe Reese, if you didn't catch it before." She wound the reins expertly around the rig's brake lever and, gathering her skirts and cloak in one hand, climbed down to stand on the frozen, rutted ground. "Come along now, Emma. You're a thin little thing. It's time you had a good meal."

Emma's throat closed, and she knew she wouldn't be able to eat for thinking of Lily, who'd probably get a withered, spotty apple and some cold tea to last her the whole day. "I-I'm not very hungry," she answered, getting down from the buggy to the wooden sidewalk.

Her rescuer touched Emma's wind-stung cheek gently. "You mean to find your sisters someday, don't you?"

Emma nodded. "Oh, yes, ma'am. I promised Caroline I'd remember everything important—"

"Well," Chloe broke in amiably, "you'll need to keep your strength up for that, won't you?"

After swallowing hard and giving the matter several moments of deep and sober thought, Emma nodded. Starving herself wouldn't keep Lily from being hungry. "Yes, ma'am," she said.

Chloe led her inside the hotel, and they were soon seated at a wooden table with a cloth as white as new snow spread over it. Pulling off her gloves and laying them aside, Chloe smiled at her charge. "Well, now, tell me what you like to do."

Delicious smells were coming from the kitchen, and a woman approached, with a pad and pencil in her hand. Suddenly, Emma knew she was ravenous.

"I like to eat," she said eagerly.

Chloe laughed again. "And what else? Do you draw pictures? Ride horses?"

Emma shook her head. "I don't know how to do much

of anything, except sweep and sing and look after Lily so she doesn't get lost."

Sadness moved in Chloe's pretty face, but she was distracted, talking to the woman with the pad and pencil. She asked for two chicken dinners, coffee for herself, and a big glass of milk for Emma.

When the food came, however, Emma could only look at it for a long time, thinking how Lily's brown eyes would have gone wide at the sight of such a feast. She and Caroline would have grabbed for a drumstick.

Emma's hand trembled slightly as she took up her fork. She didn't miss her mother, or the soldier, but what in the name of heaven was she going to do without her sisters?

# Chapter
### ❧ 1 ❧

Whitneyville, Idaho Territory
*April 15, 1878*

*T*he keening whine of the train whistle deepened Emma Chalmers' despair at the ending of *Anna Karenina,* and she sniffled as she slammed the book closed. She then hastily dried her eyes with a wadded handkerchief trimmed in blue tatting and smoothed the skirts of her prim brown sateen dress.

Grabbing up a new supply of posters she'd just had printed over at the newspaper office, Emma dashed for the door. The Whitneyville Lending Library was empty, and she didn't bother to lock up, since no one she knew would have stooped so low as to steal a book, and she'd collected only two cents in fines.

She saw a slim figure reflected back to her as she passed the spotless windows of the general store. Emma quickened her steps, as it had been her experience that some of the conductors and stagecoach drivers would evade her if given the opportunity.

As she passed the Yellow Belly Saloon, with its peeling paint and sagging porch, the smells of whiskey and sawdust and beer and sweat came out to wrap themselves around her like an insidious vine. Emma broke into **a** ladylike sprint, clutching her posters to her shapely bosom with one hand and keeping her skirts out of the dirt and tobacco juice on the sidewalk with the other. Her bright hair, pulled into a single thick plait, swung as she ran.

The railroad yard was crowded with arriving and departing passengers. Most were human, but there were some pigs and horses and an occasional crate of squawking chickens.

Emma picked her way through the throng as daintily as she could, and with a practiced eye sought out the conductor. A well-fed man with a ruddy complexion and thick white hair, he was half-hidden behind a shipment of canned meats bound for the general store.

After clearing her throat, a sound barely discernible in the din, Emma approached. "Good afternoon, Mr. Lathrop," she said politely.

"Miss Emma," Mr. Lathrop answered with a nod of his bushy head. His blue eyes revealed both kindness and apprehension. "I'm afraid there's no news today. It just seems like nobody in this whole part of the country knows anything about your sisters."

Even though she'd expected this answer—after all, she'd gotten virtually the same one every week for nearly thirteen years—Emma was stricken, for a moment, with the purest of sorrow. "If—if you would just pass these bills out, as you go along—"

Mr. Lathrop accepted the stack of crisply printed placards and held one up, with great ceremony, for his pensive perusal. It read:

REWARD! $500 CASH!
For any information leading
to the location of MISS CAROLINE CHALMERS,
dark of hair and eyes, or
MISS LILY CHALMERS, fair, and having brown eyes.
Please contact MISS EMMA CHALMERS
In care of the Whitneyville Lending Library
Whitneyville, Idaho Territory

"Perhaps I should have said 'thank you,'" Emma fretted, bending around Mr. Lathrop's ample shoulder to read the bold print.

The conductor smiled gently. "I figure it's plain enough that you'd be grateful for any help, Miss Emma."

She sighed. "Sometimes it just seems hopeless. Sort of like the ending of *Anna Karenina*. Have you read that book, Mr. Lathrop?"

He looked bewildered. "Not so as I remember, Miss Emma. A man doesn't get much chance to read when he spends his days on the rails."

Emma nodded soberly as she handed over the rest of the posters. "I suppose not. The noise would be powerfully distracting, I should think."

It was Mr. Lathrop's solemn duty to see that pigs and people found their proper places aboard the train. Therefore, he left Emma, her posters in his arms, after favoring her with a little tip of his hat. Every Christmas, Emma remembered him with a pair of knitted socks and a box of walnut fudge, and she wondered now if that was proper recompense for a man who had tried so steadfastly to be helpful.

Pausing for just a moment, Emma scanned the arriving and departing passengers, for she'd never stopped hoping to find one of her sisters among them. Walking alongside the track, she nearly collided with a ramp extending from one of the boxcars.

Not to mention the man and horse coming *down* that ramp.

Emma gave a startled gasp and leaped backwards, while the man smiled at her from the saddle and touched the brim of his battered hat. He looked like a seedy saddlebum, with no gentle qualities to recommend him, and yet Emma felt a not unpleasant tug in the pit of her stomach as she returned his regard.

"You ought to look where you're going," she said crisply.

Controlling his mount with barely perceptible movements of his gloved hands, the stranger urged the nervous horse into the dirt and cinders at the side of the tracks. Apparently, he found the fact that Emma had taken umbrage very amusing, because he was still grinning, his teeth wickedly white against a sun-browned, beard-stubbled face.

He gave a mocking bow from the waist. "My apologies, your ladyship," he said. Then he let out a low hoot of laughter and rode off.

Emma smoothed her hair, then sighed as she lifted her skirts and started back the way she'd come. It seemed to her that no one bothered to cultivate good manners any longer.

Because something about the man on the horse had disturbed her, Emma forcibly shifted her mind to the search for her sisters. Even if she came face to face with Lily or Caroline, she thought in despair, she might not recognize them. People could change so much in thirteen years. They would be grown women now.

Emma did not come out of her reverie until she was passing the First Territorial Bank. Through the window, she spotted Fulton Whitney, who made no secret of the fact that he aspired to be her husband. He was tall and blond and he looked very handsome in his gray pin-striped trousers, with a vest over his white linen shirt, and there was a gentlemanly garter on his sleeve.

He smiled distractedly at Emma's wave, and she went on walking, knowing Fulton would be displeased if she slipped inside the bank to speak to him. Business was business, he always said, and Emma belonged to another part of his life.

Emma frowned as she continued along the sidewalk. Sometimes Fulton made her feel like a straw hat stuck away on a wardrobe shelf for the winter, and it worried her that her pulse never quickened when she looked at him.

Lifting her skirts again, Emma looked both ways and

then crossed the road, wishing to avoid further contact with the Yellow Belly Saloon. It was so much pleasanter to look at the shining blue waters of Crystal Lake, hardly more than a stone's throw from the main street of town.

Fulton firmly believed that Whitneyville would some-day be a thriving resort city because of that enormous and beautiful lake, and he'd invested his money accordingly. Chloe had chosen the town for the same reason.

Cheery music flowed from the Stardust Saloon, and Emma marked the spritely beat with small movements of her head while she hurried on to the library. She found the place empty, as usual, and was just putting *Anna Karenina* back on the shelf when a thunderous explosion rocked the walls and rattled the windows in their frames.

Emma's heart did a startled double beat as she hurried to the front door to look out, fully expecting to see the Lord Himself riding on a cloud above, surrounded by His angels. The world had ended, and it only remained to be seen whether she would be taken to heaven or left behind to swim in a lake of fire.

But there wasn't a cloud in the sky, and there was certainly no sign of the Lord. Emma was quite relieved, for there were those who said she was as much a sinner as Chloe and there might not have been space for her in Glory.

People were running past her in the street, and shouts of excitement rose all around. The fire bell was clanging, and Emma caught the acrid scent of smoke.

She hadn't moved more than three or four steps when she realized that the Yellow Belly Saloon was nearly in ruins. Its front had completely disappeared, showing the men inside draped over tables like rag dolls forgotten in a playhouse. And there was a fire, picking up momentum with every passing second.

For all the clanging clamor of the bell, Emma could see no sign of the fire wagon, with its long hoses and special pump. She pressed closer to watch as townsmen dragged the injured out into the crowded street.

"Get back!" shouted Doc Waverly, who had never been known for his patient nature. "Get back, damn it, and give these poor bastards some air!"

Emma's cheeks heated at the doctor's language, but she remained where she was. It was as though she were helping somehow, just by being there.

Although she stood on tiptoe, she couldn't get a good look at any of the wounded men, but she did see Chloe and her girls flowing across the street from the Stardust Saloon in a river of brightly colored silks and satins.

"What the hell happened here, Doc?" Ethan Peters, the editor of the *Whitneyville Orator*, wanted to know.

"I've got no idea," answered the bristly old man who had been mending broken limbs and removing bullets and infected toenails in Whitneyville almost since the day of its founding, "and don't get in our way. When somebody knows the story, we'll damned well tell you about it!"

Emma bit her lip briefly as she watched some of the men carrying the wounded, under Doc Waverly's supervision, into the Stardust Saloon. She got as close as she could, but even now, at the age of twenty, Emma didn't dare defy Chloe's standing order that she never set foot inside the place.

She waited on the sidewalk until all the excitement had died down, until the smoldering remains of the Yellow Belly Saloon were drenched in water pumped from the lake, and then she went slowly back to the library.

Emma stayed there until closing time, cataloging books and consuming a page or two of *Little Women* whenever she got the chance. People came in and out all afternoon, but none of them seemed to know any more about the calamity at the Yellow Belly Saloon than Emma did.

At five o'clock sharp she closed the library door, locked it with a long brass key, and set out for home. If there was one person in the whole town, besides Doc, who would know the complete story, it was Chloe.

A fine film of sweat lay over Steven Fairfax's body when he came to. He saw a papered wall with blue flowers on it, and a pair of lace curtains that seemed to be trying to blend into each other. He started to sit up, but the pain stopped him, squeezing his ribcage like a giant fist.

He fell back onto the pillows with a muttered curse and felt at his hip for the Colt .45 he was never without. It was gone, holster and all.

His first instinct was to bellow a protest, but he stopped himself. After all, he didn't know exactly where he was, or what had happened to him. There was a damn good chance that his half brother, Macon, had finally caught up with him.

Breathing hard, he tried to think. To remember. Slowly, the events of the day began to come back to him.

He'd come into town on the train, left his horse in a livery stable, and looked for a place to have a drink and wash the soot from his throat. He'd wandered into a hole called the Yellow Belly, partly because its name had made him smile, and partly because he was too damned dirty for the Stardust, which looked like it might offer gentler comforts.

He'd ordered a whiskey and sat down alone at a table in the rear, following his rule of always keeping his back to the wall so no one could sneak up behind him. He'd learned that lesson in the war, and it had stood him in good stead ever since.

Steven hadn't taken more than a few sips of his whiskey—he remembered a slight chagrin at the realization that a glass of cold lemonade would have tasted better—when the drunk weaved in through a back entrance, singing at the top of his lungs. Nobody had paid much attention, including Steven.

It was only when the man climbed up onto a table and started singing a birthday song that Steven began to take notice. The old codger was holding a stick of dynamite in one hand. "This here's my birthday," he announced to the quiet revelers. Then, incredibly, he struck a match to the sole of his boot and lit the short fuse of the dynamite. When the men around him lunged for him, he was alternately singing to himself and puffing ineffectually at the flaming fuse, as though it were a candle on a cake.

One of the men managed to get hold of the dynamite stick and fling it away, but Steven couldn't remember much beyond that, except for an earsplitting noise, pain, and then blinding darkness.

He had to know where he was now.

He lifted his head from the soft pillow, which smelled pleasantly of starch and fresh air. "Hello? Somebody? Anybody!"

No one answered his call. Maybe this was a hotel room, instead of a house. Steven tried to roll onto his side to get a better look, but the pain was too strong. It pressed him onto his back again.

He was fighting to keep from losing consciousness when the door opened and a stranger walked in. Steven would have drawn on him if he'd had his .45; instead, his hand slapped uselessly against his thigh.

"Relax, son," said the old man, and Steven finally noticed that he was carrying a battered doctor's bag. "I'm here to help you."

"Where's my forty-five?" Steven rasped.

The doctor shrugged. "Wherever Chloe puts guns, I suppose," he answered. He was a paunchy middle-aged man with a balding pate, and he wore gold-rimmed spectacles on the end of his nose. "You won't need any firearms here. What's your name, boy?"

Steven tried to think of an alias and found that he couldn't. His brain was like frozen horseshit. "Steven Fairfax," he admitted. "And I'm not a boy, damn it. I fought in the war, same as you probably did."

His bristly response brought a smile from the doctor, who was setting his bag on a table beside Steven's bed.

"Name's Dr. Waverly," he said, "but you can call me Doc. Are you in a lot of pain?"

Steven glared up at him. "Hell, no, you damned Yankee—I never felt better in my life!"

Doc laughed at that. "Spare me the Rebel yells, Johnny. The war's been over for a long time." He was filling a syringe, holding it up to the light from the window with the lace curtains. "What brings you to Whitneyville?"

"I'm just passing through," Steven answered grudgingly. "And you keep that needle away from me."

The doctor smiled again. "Sorry, Reb. It just so happens that I'm giving the orders around here. Luckily for you, I'm on your side."

Steven's shirt was in rags on his chest, and the doctor had an easy time finding a place on his upper arm to swab with cool alcohol. The pain wouldn't allow him to struggle, so he endured the puncture of the needle.

"Just a little morphine," Doc Waverly said. "We've got to move you and wrap those ribs of yours, not to mention taking a few stitches here and there. Believe me, you'll be happier asleep."

Steven was already being pushed into a dark corner of his mind. Resisting the stuff was no good; it had him, dead to rights.

He felt himself drifting, though, and for a while he was aware of momentary stabs of pain. Then, suddenly, he was back at Fairhaven, his father's house outside of New Orleans, and he was a boy again.

He and Maman were sitting in a carriage on the road, admiring the palatial white house in the distance. It had brick walks and sprawling green lawns, and he could see a fountain rising from the garden, spewing diamonds against a bright blue sky.

"Someday you'll live here, where you belong," Maman said sadly, in her musical French accent. *"Oui,* you too will be a Fairfax—no longer will you call yourself Dupris."

Seated there beside his mother, Steven knew the first true hunger of his life. And it wasn't the sort that could be satisfied with good Cajun cooking. It was a spiritual craving, like looking upon heaven from the borders of hell.

Steven's drugged mind spun forward from that point, carrying him to the afternoon of his father's funeral. He stood beyond the high wrought-iron gates, watching as Beau Fairfax's casket was carried into a stone mausoleum. The man had never acknowledged him, but old Cyrus, patriarch of the dwindling Fairfax family, saw him there and approached, looking dignified in his black suit, despite the summer heat.

"You're Monique's boy?" he asked.

By that time Steven was sixteen years old and he'd been at St. Matthew's School for Boys for four terms. "Yes, sir," he answered his grandfather.

"I was sorry to hear that Monique passed away of the fever."

Steven hardened his spirit against the memory. New Orleans was occupied by Union troops, his mother was gone, and nothing was as it had been before. "Thank you, sir," he said.

"I'd like you to come back to Fairhaven with me. There's mention of you in your daddy's will."

Steven shook his head. "I don't want anything from him."

"You plannin' on slippin' past enemy lines and joinin' up with General Lee, boy?"

The question had caught Steven off-guard, perhaps because it was precisely what he meant to do. He hesitated between a lie and the truth, and in that moment Cyrus Fairfax discerned what he needed to know.

"Don't be a fool, Steven. Leave this fight to them that are suited to it."

Steven was not overly tall at five foot eleven, but he was solidly built and an expert at fencing. He'd been the champion for two years running at St. Matthew's. He shoved a hand through his longish brown hair, and his hazel eyes snapped with the French fire spawned in him by his mother's blood. "I could beat any Yankee," he boasted.

Despite the somberness of the occasion, Cyrus had actually chuckled at that. "I reckon you think so, anyway. Tell me, since those blue-bellies have overstayed their welcome here in New Orleans, how is it that you haven't gotten rid of them before now?"

Steven felt his face fill with color. "I would if Father O'Shay didn't lock up the rapiers after fencing class every day."

At this the old man had laughed outright. "Come to Fairhaven," he repeated when he'd composed himself. "You'll have all the fighting you need there. Your half-brother Macon will probably bloody your nose a time or two, but I reckon you'll be able to hold your own once you've developed a strategy." He leaned a little closer to the high fence that separated them. "Macon's the sneaky type, you know. Got to watch your back around him."

Steven was intrigued, in spite of himself, and the next day when a carriage came to St. Matthew's to fetch him, he went without protest. Although he had himself convinced this was only a ploy to avoid his Latin lesson, he'd become more and more curious about the man he'd scarcely known.

Sure enough, Macon had proved to be a son-of-a-bitch and a coward, never uttering a word of protest when the Yankees took over Fairhaven's ballroom as one of their command posts. Steven had stayed only two months after that, and then he'd taken the horse Cyrus had given him, along with a Yankee uniform snatched from the clothes line, and he'd ridden out.

The moment he was beyond the reach of the occupation army, he tore that uniform off as though it burned his skin and changed back into his own clothes. A week after that he became a private in General Lee's army . . .

"Say, Mister? Mister!"

Steven came back to himself, opened his eyes, and saw an aging painted face suspended above his. It was surrounded by elaborately coiffed hair of an unlikely shade of red, but it was friendly.

"Lord knows, you'd probably like a bath better than anything," the woman said companionably, "but the doc said some food would help more, so I brought you a bowl of Daisy's chicken and dumplings."

Steven looked somewhat wildly at the tray in her hands, and at the walls visible on either side of her slim, satin-clad body. The wallpaper was different here, and the bed faced in another direction. "Where the devil am I?" he demanded, easing himself upward a little way on the pillows. Although the motion was difficult, it was no longer impossible.

"My house," the woman said. "My name's Chloe Reese, and Doc says you're Steven Fairfax, so you don't need to introduce yourself."

"What a relief," Steven remarked, with only mild sarcasm. His stomach was rumbling; he wanted the food she offered.

Chloe smiled. "No need to be nasty, now. After all, if it weren't for me and my girls, you might be lying in the back of the feed store, instead of in this comfortable bed."

He accepted the tray and began to eat, and it was only then that he noticed the wrapping around his ribs and the bandages swathing his stomach and both arms. "Hell," he grumbled, wondering how long it would be before he could leave this town. Macon might already have tracked him here.

"Where's my gun?" he demanded, talking with his mouth full.

"You surely don't have the manners one would expect of a southern boy," Chloe remarked, examining her glossy fingernails. "It's locked away downstairs. I don't allow firearms in my place."

Steven was careful to finish chewing and swallow. He couldn't say he was in danger because Chloe might figure out that he was wanted, and if anybody started going through the posters down at the marshal's office, he could end up wearing a rope. Unfortunately he'd already given his name to the doctor, while his defenses were down. "Well, ma'am," he said, "the truth is, I'm a lawman, and I've got to keep that pistol handy."

"If you're a lawman," Chloe countered, "where's your badge?"

Steven thought fast. For a Fairfax, he wasn't a very good liar. "I must have lost it in the blast," he said.

Chloe didn't look convinced. "I'm still not going to let you lie in here with a gun in your hand, Mr. Fairfax. This is a respectable house."

Steven had finished his supper, and Chloe, who had been seated beside his bed in a ladderback chair, stood to take his tray. "What time is it?" he wanted to know. The darkness at the windows could have been that of twilight or of early dawn.

"Six-thirty in the evening," Chloe answered shortly. She nodded toward another chair, where what remained of Steven's long canvas coat was draped. "What we found on and around you we put in the pocket of that coat. And there wasn't any badge."

With that, she crossed the room and walked out, closing the door behind her.

Steven lay back in the flickering light of the kerosene lantern burning on his bedside table and wondered how close Macon was to catching him alone in a room with pansies on the walls, unable to defend himself.

Fulton laid a heavy hand on Emma's knee, there in the larger of Chloe's two parlors, and Emma quickly set it away.

"God's eyeballs, Emma," Fulton complained in a sort of whiny whisper, "we're practically engaged!"

"It's not proper to talk about God's anatomy," Emma said stiffly, squinting at the needlework in the stand in front of her before plunging the needle in. "And if you don't keep your hands to yourself, you'll just have to go home."

Fulton gave an exaggerated sigh. "You'd think a girl

would learn *something,* living in the same house with Chloe Reese."

Emma's dark blue eyes were wide with annoyance when she turned them on Fulton. "I beg your pardon?"

"Well, I only meant—"

"I know what you meant, Fulton."

"A man has a right to a kiss now and then, when he's willing to promise the rest of his life to a woman!"

Emma narrowed her eyes, planning to point out that he wasn't the only one with a lifetime on the line, but before she could speak, Fulton grabbed her and pressed his dry mouth to hers.

She squirmed, wondering why on earth those romantic English novels spoke of kissing as though it were something wonderful, and when she couldn't get free, she poked Fulton in the hand with her embroidery needle.

He gave a shout and jerked back, slapping at his hand as though a bug had lighted there. "Damn it all to perdition!" he barked.

Emma calmly rethreaded her needle and went back to embroidering her nosegay. It was a lovely thing of pink, lavender, and white flowers, frothed in baby's breath. It was never good to let a man get too familiar. "Good night, Fulton," she said.

Stiffly, Fulton stood. "Won't you even do me the courtesy of walking me to the gate?" he grumbled.

Thinking of the respectability that would be hers if she were to marry Fulton someday, Emma suppressed a sigh, secured her needle in the tightly drawn cloth, and rose to her feet. Her arm linked with his, she walked him to the gate.

The night was speckled with stars and scented with the fragrance of the nearby lake, and Emma had a romantic turn of heart. She stood on tiptoe and kissed Fulton's cheek.

He looked very pleased.

She touched his wounded hand in apology. "I'm sorry I stuck you with my needle," she said.

Fulton caught her hand in his and lifted it to his mouth. He kissed her knuckles lightly, and the tickling sensation made her shiver, though she felt none of the delicious things novels promised. His words were anything but poetic. "A man has certain needs, Emma," he said, after clearing his throat loudly. "I do hope you won't turn out to be so reserved in our marriage chamber."

Emma favored him with a sweet smile, but her voice was firm when she said again, "Good night." She saw no need to remind him that a formal agreement had yet to be made.

Reluctantly, Fulton left, opening the gate and disappearing down the street. Emma hurried back into the house, searching for Chloe.

She found her adoptive mother in the small parlor, listening to the delicate strains of a music box, a dreamy expression on her artfully embellished face.

When Chloe saw Emma, she closed the inlaid ivory lid of the music box and smiled. "Hello, darling. Did Fulton leave?"

"Yes," Emma answered, smoothing her skirts before she sat in the chair opposite Chloe's.

"Good. I can't think what you see in that lumbering baboon."

Emma was used to Chloe's blunt opinions, and she was unruffled. Indeed, there were times when she herself thought Fulton rather awkward. "He's a gentleman," she said, overlooking the fact that she'd had to spear the man with an embroidery needle to make him remove his hands from her person. "Tell me about the saloon explosion. I've been waiting all afternoon to hear what happened."

Chloe sighed wearily. "Old Freddy Fiddengate was celebrating his birthday. He made a wish and blew on a dynamite fuse, but the flame didn't go out."

Emma's eyes were wide, and one hand was pressed to her mouth. "Was anyone killed?"

"No, but we've got a fellow upstairs that's hurt pretty bad. Doc says he has cracked ribs, and he was cut up by broken glass."

Emma shuddered, imagining some poor derelict lying upstairs in one of Chloe's guest rooms, suffering.

Chloe went on with her account. "Charlie Simmons has a broken leg—he was standing at the bar, as usual, swilling that rotgut whiskey they sell over there—and Philo DeAngelo lost two toes. Everybody else just got the wind knocked out of them."

Touching Chloe's hand, Emma spoke softly. "You're exhausted. Why don't you go to bed, and I'll make you some hot milk."

Chloe made a face. "You know I can't stand that stuff. And besides, I've got to go back over to the Stardust and make sure things are all right. I have my girls to think about, you know."

Emma knew from long experience that there would be no talking Chloe into staying home if she wanted to go out. "Very well, then, go ahead," she said. "I'll drink the hot milk myself."

Rising from her chair, Chloe shook her head as though in amazement. "You're dull as a toothless old woman, Emma," she said. "You should be out there in the moonlight, letting some handsome young man kiss you and hold your hand. And I'm not talking about that stuffy banker, either."

"I have no desire to be kissed," Emma pointed out primly, already on her way to the staircase.

"That's part of the problem," Chloe fussed. "Personally, I think you're just trying to show the world you aren't like me."

Emma paused midway up the stairs. Despite the fact that she managed a thriving brothel, there probably wasn't a kinder soul than Chloe in the whole of the territory. "I don't care what people think," she replied, but she knew that was a lie and so did Chloe.

# Chapter
## ❧ 2 ❧

*C*andlelight flickered in Emma's spacious room as she finished her preparations for bed. The kerosene lamp would have given better light, but the soft glow of a burning wick made her feel like Jane Eyre. She could easily imagine that Mr. Rochester was just down the hallway.

Humming softly to herself, she picked up the brass candlestick and set out for a peek at the poor vagrant recovering in the guest room.

She knew she wouldn't be able to sleep a wink if she didn't look in on him first. It was the only Christian thing to do.

Emma walked carefully, so as not to spill wax on the rugs and incur the wrath of Daisy, Chloe's cook and housekeeper.

Outside her room she listened for a snore, but heard nothing. She opened the first door on the other side of the hallway, which was directly opposite her own, and crept quietly into the guest room.

Emma could see a vague shape spread out on the bed,

but she heard no breathing, and that worried her. According to Chloe, most men snored loudly when they slept.

She inched closer and closer to the bed. "Sir?" she whispered, not wanting to alarm the pitiful indigent. "Sir, are you awake?"

There was no sound from the patient.

Emma was now standing beside the bed. She bent, the candle providing the only light since there was no moon, and the unthinkable happened. The candle flame flicked against the gauze bandages covering the man's rib cage, and a blaze leaped to life.

For a moment, Emma was too horrified to move. By the time she'd recovered enough to set the candle down, the fire had gotten a good start.

The man awakened with a shouted curse, and the sound broke Emma's paralysis. Using the palms of her hands, she began beating out the flame.

The invisible stranger gave a howl and then gasped, "For God's sake, let me burn!"

Emma continued striking him until the last glowing ember of fire was gone, then turned to light the kerosene lamp with her candle. This brighter radiance showed a handsome man in his early thirties, his arms and chest covered in charred bandages, his ribs wrapped tightly with what looked like strips of an old bed sheet.

He was, in fact, the same man Emma had encountered beside the railroad tracks earlier that day, and she felt her stomach slam against her throat with a sort of sweet terror.

"I'm so sorry," Emma said breathlessly.

The man did not look the least bit receptive to apology. His brown-green eyes snapped with fury as he dragged himself to a sitting position, and even in the light of the lantern, Emma could see he'd gone pale with pain. "I knew somebody like you once. He was a guard in a Yankee prison camp."

Holding her wrapper closed with one hand, Emma dragged up a chair, ignoring his uncharitable remark.

"I'm afraid those bandages will have to be changed," she said. "Since Doc Waverly is usually only sober in the daytime, I'd better do it myself."

He regarded her distrustfully.

Emma sighed. "I said I was sorry, didn't I?"

He was squinting at her now. "Who are you?"

"My name is Emma Chalmers," Emma responded, folding her hands in her lap. "We met briefly this morning. Who are you?"

He shoved a hand through his sweaty, dusty brown hair. "Steven Fairfax."

"How do you do, Mr. Fairfax?"

"Hell, I'm just fine. I come into this damned place, looking for a drink and a . . . a drink . . . and I end up getting blown halfway to perdition by some drunk celebrating his birthday. Then you walk in and set me on fire—"

"Oh, do stop grumbling," Emma interrupted impatiently. "You're not the first man who's ever been caught in an explosion. Now, let's get rid of those bandages."

Fairfax scowled at her and pulled the singed blankets up to his chin. "I'll just wait until the doctor sobers up, if it's all the same to you."

"It isn't," Emma said in a firm voice as she rose from her chair. "I'll be back in a few minutes."

With that, she took her candlestick and left the room. When she returned she had several bed sheets from the linen closet with her, along with scissors and gauze and the bottle of laudanum Doc Waverly had given her for monthly cramps.

Ignoring Steven's intractable glare, she set the medicine on the bedside table, next to the lamp, and spread out the other things at the foot of the bed. Steeling herself against the smell and the gore that might lie beneath those bandages, Emma began cutting them away, a process Mr. Fairfax endured in wary silence.

The man's chest had more stitch marks than the sampler Emma had embroidered the month before, and the wounds looked angry. It was no wonder, since Doc

Waverly hadn't bothered to wash the patient before attacking him with a needle.

When she'd removed everything but the sheet strips girding his ribs, Emma stepped back from the bedside. "You'll have to have a sponge bath before we go on, Mr. Fairfax. There's a question of infection here."

To her surprise, the recalcitrant visitor was looking at her in a different way—his hazel eyes were twinkling with weary mischief, and his voice was lower. Smoother. "How much does that cost? A sponge bath, I mean?"

Emma frowned, puzzled. "Cost?"

Fairfax smiled at her, showing that fine set of teeth Emma remembered from their earlier encounter. He looked rather like a gentleman when he did that, instead of a trail bum down on his luck. "You know."

Emma had no time to debate. "I'm sorry," she said, on her way out the door. "I'm afraid I don't." She left the room again and came back soon after with a basin of hot water, soap, a washcloth and a towel.

"You really are a great deal of trouble, Mr. Fairfax."

"Steven," he corrected.

Emma looked at him in confusion. "Steven."

"May I call you Emma?"

"No," Emma replied, uncomfortable with his familiarity. "You certainly may not. It wouldn't be proper."

He grinned as though she'd said something funny. "Proper?" he repeated, and he chuckled.

Emma lathered up the washcloth and set about cleaning him up as best she could. Of course, she wasn't about to deal with any part of his anatomy besides his arms and chest.

"There's money over there, in the pocket of my coat," he said, when Emma was rinsing away the soap.

"Good," Emma said disinterestedly. "You'll want to buy yourself another set of clothes. I'd be glad to do that for you on my way home from the library tomorrow."

He watched her, his eyes dancing in his wan face. "How long have you been working here?"

She wrung out the washcloth. "Working here? I don't work here—I'm the town librarian. This is my home."

At that Steven gave a hoarse cough of laughter. "You're a *librarian?* That's a new one."

Emma was cutting a sheet into strips. "A new what?"

"Listen, when you're through with these bandages, I could use a little comforting."

She was bent over her work, carefully rewrapping his left arm. "We have some whiskey downstairs, but you probably won't need it because the laudanum will make you sleep. Perhaps I could read to you for a while, or—"

"*Read* to me? What kind of place is this?"

"It's a home, Mr. Fairfax," Emma answered, finishing one arm and starting in on the other. Fortunately, the patient had sustained no burns of any importance, though some of the hair on his chest had been singed away.

"You live here, don't you?"

"Of course I do. Why else would I be wandering around the place in my nightgown and wrapper?"

He feigned bewilderment. "Why, for that matter, would you set an innocent man on fire?"

Emma had finished the last bandage and was inspecting the wrapping around his ribs. It was charred in places, but she didn't want to remove it, since it appeared secure. "You're certainly one for holding a grudge, aren't you, Mr. Fairfax?"

"Steven."

"Steven, then." She poured laudanum into a spoon and extended it.

"You're not kidding, are you?" he asked, dutifully accepting the medicine and making a face. "What the devil's going on here, Miss Whatever-your-name-is?"

Emma was miffed. After all, it wasn't as though she hadn't done everything she could to rectify her earlier mistake. "What would I have to joke about?"

He started to laugh again. "You really are a librarian!" he said, and then he laughed harder.

Emma thought he must be slightly insane. Perhaps he'd escaped from an asylum somewhere. She stepped back, out of reach.

Steven Fairfax recovered his sobriety, though only with obvious effort. "What about the woman who was in here earlier? What's she, a schoolmarm?"

At last Emma realized what Mr. Fairfax had been thinking. He must have seen Chloe in her working clothes. She drew herself up to her imperious height of five feet, six inches, and fixed him in a glare. "If you weren't so sorely injured," she said evenly, "I would slap you."

The laudanum was beginning to take affect, and Mr. Fairfax yawned expansively. "You've already set me on fire and then tried to beat me to death. A simple slap would probably be refreshing."

Fury surged through Emma's system to snap in her eyes. "Don't worry, Mr. Fairfax. You'll be quite safe from me in the future."

"That's comforting."

Emma got as far as the door before duty made her pause. "Do you need to use the chamber pot?"

"Yes," Steven answered shortly.

Emma stomped back over to the bed, reached beneath it for the lidded china pot, and set it none too gently in his lap. "Good night, Mr. Fairfax," she said, blowing out the kerosene lamp with a huff and marching out of the room.

Gritting his teeth against the pain, Steven set the chamber pot on the floor beside the bed and sank back onto his pillows.

Emma.

He smiled in the darkness, thinking what a fool he'd made of himself. Because of Chloe, he'd assumed he was in a whorehouse, and he'd taken Emma for a fresh young flower in the madam's bouquet. Instead she was a librarian, and there was every likelihood that no man had ever laid a hand on her.

Steven was glad about that, even though a part of him

wished for the tender consolations a whore might have provided.

He closed his eyes and remembered how it was when she'd washed him. Just thinking about it made him harden, and he arranged his legs accordingly.

He was surprised when the door opened again, just a crack.

"Mr. Fairfax?" It was Emma's voice.

He considered pretending to be asleep, in the hope that she would come and stand at his bedside, but in the end he decided against it. For all he knew, she had a candle in her hand. "Yes?"

"I was just wondering—well—are you suffering?"

"Yes," he answered, in all truth.

The crack of light from the doorway widened. "The laudanum didn't help?"

Touched at her concern, Steven answered truthfully. "It hasn't had time, Miss Emma."

She came into the room, carrying a kerosene lantern this time, and Steven couldn't help cringing when he thought of the damage *that* could do.

But Emma set the lamp on the bedside stand, beside his own, and sat down in the chair again. He could see she was holding a book in her arms.

"I'm sorry I was so rude about the chamber pot," she said.

Steven couldn't help laughing at the somber dignity of her expression. Her very primness lured him, made him want to bring out the wildcat he expected she was hiding from the world and maybe even herself.

"And I'm sorry I was rude," he answered, tempering his amusement with a friendly smile.

"I thought perhaps you'd like me to read to you."

He bit back another smile. "That's kind of you, Miss Emma. What do you have there?"

Her guileless face glowed in the lamp light, and her voice was warm and husky. For one brief, wicked moment, Steven wished he'd been right about her in the first place.

*"Little Women,"* she said, with enthusiasm. "It's my favorite—I've read it over and over again."

Steven had heard of the book, and though he'd never had any desire to read it, he couldn't bring himself to say so. He could see now that there was something fragile in Emma, something mockery might bruise or destroy. "Why do you like it so much?"

She bit her lower lip for a moment. "I guess because it's about sisters. There are four of them—Meg, Amy, Jo and Beth."

*Sounds like a real riproarer,* Steven thought, but he kept the sarcasm to himself. He might not care to hear about any small women, but he did want to listen to Emma's voice.

She opened the worn book, cleared her throat delicately, and began to read to him about four young girls.

"I've never known anybody to call their mother 'Marmee'," Steven observed, when Emma reached the end of the first chapter and stopped reading to sniffle.

"It's common enough in the east," she said somewhat defensively.

Remembering that he'd called his own mother by the French Maman, Steven nodded. Although he wouldn't have admitted it, he was looking forward to hearing the next chapter.

"Do you have any sisters?" Emma asked, her eyes wide and sorrowful.

Steven longed to comfort her, but he didn't dare. After all, he'd practically called her a prostitute earlier, albeit by mistake, and despite the sponge bath he figured he most likely smelled like a mule fart. "No," he answered presently, "but I have a brother." He didn't elaborate because he didn't want to talk about Macon. Or Nathaniel, a cousin who had come to live at Fairhaven after losing his parents, and who was so young Steven hardly knew him. Nat hadn't even been born until after Steven had joined the army.

Emma sighed, and there was a wistful expression on her face. She looked young and very vulnerable, sitting there in her wrapper, with her reddish-blonde hair trailing over one shoulder in a thick braid. Steven wondered how he could have mistaken her for anyone other than who she was—an innocent barely past girlhood.

Somehow he knew she was pretty much alone in the world, and the knowledge ached inside him, sharper than his wounds. "I appreciate your coming back in here to cheer me up, Miss Emma."

She smiled distractedly, as though her mind were somewhere else, and rose from her chair. "I'll say good night again," she told him, and then she was gone, taking the light with her.

Back in her room, Emma blew out the lamp, laid the book lovingly beside it, and crawled into bed. She fully expected to think about Lily and Caroline, as she always did when she'd been reading *Little Women,* but instead her mind was filled with Steven Fairfax.

The man was clearly not respectable, she told herself, her chin at an obstinate angle as she wriggled down between the sheets.

Emma's thoughts turned to the limited sponging she'd given him before rewrapping his wounds. The muscles in his chest and arms had been hard and lean and browned by the sun . . .

She pulled the covers up higher and forced her thoughts to turn to Fulton. That was the only decent thing to do, since she'd been keeping company with the man for months. She had absolutely no business bathing Steven Fairfax.

But then she had never seen Fulton's bare arms, and certainly not his chest, so she couldn't very well make a comparison. Her cheeks throbbed in the darkness as she mentally undressed her fiancé.

She didn't need her highly developed imagination to tell her that Fulton would be white and soft to the touch, like a woman.

With a little groan of despair, Emma rolled onto her

side and pulled the blankets up over her head. Steven Fairfax was nothing but a saddle-bum—maybe he was even wanted by the law—and bathing him was not a ladylike thing to do.

Still, there was the way he smiled. And that glint of mischief in his eyes, overpowering the pain he must be enduring. And the soft, distinctly Southern way he spoke—it was like listening to warm rain fall on the summerhouse roof.

Emma drew a deep breath and let it out again, exasperated with her foolishness, then threw back the covers and left her bed for the window seat overlooking the lake.

On a moonlit night, the water could be magical, but tonight it was only a massive, shifting shadow, offering no comfort.

Resting her forehead against the glass, Emma sighed again. What was it about Steven Fairfax that troubled her so much?

First thing in the morning, Emma dressed, brushed and rebraided her hair, and looked in on Steven.

He grinned at her, and although he was in dire need of a shave and his hair was rumpled, Emma's heart gave a little lurch.

"I could bring you some breakfast if you'd like," she said, feeling unaccountably shy.

Steven shook his head and ran his gaze lightly over her. The sweep left a trail of heat in its wake. "Thanks, but I never eat before noon," he said.

"Coffee?" Emma inquired, reluctant to leave him even though she knew she had no business lingering.

"It's kind of you to offer," he said, and Emma took that as acceptance. She hurried downstairs, ignoring Daisy, and poured a cup of hot coffee.

When she returned, Steven had drifted off to sleep again.

Emma returned to the kitchen. Daisy was still there, expertly flipping pancakes over the griddle. A large black woman with a strong personality, Daisy had more to say about the way the house was run than Emma and Chloe put together.

"Don't know why Miss Chloe'd want to bring a stranger right into this house," the woman grumbled without so much as looking up from the skillet. "I don't like the looks of that one, I'll tell you."

Sunshine flowed through the bank of windows lining the back of the house and glittered on the royal blue waters of the lake beyond. "Don't fuss, Daisy," Emma scolded good-naturedly, pouring coffee for herself from the china pot in the middle of the table. "It's such a beautiful day."

"I'll fuss if I wants to," Daisy muttered, bringing the platter of pancakes to the table and slamming it down. "I s'pose that no good ramblin' man has to be waited on hand and foot."

Emma smiled. "Of course he does. He's bedridden."

"Well, that ain't my fault," Daisy pointed out, stomping over to the stove again.

Emma took one pancake—it was beyond her why Daisy always cooked enough for an army—and smeared it with butter.

"You bringin' the banker to supper tonight?" Daisy demanded.

Emma smiled. "I don't think so, Daisy. Fulton doesn't usually like to go out on weeknights. He says it interferes with his concentration the next day."

"I'll interfere with his concentration," Daisy muttered, mostly to herself, as she worked between the stove and the sink. "Thump him up right 'longside the head with my skillet—"

Emma nearly choked on her pancake. "Honestly, Daisy," she said, suppressing a smile, "a person would never know you were a good Christian woman by the way you talk. What would Reverend Hess say if he heard you going on like that?"

"I reckon he'd say I's an old lady and I's gotta be let alone."

"Mr. Fairfax is sleeping, and he won't be wanting any breakfast. You might check on him later in the morning, though."

"I'll check on him," Daisy said. "Give him a good wallop with my broom handle, that's what."

Emma wasn't the least bit worried, since she knew that, underneath all that mumbling and grumbling, Daisy Putnam was gentle as a new fawn. "Good," Emma answered, carrying the plate to the sink. "You give him a wallop for me."

Daisy gave her great, gleeful laugh at that, and Emma hurried through the house to the front door.

Spring was definitely in the air, and her step was brisk as she moved along the maple-shaded sidewalk toward the main part of town. Chloe's house, with its many rooms, its veranda, and its spacious yard, was one of the nicest in town. In fact, except for Big John Lenahan's ranch house and the Whitney mansion, it was the finest in the county.

The crisp skirt of Emma's blue sateen dress crackled as she walked, and today she'd worn her braid wrapped around the back of her head in a coronet, instead of trailing down her back as usual. At her throat, she wore the delicate cameo brooch Chloe had given her last Christmas, and she periodically reached up and pinched her cheeks to give them some color.

She marveled as she passed the Yellow Belly Saloon. The facade was still lying out in the middle of the street, though men were there with hammers and saws, disassembling it, and inside, the piano and bar were charred caricatures of their former selves. Beams crisscrossed the pool table, and the painting of the naked woman, so detested by the Presbyterians, had one whole side burned away, so that only the lady's head was visible.

Fate had appeased the Presbyterians.

Emma made her way to the other side of the street and would have proceeded to the library, if Callie Visco hadn't come out of the Stardust Saloon, wearing a short pink satin dress, black net stockings, and a blue feather boa.

"Hello, Miss Emma," she said. And after looking both ways to be sure no one was watching, she extended a copy of the novel she'd checked out the day before. "Could you get me another one just like this?" she asked in a whisper.

Emma smiled. "I don't know why you think you have to keep it a secret, Callie. There's nothing wrong with liking to read."

Callie squared her narrow shoulders. She'd painted a beauty mark underneath her right eye, and her yellow hair billowed around her face in big curls. "The other girls might think I got time on my hands or somethin'," she replied, with a shake of her head.

"All right, then," Emma answered, in a conspiratorial whisper to match Callie's, "you come out when you see me passing by at noon, on my way home for lunch. I'll have a book for you then."

Callie grinned broadly. It was impossible to guess her age, with all that paint on her face, but Emma had her pegged for the far side of thirty. "Thanks, Miss Emma."

Emma hurriedly unlocked the library and stepped inside. She hadn't been there more than five minutes when Fulton showed up, dressed for the bank and fiddling with his watch chain. It was always a bad sign when Fulton did that.

"I hear Chloe is keeping a man in the house," he said stiffly. "Now, Emma, you know I don't mind about Big John Lenahan stopping by every now and again, but I draw the line—"

"It isn't your house, Fulton," Emma put in reasonably.

Fulton was so startled at the interruption that he went red at the ears. "Be that as it may, I don't care for the idea of my fiancée sleeping under the same roof with somebody who'd stoop to drinking in the Yellow Belly Saloon."

Emma went to the door and began picking up the

returned books. She was careful to hide her smile. "I'm not your fiancée, Fulton," she reminded him sweetly.

"Who is he? What's his name?"

Some instinct made Emma reticent about Steven's identity. "Just a drifter," she said, carrying the books to her desk and beginning to sort through them. "He'll be gone soon."

"Well, I certainly hope so."

Emma changed the subject. "Daisy wanted to know if you planned on coming to supper tonight."

"You know I wouldn't go out on a Tuesday."

Emma sighed, staring off into the distance. He'd gone out on a Monday, but she didn't want to take the trouble to point that out. "Yes," she said, and she was thinking of the man she'd washed and read to the night before. She wondered if he was awake, drinking the coffee Emma had left for him, though it would be stone-cold by now, or swearing because no one would give him back his .45.

"What are you smiling about?" Fulton demanded.

Emma went right on sorting books. "Nothing," she lied. "Nothing at all."

# Chapter
## ❧ 3 ❧

J oellen Lenahan was one of the few people Emma had ever actively disliked. She was sixteen, with the body and manner of a mature woman, and she seemed to see other females as threats to be swiftly eradicated. She was also angelically beautiful, with her yellow-blond hair and cornflower blue eyes, though it was said that her father, Big John, despaired of getting her married before she disgraced him.

Entering the library with the regal reluctance of Queen Victoria venturing into a pest house, she bestowed on Emma a disdainful look and asked, "Are there any books here that we don't already have at home?"

Emma struggled to find some trace of Christian charity within herself as she continued dusting the shelves. "Since I don't know what books you have, I'm at a loss to answer your question."

Joellen spotted the copy of Thomas Hardy's new novel on the counter and was magnetized to it. "I want this," she announced, picking up the volume in both hands and holding it to her shapely bosom.

"I'm sorry," Emma said politely, "but that's reserved." She'd selected it for Callie, but saying so would have been asking for trouble, since Joellen would unquestionably regard herself as Callie's superior.

The girl jutted out her lower lip. "You're just being mean, Emma Chalmers," she accused in a whiny tone that set Emma's teeth on edge. "You don't like me because I come from a decent family and you—well—you're an orphan, raised in unsavory circumstances."

Emma was used to being suspect because of Chloe's occupation, so she held her tongue. Besides, she liked Big John. "You may have the book when your turn comes," she said with pointed politeness.

Reluctantly, Joellen set the volume back on the counter. She was used to getting her way, and her wide eyes snapped with irritation. "You probably don't have anything good to read in this silly little place anyway. Everybody knows Chloe got it started just to keep you busy, since the school board didn't want you to teach. It isn't a *real* library at all."

Emma's spine stiffened, and her sateen skirts crackled briskly as she walked over to stand behind her counter. Joellen's reminder of the town's belief that Emma was unfit to teach their children because of her connection with Chloe stung fiercely, but nothing could have made her reveal that. "Since this isn't a 'real' library, I can't imagine why you're staying so long."

The smirk on Joellen's face made Emma want to slap her. "There are rumors going around about you, Miss Emma. People say you're keeping a *man* in your house."

Emma could have told Joellen a few things about men visiting Chloe's house—Big John Lenahan, for example—but she couldn't bring herself to stoop so low. Nonetheless, blue fire blazed in her eyes as she replied, "What if I am, Joellen? What business is that of yours?"

"It's improper," Joellen answered in a singsong voice.

"So was what you did with Billy Baker during the harvest dance," Emma said bluntly. "Big John would have a fit if he knew."

The color drained from Joellen's china-doll cheeks. "You saw me and Billy?"

"I saw enough."

Joellen's face went from waxy white to crimson. Without another word, she turned and dashed out of the library, leaving the door gaping open behind her.

Humming, Emma closed it. In truth, she'd only seen Joellen holding hands with Billy at the dance; she'd guessed the rest.

At the stroke of noon she took up the Hardy novel and set off for home. As planned, Callie met her on the sidewalk to collect the book, then skulked up the back steps to the second floor of the Stardust Saloon, taking great care that nobody saw her.

From there Emma proceeded to the general store, where she bought trousers and a shirt that looked as though they might fit Mr. Fairfax. Her purchases were just being wrapped when Fulton came in, apparently having spotted her from the bank window.

He glanced at the trousers and shirt, just in passing, then his gaze shot back to them.

"Could you possibly help me find whatever a man wears under his trousers?" Emma whispered, leaning close to her fiancé so the storekeeper wouldn't hear. She'd been too embarrassed to ask Mrs. Birdwell, who was the town gossip and would no doubt have repeated the question in every parlor in Whitneyville as proof that the apple doesn't fall far from the tree.

Fulton looked as though she'd just thrown ice-cold water into his lap. "Emma!" he hissed, in reprimand.

Emma sighed. She couldn't think why it should be such a bother to find out a simple thing. "Never mind. I'll ask Chloe."

"Are these clothes for that—that drifter?"

A tall, thin woman with a no-nonsense bun pinned severely at the back of her head, Mrs. Birdwell quickly raised her eyes from the string she was tying around Emma's parcel. She offered no comment, but her prominent ears were practically wriggling.

"Of course they are," Emma answered impatiently. "You don't expect him to walk around naked, do you?"

Mrs. Birdwell looked incensed. She was a member of the school board, and it was she who had refused Emma a teaching position when she returned from normal school in St. Louis, on the grounds that she might be an unwholesome influence.

Fulton's ears reddened slightly. "Emma, I must insist that you watch your language!"

Emma was running out of patience fast. She told Mrs. Birdwell to put the purchase on Chloe's account—the old biddy didn't mind selling her merchandise to 'unwholesome influences'—and started for the door. "I can see we are not going to come to any rational agreement on this situation. Good day, Fulton."

He followed her out onto the sidewalk. "This is serious, Emma," he insisted. "It's bad enough that you live under that terrible woman's roof. If word of this rascal you've taken in gets back to Mother, we'll face no end of problems."

"He'll be leaving soon," Emma promised with a little sigh. "The minute he can get out of bed, I'm sure. He's no more anxious to stay than you are to have him there, Fulton."

At this, Fulton subsided a little. "You don't actually take care of him, or anything like that?"

Emma kept walking, her eyes fixed straight ahead. "I read to him last night," she admitted, leaving out the account of washing Steven and changing his bandages.

"I suppose he's illiterate, like most saddle tramps."

Emma only nodded, not wanting to say she suspected Steven was as well-educated as Fulton himself. That would only have made trouble. And speaking of trouble . . .

"Have you heard from your mother, Fulton?"

"She and Father will be home from their Grand Tour sometime in the coming month," he said a little nervously. The elder Whitneys were not going to be delighted at

42

their son's choice of a wife, and both Emma and Fulton knew it.

Since they were passing the bank, Fulton stopped. "Be sensible," he called after Emma in a stern voice, when she kept walking.

Emma looked out at the sparkling waters of Crystal Lake, because the sight never failed to soothe her. In summer she liked nothing better than wading there during the hot days and swimming, as free and naked as a nymph, when the moon rose.

Daisy was sweeping the front hall industriously when Emma walked in. "'Bout time you got here," grumbled the older woman. "That soup I made is plumb cold."

Emma smiled, thanked Daisy, and proceeded up the stairs. At the door of Steven's room, she knocked.

"Come in," he barked, sounding no more congenial than Daisy had.

Emma opened the door and stepped inside. "I brought you some new clothes," she said cheerfully. "I hope they'll fit."

The strain of lying alone, helpless and in pain, was visible in the gaunt lines of Steven's unshaven face. There was a feeling of restrained energy in the room, some power building up, about to burst through a crumbling dam. "You'll find some money in my coat," he said, shifting uncomfortably on the bed.

She drew up the chair she'd sat in the night before and sank into it, the package resting on her lap. "We'll settle up later. How do you feel?"

"Like hell," he answered, staring up at the ceiling and drumming his fingers on his bandaged chest. His hands were graceful, though sunbrowned and calloused, but they were also lethal, Emma reminded herself. Steven was almost surely a gunslinger, and men like that usually didn't trouble themselves with matters of conscience.

"Are you hungry?"

"No," he snapped. "That old harpy you call a cook has already forced two bowlfuls of soup down my gullet."

Emma smiled at the picture that came to mind. "I should have warned you about crossing Daisy. She's a woman of strong opinions."

Steven was forced to chuckle, though the sound was grim. His bandaged arms were folded across his chest now in staunch stubbornness, and his eyes moved over Emma's plain dress with an expression just short of contempt.

"Why the devil do you dress like that," he rasped, "when you're easily the most beautiful woman in the territory?"

Emma's cheeks pulsed. She started to protest, then stopped herself in confusion. Had Steven's question been a compliment or an insult?

"What's wrong with this dress?" she asked evenly, when she'd had a few moments to compose herself.

"It's plain enough for a missionary's wife," Steven replied. Although the words bit, Emma saw kindness in his eyes, and genuine curiosity.

She wanted in the worst way for Steven to find her attractive, and the knowledge surprised and shamed her. After all, she was considering marrying Fulton, and she rarely gave *his* opinions a second thought. Uncharacteristic tears swelled along her lashes.

"Hell and damnation," Steven muttered. "I didn't mean to make you cry."

Emma drew her lace-trimmed handkerchief from under her cuff and dried her eyes in the most dignified manner she could manage. "I do wish you wouldn't swear."

He sighed heavily. "I'm sorry, Emma. It's just that a woman like you—well, you should be dressed in silks and satins, with a lace ruffle here and there. And maybe some bosom showing." He narrowed his gaze for a moment, as if envisioning the change. "Yes. You have a very nice chest."

Once again Emma's cheeks burned. Shocked though she was, his words had set a fire racing through her insides, and she started out of her chair. "If you're going to be vulgar . . ."

He reached out and caught hold of her hand when she would have risen. It was as though she'd dragged her feet across a thick carpet, then touched the door knob. She flinched at the sweet shock. "Please," he said in a low, husky voice. "Don't go."

Emma sank back into the chair. His strong fingers relaxed around hers reluctantly, it seemed to her, then released their grasp entirely. "It must be terrible, being so grimy dirty."

His teeth flashed white against a suntanned face. "Kind of you to put it that way, Miss Emma."

She bit her lower lip for a moment. "I meant—well, you must be very uncomfortable. It's a pity you couldn't go downstairs and use Chloe's bathtub."

He arched his golden brown eyebrows. "I could, Miss Emma," he said quietly, "if you'd help me."

Emma's heart set instantly to pounding, and she drew back in her chair. *"Help* you?"

"Get down the stairs," he said. "I didn't mean you should help me bathe."

She smiled, much relieved, though her heart rate had hardly slowed and she still felt a little dizzy. "Oh."

"Will you?"

"I don't see why not," Emma answered briskly, smoothing the skirts of her dress before she stood. Since Steven's clothes were in shreds, she had him wait while she slipped into Chloe's dressing room and collected the robe Big John wore when he visited.

With a great deal of effort on both their parts, Steven was finally hauled into a standing position. He stood still for several moments, with Emma beneath his left arm like a living crutch, and his struggle against the pain was a visible one.

"Now the stairs," Emma said.

Progress out into the hallway was slow, since Steven could only take very short steps and he had to stop to rest every few seconds.

At the top of the rear stairwell Emma shifted to Steven's right side, so he could grip the banister with his left hand. If he were to lose his balance then, the results would be disastrous.

Daisy was in the kitchen, her Sunday hat propped on top of her head, when they reached the first floor.

"Land sakes, Miss Emma, put that man back where he belongs!"

Emma gave her longtime friend a dour look. "Mr. Fairfax wants a bath," she said.

Daisy's dark eyes narrowed. "That ain't fittin', and you know it!"

Steven ignored the cook's remark. Emma had been hoping Daisy would offer to help, but there was obviously no chance of that. She only took up her handbag and opened the rear door.

"Don't you do nothin' you shouldn't, Miss Emma," she ordered with a worried frown, and then she was gone.

The fact that she was now alone in the house with a man who was about to be stark naked was not lost on Emma, but she'd come too far to back out. She and Steven had both worked too hard getting downstairs for the effort to be in vain.

With a beleaguered glance at the clock on the kitchen mantel, she renewed her efforts at propelling Steven toward the bathroom. Half the hour she allotted herself for a midday meal was gone, and she hadn't had a bite to eat.

Ever so slowly, the two made their way down the hall toward the room Chloe was so proud of. Except for the one in the big house on the hill, where the Whitneys lived, there wasn't another bathroom like it within miles.

At the end of the darkened hallway Emma propped Steven against the wall long enough to open the door. Then she hauled him inside and set him gingerly on the seat of the flushing commode, a marvel of modern times.

He swore and grasped the edge of the porcelain sink with one hand to steady himself.

"Are you all right?" Emma asked.

"God, yes," Steven muttered. "I'm wonderful."

Emma ignored his profanity and bent to put the plug into the tub and turn the spigots. When she twisted around to face Steven, he was grinning at her.

"What?" she demanded.

"Never mind."

She realized she'd displayed her derriere, after a fashion, and the blood flowed to her face again. "Skunk," she said.

"You're crazy about me," Steven retorted with an impish grin.

"Get into the water," Emma said impatiently. "I'm due back at the library and I haven't had anything to eat."

Steven got to his feet painfully and started untying the belt of Big John's blue flannel robe.

Emma whirled away, her hands over her eyes, and Steven laughed.

"Sorry," he said.

Emma did not turn around, but stood hugging herself, her chin high.

"I'll need you to take off these bandages," Steven told her in a reasonable tone of voice.

Without looking at Steven, except out of the corner of her eye, Emma walked right past him and took a pair of scissors from the cabinet above the sink. She kept her gaze fixed strictly on his bandages as she removed them, but she couldn't help noticing the power and depth of his chest, and the ridged muscles of his stomach.

"You're pretty good at this. Have you taken care of wounded men before?"

Emma drew in a deep breath, then let it out again. The room seemed very close and very warm, and she had that familiar sense of some intangible force straining to be released. "We had a cave-in at one of the mines a few years ago, and a lot of people were hurt. Chloe let me help her and the others with the doctoring."

"Where was Doc Waverly?"

"He was around," Emma said, a little defensively, for

she liked Dr. Waverly even if he did have an unfortunate fondness for the bottle. "He just had his hands full, that was all."

"How did you come to live here, Emma?"

She helped him to the side of the tub, then turned away while he struggled out of the robe and whatever was beneath it. She caught a glimpse, despite her efforts to be circumspect, of hairy, muscled legs. "Chloe brought me to Whitneyville when I was a little girl, if that's what you mean."

"It is and it isn't." She heard him groan as he lowered himself carefully into the water. Emma wanted desperately to leave, but she didn't dare. Mr. Fairfax could easily lose consciousness, strike his head on the side of the tub, and drown. "Chloe's obviously a—lady of the evening."

Emma sighed, drying her moist brow with the sleeve of her dress. There was a peculiar sensation of aching in her most private place. "Yes."

"Is she your mother?"

"No," Emma answered immediately. "Chloe's a far better person than Mama ever was."

She heard splashing as Steven helped himself to the soap and began to wash. "That's a bitter remark if I've ever heard one."

Emma was finding it hard to breathe, and even harder to keep her gaze from skittering toward Steven's prone body. "Mama didn't care about me or my sisters. Why should I say she was a good person when she wasn't?"

Steven sighed. "Emma."

She was tapping one foot. "What?"

"I'm going to need more help."

Emma gnawed on her lower lip before answering. "What do you mean?"

"I can't wash my back, or my hair."

Squeezing her eyes shut, Emma extended her hands and groped her way to the big, clawfooted bathtub. She smacked the edge sharply with her knee, and her eyes flew open.

Steven was looking up at her with mischief in his gaze. He'd covered his private parts with a washcloth, but the rest of him was revealed in all its blatantly masculine glory.

Emma decided she'd never get the project behind her if she didn't turn to and work at it, so she rolled up her sleeves and knelt beside the tub. Trying not to think about what she was doing, she scoured Steven's back and shampooed his hair, which felt like silk between her fingers.

"The wrapping around your rib is wet."

The task of washing the rest of his body completed, Steven sagged against the back of the tub with a sigh. "I don't care," he replied, and there was a smile on his beard-stubbled face. "God, this feels good."

"I wish you wouldn't repeatedly take our Lord's name in vain," Emma protested.

"The fella that left this robe—would he happen to keep a supply of cigars here, by any chance?"

As a matter of fact, Chloe made sure there were cigars for Big John's visits, but Emma was no longer in an obliging mood. She had to get back to the library and she was hungry and soaked to the skin. Not only that, but soaping up Steven's broad, muscled back had given her a lot of odd feelings that hadn't fully subsided yet.

"No," she lied belatedly. "There aren't any cigars."

Steven unplugged the tub with a motion of his toe. "You'd better turn your back, Emma, because I'm about to stand up if I can manage it."

Emma complied quickly, praying Steven would be able to execute the feat on his own, that he wouldn't fall and crack his skull open. She held her breath.

"Can't do it," he said on a frustrated sigh, and there was a splash as he settled back into the water, which was steadily draining down the pipes. "You'll have to help me again."

"Oh, dear," Emma fussed. Then she went to the end of the tub and, keeping her eyes carefully closed, put her arms under Steven's and tried to hoist him to his feet.

This required both of them to give their utmost, but they succeeded, and Emma hastened to hold the robe out to Steven, keeping her head averted.

They were just beginning the arduous trip back up the stairs when Doc Waverly himself knocked at the glass in the back door, an affable smile on his face.

Emma had never been gladder to see anyone in all her life. Doc opened the door and came inside at her nod.

"Afternoon," he said cheerfully. "Giving our patient a bath?"

Emma flushed. "Actually, he gave *himself* a bath. I just helped him downstairs."

"Liar," Steven whispered, his warm breath caressing her ear.

"His wrapping is wet, though," Emma went on, speaking in an unnaturally loud voice, as though to drown out anything more Steven might say.

"I'll change that," Doc Waverly said. He took Emma's place under Steven's arm, and she bolted immediately for the stairs.

"I'll put fresh sheets on his bed while you're bringing him up," she called back.

She had managed the entire task by the time Steven and the doctor arrived at the doorway of the guest room, so slow was their advance. Steven was ashen with pain, but he smiled at Emma when he saw her step back from his freshly made bed.

"Thank you," he said.

"I think you could use a shot of whiskey," said the doctor, "and so could I."

After securing Steven on the edge of the bed, Doc Waverly opened his black bag and took out a fancy flask.

Shaking her head, Emma gathered up Steven's dirty sheets and left the room with them. When she returned, after exchanging her soaked blue dress for a black skirt and high-necked shirtwaist, Doc was just finishing putting new wrapping around the patient's rib cage.

"Good as new," the old man boasted.

"Not quite," Steven said, grimacing as he settled back

against the pillows. The crisp white sheets lay just covering his abdomen, and Doc bent to examine the cuts he'd stitched up the night before, frowning.

"No need to put new bandages on, Emma," the doctor said.

Emma nodded. "Is there anything you want before I go back to the library, Mr. Fairfax?" She would have called her guest Steven, except for the doctor's presence. The blaze of rumors would be fanned enough by Doc's account of Emma hauling a half-naked man from the bathroom. To address Steven informally would only have added to the problem.

"No, thank you, Miss Emma," he said distractedly, closing his eyes.

Emma felt a pang at the sight of him lying there, so exhausted by the strain of traveling up and down the stairs. "I'll read to you again tonight, if you'd like," she offered, not caring whether Doc reported her words to the general populace or not.

"That would be—fine," Steven answered. His gaze wandered over Emma's person once more, in a leisurely and slightly insolent sweep, and then he drifted into a deep, consuming slumber.

Emma descended the rear stairway with Doc right on her heels. He was probably eager to finish his rounds so he could have a drink or two at the Stardust Saloon.

In the kitchen, she lifted the lid on Daisy's soup kettle and peered inside. The stuff was cold as well water.

"You just send for me if that young fella has any trouble," Doc said generously, from the doorway.

"Thank you," Emma answered, going to the breadbox. "I will." Hastily, she made herself a jam sandwich. She ate it as she hurried along the sidewalk toward the library a few minutes later.

The place was empty, as it usually was at that time of day, and Emma put herself to work going through the stacks to make sure all the books were in their proper order. Work had always been her refuge, but that day it didn't help.

Images of Steven Fairfax sprawled in Chloe's bathtub with a washcloth over his privates filled her mind. Despite her efforts not to see, she'd noticed his hairy chest, the corded muscles in his thighs, the brown strength of his forearms. Her breath came a little faster and a fine mist of perspiration gathered between her breasts and along her upper lip.

Emma closed her eyes for a moment, determined to think of something else.

Lord, but Steven was even more appealing than before, now that the layers of trail dust, sweat, and dried blood had been washed away. His smile was as bright as the lamp on the front of a train rolling through the darkness, and his hair, while a touch on the long side, invited a woman to tangle her fingers in it.

Emma felt so warm that she went over and opened the door, just to let in some fresh air. It was unseasonably hot for April, it seemed to her.

It was just then that Big John Lenahan strolled in, whistling. He was, as his nickname suggested, well over six feet tall and powerfully built. He had thinning white hair and eyes of the same cornflower blue as his daughter Joellen's, but he was a far kinder person than his child.

"Hello, Miss Emma," he said pleasantly.

Emma smiled at him. "Afternoon, Big John. How may I help you?"

"Well, it seems Joellen took a fancy to some book you've got here, and she didn't want to wait her turn to read it. I thought I'd find out from you what it was and have old Mitch over at the general store order it up for a surprise."

Emma didn't let her opinion of Joellen show in her expression or the tone of her voice, for she wouldn't have hurt Big John's feelings for the world. "Of course. It was Mr. Hardy's new novel." She wrote the information on a slip of paper and handed it to the prosperous rancher standing on the other side of the counter. "How are things out on the Circle L?"

Big John shrugged shoulders the size of a grizzly

bear's. "We're shorthanded, as always, and Joellen's a handful. I sure wish Chloe would break down and marry me, so that girl could have a mother."

Emma smiled to think of Chloe as Joellen's stepmother. The girl's career as a brat would end in short order. "You know how Chloe is, Big John."

He nodded ruefully and tucked the slip of paper Emma had written the book title on into the pocket of his buckskin vest. "There ain't a stubborner woman in the territory, but I'll rope that filly if it's the last thing I ever do."

"It just might be," Emma warned, waggling a finger, and she and Big John laughed together.

# Chapter
## ❧ 4 ❧

$S$ame as usual, Miss Emma?" asked Ethan Peters, editor-in-chief of the *Whitneyville Orator*.

Emma was feeling melancholy that sunny Friday morning. She'd had thousands, maybe *hundreds* of thousands of posters printed up in her time, and she'd never heard a word about Lily or Caroline. Sometimes she wondered if anybody, anywhere, was reading her notices. "Yes, Mr. Peters," she sighed.

The kindly middle-aged man smiled at her as he reached for a pencil to take down the order. His long black mustache was waxed, and he'd combed what remained of his hair artfully across the top of his head. It seemed to Emma that a man was better off just going ahead and being bald than trying to hide the obvious.

"I certainly hope you aren't fixing to give up, Miss Emma. Those sisters of yours are out there someplace, and you can bet somebody who knows them is going to see your posters someday."

Emma worked up a smile. "I hope you're right."

Mr. Peters nodded. "It's only a matter of time."

Emma left the newspaper office and continued down the street toward the library. The ill-fated Yellow Belly Saloon had been burned to the ground and there had been no talk as yet of rebuilding. Chloe's place, now the only establishment in town where liquor could be had, was jumping with music and laughter.

With a little smile and a shake of her head, Emma proceeded past the Stardust at a respectable pace, though secretly she yearned for a look inside. She was especially curious about the upstairs, where girls like Callie received their amorous callers.

While plundering her jet-beaded handbag for the key to the library's front door, Emma once again accepted the fact that she'd probably never see any part of the Stardust Saloon, upstairs or downstairs. Chloe had sworn to skin her alive if she put one foot over the threshold. Although Chloe had been the gentlest of adoptive mothers, Emma knew the legendary Miss Reese was immovable where this subject was concerned.

Emma was just fitting the key into the lock when Fulton appeared, wearing his usual suit and derby hat. He looked very agitated indeed.

"I must speak with you," he said in an earnest whisper, as though the whole town might be bending its collective ear to hear whatever passed between them.

For the second time that morning Emma sighed. "Come in off the street, Fulton."

He followed her into the cool, musty confines of the Whitneyville Lending Library, which was founded by Miss Chloe Reese and patronized by people who wouldn't have spoken to the woman to save themselves from the fiery pits of hell. "Emma," he began, taking off his hat and turning its brim nervously in his fingers, "something must be done about the rumors."

"What rumors?" Emma asked, though she knew full well why Fulton was there. She'd guessed the moment she saw him that he was going to lecture her about Steven.

Fulton paused to run appreciative blue eyes over her

trim green skirt and pristine white shirtwaist. "You do look real nice this morning," he allowed.

Emma slipped behind the desk, mostly to put a barrier between them, and pretended to be busy with the card file. "Thank you."

He took the plunge. "It's that outlaw you and Chloe are putting up. He has to go, Emma."

She thought of Steven listening with real interest to another chapter of *Little Women* the night before, and lowered her eyes so Fulton wouldn't see the memory there. "The man is quite harmless," Emma lied. Steven wasn't just passing through her life, she knew that. He was just cussed enough to have some lasting, and probably devastating, effect on it.

"I've talked to some of the people who were in the Yellow Belly when he rode in, Emma," Fulton rushed on. "They said he wore a forty-five, and there wasn't a man in the place who would have challenged him."

"There probably wasn't a man in the place *sober* enough to challenge him," Emma reasoned a little impatiently, as her fingertips flicked over the card file.

"He's a gunslinger," Fulton asserted, placing his hands against the counter and leaning toward Emma. "I must insist that you ask him to leave."

Emma had a slight headache. Fulton had no right to insist on anything, since he and Emma had made no formal agreement to marry. "I don't see how he could leave," she said, "when he can't even walk on his own."

"Then send him over to stay with Doc Waverly."

"That's a grand idea, Fulton. Whenever the doctor happens to be sober, he can see to his patient's needs."

Emma's sarcasm was not lost on Fulton, nor did it move him. He knotted one hand into a fist and slammed it down hard on the counter. "Damn it all to hell, Emma, people are saying you're intimate with the man—that you bathed him, for God's sake!"

Emma's headache was now full-blown. So Doc Waverly had spread the word. Well, when she saw him again, she'd give him a piece of her mind for being such an old busybody. "I think you'd better take your case to Chloe," she said, fumbling underneath the counter for the box of headache powders she kept there.

They both knew what Chloe would say: that Fulton should go count his money and stay out of her business. Only, she wouldn't put it so politely.

Emma drew a deep breath, to embolden herself. "Furthermore, I don't think you and I should see quite so much of each other for a while. We both need time to gain some perspective."

Fulton glared at her for a moment then, seething, he stormed out of the library and slammed the door behind him.

Emma got water from the temperamental spigot in the backroom sink and stirred in a packet of headache powders. She was busy all morning, and when she walked home at noon she found a plate of chicken sandwiches on the kitchen table, covered with a checkered napkin. There was no other sign of Daisy's presence.

After making sure her braid was tidy, and pinching her cheeks for color, Emma took the plate of sandwiches up the rear stairs and knocked at Steven's door.

He sounded irritable when he told her to come in.

"How are you feeling?" she asked.

He slammed shut the book Emma had brought him from downstairs that morning. "Fine," he said, glowering.

Emma laughed, taking her customary chair, the plate of sandwiches balanced on her knees. "I know you can be pleasant if you try, Mr. Fairfax. You were a perfect gentleman last night, when I was reading to you."

Steven's glance at the sandwiches made her extend the plate, and he took one of Daisy's creations with a sort of reluctant gratitude. "I need my forty-five," he said.

Emma smoothed her skirt, the sateen slick and shiny under her fingers. The movements of Steven's throat as he chewed and swallowed gave her a strange, heated feeling. "This seems to be my day for dealing with impossible demands," she said.

Steven frowned even as he continued to consume the sandwich, and Emma suppressed an urge to fan herself with one hand. "What's that supposed to mean?" he snapped.

"I think that's obvious. It means I'm not going to give you the gun."

He didn't take another sandwich, and when he ran his tongue swiftly over his lips, Emma felt a stab of what could only be raw desire. "Has anybody ever told you what a hardheaded little spitfire you are?"

"Yes," Emma replied primly, "and it's never done them a mite of good."

Steven sank back against his pillows, and Emma knew by his involuntary grimace and the paleness of his skin that he was in severe pain.

Gently, and without thinking, Emma reached out to touch his forehead. His hand rose and closed around her wrist, and his fingers were at once strong and gentle. "Come here," he said gruffly.

He was like the mystical, superhuman creatures Emma had read about, captivating their victims with their eyes. She put the sandwich plate on the bedside stand and allowed him to pull her nearer, so that she sat on the edge of the bed.

Her breasts rose and fell beneath her very proper bodice as he ran the calloused pad of his thumb up and down the inside of her wrist. A shiver went through her, and she swallowed hard, feeling like a field mouse facing a cobra.

Steven's hand left her wrist to lightly grasp her thick, red-blond braid and run it between his fingers. Then he traced her jawline and the full moistness of her lips, and she trembled and started to move away.

He wouldn't allow her to go. He cupped her chin in his hand and said, his voice low and mesmerizing, "You're a wildcat underneath those librarian's clothes, Emma

Chalmers." When her indigo eyes widened in surprise
and the beginnings of offense, he smiled and continued.
"And one of these days, I'm going to prove it's true."

Having said that, he brought Emma's face down to his
and he kissed her, bold as you please. A sweet shiver went
through her as he touched the sides of her mouth with his
tongue, seeking something she'd never been asked to
give.

Feeling a flame ignite in the depths of her femininity,
Emma made up her mind to pull back and instead
opened her mouth for Steven. He immediately mastered
her with his tongue, and Emma gave a helpless sigh as she
sank against him.

"Steven," she protested when he somehow maneuvered her so that she was lying beside him on the guest
room bed, her hair coming out of its braid and rising
around her face in gossamer strands of coppery gold.

"Sweet," he said in a sleepy tone, just before he
covered her mouth with his again.

Emma felt much the way she had the summer she was
fifteen, when she'd gotten into Chloe's Christmas cordial
and drunk herself silly. She didn't seem to have any
anchor in the real world, and her head swam. When
Steven laid a gentle hand on her breast she whimpered
and arched her head back on the pillow.

"Does your banker touch you like this, Emma?"

"Oh, God," Emma whispered, too deliciously dis-
traught to wonder how much Steven knew about Fulton.

Steven bent his head and nipped at a hidden nipple
with his teeth, and the pleasure made Emma plunge her
heels into the mattress and try to raise herself for more.

He was kissing her neck, nibbling at it, teasing her
pulse point with his tongue even as he began unfastening
the tiny pearl buttons that held her shirtwaist closed.

"Mr. Fairfax!"

"I'm not going to hurt you," he assured her quietly,
and she believed him. "All I want to do is show you who
you really are." He punctuated each word with some

amorous attention to her tingling neck, and when Emma felt herself bared—except for her thin camisole—he slid down her body until his face was even with her straining breasts.

With the utmost tenderness, he uncovered one, giving an admiring sigh before he cupped the fullness in his hand and laid his tongue to the nipple.

Emma gasped with pleasure as he sucked, her head moving from side to side on the pillow in sweet delirium. His words echoed in her fevered spirit. *All I want to do is show you who you really are . . .*

Presently he bared the other breast and busied himself at its peak, and Emma could hardly keep herself from thrashing on the bed. When he lifted her skirt and laid his hand over the soft place where her bloomers were moist, however, she was startled and sat bolt upright, springing off the bed to stand on the other side of the room.

The expression in Steven's eyes showed both understanding and amusement, and he watched with undisguised interest as Emma hastily covered her still-pulsing bosom.

"I know," he sighed, with a crooked, teasing grin. "You're not that kind of girl."

Emma knew her face was crimson with embarrassment and umbrage, and only then, when it was too late, did she think to do her buttoning with her back turned. "I most certainly am not!"

"You liked it," Steven said, settling back with a smug sigh. "And from now until the day I take you, you're going to be wondering what else I might have made you feel."

"You are insufferably arrogant, Mr. Fairfax!"

"But right, nonetheless," he responded easily. And then he had the bald effrontery to yawn. "You're all warm and wet, and certain parts of you are feeling downright disappointed, whether you'll admit to the fact or not."

A lame protest died in her throat. Everything Steven

said was true, and she couldn't deny it because she knew he'd see through the lie.

"Emma the librarian," he said huskily. Then he chuckled as though he found her occupation extraordinarily humorous.

Emma's knees felt weak as noodles, and a soft whimper rose in her throat at the brazen truth of his words. She swallowed it. "You overestimate your appeal, Mr. Fairfax," she said. And then she turned on one heel and left the room, slamming the door shut behind her.

Only when she was seated on her favorite rock down by the lake did Emma's flesh begin to cool and her breathing start to slow. She'd wanted to stay on that bed with Steven, to allow him even further liberties, and the fact terrified her. More than anything, except of course for finding her lost sisters, Emma wanted to be accepted as a decent and upright woman.

She put her hands to her throbbing cheeks. Instead, she'd behaved like a wanton. She could still feel the warm wetness of his mouth on her nipples. Misery knifed through her, even as remembered pleasure made her bunch up the fabric of her skirt in both hands.

Much later, when she'd regained her dignity, Emma returned to Steven's room to confront him.

"How dare you touch me like that?" she breathed.

He had settled back on his pillows, looking comfortable as you please, and he marked his place in the book he'd been reading with an index finger. "Wait until you see the other ways I mean to touch you," he drawled.

Emma's face flamed bright as her hair. "You most certainly will not," she said, bristling.

Steven nodded toward the chair. "Sit down, Emma," he said gently. "Please."

Emma sat after pulling the chair well out of his range.

"Stop acting as though you've been besmirched or something," he scolded good-naturedly. "You're not the first girl who's ever had her breasts kissed."

*"Please,"* Emma gasped, looking away.

Steven laughed. "I'd like to meet this beau of yours,"

he said, opening the book again. His eyes narrowed as he fastened his attention on the page. "I figure he's probably something of a curiosity."

Incensed, Emma shot from her chair and barely kept herself from batting the book out of his hands. "Fulton is a gentleman," she said, wondering why she felt compelled to defend the man so strenuously when she'd all but broken off with him just a short time before. "He is well-mannered and educated and he is *not* a 'curiosity'!"

The patient smiled politely and turned a page. "He's never made you feel like a woman," he said, with insultingly accurate perception. "You're as luscious as a ripe peach, and the fool's left you on the vine. To my way of thinking, that makes him an oddity, like the mummified Indian I saw once." He turned another page, frowning thoughtfully. "Somebody ought to sell tickets."

Emma wanted to stomp over to that bed and slap Steven Fairfax squarely across the face, but he was a wounded man, after all. Besides, she didn't dare come that close to him. Without another word, she whirled on one heel and fled, taking satisfaction in closing the door with a slam that made the paintings and photographs in the hallway rattle on their hooks.

Downstairs, Emma fairly flung the teakettle onto the stove, and she was just standing there, full of helpless fury, when Chloe came in from the small parlor.

She looked at Emma's disheveled hair and wrinkled skirt in surprise, then asked, "Are you all right?"

"No," Emma answered, hugging herself. "No, I'm not all right. I'm not all right at all!"

"May I ask what happened? You look like you used to when you were eleven or twelve, and you'd spent the day playing on the island."

Emma knew real misery as she watched the truth dawn on Chloe. The older woman's eyes, green as an Irish meadow, flashed with good humor.

"Why, Emma Chalmers. You let Steven kiss you. And pretty thoroughly, too, by the looks of you!"

"I'm no better than my mother!" Emma whispered brokenly.

Chloe's manner immediately became firm. She went to the stove and with a practiced finger, tapped the side of the kettle Emma had just put on, to see if it was hot enough for tea. "Nonsense," she answered, taking a china pot and a tin of orange pekoe from the shelf beside the stove. "You'd never abandon anyone who needed you, like she did. Why, look at the way you've searched for those sisters of yours."

Emma collapsed into a chair at the table. She didn't see how she could face going back to the library, considering the state she was in. Her hands closed around the delicate china cup Chloe set before her, even though the water wasn't ready yet. Her throat was constricted with a riot of clashing emotions, and she couldn't have spoken for anything.

Chloe smiled kindly, sitting down next to Emma. "Why don't you lock up the library tomorrow and spend the day doing something frivolous? You're far too practical for your own good."

"What could I do?" Emma asked forlornly.

Chloe's shapely shoulders moved in a shrug beneath her pink feather boa, which complemented her cranberry-colored dress. "I'm going out to Big John's for the afternoon. You could come along."

Thinking of Joellen, Emma made a face. "No, thanks. You and Big John don't need me underfoot." At that, Emma promptly covered her eyes with both hands and began to sob.

"Emma, what happened up there? Surely a simple kiss wouldn't upset you like this!"

For the first time since Emma had known Chloe, she found herself unable to confide in the woman. She was simply too ashamed to admit what she'd allowed Steven to do to her—or how much she'd liked it. "I'll be all right," she said suddenly, bolting out of her chair, the prospect of tea forgotten.

In her room she brushed and rebraided her hair, then wound the plait into a conservative coronet at the crown of her head. She didn't pinch her cheeks or spray herself with perfume, either.

As she was leaving, having determined that even going back to the library would be better than staying in that house and remembering what a hussy she'd been, Emma froze in the hallway. She was possessed of the most insistent need to look in on Steven, and after all he'd done, too.

She crept to the door and reached for the knob, but her courage wavered. Then, after a moment of collecting herself, Emma rapped lightly and stepped inside.

Steven had put on the clothes she'd brought him, and he was clasping the bedpost in one hand in an effort to hoist himself to his feet. His jawline was set and his eyes were closed against what had to be a wrenching agony. Although he was surely aware of Emma's presence, he paid her no mind at all.

Hastily, Emma hurried over to take his arm. "You shouldn't be out of bed!" she blurted.

Steven scowled at her, as though it were somehow her fault that he couldn't move about as he liked, and collapsed onto the mattress. He sagged back against his pillows, his skin gray with the strain of trying to rise, a muscle in his jawline standing out with hard annoyance.

Emma relaxed a little, and even managed a smile. Just as she'd pretended to be Guinevere or Joan of Arc as a young girl, she now pretended to be a person who had never lain beside a man or allowed him to open the bodice of her dress.

"How are you feeling?" she asked in the same tone she used on summer afternoons, when some of the town's children came to sit beside the lake with her and listen while she read stories.

He ruined everything by saying, "I don't like your hair that way. It makes you look like a spinster."

Emma couldn't help bristling. "Did it ever occur to you that I might *want* to look like a proper lady?"

"Why?" grumbled Steven, reaching for his book.

"I don't have to stand here and be insulted!" Emma flared, wounded because a lady was what she most wanted to be. "Honestly, Mr. Fairfax—you are the most arrogant, impossible man!"

He smiled mischievously. "I'd like you to call me that from now on—in public, at least. *Mr. Fairfax.*" He paused to relish the name. "Yes, I'd like that very much."

If there had been anything in Emma's hand, she would have thrown it at him. "You can't possibly think I mean to speak to you at all after this!"

He laughed. "You'll do a whole lot more than speak, Miss Emma."

Emma gave a strangled scream of fury and once again fled the room, striding along the hallway and down the rear stairs. Chloe was gone, but Daisy had returned from wherever she'd been, and she was rolling out pie dough on the work table.

She laughed when Emma hurtled into the kitchen. "What's the matter, chile? The debil chasin' after you?"

Emma paused to take a deep breath and recover her dignity. "Yes," she said. "Do you know where Chloe put Mr. Fair—Steven's pistol?"

"She done locked it up in her desk drawer with the derringer. Why? You gonna give it back to him?"

Emma nodded, then proceeded toward the hallway. "I most certainly am."

"Why you wanna do that?" Daisy fussed, following her out of the kitchen and into Chloe's study.

Finding the key in its customary hiding place, Emma unlocked Chloe's desk and lifted the formidable Colt .45 gingerly from its depths. "There's always the hope that he'll shoot himself," she said cheerfully.

Daisy shrank back against the doorway. "Miss Emma, you put that thing down right now, or I's gonna take you over my knee and paddle you!"

Emma raised the gun and sited in on a book shelf across the room. She wondered what it would be like to fire the weapon. In the next instant she found out, for the gun went off with no intentional help from Emma, and several of Chloe's leatherbound books exploded into a single smoldering tangle of paper.

Daisy screamed and so did Emma, who dropped the gun in horror only to have it fire again, this time splintering the leg of Big John's favorite chair.

"Don't you dare touch that thing again!" Daisy shrieked, when Emma bent to retrieve it.

Emma left the pistol lying on the rug and straightened up again, one hand pressed to her mouth in shock. The two women stood in their places for a long time, afraid to move. Emma, for her part, was busy imagining all the dreadful things that could have happened.

She was amazed to see Steven stumble into the room, fully dressed except for his boots, drenched in sweat from the effort of making his way down the stairs in a hurry. The expression in his eyes was wild and alert, almost predatory.

"What the hell's going on in here?" he rasped.

Emma pointed to the pistol as though it were a snake coiled to strike. "It went off—twice."

Steven was supporting himself by grasping the edge of Chloe's desk. "Pick it up very carefully and hand it to me," he said.

Emma bit her lower lip, remembering what had happened when she'd handled the gun before.

"You can do it," Steven urged. "Just make sure you don't touch the hammer or the trigger."

Emma crouched and picked it up cautiously. The barrel was hot against her palm.

"Here," Steven said, holding out his hand.

Emma surrendered the gun, and leaning back against the desk, Steven spun the chamber expertly, dropping the four remaining bullets into his palm. He gave a ragged sigh, then just stood there, cradling the pistol in his hands like a kitten or a puppy.

"I was going to bring it to you," Emma confessed in a small voice.

"She was hopin' you'd blow your brains out with it," Daisy muttered, before she turned and went back to the kitchen.

Steven's voice was ominously quiet. "What changed your mind, Emma? The last time I asked for this gun, you refused to get it for me."

Emma ran her tongue nervously over her lips. The truth was, she wasn't quite sure why she'd wanted to touch and hold that terrible weapon. She guessed it probably had a dangerous fascination for her, just as its owner did.

"Answer me," Steven insisted.

"I don't know," Emma replied.

"Where's the holster?"

Emma went woodenly to Chloe's desk drawer and collected the item he wanted. It was made of plain, creaky leather, and it had obviously seen long use. "You're an outlaw, aren't you?" she whispered, holding out the holster.

Steven took it and immediately sheathed the gun. He was weakening rapidly; Emma could see he was barely able to stand. "That depends on who you're talking to, Miss Emma."

She wet her lips again. "Give me the gun, Steven. We'll put it away."

He shook his head, dismissing the suggestion. "Will you help me back up the stairs?"

Emma nodded and Steven put his arm around her shoulder. She probably wasn't much steadier than he was, since she was still trembling with fear, but somehow she managed to get him back to his room.

There Steven stretched out on his bed, the pistol at his side on the mattress, and closed his eyes. "I'm not a criminal, Miss Emma," he said wearily. "You're safe with me."

"Safe" was hardly the word Emma would have used, especially after what they'd done together, but she didn't have the strength to argue. There was a great hammering at the front door, and Emma knew it would be the marshal and some of the townsmen, come to find out why two shots had been fired inside Miss Chloe Reese's house.

There was an appeal in Steven's hazel eyes when he opened them to look at her. "Lie if you have to," he said, "but don't mention me."

# Chapter
## ❧ 5 ❧

*E*mma smoothed her hair before wrenching open the front door to greet the marshal. With him, to her chagrin, was a very concerned Fulton.

"Great Scot, Emma," the latter boomed, pushing past her into the house. "What happened here? Are you hurt?"

"No," she said quietly, pushing the door closed. "No one was hurt. I—I was handling a gun Chloe keeps in her desk. I shouldn't have touched it."

Fulton proceeded to the study, the elderly, forgetful marshal following after him. Together they inspected the demolished books and Big John's broken chair.

"Where is this gun now?" Fulton demanded.

"I put it away," Emma lied. She felt foolish over the shooting episode, but she was also annoyed. She'd told Fulton very firmly that she believed they shouldn't be quite so friendly as they had been, and he was behaving as if nothing had changed between them.

"I want to see it."

"Well, you can't," Emma retorted stubbornly, squaring her shoulders even as she gripped the back of Chloe's desk chair for support. "No crime was committed here. There was an accident, that's all."

"All this has something to do with that damnable drifter!" Fulton accused, his face red with fury.

Old Marshal Woodridge just looked back and forth between Fulton and Emma.

"No, it doesn't," Emma insisted. If her hands hadn't been in plain view, she would have crossed her fingers. "I told you—there was an accident."

Fulton glared at her and pointed toward the upper floor. "I think the marshal and I should just go upstairs and have a little talk with your friend."

Emma swallowed. She'd promised not to mention Steven, and she hadn't. "Go ahead, then."

"Just one damned minute," another voice interceded, and Emma turned to see Chloe standing in the doorway. Her color was high, her artfully styled hair mussed, as though she'd made great haste to get home. "This is my house, and I'm choosy about who goes poking around in it."

Marshal Woodridge, with his rheumy eyes and missing teeth, wasn't inclined to argue with Chloe. He smiled at her. "No call to get riled, now," he said. "We just came on account of the shots."

Chloe's gaze locked with Emma's. "Was anyone hurt?"

Emma shook her head and realized she was still trembling.

"Then I don't see any need for you two to hang around here," Chloe told the marshal and Fulton. "Good day, gentlemen, and thank you for your concern."

"I'll come calling tomorrow afternoon," Fulton told Emma in a somewhat petulant tone. He made his retreat quickly, giving her no time to protest.

The marshal, who hadn't bothered to remove his battered old hat, tilted the brim politely and followed Fulton out.

"What happened?" Chloe demanded the moment the men were gone.

Emma explained as well as she could.

"You know I forbid anyone to carry a gun in this house. Why did you even touch the thing?"

As she recalled the deadly expression in Steven's eyes when he'd come downstairs to investigate the gunshot earlier, it came to Emma that his reasons for constantly pestering her to give him the pistol might be more far serious than she'd guessed. He'd clearly expected trouble.

"Steven needs to have it close at hand," she said softly, frowning as some very disturbing possibilities presented themselves in her mind. "He's—I think someone's hunting him."

Chloe didn't look entirely convinced, but some of her anger had subsided. She went to the liquor cabinet and made herself a strong drink. "Who? A lawman? A bounty hunter?"

Emma was miserable. "I don't know."

Chloe gave a long sigh, then tossed back her drink with dispatch. Despite the fact that she didn't receive callers herself, she had a lot of work to do at the Stardust, and the incident had been an interruption. "I'd ask Marshal Woodridge if he's seen any posters or received wires about a man answering Fairfax's description, but I don't expect that old fool would recognize Billy the Kid or Butch Cassidy, let alone an outlaw who might not have made a name for himself."

Although her opinion of the marshal's competence was no higher than Chloe's, Emma felt the color drain from her face at the prospect of drawing undue attention to Steven. "He'll ride out soon," she said hastily. "Can't we just leave well enough alone?"

Already on her way to the door, Chloe frowned, then nodded. "I guess so, as long as there's no more trouble." She paused, her hand on the knob, her green eyes meeting Emma's. "Mind you don't fall in love with him, Emma. I've got Fairfax pegged for a good man, but I suspect you're right in thinking he's in some kind of trouble. I won't have you caught in the middle of somebody else's fight."

Emma swallowed, unable to promise she wouldn't give her heart to Steven, when she'd very nearly given him her body. "I'll be careful," was the best she could do.

When Chloe was gone, Emma found she had no spirit for returning to the library. Instead, she went to the piano, which stood in a corner of the small parlor, to play and sing the old-fashioned song she and Lily and Caroline had once sung in harmony.

> *Three flowers bloomed in the meadow,*
> *Heads bent in sweet repose,*
> *The daisy, the lily, and the rose . . .*

When she rose from the bench, she felt lonelier than ever, but she was in a calmer state of mind.

She was just beginning to think she could cope when there was a ruckus in the kitchen. Hurrying to investigate, Emma found Callie at the back door, looking intimidated by Daisy's upraised skillet and warning glower.

"I gotta come in, Miss Emma," Callie blurted, when she saw her friend. "Miss Chloe done told me to come over here and take care of that drifter man."

Emma reached out and clutched the back of a kitchen chair for support, but revealed no other sign of her true feelings in the matter. In fact, she smiled when she said, "Daisy, put down that skillet this minute and leave me to talk to Callie in private."

Daisy complied, muttering about what this world was coming to when a decent woman was called upon to let a strumpet walk right into her kitchen.

"What do you mean, you're supposed to 'take care of' Mr. Fairfax?" Emma asked pleasantly, lifting the teakettle from the back of the stove.

Callie wet her painted lips nervously with her tongue. "Well, Miss Emma, I reckon I'm supposed to dump the slop jar and keep him company and such as that."

Emma poured hot water over leaves of fragrant tea she'd sprinkled into the bottom of her favorite teapot. Although her demeanor was pleasant, she was still spinning inwardly in the whirlwind of jealousy that had possessed her from the moment Callie had stated her purpose. "What else were you told to do?"

Callie's kohl-lined eyes scanned the kitchen as though expecting to find the answer written on a spice jar or a flour bag. "That's all Miss Chloe said, but I reckon if he wanted some comfortin', I'd see to that, too."

Dropping into a chair facing Callie's, a fixed smile on her face, Emma asked confidentially, "Just exactly how would you 'comfort' a man like Mr. Fairfax?"

The one task Callie probably felt competent at had been presented, and she beamed. "There's things they all like, Miss Emma—don't matter much what kind of man they are."

Emma felt color pounding in her cheeks as she poured tea for Callie, then for herself. "Like what?"

At this, Callie actually blushed behind her heavy rouge. "You're a lady," she protested. "A lady don't want to know things like that."

"I suspect she does," Emma replied wistfully, lifting her teacup to her lips, "if she wants to keep her husband from frequenting the Stardust Saloon."

Callie squirmed a little in her chair, hesitating to pick up her cup even though it was obvious she wanted to. "Not many men in town do that, Miss Emma—stay away from the Stardust, I mean."

"Nonsense," Emma countered. "Fulton doesn't go there."

Callie overcame her hesitancy in that moment and took a slurping gulp of her tea.

"Tell me what you do to them," Emma pressed, "that they find so appealing."

After looking carefully around her to make sure Daisy wasn't lurking somewhere, ready to descend on her like a wrathful angel, Callie leaned forward in her chair and whispered something that made Emma's eyes go round.

She set her teacup down in its saucer with a rattling *clink*. "You don't!"

"Yes, we do," Callie insisted. "And they like it."

Emma took a long, deep breath. Her cheeks felt as though they'd been doused in kerosene, then set afire, and her stomach seemed to be perched on the edge of some unseen precipice, ready to drop off into space. "If you do anything like that for Mr. Fairfax, Callie Visco, I'll never fetch you another library book as long as I live!"

Callie reared back in her chair, her expression a mingling of bafflement and concern, but she didn't say anything.

Emma found that unsettling, since she wanted a promise written in blood. "You can just go back to the Stardust Saloon," she said with prim dispatch. "We don't need you here."

At this, Callie shook her peroxided head. "And have Miss Chloe turn me out for disobeyin' her orders? Not on your life—I've got no place to go from here!"

"I suppose there's nothing to do but let you stay, then," Emma said with a sigh. Although she was now ashamed of her proprietary feelings toward Steven Fairfax, they hadn't changed in the least. She assessed Callie's wild hair and revealing red satin dress with a thoughtful eye. "We'll have to do something about the way you look, though."

And so it was that Miss Visco was presented to Steven a full hour later, wearing a plain calico dress, her face scrubbed clean of paint, her billowing yellow hair brushed and tucked into a matronly snood.

Steven maddened Emma by smiling at Callie as though she were an angel of mercy come to save him from ceaseless torment. "Hello, there," he said.

Callie gave an awkward little curtsey and tossed a wary glance in Emma's direction. "Hello," she responded.

"Mr. Fairfax," Emma said formally, "this is Miss Callie Visco. She's going to look after you since—since I'm so busy at the library."

Steven closed the book he was reading. "Whatever you say, Miss Emma."

Emma didn't like the way he was studying Callie. "I know I can trust you to be a gentleman," she said, in a strait-laced tone of voice.

"Whatever gave you that idea?" Steven replied, his eyes laughing as they moved, a little reluctantly, it seemed to Emma, from Callie's body to Emma's face.

In another minute Emma knew she was going to have a childish jealousy fit and disgrace herself. Determined not to give Steven that satisfaction, she squared her shoulders and said, "Good day, then." After that, she slipped out of the room and closed the door firmly.

There was nothing to do then but go to the library. Once there, however, Emma couldn't keep her thoughts on books. No, they kept straying back to Chloe's guest room, where Callie might even now be doing to Steven what men supposedly liked so much. The thought made Emma spitting mad, and her color was high when Fulton strolled in unexpectedly.

"I brought you a present," he said in a tone that was, for him, quite meek. Doffing his hat, he stepped over the returned library books Emma had yet to put away and extended a blue satin box to her. "I'm sorry about that little spat we had earlier, Emma. Will you go walking with me tonight, after supper?"

Emma looked at the box of chocolates but did not accept it. "Fulton, I thought we agreed not to see each other for a while."

He set the candy on the counter and, although he couldn't hide the muscle that flexed in his jawline, he did seem to be making an effort at calmness. "We agreed to no such thing," he said reasonably. "Emma, that man is not suited to you. He's a saddle-bum, a drifter. He can't give you a home and family, the way I can."

Emma thought of the sweet, piercing things Steven had made her feel in his arms, and she suffered a twinge of sorrow. She ran her fingers over the letters of a title embossed on the cover of a book. "This has nothing to do with Mr. Fairfax," she said quietly. And sadly. For Fulton was at least partly right—Steven couldn't give her the respectable life she longed for, he probably didn't even want to settle down and start a family. But the few kisses Fulton had stolen from her over the course of their friendship had never stirred a response inside her, either. And she could no longer convince herself that her coolness to his touch didn't matter.

Fulton sighed. "I hope you'll give me an opportunity to change your mind, my dear. After all, we are still friends, aren't we? Or have we become enemies?"

Emma shook her head. "Of course we haven't," she said in a small voice. Although Fulton was a little stuffy and quite fond of getting his own way, Emma liked him.

"Then there's no reason why you shouldn't take the chocolate," he said, holding the candy out to her again.

"Thank you," she said, having no choice but to take the box.

Callie Visco, Steven decided, was a good sport. She'd helped him out of bed, even though he could see the idea was against her better judgment, and spent a good part of the afternoon escorting him back and forth across the floor while he practiced walking.

Now, with the sun sinking in the sky, he was half-sick with exhaustion. He collapsed gratefully onto the bed and let Callie cover him with the blankets like a weary child.

Laying her small hand on his forehead, she smoothed his hair back. "You'd like some soothin', wouldn't you, Mr. Fairfax?" she asked in a sympathetic voice.

A raw chuckle left his throat as he thought of Emma forcing this poor little minx into a calico dress and an old lady's snood. "I sure would, Callie," he answered honestly, "but I'm afraid there's only one woman I want."

A mischievous grin curved Callie's mouth. "Miss Emma?"

"The same," Steven admitted with a sigh, "but don't you tell her. I want this to be our little secret."

Callie sat down in the chair Emma always occupied when she read to him. He found himself missing that redheaded hellcat with a fierce keenness, as though they'd been parted a month instead of a few hours. "She got real upset, Miss Emma did," Callie confided in a happy whisper, "when I came over here and told her Miss Chloe'd sent me to look after you."

Steven laughed. "Good," he replied, staring out the window at the sun. It seemed to be immersing itself in the far side of the lake. "I'm making progress."

Callie was fidgeting with the snood that bound her yellow hair. "I guess I'd better be gettin' back to the Stardust, Mr. Fairfax."

He reached out to clasp her hand and give it a friendly squeeze. "Steven," he corrected.

She looked delighted. "Steven, then." Callie paused to peer at him, squinting as though she needed spectacles. "You don't look like a man anybody'd call 'Steve,' I reckon."

"I reckon I'm not," Steven said smoothly. "Callie, there is one thing you could do for me, if you wouldn't mind."

Callie's eyes lit up. "What?"

"There's some money in the pocket of that coat over there. Take what you need and get me a box of cigars, will you?"

"Anything else?" she asked, and Steven thought he heard a note of hopefulness in her voice as she headed toward Steven's long canvas coat, which was still draped over the back of a chair near the window.

Steven grinned. "Yes. Buy yourself a handkerchief or something—whatever you'd like."

Callie looked back at him, the money in her hand, a touching expression of surprise on her face. "Thanks, Steven—for everything."

"Thank you," Steven answered, settling back on his

pillows and closing his eyes against the glare of the sun on the lake.

"See you tomorrow," Callie replied, and then he heard the door close behind her.

Emma stood stock-still in the hallway, her eyes wide as she watched Callie leave Steven's room, clasping a ten-dollar bill in one hand.

"Hello, Miss Emma," Callie said brightly.

It required all Emma's Christian forbearance not to grab the woman by the hair and snatch her baldheaded. "How is Mr. Fairfax?" she asked, her voice stiff with the effort it took not to scream.

Callie smiled. "He's right happy, but he's pretty tired."

Emma must have looked ferocious at that point, for Callie shrank back in surprise, then scurried toward the front stairway like a field mouse with a cat on its tail.

After taking a moment to compose herself, Emma knocked at the guest-room door in an unquestionably proper fashion.

"Come in," Steven called from inside. It wasn't his usual bark; indeed, Emma thought, he sounded "right happy."

She stormed into the room and stood at his bedside, her hands on her hips, her blue eyes shooting sparks. There was a silly grin on his face and he had the audacity to add insult to injury by following that with a yawn.

"Deviant!" Emma hissed.

"Jealous, Miss Emma?"

"Hardly, Mr. Fairfax."

"I think you are," he countered matter-of-factly. "You're breathing fire, and Callie's got to be the reason."

Emma still wanted to stomp her feet and scream in frustrated rage, but she managed to keep her composure. She didn't speak because she couldn't think of an argument Steven wouldn't see straight through.

To her surprise he smiled at her, and there was no sign of mockery in his eyes or the set of his mouth. "You saw

Callie leaving this room with money in her hand, didn't you?" he asked.

"Yes!" Emma spat, moving her coppery braid from her right shoulder to her left, and then back again.

"I sent her to buy cigars."

Emma stood very still. "You what?"

"You heard me, Emma."

Sinking her teeth into her bottom lip, Emma groped for a chair and sank into it. She swallowed hard. "She'd better have them with her when she comes back," she warned.

Steven chuckled. "So you do care about me, just a little?"

"Just a very little," Emma said primly, sitting up straight and smoothing her skirts.

"We'll see how little you care," Steven told her, his eyes slipping from her mouth to her breasts and back again, "when I've got these damn sheets off my middle."

"You presume a great deal, Mr. Fairfax. It just so happens that my interest in you is no more than ordinary Christian charity."

Steven smiled a slow, leisurely smile that made Emma's heart and stomach collide with a jolt. "It's been my experience that 'Christian charity' isn't all that ordinary," he said. "And it generally doesn't involve letting a man take his comfort in quite the way I did with you."

Emma flushed hotly, for she could not deny having allowed Steven to bare her breasts, then kiss and fondle her in a most intimate way. Nor could she claim she hadn't reveled in every caress. "There is no need to remind me of my—error in judgment," she said, clasping her hands together and lifting her chin. She thought of the things Callie had told her men liked, and her color deepened even more.

"Come here," Steven said evenly. The formidable pistol was close at hand on the bedside table.

Emma was backing toward the door. "No," she said,

with breathless resolution. But she wanted desperately to go to Steven, to lie with him and let him kiss her and touch her the way he had before.

He only smiled, shrugged, and closed his eyes.

The task of carrying up his supper fell to Emma that evening, since Chloe was busy at the Stardust and Daisy had gone home with a headache soon after the meal was cooked. Although Emma told herself she would have preferred to avoid contact with Mr. Fairfax, the truth was that she felt a certain dizzying excitement at the prospect.

Steven looked weary and suspiciously docile when she walked into the room, carefully balancing the tray. She made sure she left the door wide open.

"That smells good," he said.

Emma was inordinately pleased. Although she hadn't cooked the savory meat and vegetable pie herself, she found herself wanting to take the credit. "Sit up, please," she said in a remote tone.

The patient raised himself with great effort, and when Emma set the tray across his lap, he made no move to pick up his spoon or fork. "It's been a long day," he said with a heavy sigh. "I'm not sure I want to make the effort to eat."

She sank into the chair beside the bed. "But you *must* eat," she replied. "You'll never get your strength back if you don't."

Steven lifted one shoulder in a dispirited shrug and looked away.

After drawing a deep breath and letting it out again, Emma reached for his fork, stabbed a piece of Daisy's meat pie, with its thick, flaky crust, and raised it to Steven's lips.

He smiled wanly and allowed her to feed him. In fact, it seemed to Emma that he was enjoying this particular moment of incapacity.

The experience was oddly sensual for Emma; she found herself getting lost in the graceful mechanics of it. When Steven grasped her hand, very gently, and lightly kissed her palm, the fork slipped from her fingers and clattered to the tray. Her breasts swelled as she drew in a quick, fevered breath.

Steven trailed his lips over the delicate flesh on the inner side of her forearm until he reached her elbow. When his tongue touched her at the crux, the pleasure was so swift and so keen that she flinched and gave a soft moan.

His eyes locked with hers and he told her, without speaking aloud, that there were other places on her body he wanted to kiss. Places he fully intended to explore and master.

Emma took hold of the tray with a hasty, awkward movement and bolted to her feet, feeling hot and achy all over. "Well," she said with a brightness that was entirely false, "if you're not hungry any longer . . ."

"I didn't say that, Miss Emma," he interrupted, his voice as rough as gravel. "It's just that it isn't food I'm hungry for."

Only her fierce grasp on the sides of the tray kept Emma from dropping it to the floor—plate, cup, leftover food, and all. "What a scandalous remark!"

Steven smiled and stretched, wincing a little at the resultant pain. "I can think of plenty of 'scandalous' remarks," he said, "if you'd like to hear more."

Emma was painfully conscious of the pulse at the inside of her elbow, where Steven had kissed her. A number of other fragile points, such as the backs of her knees and the arches of her feet, tingled in belated response. "Good night, Mr. Fairfax," she said, with feigned dignity. And then she turned and walked out of the room.

# Chapter
## ❧ 6 ❧

$S$teven didn't see Emma again for a full week, and while he told himself it was for the best, he ached to see her every moment of that time. He spent his days pacing the room with Callie Visco under his left arm for support, and his nights cleaning the .45 and listening for Emma's footsteps in the hallway.

He supposed she was either embarrassed to face him or meting out punishment for the hard time he'd given her. He sure as hell hoped she hadn't pegged him as a bad influence and decided to stay away from him.

Of course, he reflected ruefully, he probably *was* a bad influence. He'd seen innocence in Emma's dark blue eyes, as well as passion, and experience told him she'd never before allowed a man to touch her in quite that way.

His blood stirred as he considered some of the *other* ways he wanted to caress Emma. Damn, but he was tired of being confined to that bed—at least, alone.

It was Saturday morning when he finally dragged himself out of bed and into the clothes Emma had bought for him. While any sort of motion hurt intensely, especially bending over to pull on his boots, Steven was determined not to spend another day lying around waiting for Macon to close in on him.

Gripping the bedpost, he shut his eyes against the last crushing wave of pain. When it had ebbed, he collected his gunbelt from the drawer of his bedside table and strapped it on, tying the rawhide strip loosely but firmly around the lower part of his thigh. Then he crossed the room to the wardrobe and reached up, again at great cost to his rib cage, to take his .45 from the hat shelf.

Because he'd cleaned it repeatedly during the long nights when Emma was avoiding him, it glistened with a cold, lethal beauty. Steven spun the chamber with his thumb, then loaded it with bullets from his belt. He was spinning the six-shooter on his finger, getting reacquainted with the feel and weight of it, when there was a knock at the door. Quickly, he slipped the gun back into its holster. "Come in."

After all this time, he still hoped the visitor would be Emma, but it was Daisy, bringing his breakfast.

"You goin'?" she asked in her blunt way, and Steven smiled and nodded.

"That'd be the best thing," Daisy agreed with a nod, putting the tray down on his bedside table. "But you better eat somethin' first."

Steven was anxious to leave, since he'd been cooped up in that room for nearly two weeks, but he didn't want to hurt Daisy's feelings. If she'd gone to the trouble to cook him a meal, he'd eat it. "Thanks," he said.

"You goin' to see Miss Emma afore you move on?"

He sighed, sitting down on the edge of the bed and reaching for the fork Daisy had brought along. There were scrambled eggs, sausage links and biscuits on the plate. "I'm not sure. I think maybe it would be better if I just rode out without bothering her."

Daisy narrowed her eyes. "You done trifled with that girl, ain't you?"

Steven swallowed a bite of sausage before answering.

"In a manner of speaking," he confessed, remembering the warm softness of Emma's breasts, and the way their peaks had hardened for him like sweet candy.

Daisy's hardworking hands were resting on her generous hips. "There gonna be a baby?"

Steven shook his head. Things hadn't gone quite that far; no, Emma's babies would probably look like that banker Callie had told him about, not him, and the realization filled him with sadness. "No chance of that, Daisy, so you don't need to worry."

"Well, I *is* worried," Daisy insisted. "Miss Emma ain't herself. She's off her food, she don't sleep at night. Not only that, she don't argue back with me or Chloe when we bosses her around. Somethin's wrong."

Steven's appetite was gone, and he laid down his fork. "She'll be all right," he promised gently, but he wasn't at all sure of that. Some women couldn't forgive themselves for even the slightest intimacy with a man. He didn't want Emma suffering that way. "Where is she?" he asked, rising to his feet.

"The library," Daisy answered in a tone that said any idiot could have figured that out.

Steven nodded and collected his hat and canvas coat from the chair. They'd both seen better days, all before the explosion at the Yellow Belly Saloon, and he supposed it would be a good idea to replace them. "Thanks for everything, Daisy," he said, and as he passed the big woman, he kissed her lightly on the cheek. "You're the best cook north of New Orleans."

She beamed at the compliment, then made herself glower. "You just get on out of here and stop takin' up my time, you fancy-talkin' man!"

Steven laughed and left the room, his boot heels making a steady sound on the hallway and the front stairs. Crossing the entry hall, he opened the front door and was met by a rush of fresh, spring-scented air. Being outside again was even better than he'd thought it would be.

His first stop was the livery stable, where he paid for the care of his horse, a gelded paint named Cherokee. He left both the horse and his coat with the stablemaster and walked the short distance to the Stardust Saloon.

Out of the corner of one eye, he saw Emma standing on the wooden sidewalk in front of what must be the lending library, but he pretended he hadn't noticed her. Emma had made her feelings plain enough by staying away.

The Stardust was jumping with laughter and piano music, and Chloe's girls, in their bright dresses, were everywhere. There was a redhead in a skimpy yellow gown seated on top of the piano, and a brunette in royal blue perched at one end of the bar. Various other birds of paradise graced the laps of the men drinking at tables, and a few hovered around the pool table, cheering on favored patrons.

Steven couldn't suppress a slight shudder, remembering what had happened to him the last time he'd ventured into a saloon; it was enough to turn a man off drinking and wild women forever.

When Steven's eyes had swept the room carefully, making sure Macon and his men weren't waiting there for him, he approached the bar and spoke to the brunette in blue. "Where can I find Chloe Reese?"

The pretty young woman took his hat off and resettled it on his head. "You don't need Chloe, cowboy. What you need is right here."

Steven grinned. "Begging your pardon, ma'am, but it's Chloe I have to see, all right."

The brunette thrust out her moist red lower lip in a pretty pout. "Okay, but you're going to find out she don't turn tricks, not even for lookers like you. Big John Lenahan's the only man ever touches Chloe."

"Thanks for the warning," Steven replied. He took a folded bill from his pocket and laid it on the lady's bare knee, and she brightened instantly. "Now," he said softly, "where's Chloe?"

"Upstairs in the parlor," was the pert answer. "You

can't miss it." The bill disappeared down her bodice. As Steven headed toward the stairs, she called after him, "If you change your mind, honey, I'll be right here."

Steven touched his hat brim in acknowledgment and climbed the stairs.

He found Chloe holding court in a parlor filled with red velvet, gilt, and tassels, beads, and braids. There were paintings of nudes in various interesting positions on the wall, and Chloe herself was resplendent in an elegant purple velvet dress.

"Well," she said when Steven entered her parlor. Then, with a flutter of her fingers, she dismissed the unoccupied girls who'd been seated around her, chattering.

Steven took off his hat. "Hello, Chloe," he said quietly.

Chloe smiled and gestured toward a nearby chair. "Sit down, Mr. Fairfax."

He lowered himself carefully into the chair.

"Still a little stiff, I see," Chloe commented, fluttering a pearl-studded fan in front of her face.

"I'll be all right," Steven assured her, "thanks to you. What do I owe you?"

Chloe looked benignly insulted. "That's a rude question, Mr. Fairfax. Don't people take in wounded strangers down south?"

He smiled. "Not in my family, they don't."

Before Chloe could make a comment on that, a door opened and a tall, heavyset blond customer came out, derby hat askew, fingers clumsily buttoning his vest as he moved. Not one, but two women followed moments later.

Some instinct told Steven who the ladies' man was even before Chloe spoke. "You've been so curious about Mr. Fairfax, Fulton," she said, in an idle tone. "Here he is."

The banker. Steven got to his feet, not as a gesture of courtesy, but so the man couldn't look down on him.

"Fulton Whitney," the banker said by way of introduction. His tone was grudging.

Steven didn't put out his hand, or speak. He was

wondering what kind of polecat would cozy up to a woman like Emma, then spend a sunny April morning rolling in the sheets with a couple of floozies.

Whitney cleared his throat and shifted awkwardly on his feet, while Chloe left the sofa where she'd been sitting, her fan still fluttering.

"I'd better see how things are going downstairs," she said, and then she was gone.

"So you'll be leaving now, I suppose," the banker said, breaking the strained silence. "I don't imagine a man like you cares to stay in one place too long."

Steven folded his arms. "Until just a few minutes ago, I figured on riding out," he answered. "Now I'm not so sure."

Color blossomed in Whitney's pasty cheeks. "What possible reason could you have to stay?"

"Just one. Her name is Emma."

The banker stared at him with undisguised contempt, and Steven figured he must look pretty seedy, all things considered. It had been days since he'd shaved, and two months since he'd had a haircut. "You aren't good enough to lick her shoes."

Steven indulged in a slow, obnoxious smile. "Let me understand this," he drawled. "I'm not good enough for Emma, but you, her fiancé, just crawled out of bed with two whores?"

Again, Whitney's face flooded with blustery color. "I don't have to explain anything to you," he rasped. And then he started to walk away.

Steven was possessed of a rage nobody but Macon had been able to arouse in him before. He grasped the banker by the arm, whirled him around, and threw his fist into the middle of the bastard's face.

Fulton gave a startled yelp as he struck the wall, then slowly slid down it, one hand to his bleeding mouth.

"Now," Steven said calmly, "we know exactly where we stand, you and I." With that, he turned and left the whorehouse parlor, moving steadily down the stairs.

Until he'd seen Fulton Whitney walk out of that room

upstairs, he'd fully intended to get on Cherokee and ride out, heading for California, maybe, or Oregon. Sooner or later, given enough whiskey, hard work, and women, he'd have been able to put Emma Chalmers out of his mind.

Now everything had changed. He couldn't leave her to that fool of a hypocrite she planned to marry; if he did, the blue fire in her eyes would falter and die one day in the not too distant future.

Outside in the fresh air, he crossed the street to the general store. If he was going to stay in Whitneyville for a time, he'd need money. Since he didn't dare wire his grandfather in New Orleans—Macon's people would be watching for just such a message—he'd ask around about a job. The mercantile seemed to be as good a place to start as any, since storekeepers usually knew everybody for miles around.

Emma bit her lower lip and dove into the cool, shaded privacy of the library. Just seeing Steven again had shaken her, but watching him stroll into the Stardust Saloon nearly destroyed her composure.

She lingered inside the empty library for only a moment before a need to know drove her back out onto the sidewalk and down the street to the swinging doors of Chloe's saloon. She watched in horror as Steven strolled away from a trollop in a blue dress and up the stairs to the infamous second floor.

Emma drew in her breath and spread one hand over her pounding heart, as if to slow its furious beat. It was all she could do not to follow Steven up those stairs and demand to know what he thought he was doing.

Pride and jealousy warred within Emma, and pride finally prevailed. Biting her lower lip to keep from crying, she forced herself back down the sidewalk to the library.

Over the coming hour she was aware of every tick of the clock and every beat of her heart. She stiffened in relief and shock when the door opened and Steven walked in.

He actually had the audacity to grin at her as he swept off his hat. "Hello, Miss Emma," he said.

Emma felt heat surge from her breasts to her cheeks. A full sixty minutes had passed since she'd seen him go up Chloe's stairs, and it was plain enough what he'd been doing.

When she didn't speak, Steven walked over to the counter she was standing behind and laid his hat down on it. "Aren't you going to say hello?"

She glared at him. "I think 'good-bye' would be more suitable to the situation, don't you?"

He reached out, bold as could be, and grasped her braid lightly in one hand. "It's like spun fire," he mused. "You're a very beautiful woman, Miss Emma."

"Am I?" Emma countered sweetly. "Tell me, Mr. Fairfax—how do I measure up against the girls over at the Stardust?"

His grin was maddening. "If what we did a week ago was any indication, you can definitely hold your own."

Emma flushed at the reminder and turned her head away, but Steven caught her chin in one hand and forced her to look at him again.

"Is that why you've been avoiding me, Emma? Because of what happened?"

All her life Emma had wanted to be decent and respectable. And what had she done? She'd let the first gunslinger who rode into town make her act like a strumpet within a matter of days. "Yes, damn you!" she blurted out, her eyes filling with angry tears.

Still holding her chin in his hand, Steven rounded the counter. "You'd better get used to seeing me," he said huskily. "Because I'm going to be around a while."

Emma swallowed hard. "You said someone was after you—"

"Maybe it's time I let him find me," Steven said, his lips only a fraction of an inch from hers.

His kiss jolted Emma through and through, and she wasn't able to push him away, no matter how badly she wanted to. She submitted, as she always did with Steven, and a few more kisses stole her reason and fairly stopped her breathing.

She found herself crushed between Steven and the library counter, and the very hardness and strength of him made her lightheaded enough to swoon. Emma closed her eyes and gave herself up to the storm of sensation his touch aroused in her.

The moment he released her and stepped back, however, she was wild with fury. After all, someone might have walked in and caught her kissing Mr. Fairfax—and had that happened, Emma would have been completely ruined.

"I see things haven't changed much," he drawled, resetting his hat. "Good day, Miss Emma."

Emma gave a strangled cry and would have stomped on his instep if she hadn't been afraid she'd break his foot. She didn't mind hurting him, but there was always the chance that Chloe would take him back into the house again. Color stung her cheeks. "Get out."

Steven's hazel eyes danced. "I guess I'd better. The way you were clinging to me just now . . . well, you might not be above taking advantage of a man."

Emma longed for a heavy book to clout him with, but she'd long since put them all away. She pointed toward the door with a trembling index finger and tried to look fierce.

He chuckled and, without another word, rounded Emma and walked out of the library, whistling.

Emma was so undone, she couldn't stand still for another moment. As soon as she saw Steven disappear into the barber shop, she bustled over to make sure the encyclopedias were in proper order. After that, she rearranged the card file. There was still too much time left in the day.

A flurry of late-afternoon visitors was Emma's salvation, and at five o'clock exactly she locked the place up and marched out the front door.

As she passed the bank's window she saw Fulton. He was sitting at his desk, head bent over a ledger, but he must have sensed Emma's passing, even though she was trying to hurry by unseen, for he looked up and smiled sadly.

Emma nodded a distant greeting—simple politeness decreed that she could do no less—and hastened along the sidewalk.

Alas, Fulton pursued her, shouting her name from the doorway of the bank, so that she was forced to stop and turn. Her arms tightened around the book she'd selected for that night's reading.

"I'd like you to have supper with me this evening," he called out, in jovial expectation of her ready agreement.

Emma walked circumspectly toward him, so that she wouldn't be forced to shout her refusal for the entire town to hear. "Fulton," she said in a moderate tone, "we have already discussed this matter. And I've told you that I think you and I have spent entirely too much time together."

He looked more annoyed than disappointed. "I would have thought you'd be over that nonsense by now. I'll come by for you at seven, and we'll dine at the hotel."

Although she could feel her color rising, Emma kept her temper. "Please do not trouble yourself, Mr. Whitney. I will be dining alone and retiring early." With that, she turned to walk briskly away.

Fulton's fingers bit into her upper arm, hard enough to leave bruises, and when Emma looked up into his eyes in furious surprise, she was frightened by the cold anger she saw there. "Don't make the mistake of thinking I'll give you up so easily, Emma," he breathed, "because I won't."

She rubbed her arm as she walked away, torn between puzzlement and outrage. Uneasiness quivered in the pit of her stomach.

When Emma arrived at home, however, all thoughts of Fulton were driven from her mind, for she found Steven Fairfax waiting in the large parlor. He'd been barbered and shaved, his shirt and trousers were new, and he looked so handsome that Emma's knees weakened.

"You are no longer welcome in this house," she said pleasantly.

His smile didn't waver, but he took off his disreputable old hat. "Is that any way to treat a law-abiding citizen of Whitneyville, Miss Emma?"

"If I should encounter one," Emma said stiffly, "I'll be sure and deal with him kindly."

Steven chuckled. "You're a saucy little hellcat," he said, strolling toward her. "And I've got half a mind to kiss you again."

Emma's palms went moist at the memory of their last kiss. "Doesn't it bother you at all that I belong to another man?"

He came to a stop not a foot away, turning his hat in his hands. It was a gesture of habit, Emma discerned, rather than of nervousness, as it was with most men. "You don't belong to anybody but me," he replied, in a low, steady voice, "and I've proved that more than once."

"Why are you here?" Emma bit out the words, frustrated beyond all bearing.

"Because I forgot to thank you for looking after me when I was hurt, for one thing," Steven answered.

Emma knew there was more. She folded her arms and snapped, "And for another?"

He reached out and traced the outline of her lips with his fingertip. "For another, Miss Emma," he went on, his eyes laughing even though his mouth was serious, "I wanted to let you know you're going to be keeping company with *me* from now on, not the banker."

# *Chapter*
## ❧ 7 ❧

*Y*ou can't be serious," Emma said. "We have absolutely nothing in common."

His gaze drifted lazily over her, igniting a fire under Emma's skin. The heat was suffocating, as if her clothes were burning. "Oh, but we do," he argued reasonably, glancing in an idle fashion at the piano, the bookshelves, the silk-upholstered furniture and clutter of bric-a-brac. "Some very good marriages have been built on passion."

Emma struggled to keep her equanimity. Suddenly, she didn't want Steven to know she had any doubts at all where Fulton was concerned. "I believe that's what Mr. Whitney is offering me," she said evenly. "You recall Mr. Fulton Whitney, I presume? He's the man you always refer to as 'the banker.' He is a solid, steady sort, too, with excellent prospects and a good home." There was no need to point out that expectations for a gunslinger could not possibly compare; the message got through as efficiently as if it had been sent by Western Union.

Emma knew that by the way the muscle tightened in Steven's smoothly shaven jawline.

"The banker isn't good enough for you," he said, carefully inspecting one of Chloe's china shepherdesses as he spoke.

His blithe confidence nettled Emma, and so did the tantalizing scent of bay rum he'd brought with him. He was completely disrupting the sanctity of that parlor where Emma had always felt so safe.

"But you are?" she inquired, raising one eyebrow.

"Yes."

"You're a drifter—an outlaw!"

Steven's gaze never left hers. "Until now I didn't have a reason to stay in one place. And I'm not an outlaw."

"You're wanted—you admitted yourself that someone is looking to kill you."

He gave a ragged sigh. "All right, it's true—I'm wanted in the state of Louisiana. But I'm innocent."

"Criminals always declare their innocence," Emma said stubbornly, even though, deep inside, she knew Steven would not have deliberately broken the law. Still, she longed to know what he'd been accused of.

That maddening grin was back. "You're wasting your breath trying to discourage me, Miss Emma. Once I decide I want something, I don't ever give up on it. If it takes from now till the crack of doom, I'll bed you properly, and I'll prove you were born to love me."

Emma's hands flew to her hips. "If you aren't the most arrogant and impossible man I've ever met—"

Before Emma could finish the sentence, Chloe arrived home.

"Hello, Emma," she said warmly, flowing across the room in a graceful motion of silk and bright green feathers to pour herself a drink. "Mr. Fairfax," she said, in a cooler, slightly questioning tone.

Much to Emma's pleasure, Steven's aplomb was jarred by Chloe's appearance.

"Nice to see you again," he managed.

The reminder that Steven must have encountered Chloe earlier in the day, inside the Stardust Saloon, pierced Emma's composure. "You wanted to thank me for nursing you," she said abruptly and her face went crimson the moment the words left her tongue. She cleared her throat sharply and squared her shoulders. "You've done that, Mr. Fairfax. You're welcome, and good-bye."

Chloe was watching the tableau with interest from beside the liquor cabinet, a snifter of brandy in one hand, and she offered no contribution.

"Not good-bye, Miss Emma," Steven drawled, and his brazen gaze rested on her breasts for a moment, to remind her, she was sure, that he'd bared and enjoyed them with practically no protest from her. "Like I said, I'll be around." With that, he nodded slightly in Chloe's direction, put his hat on, and walked out.

Emma followed him out onto the porch, incensed at his gall, and spoke in an angry whisper.

"You're a drifter! You should be drifting!"

He chuckled and leaned one powerful shoulder against one of the white painted pillars that supported the porch roof. "You're right. I should move on and forget I ever saw this backwater town. But I mean to stay, Miss Emma." He straightened and looked struck by some startling thought. "Now that you mention it, I guess I'll be needing a library card."

"I didn't mention it!" Emma snapped, folding her arms. She searched her mind for some protocol that would prevent him from coming into the library and kissing her again. Every time he touched her, it was harder to stave off the seduction she was sure was coming. "You can't borrow if you don't have an address," she added priggishly.

"Well, Miss Emma," Steven responded, mischief flickering in his eyes, "it just so happens that I do. I'm staying in the foreman's cottage on Big John Lenahan's ranch."

Emma's mouth dropped open for a moment, then closed again. "You can't work for Big John with your ribs bound!" she protested, when she'd recovered somewhat. "How will you ride?"

"I'm glad you're concerned about my well-being,"

Steven replied in a voice meant to carry beyond the fence, where two women were strolling by, pretending not to notice that Emma Chalmers was entertaining the much-talked-about stranger.

"I wish you'd just go away and leave me alone!" Emma reached for the screened door, and the hinges squeaked loudly as she wrenched it open.

Steven grinned broadly. "Like I said before, Miss Emma—you're going to be seeing a lot of me from now on. In fact, I mean to come calling again as soon as I can."

One of the curtains moved behind Steven, and Emma wondered who was eavesdropping—Chloe or Daisy.

Emma's desperation drove her to lie. "That would not be proper, I'm afraid. You see, I plan to become engaged to Mr. Whitney very soon."

Steven caught hold of her hand and dragged it to his mouth, where he kissed the knuckles. It was as though she hadn't spoken. "Good night, Miss Emma," he said fondly. "Sweet dreams."

There was a full moon that night; its light glimmered on the dark waters of the lake. Emma stood stiffly beside Fulton, looking out at the silent ballet of light and shadow and hating herself for relenting and agreeing to go walking with the man. She wasn't sure why she'd done that, but she suspected it had to do with Steven Fairfax.

In spite of her better judgment, all Emma's thoughts and feelings were for quite the wrong man.

Fulton seemed nervous, and his boots made a crunching sound in the pebbles along the lakeshore as he shifted uneasily. He tried to take her hand, but Emma was careful to stay out of reach. "I imagine you're relieved to have that gunslinger out of the house," he said, his voice too earnest and too loud.

Emma looked up at him, hoping he couldn't see contrasting emotions in her face. She was glad Steven was gone from Chloe's house, yes, but she also missed him dreadfully. Thus her response was only a partial untruth. "It will be much easier, now that he's gone." *And much more difficult,* she reflected to herself.

"He didn't say anything about me?" Fulton asked, in a curiously uncertain tone.

Emma turned her head to hide the forlorn little smile that curved her lips. "Only that you were all wrong for me," she answered in a soft, thoughtful voice.

Fulton stiffened instantly. "What else?"

Emma turned her gaze to Fulton's face, puzzled. "Nothing else," she said. "Why?"

He sighed and averted his eyes. "No reason."

Emma folded her arms and stood looking out over the moonlit water. Fulton was hiding something, but she didn't care to pursue it. In fact, she didn't really want to talk at all.

Fulton insisted, however. He cleared his throat and announced, "There was a wire from Mother and Father today. They'll be home within the week."

"I see."

Without warning, he reached out and took her arm, forcing her to face him. "I don't think you do," he said urgently. "Emma, we've got to elope—now. Tonight. That way, I'll be able to present you to Mother as a *fait accompli.*"

Stunned, Emma jerked her arm from his grasp. "Fulton, I've told you . . ."

He laid a fingertip to her lips. "Don't say it. I know Mother intimidates you, Emma, but once you're my wife, she'll accept you, I know she will."

The pain Emma felt must have been visible in her eyes when she looked up at Fulton, but if he saw it, he didn't react. Perhaps he would listen if she approached the subject from his point of view, rather than her own. "Fulton, there's a lot of talk about me, and—"

His hands grasped her shoulders. "I don't care, Emma," he whispered. For the first time, she noticed that his lower lip was cut and slightly swollen.

She touched the wound gently. "What happened?"

Again his eyes skirted hers. "It's nothing you need to worry about, darling," he said. "Now, listen to me. We must get married right away!"

"I can't do that," Emma said miserably.

"I know women like a church wedding, but—"

"That isn't the reason. Fulton, I don't love you. It would be a dreadful mistake for us to marry."

He was still holding her shoulders, and he gave her an angry little shake. "You'll have tender feelings for me soon, Emma, I promise you. Come away with me to-night!"

Emma pulled free. "I can't."

"Is it true, then, Emma—what everybody's saying about you and Fairfax?"

The question was so direct that it startled Emma. "I guess that depends on what's being said," she replied sadly. Then, holding her shawl more closely around her against the evening chill, she started up the bank toward Chloe's house. Fulton had no choice but to follow.

He stopped her at the edge of the lawn, again by taking her arm. This time his hold was too tight for her to pull out of. "I don't care if it's all true," he sputtered. "Do you hear me, Emma? *I don't care.* I still want you more than I've ever wanted anything!"

Emma sighed. "What *are* they saying?" she asked, braced for the worst.

Fulton's hand dropped from her arm and he lowered his head. "That you spent the nights in his room."

Emma's cheeks flamed, but her chin rose to an obstinate level. "That's a lie."

A bright smile broke over Fulton's face. "I knew it was."

Guilt pummeled Emma like an invisible fist. "You'd want to marry me, even if I'd said the rumors were true?"

Fulton nodded. "It's no secret that I'm eager for the—solaces of marriage, Emma. I'm willing to overlook a great deal to have you."

The lights of home flowed golden into the night, and Emma longed to be inside, away from Fulton and his too-generous forgiveness. But where could she go to get away from herself?

The answer was nowhere. Steven was a drifter, a wanted man. He'd soon grow bored, or restless, and move on without her, despite his protests that nothing could turn him aside from an objective once he'd made up his mind.

"If you won't marry me right away, then promise you'll come to next Saturday's dance with me." There was a frantic element in Fulton's request.

In time, Emma reflected, she might even forget Steven Fairfax entirely. For now, she had to give her future very careful consideration, and besides, she wanted to discourage him from pursuing her in any way she could. "I'll buy a length of fabric and start sewing up a new dress tomorrow," she said with sorrowful resolve, "and we'll go to the dance as friends. Your parents will be home by week's end, won't they?"

Fulton started to say something, then stopped himself. "Yes," he answered finally.

Emma started up the steps that led onto the screened mud porch. The kitchen was just beyond.

"Wait," Fulton said, and he climbed the steps until his face was level with Emma's. Derby hat in hand, he kissed her carefully on the mouth.

Emma waited for the delicious sensations she felt when Steven kissed her that way, but they didn't come. There was no revulsion, either, just—nothing—and Emma was much relieved when Fulton drew back, looking very pleased with himself.

He took her hand, his eyes glinting in the moonlight. "We could slip into the summerhouse—"

Emma opened the back door. "Good night, Fulton," she said firmly, and then she hurried inside the house.

Chloe was in the kitchen, sipping hot chocolate, but Emma didn't stop to chat with her as she would have done on almost any other night. Instead she raced up the back stairs and locked herself in her room.

Steven would have preferred to eat his dinner in the cook shack with the other men so he could get to know them, but he ended up at Big John's table instead. He found himself seated straight across from the friendly widower's sixteen-year-old daughter, Joellen.

"It isn't easy to find a man with your references," Big John said as he scooped a mountain of mashed potatoes onto the plate he'd already cleared once and drowned them in gravy. He'd come by his nickname honestly, for he was the size of a grizzly, but Steven could see his bulk was muscle, not fat. "You must have been punchin' cows most of your life."

Steven smiled, avoiding Joellen's efforts to attract his notice, and took a sip of his wine before answering, "Since just after the war, anyway."

Joellen's glass toppled over, spreading a purple stain over the white linen tablecloth. "Oh, I'm so clumsy!" she cried, and Steven bit the inside of his lip to keep from laughing out loud at her obvious bid for attention.

Big John just shook his white, weathered head, and the plump Mexican cook, Manuela, rushed in, prattling in Spanish as she elbowed aside the daughter of the house to dab at the stain with a corner of her apron.

"Leave that, Manuela," Big John ordered quietly.

With one dark, reproachful glance at Joellen, Manuela hurried out of the room again.

Joellen batted her enormous eyes at Steven as she sank with feigned dejection back into her chair. She was probably the prettiest child Steven had ever seen, but she was exactly that—a child. "Did you fight in the war, Mr. Fairfax?" she asked, the light of the lamps flickering in her white-gold hair, which trailed down over her shoulders in a smooth cascade.

Steven pushed back his chair. "Yes."

Joellen quirked one perfect eyebrow. "On the losing side?"

"That's most people's opinion, yes," Steven agreed, fighting back another smile. "Of course, my granddaddy swears the south will rise again, and he's got a stack of Confederate bills stashed away for the occasion."

Big John grinned and offered Steven a cigar, which he accepted graciously. "Who'd you serve under, young fella?"

"Jeb Stuart," Steven answered. He didn't like to talk about the war the way some men did. As far as he was concerned, it was best forgotten.

"Best damn horseman in either army," Big John reflected.

Steven agreed without question.

"I was in to see Emma Chalmers at the library the other day," Joellen piped up, and that brought her the regard she'd been seeking all evening. Both Steven and her father were looking straight at her. "I wanted to check out a book and she got saucy with me," Joellen continued. "But I put her in her place and reminded her that she's nothing but an orphan."

Big John looked disgusted. "Now, Joellen," he said, with heavy patience, "that wasn't very kind of you."

Joellen's gaze shifted to Steven's face. Her eyes were half closed as she asked, "And what do you think?"

Steven turned the unlit cigar Big John had given him between his fingers. "That Emma Chalmers is the prettiest woman I've ever seen."

At that, Joellen's china-doll complexion turned the color of cranberry cordial. "You can't be considering *marrying* her or anything—she's practically engaged to Fulton Whitney!"

"The time will come when she doesn't recall his name," Steven said, and when he rose from his chair, Big John stood, too, offering a strong work-calloused hand. Tucking the cigar into his shirt pocket, Steven shook the rancher's hand, then made his excuses and left.

He didn't get halfway to the cottage Big John had assigned him before Joellen caught up to him. She was wearing a divided riding skirt, high black boots, and a white blouse that glowed in the moonlight just the way her hair did.

"Are you mad at me?" she asked, scurrying to keep up with Steven's long strides. "For saying what I did about Emma Chalmers?"

"No."

"She won't marry you, you know," Joellen hastened to say. "She wants to live in a grand house, like the Whitneys do."

"That a fact?" Steven asked, glancing up at the spectacular array of stars shimmering against the sky.

"She wants money, too, and respectability. She'd never marry a ranch foreman."

Steven had reached the door of his cabin, and he wasn't about to invite Joellen in, though she seemed to expect it. "Good night," he said pointedly.

Joellen's lower lip jutted out, and she turned and stormed away.

Steven chuckled as he watched her stride back toward the towering ranch house with its pillared porch and climbing rose bushes. Then he took matches from his vest pocket, sat down on the step, and lit the cigar Big John had given him. His thoughts immediately turned to Emma, and the way she'd felt, all soft and warm against him, when he'd kissed her last.

He puffed on the cigar for a few moments, speculating. He wondered if she would really be fool enough to marry that dough-faced banker.

Emma was stubborn, and she probably thought Whitney could give her what she wanted—money, respectability, comfort. That willfulness of hers just might land her in the wrong bed, and Steven wasn't willing to let that happen.

He stubbed out the cigar and went inside, where he didn't bother to light a lamp. The glow of the moon flowed in through a window, brightening practically every corner of the tiny one-room house.

After tossing what remained of the cigar into the stove, Steven stripped off his clothes and collapsed onto the double bed that dominated the room. He kept his .45 within easy reach on the mattress beside him, and made himself quiet. Deep within him, he could sense Macon's approach, but this time he wasn't going to run. He had a reason to stand and fight, a reason to risk everything, and he was tired of always looking over his shoulder. No matter what happened, he meant to stay.

His ribs were still tightly wrapped, and they still hurt like hell when he made a sudden move. Steven turned slowly onto his side to lie facing the locked door.

The moment he closed his eyes, his mind shifted to Emma. He imagined her beneath him, her naked skin as smooth as velvet, and he hardened painfully. He'd have given anything he owned, including his .45 and the fortune waiting for him in Louisiana, to have her there beside him in that bed.

Despite the ache in his groin, Steven was tired, and in less than a minute he was asleep.

As so often happened in his dreams, he found himself back in Louisiana. This time he was standing on a grassy knoll, an early morning fog wafting around him, a dueling pistol in his hand. His opponent was Macon's bastard son, Dirk.

"No!" Steven protested out loud, but the word didn't pull him out of the nightmare. He could feel the butt of the pistol in his hand, the soft dampness of the ground under the soles of his boots. All his senses were heightened.

Dirk, just barely twenty, was no older than Steven. Small, with dark hair and dark eyes, like his father, he was hotheaded and jealous of Steven's close relationship with Cyrus. The pistol trembled in his hand as he raised it to fire, and his face was contorted with hatred.

The shot went wide of Steven, making a shrill *ping* as it struck the trunk of a tree on the edge of the clearing.

"Go ahead," Dirk shouted, like a crazy man. "Shoot me!"

Steven shook his head. "Walk away, Dirk," he said quietly. Gravely. "We'll forget about this."

"I'll never forget it," Dirk vowed as his second handed him another pistol. "I loved Mary—and you damned well *knew* it, you skulking, back-street bastard! And still you bedded her!"

No amount of denial or explanation would have convinced his nephew that Mary had entered Steven's bed at Fairhaven after he was asleep. He hadn't even known she was there until Dirk had come crashing in the next morning, demanding retribution.

Facing that second dueling pistol, wavering wildly in Dirk's hand, Steven knew he wasn't going to be lucky again. Grimly he raised his own weapon and shot his nephew neatly in the left shoulder.

Dirk went down, blood soaking his shirtfront and turning it crimson, a cry of abhorrence and pain on his lips.

Steven handed his gun to his own second and approached his brother's son, crouching on the ground beside him. A doctor, a stranger wearing an ulster and a beaver tophat, was already peeling back the bloody shirt.

"Why didn't you listen to me?" Steven rasped, his gaze linking with Dirk's.

By then Dirk was only half conscious. He spat at Steven and closed his eyes, his face going pale as wax.

Steven felt strong hands on his shoulders and looked back to see his best friend and second, Garrick Wright. Garrick's voice seemed to echo through the isolated clearing, even though he spoke quietly. "Let's go. It's over now."

Slowly, reluctantly, Steven rose to his feet again. When he spoke he addressed his words to the doctor. "He'll be all right?"

The older man looked up at Steven with grim gray eyes. Early morning moisture beaded his salt-and-pepper hair and mustache. "Men like Dirk are never 'all right,'" he replied. "They cannot be content until they've challenged the world and brought about their own deaths."

Steven swallowed hard. "He'll die, then?"

"Not this time," the doctor replied.

And Steven turned and walked away to begin the dream again. It always repeated itself, over and over, for one night or a hundred nights, as it might choose.

Emma was waiting when Mrs. Birdwell opened the general store at nine o'clock Monday morning. She went immediately to the bolts of fabric, as though by selecting material and sewing a dress for Saturday's party, she could make everything right.

"I'd have thought you'd be opening up the library by now," Mrs. Birdwell trilled, flipping through a stack of invoices at the counter. She wore a smug expression on her plain face, suggesting she was privy to some defamatory secret.

"I'm taking the day off," Emma announced, taking pleasure in the way Mrs. Birdwell pushed her spectacles the length of her nose, until their rims pressed against her forehead.

"Next you'll tell me you're not meeting the train!"

Emma shook her head. "Oh, no. I've got a fresh batch of posters waiting over at the depot right now. As soon as I hear the whistle, I'll be headed that way."

Mrs. Birdwell pretended friendly concern. "Don't you think you should give up trying to find those sisters of yours? After all, they're surely either married or dead, after all this time."

Emma, who had been examining a bolt of green watered silk, laid it down on the yardage table to turn and face Mrs. Birdwell squarely. "Lily and Caroline might well be married—they'd have grown up to be beautiful women—but they're not dead. I would have known it if they were."

Mrs. Birdwell subsided slightly, not daring, apparently, to ask how Emma would know such a thing.

Emma, not sure how she knew but bone-certain that she did, all the same, snatched up the bolt of watered silk, and carried it to the counter, where she set it down sharply. "Is there any lace for trim? I didn't see it there."

The storekeeper strode through the well-stocked mercantile, as though it were a trial to have to wait on such a tiresome customer, and opened a drawer in the notions table. "White or ecru?" she snapped.

"Ecru," Emma answered, hiding a smile. "And some of your best silk thread as well."

"Have you a pattern?" Mrs. Birdwell demanded, returning with a length of ecru lace and two spools of green thread.

Emma nodded. "I ordered one from a magazine, months ago."

Mrs. Birdwell was duly offended. "You know, Mr. Birdwell and I try our best to stock the store with everything a person could want," she complained. "I can't think why you'd want to send away for anything."

"It has to be a special dress," Emma answered sweetly. "It's not every night one attends a party at the Crystal Lake Hotel."

Mrs. Birdwell's small eyes narrowed behind her spectacles. "I can just imagine what Cobina Whitney will say when she finds out who her boy's been consorting with," she huffed.

Emma smiled remotely and took money from her handbag to pay for the fabric.

In the distance a train whistle sounded. Emma knew from long experience that it was still a good way off, just rounding the far side of the lake, no doubt. She waited patiently while Mrs. Birdwell measured the length of silk and totalled up the bill.

Fifteen minutes later, her purchases wrapped in brown paper and string, Emma arrived at the railroad station.

Mr. Lathrop waved at her as he stepped down from the train. "More posters?" the conductor asked good-naturedly as she hurried up to him.

She handed over a ream of freshly printed notices. "Here they are," she said, smiling. "Any news?"

He shook his head. "Not this time. I'm sorry, Miss Emma."

Emma's disappointment was as keen as ever, but it

faded quickly. There was always the next train, and the one after that. One of these days, somebody who knew Lily or Caroline was going to see one of those posters.

After exchanging a few pleasantries with Mr. Lathrop and walking up and down the aisles of the passenger cars once, to look for familiar faces, Emma took her parcel home. There she spread the fabric out on the long dining room table, pinned the pattern into place, and cut out her dress.

By lunchtime, she had completed the arduous task and sewn tiny whip stitches around most of the pieces so the fabric wouldn't ravel.

She was outside in the back yard, seated in the swing Big John Lenahan had made for her when she was eleven, and watching the spring sun shimmer on the lake when she felt masculine hands encircle her waist.

"Want a push?" Fulton asked.

Emma would never have confessed to the disappointment she felt. She forced a smile to her lips. "No, thanks," she said. "What are you doing here? It's the middle of the day."

"I couldn't think of a better time to catch you alone." He took hold of the swing's ropes and twisted them so that Emma was facing him. His eyes moved hungrily over her breasts, her trim waist and womanly thighs. "Let's go into the summerhouse, Emma. I'll make you forget that gunslinger once and for all."

Emma swallowed and then forced herself to smile. "What gunslinger?" she asked, to prove she'd forgotten Steven Fairfax already.

# *Chapter*
## ❧ 8 ❧

*E*mma hummed as she stitched a bodice seam on her new silk dress. The evening was fairly cool, so there was a fire snapping on the parlor hearth, and a cup of hot, sweet tea waited at her elbow. An authoritative knock sounded at the front door, and some instinct made her stiffen. She sat rigid in her chair while Daisy went to answer the imperious summons.

"Someone to see you, Miss Emma," the housekeeper announced, with uncommonly good cheer.

Emma's heart fluttered when she rose from her chair —the silk bodice in her hands—to see Steven walk through the parlor doorway, his hat in his hands. His clothes, though they were the rough, practical garments of a rancher, were clean. For all of that, he was wearing that pistol of his, riding low on his hip, in just the way a gunslinger would.

"Hello, Emma," he said with a grin, when she found she couldn't speak.

She sank back into her chair, and Steven went to stand by the fire, one arm resting on the mantel.

"That color will look good on you," he observed, speaking of the green silk in her lap. She was busily stitching again.

"Thank you very much," she said coolly. She didn't ask Steven to sit down because she didn't want him to stay. She'd only just managed to put her scandalous encounters with him out of her mind.

"Don't you want to know why I'm here?"

Emma made herself meet his eyes. "No," she said. "I do not."

He chuckled, unmoved, as always, by her discourtesy. "We're going on a picnic Saturday," he announced.

Emma had had all she could take of Steven Fairfax's audacity. She glared at him, her cheeks throbbing. "I hardly think that will be possible. You see, I've agreed to attend a party with Fulton on Saturday evening."

Steven sighed. "So you're still seeing the banker, huh?"

"Honestly," Emma snapped, amazed, "you are insufferable. And I'm not going on any picnic with you, now or ever!" The silk crumpled between her clenched fingers, and she nearly stuck herself with the needle. "Perhaps I have finally made myself clear?"

He smiled. "I do comprehend what you're trying to say, Miss Emma. I just disagree with you, that's all."

Emma hurled down the bodice of the dress she'd been sewing and bolted out of her chair. "What on earth gives you the idea that it matters, whether you and I agree or not?"

His eyes glittered with firelight and humor as he watched her. "You are indeed a beauty, Miss Emma—the kind of prize a man dreams of winning. Win you I will, and when I do, I intend to have you well and often."

A tremor of mingled fury and desire coursed through Emma's slender frame. "What will it take to make you go away and leave me alone?" she whispered, clasping her hands together as though she were praying.

Steven drew her to him without moving, without extending a hand. Before she knew what was happening, Emma was standing on the hearth, looking up into his face. He touched her lips, very lightly, with his finger, sending a storm of fire all through her. "Go on the picnic with me," he said quietly. "Then if you still want me to leave, I will."

Emma's eyes widened. She felt hope, but also a raw sort of dismay. "You mean you'll actually saddle your horse and leave Whitneyville entirely? You won't even work on Big John's ranch anymore?"

"That's right," Steven answered hoarsely, winding an escaped tendril of Emma's blaze-colored hair around the same finger that had caressed her lips. "If you can tell me you never want to see me again after our picnic, I'll ride out."

Emma bit her lip and laid one hand to her heart, as though to slow its rapid beat so Steven wouldn't hear it. "But the dance . . ."

"You'll be back in plenty of time for that."

Within Emma's breast, reason and whimsy did battle. And as so often happened where this man was concerned, whimsy won. "All right," she sighed with resolution. "But I expect you to keep your word." She waggled a finger at him. "There'll be no backing out after I say I never want to see you again."

He bent his head and kissed her lightly, tantalizingly, on the lips. "You have my word of honor," he told her between soft samplings of her mouth that sent sweet shocks jolting to her nerve endings.

Emma wanted desperately to be held and soundly kissed; she longed to melt into Steven's hard frame and lose herself in the riotous pleasure of his touch. But saying so outright just wouldn't have done. Especially not under the circumstances. "Good night, Mr. Fairfax," she said in a shaky voice.

Steven laughed and tossed his hat onto a settee to pull her against him. Her heart raced and heat climbed from her stomach to her chest at the intimacy of their contact —Emma could feel his rocklike masculinity pressing against the soft flesh of her thigh.

*"Mr.* Fairfax," she protested. "I must insist—"

Her words were smothered by the warm, moist conquest of his mouth. His tongue teased the corners of her lips, and when they opened for him, he consumed her. Emma whimpered and sagged slightly in surrender, as he plundered her sweetness. By the time the kiss ended, the room was spinning so that she could barely stand, and Steven deposited her in a nearby chair.

"See you Saturday, Miss Emma," he said with a low chuckle.

"Go to perdition, Mr. Fairfax," Emma replied breathlessly, not daring to meet his eyes. But she knew she'd go on the picnic with him, and so did he.

Chloe swept in almost the moment the front door had closed behind him. "I'll make sure there's a basket packed," she said, making no pretense that she hadn't heard all or most of the conversation.

Emma snatched her bodice from the floor, took up her needle and thread, and began making furious, stabbing stitches. "If you cared about me at all, Chloe Reese, you would forbid me to be alone with that man for a minute, let alone a whole day!"

Chloe laughed. "Would you obey me if I did?"

The look Emma gave her was sheepish. "No," she answered honestly. "I probably wouldn't."

Green eyes flashing with amusement, Chloe sat down in the chair nearest Emma's. "The way he kissed you made me think of Big John. Now, there's a man."

Emma sighed, mortified that Chloe had witnessed such a personal moment. But her guardian had offered her a chance to change the subject, and she wasn't going to overlook it. "Why don't you marry John? It's obvious you love him."

Chloe's rich taffeta skirts swished and rustled as she settled herself in the chair and crossed her shapely legs. "Mr. Lenahan is a proud man," she answered, her tone sad. "I won't have people making fun of him because he took a whore for a wife."

Emma's gaze shot to Chloe's face. "But you're not—you don't—"

"I might as well be, Emma. Folks take the same view of me as if I did."

Given all she'd suffered over the years because of Chloe's occupation, there was no denying her assertion. "Has he ever proposed?" Emma asked, her needle suspended.

Chloe smiled. "Oh, yes, once or twice."

"I think you should marry him," Emma announced with certainty. "And hang what everybody else has to say about it!"

"And I think you should stay plumb away from Fulton Whitney. It isn't right, Emma, using one man to hold off another like that."

Emma bit her lower lip and went back to sewing her seam. She still had a lot to do if she wanted to wear the dress on Saturday night. "Who says I'm using anyone?"

Chloe gave a rich burst of laughter. "I do." She was a vivid woman, still beautiful despite what seemed to Emma an advanced age, and she was smart. It was no wonder a fine man like Big John Lenahan wanted her for his wife. "I suppose you're thinking you'll be an old maid if you don't tie the knot with Whitney—still puttering around that library and meeting every train with a stack of posters when you're ninety."

Dismayed, Emma let her hands rest in her lap. "You sound as though you don't think I'll ever find my sisters."

Chloe's eyes softened. "I didn't mean it that way," she said gently. "You'll find them, all right, if there's any justice in this world."

Emma was relieved that Chloe thought so, and she managed a smile. "Why do you dislike Fulton so much? I do believe you're pleased that I'm going on a picnic with an outlaw—a man you said yourself was probably just one step ahead of real trouble."

"My reasons for not liking Fulton are my own business," Chloe replied. "You'd see what's wrong with him for yourself if you'd just open your eyes. And I've changed my mind about you seeing Mr. Fairfax because

Big John says he's solid as bedrock. Fact is, I think he could bring out a side of you the rest of us have never seen."

Reflecting on the way she'd responded to Steven's kisses, Emma dropped her eyes. "Maybe that side is better left alone," she said, feeling a stirring of desire as well as shame.

"Nonsense," Chloe said briskly, "it's as much a part of you as that lovely copper-colored hair of yours and your blue eyes. You're a woman now, Emma, and it's time you stopped trying to mold yourself into a blue-stocking."

*I'm terrified of that other Emma,* she thought. "My mother had a passionate side," she observed aloud. "It brought her to ruin and made her give up her own children."

"She was weak," Chloe insisted.

Emma recalled how easily Steven had been able to make her submit to him. "Perhaps I'm weak, too."

"Only where one man is concerned, I think," was Chloe's reply. She rose from her chair and yawned daintily. "I'll be off to bed now. It's been a long day."

"Good night," Emma said, standing.

Chloe kissed her cheek. "Good night, Emma, dear. And don't stay up half the night berating yourself because some cowboy can make your knees melt. It just means you're a normal, healthy woman, that's all."

Emma reflected that the Presbyterians would probably argue that point, but she didn't say so out loud. She just sat back down and went right on sewing her party dress.

His cattle were still spread all over the ranch, and Big John Lenahan watched with interest as Fairfax dispatched men for the roundup. He was a born leader, that young Reb, despite his soft-spoken ways and gentlemanly manner. Although some of the men begrudged him his authority, none of them wanted to cross him.

Fairfax was just about to mount his own horse and ride out when Big John hailed him.

He turned, pushing the beat-up old hat to the back of his head, and stood beside his gelding, watching the rancher approach.

"The army's just put in an order for a couple hundred head of cattle," Big John said, patting the pocket of his shirt where the telegram rested. "How'd you like to head up a drive?"

Fairfax was clearly interested, but there was a look of reluctance about him, too. "Where to?"

"Spokane, over in the Washington Territory," Big John answered. "The army'll take 'em from there to Fort Deveraux."

"That's about ten days from here," Fairfax mused.

"Maybe as long as two weeks," Big John allowed. "After all, two hundred cattle and a couple of supply wagons can't be expected to move as fast as one man on horseback."

Fairfax nodded in agreement, and Big John knew he hadn't said anything to surprise the man.

"All right. When do you want us to head out?"

Big John scratched the back of his neck. It didn't itch, but it was his habit to scratch something when he was thinking. "Sunday morning, I reckon. I'm depending on the Lord to forgive us for working on the Sabbath Day."

"How many men?"

"Twelve good ones ought to do you. You can choose them yourself, of course."

Fairfax nodded his head. "Fine," he said, and the two men shook hands to bind the agreement.

As Big John strode away back to his study and the book work he hated, he allowed himself the fanciful wish that Steven Fairfax would fall in love with Joellen and marry her. She was just sixteen, of course, but it wasn't unheard-of for a girl that young to tie the knot, and God knew it would be nice to let somebody else take the responsibility for her.

But Big John was nothing if not pragmatic, and he'd heard Fairfax express a yearning for Emma Chalmers last night at supper. If John Lenahan knew anything about people, and the years had taught him a good deal, that pretty little librarian had just better start herself a hope chest.

Steven swore as he raised himself painfully into the saddle. The last damn thing he needed now was a two-week ride into the Washington Territory. For all he knew, he might come back and find Emma married to that piss-ant banker she seemed to think of so highly.

Riding after one of the groups of men he'd sent to round up stray cattle, Steven wondered if he shouldn't have told Emma about seeing Fulton upstairs at Chloe's. Even before the thought was completed, he knew he'd done the right thing by keeping quiet. There were some things a woman had to learn about a man all on her own, instead of hearing about them from somebody else.

Steven's mind shifted to Macon; his brother was a tireless, inflexible bastard, and he was undoubtedly closing in by now. Still, he might not stop in Whitney-ville at all.

Steven spurred the gelding lightly, and it shot forward across the grassy ground. There were snowcapped mountains visible in the distance, and stands of good timber in the foothills. He was going to miss this part of the country when he had to leave it.

But everything would be all right if Emma was with him when he left.

The week had passed much too rapidly for Emma's comfort, but her dress was finished and hanging on the front of her wardrobe, a thing of splendor with its lace trim and yards of glossy silk. Daisy was in the kitchen, filling a basket with picnic foods, when Emma came down the stairs in a crisp white cambric dress embroidered with small pink roses.

"Fasten my buttons, please," she said, turning her back to Daisy.

"I'll fasten your buttons, all right," Daisy muttered, but she couldn't hide her amusement at Emma's good mood. "You just see that young cowboy don't *un*fasten 'em again."

Emma stiffened. "Daisy! How could you say such a thing?"

"I wasn't always old an' fat," Daisy chortled. "No, siree, I was young once, just like you. Now, you mind your manners and behave like a lady, or I'll paddle your bottom."

"Fiddlefaddle," Emma said, but she was smiling when she whirled around to face Daisy, her skirts swishing as she moved. "How do I look?"

"Like a tiger lily," Daisy answered fondly, gathering her apron into her hands. "Lord, but you're a beauty, chile—no wonder some young fella's always tryin' to lead you down the primrose path!"

Emma's smile faded as she wondered how on earth she would resist Steven Fairfax if he got her alone and kissed her.

But Daisy laughed at her expression and patted her briskly on the cheek. "Don't look so fretted up, now— the fella what succeeds, I reckon he'll be the right one."

To distract herself, Emma went to the table and peered into the large wicker picnic basket. She could see a pie, an entire chicken—fried up crisp—cold potato salad, and some of Daisy's special wheat-flour rolls. She looked at the cook in amazement. "Daisy, we're just going on a picnic, not spending two weeks in the wilderness."

Daisy frowned and shook her finger at Emma. "Nobody's gonna say *my* chile didn't get enough to eat," she vowed, and that was the end of the subject. She took a pitcher of cold lemonade from the icebox and filled a jar with a tight-fitting lid, then added that to the basket, too. "What you gonna do when Mr. Fulton Whitney hears about this debilment?"

"It isn't devilment," Emma protested, bending close to the little mirror beside the door and pinching her cheeks to make them pink. "It's a picnic and nothing more—the whole thing is perfectly innocent."

Daisy chortled, her great bulk quivering with amusement. "I declare that's what Eve said to Adam. 'The whole thing is perfectly innocent.'"

Before Emma could offer a reply to that, there was a knock at the front door. Emma raced through the house to the entryway, where she stopped with a lurch and smoothed her hair, which was braided into its customary plait. After that, she pinched her cheeks again, but when she opened the door the expression on her face was purposefully dignified and remote.

Steven grinned as though he could see right through her. He was finely dressed, but she could see the bulge of his .45 beneath his suitcoat. "Hello, Miss Emma," he said, taking off his new beaver hat.

"Mr. Fairfax," Emma replied, stepping back to admit him.

There in the shadowed light of the entryway, he brought a very small box from the pocket of his vest and held it out. "This is for you."

Emma fairly lunged for the package, before remembering it wasn't polite to go grasping at things in other people's hands. "You shouldn't have," she said.

Steven's eyes glittered with silent laughter. "But I did," he reasoned.

"That's true," Emma replied, snatching it from his fingers and ripping off the paper.

The package contained a tiny bottle of real French perfume, and Emma's eyes went round at the sight of it. Uncorking the little crystal lid, she held the splendid stuff to her nose and sniffed.

Surely heaven didn't smell any better. "Thank you," she breathed, amazed that a cowboy could give such an elegant, costly gift. Even Fulton, with all his money, had never presented her with anything so dazzlingly extravagant.

117

Steven smiled. "You're welcome, Miss Emma. Now, are we going on that picnic or not?"

Emma led the way back through the house. "Daisy's fixed us a grand basket."

"We'll have plenty to eat then, darlin', because I just picked up a full meal from the hotel."

Emma turned and looked at him in surprise. "But the lady always provides the food," she said.

"That doesn't seem quite fair, since it was the gentleman who did the asking," Steven replied in a mischievous whisper.

Daisy was still lingering in the kitchen when they arrived, and when she saw Steven she shook a wooden spoon at him. "I raised this chile to be a good girl," she warned. "Don't you go messin' with her, hear?"

The beginnings of a grin quirked Steven's lips, but he didn't quite give in to it. "Yes, ma'am," he said.

Emma reached for the basket, but Steven's hand caught hers and forestalled the motion.

"We won't be needing that," he declared politely. Then for Daisy's benefit he added, "I had a basket made up at the hotel."

To Emma's surprise, a broad smile spread across Daisy's smooth mahogany-colored face. "I'll just give this here food to the Reverend Hess. That boy's always hungry."

Emma didn't protest. Food was the last thing on her mind that sunny day in early May, and she wouldn't have begrudged the pastor anything. She took up the cream-colored shawl she'd crocheted two winters back and draped it nervously around her shoulders. "I guess we'd better get this over with," she said.

Steven laughed softly at that and put his hand on the small of her back to guide her toward the front door. His smile, however, was for Daisy. "Mind you don't flirt too much with the reverend, now," he warned.

The cook gave a rich chortle at that and called out, "You just get out o' my house right now, Johnny Reb."

Steven was grinning as he closed the front door and

shepherded Emma across the porch, down the steps and the walk to the gate. A horse and buggy, no doubt rented at the livery stable or borrowed from Big John Lenahan, waited in the sun-dappled shade of Chloe's towering maple trees.

Emma gave him a sour sidelong look as he opened the gate for her. "It's plain that Daisy never learned not to trust a flattering rogue," she remarked.

Steven closed his hands around Emma's waist and lifted her none-too-gently onto the leather seat of the rig. "If that's what you think of me," he demanded, pushing his hat to the back of his head to look up at her, "what are you doing going on a picnic with me?"

Emma took great delight in prickling his overblown pride. "You know very well what I'm doing," she answered in the same haughty tone she'd used on the school grounds as a girl, when the other children had tormented her about Chloe's method of earning a livelihood. "I'm honoring my end of our agreement. I'll still detest you when this picnic is over, and you'll ride out of this town forever, just as you promised."

His grin was downright maddening. "Or," he retorted, "you'll end up asking me to stay. In fact, I expect you'll ask real nice, Miss Emma." He took a few moments to watch the color flood her face, laughed again, and rounded the buggy to climb up in the seat beside her and take the reins.

"Just where are we going for this picnic?" Emma asked stiffly, pulling her shawl still more closely around her, until she suspected there were little imprints of its design appearing on her upper arms. "The churchyard? There's a good place down on Cold Creek, too."

"Are you waxing helpful all of a sudden?" Steven countered, feigning surprise and driving the horse and buggy straight toward the center of town. In another two minutes, if he didn't turn to the right, they were going to pass directly in front of the First Territorial Bank.

Emma clutched his upper arm and immediately withdrew when she felt the granite-hardness of his muscles beneath her fingers. "I don't want Fulton to see us!" she protested in a somewhat frantic whisper, as though Fulton might have spies stationed in the branches of the elms and maples along the sides of the street.

"I'm afraid he probably will," Steven lamented without any conviction at all, as he continued past the last turn that would have saved Emma from certain exposure. "Sorry, Miss Emma, but there was nothing in our agreement about avoiding the banker."

Emma looked down at the hard-packed dirt of the road and calculated that she'd probably turn an ankle if she jumped, not to mention ruining her favorite spring dress. She folded her arms. "You're deliberately trying to compromise me."

"Oh, no, Miss Emma," Steven assured her suavely, tilting the brim of that obnoxious hat just for a moment. "I haven't even started on that yet."

Emma folded her arms across her bosom and glared straight ahead. "I will not miss you when you leave," she said coldly. "In fact, I will *celebrate.*"

They were passing the First Territorial Bank, and Steven waved at someone inside. Emma didn't dare look to see who it was, but her cheeks went red and she stomped one foot against the floorboard of the buggy.

To make bad matters worse, Steven headed straight toward the center of town, stopping only when they came to the base of the wharf where the mail boat tied up when it wasn't making its rounds of the two other small communities situated on Crystal Lake. It was there, bobbing on the glistening blue waves, its steam engine chugging and chortling away.

"What—?" Emma began lamely as Steven secured the brake lever, jumped down to the ground, and collected the picnic basket from underneath the seat.

With a smile on his face, he extended a hand to Emma.

She would just as soon have bitten him as let him help her down, but she kept their bargain firmly in mind and laid her hand in his.

They boarded the mail boat with half the town of

Whitneyville looking on from windows and sidewalks; Emma could feel their gazes burning into her back. By the end of the day Fulton would be a raving maniac.

The cumbersome little boat pulled slowly away from the wharf, bound across the lake to the little town of Onion Creek, which boasted three houses, a public privy, and a one-room schoolhouse.

"Mornin', Miss Emma," said the captain of the small craft. Tom Fillmore was one of the few people in Whitneyville who had treated Emma with respect even before Fulton had taken a fierce and sudden fancy to her. "Fine day for a picnic."

Emma considered asking Tom to take her straight back to shore, but in the end she just turned her back on both him and Steven and stood morosely at the railing, staring at the island in the middle. It was an enchanted place to her; she and Chloe had often rowed over when she was a girl, to have picnics and fish for fat lake trout that melted on the tongue when Daisy fried them up.

Surprise overtook Emma when the mail boat suddenly veered toward the middle of the lake. Since there were no houses on the island, she turned in consternation to see Tom inside the wheelhouse, swinging the vessel toward its shore.

Steven had been leaning against the jamb of the wheelhouse door, talking with the skipper. Now he strolled to her side, grinning as though he hadn't just utterly ruined her reputation.

"Scoundrel!" she accused through her teeth. "You deliberately let everyone see me with you—including Fulton!"

Steven arched his eyebrows in a counterfeit expression of surprise. "Don't tell me Mr. Whitney was slaving over his accounts on a fine day like this one!" He took off his hat and slapped it against one thigh, as if in self-admonishment, but his smile was downright insolent. "I do apologize, Miss Emma. I keep forgetting these Yankee boys don't know how to slow down and enjoy life."

Emma felt a pull deep inside. She wanted with all her

heart and soul to slap him, but that would only have proved that his impudent comments had found their mark. In stiff silence, she turned her face away from him, toward the island that as a child she had whimsically called the Garden of Eden.

And a portent of something that lay not only in the future, but in the ancient past, reverberated in her heart like the chime of a mystical bell.

# Chapter
## ❧ 9 ❧

*J*oellen Lenahan stood with one hand resting on her hip, her plump lower lip jutting out. "Where is he?" she demanded.

Big John didn't look up from the paperwork he was fussing over. He just sat there, behind that imposing desk of his, his head bent, his right hand gripping the stub of a pencil. "Who, darlin'?" he asked pleasantly enough.

Joellen wanted his full attention. She stomped one expensively booted foot, and he raised his head. His blue eyes revealed good-natured bafflement. "Where is Mr. Fairfax?" she pressed, standing directly in front of her daddy's desk now. "You sent him away, didn't you? He's going on that dratted cattle drive!"

Big John sighed and laid down his pencil. "Sit down, Joellen," he said, his voice a patient rumble.

Joellen sank petulantly into the large leather chair and folded her arms across her shapely breasts. She glared at her father, her large green eyes brimming with crystal tears. She was dressed in a pristine white blouse artfully

123

open at the throat and a green velvet skirt, divided so she could ride astride. Her greatest glory, the blonde hair that was the legacy of some Scandinavian ancestor, tumbled free around her shoulders, reaching all the way to her elbows. A green ribbon drew it softly back from her face. And all to impress a certain foreman.

"You're forgetting," her father pointed out reluctantly, "that Steven Fairfax is spoken for. He's got his eye on Miss Emma Chalmers."

Joellen was horrified. "That dowdy little snippet who runs the *library?* He's just toying with her, that's all."

Big John shrugged his powerful shoulders. "Miss Emma tries to conduct herself proper-like, and dress the way a lady should, but she's not dowdy, Joellen, not by a far sight."

Miss Lenahan was in no mood to hear a recital of that dreadful woman's virtues. She steered the conversation in a slightly different direction. "If Steven's taken up with her, it's only because he knows she's loose, and he's out for what he can get. When it comes time for marrying, he'll want another sort of woman entirely."

Two patches of color appeared on Big John's leathery cheeks, and his eyes snapped. In that instant, Joellen knew she'd gone too far. "I won't hear another word against Emma," he said tightly. "Now, you just run along and forget chasing after Fairfax—do you hear me?"

Even Joellen didn't dare cross Big John when he had that look in his eyes. She nodded glumly. "Is he going on the drive?"

"Yes," her daddy answered, bending his head over that infernal ledger book of his. "Now, go on about your business, Joellen, and leave me to mine."

Joellen thrust herself from her chair and strode out through the gaping doorway of Big John's study. She didn't see why he had to send Steven away on a drive; after all, he was practically the newest man on the place.

But if Steven had to go, well, there were ways of dealing with a problem like that. A smile brightening her face, Joellen marched confidently out of the house and over to the stables.

Her new palomino mare trotted to the paddock fence to greet her, golden in the bright spring sunshine. The animal's mane and tail were just the color of new cream. Climbing up onto the lowest rail of the fence, Joellen reached out to pat the horse's velvety nose.

"Hello, Songbird," she said.

Songbird whinnied a response, and Joellen forgot all about Steven and Emma Chalmers and the cattle drive— for the time being.

The mail boat chugged up to the rotting wharf that reached way out over the sparkling blue waters, and Tom Fillmore throttled down the engine.

Steven tossed the picnic basket over the railing, onto the creaking dock, and vaulted after it. There was an insolent grin in his eyes as he held a hand out to Emma.

She drew a deep breath and let it out again. Catching the skirts of her white cambric dress in both hands, she eyed the railing with trepidation. If ever there was an idea born in perdition, it was this one. Her blue eyes locked with Steven's, repaying his friendly mischief with pure sourness. "There's no way I can climb out of this boat and still behave like a lady," she said.

Just when she was thinking she might have gotten herself out of this awful situation, that she might not have to spend the day picnicking with Steven Fairfax after all, Tom Fillmore went and produced a sturdy-looking apple crate.

He set it carefully on the deck, made sure it was steady, and grinned, squinting his eyes in the sunshine. "There you are, Miss Emma," he said proudly, offering her a grubby hand to grip.

Resigned, Emma took his hand and stepped up onto the crate. Steven immediately took her elbow, and she stepped down onto the creaky wharf.

In another moment the mail boat was chortling away

on its journey to Onion Creek, and Emma was alone on an island with Mr. Fairfax. She couldn't think why on earth she'd agreed to do such an outrageous thing, and glanced nervously toward town.

Sure enough, there were people gathered on the docks —Emma couldn't quite make out who, given the distance and the glimmer of sunlight on the water, but she knew why they were there. Within twenty minutes everybody in Whitneyville would know Emma Chalmers was out there alone with a gunslinger.

"No sense in looking back, Miss Emma," Steven said, his voice low and husky.

Emma made herself meet his eyes, but she couldn't speak for the life of her. There was something about him that made her breath catch and her heart miss a half-beat.

Steven took her arm. "I think we'd better get off this wharf before it collapses," he said practically.

Emma was jarred out of her reverie. She whirled, one arm in the air to flag down the mail boat. She meant to get herself straight back to Whitneyville before everything was lost, but Tom misread her gesture. He waved exuberantly and then turned back to the wheel again.

Fingers curled around her elbow, Steven led her over the wharf, which shifted and groaned beneath them, to the shore. Tiny pebbles crunched under Emma's feet as she advanced up the beach with Steven, toward the inner part of the island.

Nervousness made her smile too brightly and speak in a voice that was a touch too loud. "Couldn't we just have our picnic on the wharf?"

Steven continued up the grassy embankment, pulling Emma behind him, and all she got in answer to her question was a look of moderate disdain and a slight shake of his head.

There was a tumbledown shack a few yards up ahead, with just two weathered walls left, and a fireplace. Some small creature had made a nest in the hearth, and green grass poked up between the remaining floorboards.

"Who lived here?" Steven asked, slowing his pace now that they'd reached level ground.

Emma reached back to be sure her braid wasn't coming undone. "Just some homesteaders. I don't know what their names were."

Steven released her hand and gave the remains of the house a thorough assessment, as though it might be important to remember what he saw. "It must have been nice, living out here—just a man and his wife, and maybe a couple of kids."

"It must have been *lonely*," Emma countered. "Besides, you don't know what this lake is like in winter—it freezes solid in some places. These people might easily have been marooned here for weeks at a time." She shivered, even though there were bees buzzing in the warm May air.

"I imagine they found things to do," Steven said quietly. He held out a hand to Emma, and she went to him, just as she always did.

Emma flushed as she lowered her eyes, unable to help picturing herself and Steven in such a situation. "I imagine," she conceded.

Just past the old house was a privy, leaning decidedly to the right and almost completely covered by a wild rose bush sporting the tiniest pink buds. Beyond that was a split rail fence, turned a dirty coffee-brown by the weather, like the privy and the house.

Steven set down the picnic basket and released Emma's hand to take down the two upper railings. Lifting her skirts as modestly as she could and still get over the lower bar of the fence without snagging them, Emma climbed awkwardly to the other side.

Steven immediately handed over the picnic basket and folded blanket and followed.

"Just how far do we have to go?" Emma wanted to know. "Most people like to picnic by the water, you know."

He grinned. "Do they, now? Well, we're going to have a good look around before we choose a place."

Emma thought of that crowd of people on the wharf across the water at Whitneyville. Heaven only knew what speculations they were up to by now. "Fulton might be rowing over here at this very instant," she warned, just in case Mr. Fairfax had any ideas. And she was dead certain he did.

His smile confirmed it. "You don't need to worry about him, Miss Emma. He wouldn't confront his own grandmother unless he was sure he could get the drop on her."

Emma's cheeks reddened as she followed Steven through the deep grass and between towering fir and pine trees. "I resent your insinuation that Fulton is a coward," she said. "He's a very fine man."

Suddenly, Steven stopped right in the middle of the trail. Emma, who had just built up a good head of steam, collided with him—hard.

For a long moment, Steven held her to him without even using his arms. No, it was the look in his eyes that gripped her, that made her feel as if something warm was spilling over within her. "If he's such a fine man," he reasoned, his voice hardly more than a rasp, "how come you're out here with me?"

Emma was so flabbergasted by the question, and by the obvious answer, that she just stared up at Steven's face. She felt like a field mouse looking into the eyes of a tomcat.

"Well?" Steven prompted, his lips just a hair's breadth from hers.

Coming to her senses at the last second, Emma leaped backward, causing her handbag to thump painfully against her thigh. "I'm here with you because we have a bargain, Mr. Fairfax," she blurted out. "You promised to leave Whitneyville forever, remember?"

"If you still want me to," Steven pointed out, and then he was forging his way through the wilds of that overgrown island again, dragging Emma after him.

He finally settled on a grassy rise on the opposite side from Whitneyville. There was a fine view of the lake, and far behind them a conglomeration of hemlocks, cedars, and Douglas fir made a horseshoe shape. The trees harbored a clearing where a multitude of white daisies with centers as yellow as pirate's doubloons rippled in the breeze.

Looking at them, Emma forgot her troubles. "There must be one for every angel in heaven," she breathed.

Steven, who had been spreading the picnic blanket on the ground, came to stand behind her. His hands rested lightly on her shoulders, and he bent to plant the lightest of kisses on her nape. "Today they all belong to just one angel—you."

She turned to look up at him, and his arms slipped naturally around her waist. He'd tossed his hat onto the picnic blanket, but the imprint of the band showed in his glossy brown hair, and Emma couldn't resist touching it with the fingers of one hand. "Why did you have to go and get yourself blown up in Whitneyville?" she asked softly. "Life was so simple before I met you—I knew what I thought about everything."

A trace of a smile touched his lips. "And now?"

"I'm confused, Steven. I've spent all my time with one man over the last few months and now here I am, standing in an ocean of daisies with quite another."

He brushed her mouth with his own. "If it helps, Miss Emma, I'm as muddled up as you are. A few weeks ago I just wanted to keep on moving. Now it's like I've got lead in my boots."

Emma knew what was going to happen if she didn't break away, and she used every shred of her willpower to turn from Steven and run through the daisies, her arms outspread. She'd gone only a few yards when she stumbled over something and went sprawling.

She was laughing when she rolled over and started to sit up, and her plump breasts strained against her bodice. Before she could begin the arduous process of untangling herself from her skirts and struggling back to her feet, Steven was kneeling beside her on the ground.

He reached out slowly to touch her braid. "God in

heaven, but you're beautiful," he rasped, and it was as though he begrudged the words. "Who are you, Emma? Where did you come from?"

She smiled, even though her stomach felt just the way it had once long ago, when she'd raced down an icy hillside on a runaway sled. Speaking softly, her words interspersed with small sighs, she told him how her mother had decided three daughters were too much trouble and sent them west on an orphan train. Her throat tightened as she recounted being separated, first from Caroline, then from Lily.

Steven shifted so that he was straddling her hips, but there was nothing threatening in the motion. He'd listened to every word Emma said with genuine interest and carefully veiled sympathy. When she was finished, he told her about growing up as the bastard son of a land baron and his mistress.

The first kiss seemed to flow naturally from there, like a river from its headwaters.

Emma knew she was lost, but to her credit, she did put her hands behind her and tried to scoot backwards; the motion only served to bring the neckline of her dress to the very perimeters of her nipples.

Halting her escape with pressure from his knees, Steven reached out and plucked a single daisy from the host surrounding them. Holding it by its sturdy green stem, he slowly drew the white petals across the upper curves of her breasts.

Emma trembled, even as that strange, familiar heat began pulsing deep within her, and her breath came quickly, making her bosom rise and fall under Steven's eyes.

He drew the daisy lightly from the base of her chin to the deep plunge of her cleavage then, and Emma's nipples leaped to attention beneath her dress.

The flower touched her lips, making a feather-light circle around them. The sensual side of Emma's nature, hidden away behind a prim facade until this man's appearance in her life, took over completely. Her head went back, as though an invisible fist gripped her hair, and her nipples sprang free of their tenuous bonds.

Emma was shocked back to her senses by this occurrence, but before she could cover herself, Steven's daisy came to rest against one hardened morsel and turned like a velvety pinwheel. The sensation was one of delicious abandon, and Emma's brazen side was in command again.

She arched her neck and gripped the sweet green grass with both hands as Steven touched the flower to her other nipple in just the same way. He leaned over her and found her mouth with his, shutting out the sun with his shadow.

Emma's lips opened for him, so easily trained to his bidding, and their tongues writhed like lovers locked together. His fingers gently pulled down her bodice until her breasts were fully revealed.

She felt herself straining brazenly against his hand, but there was no going back. It belonged to Steven, this kingdom of daisies, and his rule was absolute.

He withdrew his mouth from Emma's, finally, but his hand still cupped her breast. His thumb shaped her nipple for a gentle conquest. "Where is the perfume?" he asked huskily.

Emma blinked, barely able to speak for the lump tightening in her throat. "Perfume? Oh—it's in my handbag—"

"I want you to wear it," Steven said.

She was confused, impatient. She lifted one arm to show the pretty drawstring bag dangling from her wrist, and the movement would have made her fall to her back if Steven hadn't supported her by sliding his free hand around between her shoulder blades.

With groping, awkward fingers, she found the small crystal bottle inside her bag and brought it out. The facets trapped the sunlight in tiny bits and transformed it to rainbow colors.

Steven laid Emma gently on the carpet of daisies to take the little flagon from her hand. She watched, half bewitched, as he removed the stopper and touched it ever so lightly to the pulse point at the base of her throat.

The lush woodsy scent rose to her nostrils, and Emma closed her eyes to savor this new pleasure.

Steven stretched out beside Emma and kissed the place he had just perfumed, one hand resting brazenly on her bare breast. She swallowed a moan, for there was still some vestige of pride held prisoner in a dark part of her heart.

The perfume touched the sensitive place beneath her right ear then, and as before, Steven followed the scent with his lips.

Emma's pride rattled the bars that confined it, but its protest went unheeded. Another part of her—the part that was a harlot's daughter—had taken her over, body and soul.

When the stopper touched between her breasts, Emma was fevered. Her back arched, her nipples reached. She entangled her fingers in Steven's hair, trying to guide him to the sustenance she needed so badly to give.

He brought her skirts and petticoats to lie around her waist in a billow of white, drew her right knee up and wide of her left. Through the taut cloth of her drawers, he teased that moist junction that was already preparing itself for him.

"Listen to me," he grated out, grasping her chin in his hand. "I'm going to take you when you're ready, Emma Chalmers, and make you into a woman once and for all. If you have any objections, you'd better speak up now, while I've still got enough control to stop myself."

Emma bit down hard on her lower lip, lest her pride escape and save her from the fate her body craved.

"All right, then," Steven said in a tone of gentle finality. And he began unlacing Emma's shoes.

The spring sunshine warmed her breasts and her face as she lay in the field of daisies, surrendering her clothes garment by garment. Soon she lay before Steven wearing nothing but the freckles God had sprinkled over her body like gold dust.

Steven took off his own clothes and lay beside her on the bed of flowers, one hand splayed on her belly. His other arm lay under her shoulders, and his fingers played with her braid.

Emma gave a little whimper as he took the silky end of her plait and brushed each nipple with it. She stretched both arms above her head and gripped handfuls of daisy stems, laying them before him like Vikings' plunder.

He rolled a nipple between index finger and thumb until Emma, remembering that pleasure only too well, begged him in a breathless gasp to take it into his mouth. He did so greedily, lustily, and the hand that had been under her shoulders shifted to lift her hips.

He trailed his lips lingeringly to the other breast, where he sucked and teased until Emma was tossing her head from side to side. When her hands grasped at him, trying futilely to pull him close, to make him lay his weight upon her, he strung kisses down her belly in a velvety ribbon of sensation, then shifted, so he was between her legs.

Emma felt his hands on the insides of her thighs, stroking her, soothing her, setting her ablaze. Her heartbeat seemed to throb in her throat, her tongue, even her lips. "Steven," she pleaded, and it didn't matter that she didn't know what she was asking for.

He touched the damp mound of tangled silk, and his thumb burrowed through to make a sensuous circle around the small, hardened nubbin he found trembling there.

Emma gave a soft cry and gazed at the sky, losing herself in its gentle blue. "Please—"

No plea would be enough, it seemed, for through the haze of an azure sky fringed with daisies, she saw Steven shake his head. "Not yet, sweetheart. Not before you're ready."

Emma was near to weeping with frustration when he fell to her, his head resting between her thighs, and drank the nectar no other man had ever tasted.

In her need, Emma bucked like a wild mare, her hips

tossing up and down, back and forth, without pattern or reason. And Steven rode her until she hurled herself high in surrender, crying out in her triumph, and he extracted the last shuddering sigh of pleasure from her before letting her settle back to the soft ground.

Blindly, her breath a series of gasps tearing in and out of her lungs, she reached up and found his bare chest with her fingers. She found the tiny buttons hidden in downy maple silk, and teased them.

The groan this drew from Steven made her exultant. She laid her hands to his back as he came to rest between her legs, and there was no fear in her, only anticipation, when she felt his rod pressed between his belly and her own.

He kissed her ravenously and then whispered, "It'll hurt just this once. But after that, there'll be nothing but pleasure."

Emma would have trusted him with her soul, let alone her body. Nothing else existed for her except Steven and herself, and their bed of wild spring daisies. She nodded, her hands resting on the small of his back.

The first taste of him was a surprise that made her widen her eyes and start a little. Steven stopped and soothed her with tender words and kisses until she lay back, feeling herself draw at him from deep inside.

He groaned and advanced again, and Emma felt something tear inside her and then give way. Steven rested, braced on his elbows, until she'd gotten over that momentous sacrifice, then eased full inside her.

Emma couldn't believe the size and power and heat of him, and she pushed the pain to the back of her mind and gave herself up to the pleasure. Her fingers moved lightly from the bulging blades of his shoulders, over his middle to his hipbones and his buttocks. Briefly she registered that his ribs weren't wrapped, but instinct told her that he was withholding something precious, and she clasped at the taut, rounded muscles beneath her hands, urging motion.

Steven groaned her name and withdrew slightly, and the closer he came to leaving her, the more Emma despaired. Just as he would have become a separate being again, he lunged deep into her again, and the friction was like the meeting of kerosene and fire.

Emma arched her back and thrust herself at Steven, wanting another stroke, and another. He gave them, but with excruciating slowness, pausing now and then to take suckle at her breasts, her lips, her earlobes. He savored her like a confection, and when she was sure she could bear no more delays, no more teasing, he sensed that and hoisted her upright, while he knelt.

She shuddered at the glorious splendor of his total possession, and her own. Her hair had come partly free of its braid, and tendrils of it rioted around her face, ablaze in the sun.

He caught her cheeks in his hands and kissed her roughly, for they were both savages in those moments, and his tongue swept her mouth and her lips before he moaned, "My beautiful, blue-eyed tigress—"

Emma began to rise and fall upon him because she craved the friction, and his moan of helpless pleasure filled her with a rush of sweet power. She wanted to shout her exultation, but she hadn't the breath for it, so she simply gripped Steven's shoulders and worked her instinctive magic.

She sheathed and unsheathed him, and felt the moisture on his flesh as he strained toward something Emma only partly understood.

Her own pinnacle came upon her by surprise, ambushing her in the act of possessing him. She flung her head back and called, without words, to the sky, as a string of fireworks went off between her hips. Every sensation was intensified when Steven's mouth closed over her nipple.

He sucked until something happening inside his own body made him fling back his head and shoulders like a stallion. His hands gripped Emma's hips and held her to him as he stiffened violently.

She felt his warmth spill within her and laid her forehead to his shoulder, cherishing the rapid rise and fall of his chest, the steady thud of his heartbeat.

Sitting up was too much for both of them, and they collapsed onto the springy cushion of flowers, arms and legs entwined. It was a long time before either of them stirred at all.

Steven raised himself on an elbow, plucked a daisy, and put it through Emma's loose braid. He continued until a trail of white flowers paraded from her scalp to the place beneath her breast where her hair made a coppery fan.

His fingers strayed naturally, lightly, from there to her breast, and Emma sighed as he caressed and weighed her in his hand.

"I want to watch you take your pleasure, little tigress," he said gruffly, and his fingers moved from her breast to the junction of her thighs. Because he was her king, in that fanciful time and place at least, Emma parted her legs for him.

Her teeth sank into her lower lip as he found the hidden pearl and bared it to be his plaything. Her right knee drew up, then fell wide of her hip.

Steven bent to nibble at her lips for a few moments, but after that he watched the different expressions chasing across her face like clouds drifting past the moon.

When his fingers went inside her, Emma could find nothing to do with her hands. They moved from the ground to her breasts to Steven's shoulders.

He laid them gently back on her breasts, and Emma felt her nipples harden fiercely against her palms. "Steven," she whispered, his name both a plea and a prayer.

He worked her into a frenzy, and soon Emma's thighs were thrashing on the soft, fragrant earth, and Steven watched her passion play naked in her face until it was spent. She lay still, her head turned to one side, unable to look at him.

He kissed the soft expanse of her neck. "Don't be ashamed, tigress," he whispered. "There's never been anything more beautiful than a woman willingly surrendering her body to a man."

There were tears in Emma's eyes when she forced herself to meet his gaze. "What if she's nothing more than a pretty toy to that man?"

Steven found Emma's drawers and gently drew them over her ankles, her calves, her thighs. She lifted her bottom so he could bring them to her waist. "If I wanted a plaything, Miss Emma," he said hoarsely, "I'd go over to the Stardust and lay my money on the bar."

Emma scrambled to her feet and began pulling on her petticoats, her back turned to Steven. "Daisy always says men don't buy the cow when they can get the milk for free," she confided, and a little sob followed the words out of her throat.

Steven gripped her arm and turned her to face him. He was wearing his trousers but nothing else, and Emma's fingers ached to spread themselves over his chest. "Do you have any idea how beautiful you are with your hair all tumbled and filled with daisies?"

"You're deliberately changing the subject!" Emma accused, as it began to dawn on her what she'd done, what she'd sacrificed.

"All right," Steven barked, "I'll marry you as soon as we get back to Whitneyville!"

"Well, *that's* damn generous of you, considering that you just ruined me for any other man!" Emma shouted as the librarian chased the tigress back into her cage. She limped around in a circle in that ocean of daisies, searching in vain for her shoes.

Finally, Steven stopped her restless prowling by holding them aloft. "Tell me to leave, Emma," he said, when she flung herself at him, grabbing for her shoes. "That was our deal, remember?"

Emma stopped the struggle and stared at him. As furious as she was with this man, as used as she felt, she couldn't bring herself to say the words that would end her torment and perhaps allow her to salvage something of her dreams.

He took her chin in his hand and held it, leaving her nowhere to look but directly into his eyes. "Say it," he ordered.

# Chapter
## ❧ 10 ❧

$S$tay," Emma whispered, in response to his command. "I want you to stay."

Satisfied, Steven opened the picnic basket he'd had packed at the hotel and began lifting out various flavorful dishes to tempt his willing captive.

Emma tried, but she had no appetite, not after what she'd done. She sat there on the blanket with her head down, her lower lip caught between her teeth, her hair trailing over her breasts and down her back like a hoyden's. Her beautiful white dress was stained with grass and dirt, and her shoes weren't laced all the way up.

Steven didn't speak again, didn't try to erase what she was feeling. Instead, he found a comb in her handbag, knelt behind her, and gently began working the tangles out of her hair.

"Maybe the women of Whitneyville are right about me," she muttered in genuine despair, and daisy petals fell like rain around her as Steven continued to comb her hair.

"They might be right about some things," Steven answered gently. "But they're dead wrong about you." There was something soothing in the feel of his hands in her hair, even though the pulling of the comb hurt now and then. "Tell me, Emma—do you really mean to marry the banker?"

In that instant Emma realized that Steven had compromised her only to keep her from marrying Fulton, that he had no plans to offer her anything lasting. She stiffened. "Yes," she answered to repay him, even though she'd known for days that she would never be Mrs. F.W. Whitney.

Steven began rebraiding her hair, and the motions of his hands were slightly rougher now. "I'm taking a herd of cattle over into the Washington Territory for Big John," he said evenly. "I'll be gone a couple of weeks, probably. I want your word that you won't do anything stupid while I'm away."

Emma was still angry, and she still felt used and manipulated. "I'll promise you nothing, Steven Fairfax."

He bound the bottom of her braid with a clip she produced from her bag, and gave it a little tug before moving around to sit facing her, cross-legged like an Indian. "If you marry the wrong man," Steven warned, in a voice all the more ominous because of its quietness, "you'll regret it into your old age. You'll never pass a day—or a night—without remembering how it was when we made love in a field of daisies, and wishing to God it could be that way with him. But it won't be, Emma—no matter how hard you wish."

She knew what he said was true, and that made everything infinitely worse. "When will the mail boat come back for us?" she asked, avoiding Steven's gaze.

A motion of his hands told her he was checking the watch he carried in his vest pocket, and she saw his suitcoat push backwards to reveal the Colt resting with deadly ease in its holster. "In an hour," he answered, and he got up off the blanket to walk away.

Emma didn't lift her eyes until he returned with an

armload of daisies. He knelt behind her again, and when she tried to move away, he stopped her by reaching around and closing his hands over her breasts.

Emma gave a little whimper and let her head fall back against his shoulder.

He chuckled, and caressed her for a few moments longer, then began weaving daisies into her braid until it almost looked as though she had flowers for hair. When he was through he laid the plait over one of her shoulders and came around to admire her.

Because she couldn't imagine Fulton doing a thing like that, and because she'd probably ruined her life, Emma began to cry.

Steven smiled and brushed her tears away with the edges of his thumbs. Then he took a piece of fried chicken from the basket and held it to her lips.

At first she resisted, but her hunger had been stirred and she nibbled at the chicken. Slowly, systematically, Steven fed her, and there was such sensuality in the ritual that Emma ached to be possessed all over again. Who would have thought a man could seduce her by simply putting flowers in her hair and food into her mouth?

"Steven—" she whispered.

He smiled gently. "I know, tigress. But you're too sore for that." His finger traced her cheek lightly, sending a delicious shiver through her. "I'll take proper care of you when I get back from the cattle drive."

The quiet arrogance of the remark forced Emma to challenge him. "What if I'm married to—someone by then?"

"You won't be," he answered with absolute confidence, and he slid Emma's dress down off her shoulders until her breasts stood bare and firm before him. He caressed each nipple with his fingertips until it tightened and protruded, sucked much too briefly at both, and then covered Emma again. "You'll wait."

Emma's cheeks were crimson, and she began gathering up the food and tucking it back into the basket, just to have something to do. With extreme effort she turned her

141

mind from the pleasures she craved and asked, "Who is it that's after you, Steven? Who wants to kill you?"

"Nobody important," he answered, watching her as though her every motion brought him to some joy too profound to speak of aloud.

"I have a right to know," she said, even though she knew she had no rights at all where this man was concerned. She was a serf in his kingdom, destined to do his bidding. He'd just taken her in a daisy field, after all, and made her howl like some creature of the jungle in the process.

Steven sighed. "Someday I'll tell you. But this isn't the time."

Emma had to settle for that, and it rankled. She slammed the lid of the picnic basket down and snapped, "And in the meantime, I may be consorting with a criminal!"

He laughed. "Is that what you were doing, Miss Emma? Consorting?"

If she could have summoned a genie and wished for one thing in that moment, it would have been the power to bend Steven to her will the way he bent her to his.

Some passing fairy must have granted her whim, because she remembered the secret Callie had told her in the kitchen that day, concerning what men liked.

And an hour was plenty of time.

There was a small jug of water inside the picnic basket, and Emma got it out. Steven frowned, puzzled, when she turned to him and brazenly lowered her bodice. When she brushed his lips with the taut pink tip of a breast, he resisted as long as he could, then moaned and caught it in his mouth.

As she nurtured him, he gradually sank backwards onto the blanket, and Emma found the buckle of his gunbelt with her fingers. She opened it deftly, and Steven moaned against her nipple when he felt it fall away.

After that, she unfastened the buttons of his trousers. He gripped her hand for a moment to stop her, but then his fingers relaxed, and he drew harder on her breast.

She found his manhood, freed it, and caressed it until it stood proud and hard against her hand. When she knew Steven was beyond the point where he might have turned back, she eased his trousers down over his hips.

With the tepid water from the jug and a checkered table napkin, she gently bathed him, taking her sweet time. Steven endured that, but he cried out hoarsely when her lips finally closed around him.

She teased and tempted him until he was half delirious, and muttering words that made no sense, and then she straightened, giving him a little pat. "Never fear, Mr. Fairfax. I'll take proper care of you when you get back from the cattle drive."

It was a moment before her words penetrated his daze. When they did, he swore and began righting his pants.

With a smile, Emma stopped him. She bent to him, and he groaned her name when she took him back into her mouth. "God, Emma," he rasped out, "do you have any idea what you're doing?"

She was too busy enjoying him and her precious moment of power to answer.

Fulton watched furiously from the sidewalk as the mail boat made its laborious way toward the wharf. He wasn't the only one looking on; half the town was watching from various surreptitious vantage points. That was the hardest thing of all.

Emma's dress was rumpled and grass stained, he noticed, as Fairfax helped her over the railing onto the dock. And there were daisies jutting out of her braid, giving her the look of a storybook princess. Even from that distance—some twenty yards or so—Fulton could see that her blue eyes had a tired, dreamy expression in them, while her cheeks were flushed pink.

Suppressing an urge to kill, Fulton rubbed his chin and reflected that there could be no doubt as to what had happened on that infernal island out in the middle of the lake. Fairfax had compromised Emma, and he'd pleasured her in doing it.

But Fulton was a man who knew how to look at the debit side of a situation as well as the credit side. If Emma had given herself to Fairfax, it meant the townspeople were right. She was a hot-blooded little tramp, and a woman like that would be better in a man's bed any night of the week than some prim and proper bluestocking. She might even be amenable to the games he liked so much.

Fulton's blood heated in his veins. He wanted Emma to be at his mercy, to stretch naked in his bed every night while he took his pleasure, and he wanted her badly enough to marry her in spite of what she'd done with that gunslinger.

He felt himself go hard under the trousers of his impeccable gray suit. Until that day, he'd been compelled to treat Emma like a lady. Now, he realized his objective could be gained by just a little persuading, and he could hardly wait to get her alone and exercise his rights.

Anticipation gave him the strength to ignore the public humiliation she'd subjected him to, and he found reason to rejoice in the fact that his mother wasn't there to see the kind of daughter-in-law she was about to get.

Drawing a deep breath, Fulton turned away and strolled resolutely back to the bank, ignoring the glances of sympathy or contempt tossed his way as he passed along the sidewalk. There were times when it suited a man to pretend he was blind as a miner in bright sunshine.

That night the dining hall at the Crystal Lake Hotel was turned into a ballroom. Streamers had been hung from every high surface, and at first the place smelled of early flowers and beeswax. A small band of men with red noses and glassy eyes played awkward music on a platform at one end of the room, and the place was so hot and so full of the scent of sweating bodies and perfume that Emma's ivory-handled fan was working overtime.

She stood miserably at Fulton's side in the green dress she'd made for the occasion, wishing she hadn't agreed to let him escort her. She'd done it only to spite Steven, and now the evening would be interminable.

Emma repeatedly scanned the crowd for him, though she was certain even he wouldn't be crass enough to present himself in public after the events of the afternoon.

"You look lovely tonight," Fulton whispered, his breath warm and scented with alcohol as it brushed past her cheek. His hand fumbled for hers, gripped it, squeezing too tightly.

"Th-thank you," Emma muttered. She was bitterly aware of her mistake; discouraging Fulton would be more difficult now than before.

"I have a surprise for you," Fulton went on, practically breaking her fingers.

Emma couldn't keep herself from wincing. "What?" she asked fearfully, sensing the approach of disaster.

"You'll see," was his cryptic, frustrating answer.

Fulton smiled indulgently down at her, although she thought she saw a shadow of animosity in his eyes, then he moved to the front of the room and stood up on the crude wooden dais with the musicians.

Probably because half the people at the dance owed him money, everyone stopped to pay Fulton proper attention as he smiled jovially and held up both hands, palms out.

"I have a very happy announcement to make," he said, and the blood drained from Emma's face. "Miss Emma Chalmers and I will be married before the summer's out."

Emma sucked in her breath and closed her eyes as a murmur of speculation moved through the crowd. This was followed by a burst of somewhat hesitant applause, and while the women held back, fanning themselves, the men pushed forward to shake Fulton's hand.

Emma felt as though she might throw up. God knew,

145

Fulton was used to getting his own way, no matter what objections might be raised, but this time he'd gone too far.

He came to her like a conquering hero and steered her toward the door. "Come now, Emma, dear," he said through his teeth, his hand tight on her elbow. "It's time we were alone together."

Fury mingled with the bile burning the back of Emma's throat. "You will go back up there, Mr. Whitney, and explain that you were only joking. There will be no wedding!"

His fingers bit into her flesh, and again she saw that hostile wraith move in the depths of his eyes. "I've had one humiliation already today," he said, pulling her along like a half-wit who couldn't be expected to find her own way. "And I will not suffer another."

Emma looked around worriedly, finding no one who looked likely to come to her aid. Big John Lenahan hadn't arrived yet, and Chloe avoided such gatherings. Emma had no other champions.

Fulton promptly linked her arm through his and propelled her through the doorway. His motions were rougher than before, and Emma sensed repressed violence in him. Then, in the next instant, she decided she'd imagined it all.

She was just about to tell him about Steven, right there on the sidewalk in front of the hotel, when Big John arrived, nicely dressed and driving the fancy surrey that had belonged to his late wife. He was accompanied by Steven and Joellen.

The rancher's daughter was wearing a sky-blue dress that shimmered in the bright moonlight and made Emma's carefully stitched frock look dowdy. She clung to Steven as he helped her down.

Joellen saw Emma at the same time Steven did, and Emma stiffened beside Fulton.

"Who invited him?" he asked in a loud whisper.

"It's a public dance," Big John pointed out affably, pausing to nod at Emma. He was one of approximately

146

three people in the town of Whitneyville who didn't feel intimidated by Fulton's power.

Emma was pretty certain Chloe had suggested to Big John that he should bring his new foreman along to the gathering, so he could become acquainted with the community. Her goal had surely been to distract Emma from Fulton.

The banker was seething behind the cordial smile he offered Big John. Emma's gaze shifted from her escort to the smiling Joellen and finally to Steven, who was watching her steadily. She thought she saw herself reflected in those unflinching hazel eyes, lying naked in a field of daisies.

"I don't suppose I could have a dance with Miss Emma," Big John thundered, his beaming smile full of friendly confidence.

Even in the worst of circumstances, Emma would have had a smile for Big John. She moved easily into his arms as the band tuned up inside, leaving Fulton, Steven, and Joellen on the sidewalk.

"I confess to some confusion, Miss Emma," John Lenahan told his dance partner as they swept around the floor at a reckless pace. "I thought you and Fulton, Jr. were all through."

Big John had always been kind to Emma during his visits to Chloe, and she'd come to look upon him almost as a father. "We are," she answered, only then realizing that her partner had steered her from the front of the dancehall to the back.

They stepped out into the starlit night, and Emma was grateful for the cool breeze from the lake and the moments of relative privacy. People had been staring at her ever since the dance started.

"I'm so confused," Emma confessed, and then she began to cry.

Big John took her into his strong arms. "There now, little one, don't you feel bad. Junior'll get over the loss of you soon enough."

Emma pulled her handkerchief from under her sleeve

and blew loudly. "Yes, but will I get over the loss of him?" she wailed. "It's true that I don't love him, but who am I to be so choosy?"

The rancher laughed. "Can't say as I really think you're going to be losing much by cutting Whitney loose, Emma."

"Just respectability," Emma said, sniffling again. "And a home of my own. And children."

Big John put his hand under her chin and lifted. "Respectability's got to come from inside you, Miss Emma. Nobody else can give it to you."

Emma dabbed at her eyes with her wadded handkerchief. Big John was right, though she didn't want to admit it. Respectability wasn't an honor someone else could confer on a person. It had to be earned.

She gave her friend a shaky smile. "It isn't going to be easy, you know. Fulton is a persistent man."

"The right way may not be the easiest, but it's always the best," Big John replied. Coming from anyone else, the words would have sounded preachy. From him, they were rock-solid.

Emma drew in a breath of the night air and held its sweetness in her lungs for a long moment, then released it. "I think I'm in love with Mr. Fairfax," she said all in a rush, and the admission surprised her more than it did Big John.

In fact, he didn't seem the least bit taken aback. He nodded and said, "I guess we'd better be getting back inside, Miss Emma. Junior doesn't worry me, but I wouldn't like to find myself on the wrong side of Mr. Fairfax."

Emma took Big John's arm and he led her toward the door. "Has he ever told you what—or who—he's running away from?"

"No, Miss Emma," the rancher answered, pushing open the door. "My guess would be, you'll be the one he tells, and that won't be until he's damn—darned good and ready."

Emma preceded Big John through the doorway and

came face-to-chest with an agitated Fulton. For one terrible moment she thought Steven had told him what had happened on the island that day, and she swung breathlessly between horror and relief. Then she caught a glimpse of Steven, dancing with Joellen, and knew instinctively that he'd left the task to her.

"I've been looking all over for you," Fulton complained to Emma, though he had a banker's smile for Big John. "I thought you'd fallen ill or something."

Emma shook her head. "I'm fine, Fulton," she said. "I just need to talk to you in private, that's all."

"Certainly, darling," he said icily, again leading her toward the front door.

Panic seized Emma as Big John disappeared into the crowd. It was then that Steven, watching her over the top of Joellen's glowing blonde head, caught her eye and held it.

She knew she couldn't live a lie, even for one more day. "About today . . ."

He cut her off in mid-sentence by pulling her out the door and hoisting her into a nearby buggy.

"Fulton, wait!" she gasped, but he only reached for the reins.

A polite but reluctant spattering of applause sounded from inside, on the dance floor.

"Stop!" she said again. It was true she'd wanted to speak with Fulton where no one else could hear, but she didn't like his manner or his eagerness to be alone with her.

Fulton released the brake lever and would have driven off if Steven hadn't suddenly appeared to take a firm hold on the harness and stay the horse.

"I believe the lady wants to stay right here," he said smoothly.

Fulton's jawline went taut with some inner violence, but then his gaze dropped to the bulge on Steven's hip—the ever-present .45—and laid the reins down.

The banker swallowed visibly. "You've done enough, Fairfax. Leave us alone."

Steven approached and held out a hand to Emma, and she took it, at once relieved and terrified. "Miss Chalmers owes me a dance," he said and then, calm as you please, he turned his back on Fulton and ushered her back inside.

She collided with his hard masculine chest as he pulled her into position for a waltz, and Emma suffered no illusion that the contact had been accidental. Rather, it had been an all-too-poignant reminder of what had happened between them that day.

She looked up into Steven's eyes, helpless to turn away.

"Were you going somewhere, Miss Emma?" he asked.

She sighed and tried to pull free, but his arms were as immovable as if they'd been carved from tamarack. "I was going to tell Fulton the truth about what happened today," she said finally. "Once I'd done that, he would have been more than happy to take me home."

He arched an eyebrow skeptically but said nothing.

Emma was fast losing her patience. "Let me go, Steven."

"Mr. Fairfax," he corrected, to her utter amazement.

"What?"

"I told you before," he said, pulling her back into his arms when she would have fled. "In public, I want to be addressed as Mr. Fairfax. You may call me Steven in private."

It took all Emma's resolve not to stomp on his instep. "That is both arrogant and old-fashioned!" she hissed.

Steven shrugged. "Then I'm old-fashioned. We'll argue about the arrogant part later."

Emma was shaking her head. "You really mean it, don't you?"

He nodded. "Yes," he said.

"Well, I'm not going to do it!"

He made a tsk-tsk sound. "Now, Emma, you know better than to challenge me like that. It just won't get you anywhere."

Emma's breath was coming in hard, ragged gasps, and it wasn't because the dancing was strenuous. "I have enough on my mind without you giving me ridiculous orders, *Mr.* Fairfax."

Steven glanced toward Fulton, who was watching them from the doorway, his eyes so hot with anger, they seemed to glitter in the half-light. "Furthermore," he went on, with a longsuffering sigh, "I'll thank you not to go out riding in the middle of the night with men such as Fulton Whitney. Your becoming his wife doesn't even bear thinking about."

"I don't remember getting a better offer from you," Emma pointed out sourly.

He chuckled. "And you won't, darlin'. But you will get everything you need."

Emma would have slapped him then and there if it weren't likely to cause a scene that would be talked about for years. "Maybe I still want to marry Fulton. Did you ever think of that? Maybe he'll understand and—and forgive me for what I did with you."

Steven laughed outright at that. "Forgive you? No man forgives *that,* Miss Emma, not unless he's a real fool. Face it, your chances of becoming a Whitneyville Whitney are too dim to read by."

Blessedly, the music stopped at that moment, and Emma propelled herself out of Steven's arms and marched over to Fulton, who was standing sullenly beside the pastor's spinster sister.

"Fulton," Emma said forcefully, taking his arm. "I must speak with you. *Right now.*"

Fulton looked furious, then surprised, then pleased. "All right, my darling." This time, he knew better than to take her outside, so they slipped into the darkened hallway leading to the hotel kitchen.

There was a window, and Emma could see that the moon was high in the sky, riding between the tops of the First Territorial Bank and the Stardust Saloon, looking like it was going to roll right down the street, all big and glowing. The craters and mountain ranges were etched on it like veins on a baby's head.

This was no time for admiring the moon, however.

Fulton obviously had other ideas. He gripped Emma's arm and twisted her around to face him.

"What kind of game are you playing?" he demanded in a harsh whisper.

Emma swallowed. "I have something to say," she said, trying to maintain a little distance even though Fulton was towering over her and standing so close that she could hear his watch ticking over the noise and music in the dancehall.

"What?" he snapped.

Emma tried to squirm away, but it was no use. Fulton was right there, breathing in her face. "If you could just step back a little . . ."

Fulton remained exactly where he was, and with a groan he bent his head and began nibbling on her earlobe. "You don't know how long I've wanted to get you alone like this."

"We're not alone," Emma pointed out, beginning to realize that she could be facing certain very unpleasant difficulties. "The whole town is in the next room, remember?"

"They won't hear us over the music."

Emma wriggled under Fulton's arm and landed with a breathless thump on the other side of the hallway. "In the name of heaven, Fulton Whitney, *will you listen to me?!*"

He raked his hands through his usually neat hair. "Very well, Emma," he said, with an indulgent sigh. "I'm listening."

"You must know that I went to the island for a picnic with Steven Fairfax today," Emma blurted out.

Fulton nodded. "I know," he said.

Emma gnawed at her lower lip, searching her mind for the right words to tell Fulton the truth and get him to leave her alone without being unkind. "You see, Mr. Fairfax and I talked and, well, there was this field of daisies—"

Fulton wasn't looking at her face, he was looking at her bosom. And she would have sworn he still wasn't listening. "Daisies?"

Emma could hear the merriment and the raucous fiddle music beyond the hallway door. She wondered whether Steven was back in Joellen's arms or waiting somewhere nearby.

"You don't need to tell me what happened," Fulton said in a low voice, trailing a fingertip from the pulsepoint at the base of Emma's throat to the delicate underside of her chin. "I've already guessed."

# Chapter
### ❧ 11 ❧

You've guessed?" Emma wasn't really surprised; she figured the entire town probably had a pretty accurate idea of what had transpired while she was on the island with Steven that day. It was Fulton's collected manner that took her aback.

He neither recoiled nor exploded. He simply stood there, his features all in shadow, his voice low and even. "You and the gunslinger?"

Emma looked away then, and nodded. "Yes."

"On the island today," he clarified calmly.

By then Emma was beginning to sense the suppressed fury that lurked beneath his placid demeanor. "Yes," she said again, swallowing. Lord knew, she had no desire to hurt Fulton, but it wasn't as though he'd ever had any real claim on either her affections or her loyalty.

Fulton's hand grasped hers, and it was not a reassuring contact. His fingers squeezed until her knuckles bunched together, sending a piercing ache shooting up her arm.

"Why?" he ground out. "Why did you let him—let

him have you, when you've hardly allowed me to hold your hand all this time? Good God, Emma, we've been seeing each other for months, and it was only a few days ago that you finally let me kiss you!"

She tried in vain to pull away. "You're hurting me," she whispered.

*"Tell me why!"* Fulton rasped, increasing the pressure until Emma thought she'd surely faint from the pain.

"Because I love him!" Emma cried in desperation and sudden, terrible fear. "Please—let me go—"

He released her, but not before applying the excruciating pressure once more. "You love him," he said. "He's a saddle-bum, an outlaw—a gunslinger! And you *love* him?"

Emma was too frightened, for the moment, to speak or move.

"Damn you!" Fulton breathed, and suddenly he gripped her again, this time by the waist. He hauled her roughly against him, and she felt his desire for her, but the feeling wasn't the same as it had been with Steven. This was frightening.

"Fulton!" she gasped, and the struggle to free herself took so much of her energy that she had none left for screaming.

He crushed her against the wall and began pulling up her skirts, and Emma ceased fighting long enough to drag a breath into her lungs. Before her shriek could escape, however, Fulton covered her mouth with his own, grinding his lips against hers, invading her with his tongue.

Again there was nothing of the sweet warmth she'd known in Steven's arms. Born in the roughest part of Chicago, raised by a worldly woman who knew the dangers a young lady might be called upon to face, Emma drew her knee up hard into Fulton's groin.

The impact made him release his hold on her. He doubled over, groaning. She watched him turn sideways and brace one shoulder against the hallway wall, his breath tearing in and out of his chest, his eyes feral with fury in the half-light. Emma marveled that she had never seen this side of him, never guessed at the cold brutality secreted behind that bland facade.

Squaring her shoulders and smoothing her skirts, Emma forced herself to walk away slowly, hiding her fear as she would from a growling dog. Her first and foremost instinct was to break into a frantic run.

She half-expected to find Steven waiting for her when she returned to the dance. Instead, he was squiring Joellen around the floor, smiling down at her and laughing at something she'd said.

For Emma, the evening had been disastrous. Looking neither left nor right, she marched toward the front door and out into the cool sanctity of the spring night.

The music seemed to follow her down the street, and the surface of the lake, doing its glittering moon-dance, failed to offer its usual solace. Reaching the safety of Chloe's front porch, Emma dropped into the shadow-draped swing and gave vent to all the emotions she'd been holding in.

She'd given her heart, as well as her body, to a man who could offer her virtually nothing except sensual abandon. And Fulton, a man she had once liked and trusted, had betrayed her in the most fundamental of ways. Her dreams of a respectable life, a solid marriage, a happy family, were all shattered.

Her tears did nothing to cool the heat of shame in her face. Nearly sick with grief, Emma wrapped both arms around herself and rocked. For all her efforts, she was really no better than her mother had been. All it had taken to steal her virtue was one handsome, sweet-talking man.

The hand closing around her elbow made her give a startled gasp, for she hadn't heard the usually squeaky hinges on the front gate or the sound of footsteps on the walk.

She drew in her breath to scream, but a moment before the cry would have escaped, Steven sat beside her, draped in the lace-strained light of the parlor window.

"You told him," he said.

Emma wrenched her arm free. She was tired of being grabbed, wrestled, and jumped. "Yes," she spat. "And he didn't take the news well."

"Can't say I blame him," Steven responded in a slow, barely discernible drawl. His grin flashed bright as lightning against an ink-black sky, and Emma felt herself melting in its heat. "You're not the kind of woman a man likes to lose."

She slid back against the arm rail of the swing, as though to slacken the power he wielded over her, but he only pulled her close again. "Steven, I'm really very ti—"

He cut her off with a kiss that made her fling her arms around his neck and give a sigh that vibrated all the way down to the soles of her feet.

Emma's toes curled inside her dancing slippers, and when Steven's tongue teased the corners of her mouth, she opened herself to him. At the same time, he raised his hand from the side of her waist to cup her breast, the thumb lightly brushing her nipple to taut attention. Wanton heat rushed through Emma's veins and muscles, and she wanted nothing so much as to lie down in that shadowy swing and give herself to Steven without reservation.

But just as suddenly as he'd begun the kiss, Steven ended it, holding Emma back from him so that the light from the front window splashed over her face. He studied her for a long moment, then laid the tip of an index finger to the very spot on her neck where Fulton had touched her earlier. "What happened?"

Emma averted her eyes briefly, then looked straight into Steven's face. "Fulton became—overexuberant."

"Overexuberant?" Steven mocked, but there was a funny half-smile tugging at the corner of his mouth.

Emma bristled, and her eyes dropped to the ever-present holster and pistol on his hip, then shot back to his face. "Don't you ever take that thing off?"

He grinned. "Yes, ma'am," he replied huskily. "I take

it off when I go to bed." He took Emma's braid lightly in his hand and rubbed his thumb over it, as though memorizing the feeling the gesture produced. "I've got to leave on the drive tomorrow, early. I'm here to say good-bye."

Although Emma knew he'd be back in two weeks or so, she was as filled with grief as if he were leaving forever. Still she bridled. "You needn't think that troubles me," she lied. "I'll be glad to see you go."

Steven chuckled. "I suppose you will," he agreed. "But I dare say, Miss Emma, that you'll be happy to see me come back, too. Maybe I'll take you over to the island again and have you in the daisy field."

Color pulsed in Emma's cheeks, for he'd evoked a tangle of sensations within her just by reminding her of the wild pleasure he'd shown her on the island that day. She bit down on her lower lip and looked at him despondently.

"Two weeks isn't that long," he reasoned gently, drawing her close again and resting his chin on the top of her head. "Besides, when I get home, it'll be summer."

Emma trembled, imagining more of Steven's deft kisses and caresses beneath a gaudy midyear moon.

"It'll be better for you next time," Steven went on hoarsely, his hands moving lightly, soothingly up and down her back. "There won't be any pain. Only more pleasure than you'll know what to do with."

Emma looked up at him, wondering if he knew the ecstasy he caused her had been so intense that it was nearly pain instead. "Couldn't you stay?" she whispered. "Couldn't someone else go on that cattle drive?"

He shook his head, then bent to kiss her lightly on the mouth. "Be ready," he told her, when it was over, "because when I get home, I plan to take you wherever I find you." With that, he gave Emma a little pat on the bottom, put his hat on, and went whistling down the walk to the gate.

Emma rose from the swing to stand on the porch, her

fists clenched at her sides, the blood burning in her veins. Steven wanted her to think of him the whole time he was gone, and he'd made sure she would with his kisses and his words. She longed to spite him for his arrogance, but she knew she'd spend the next two weeks wondering where she would be when Steven returned, and what she'd be doing. And which delicious things he would do to her.

Whirling on one heel, Emma hurried into the house and turned sharply into the large parlor, where she caught Chloe and Big John Lenahan in the middle of a kiss.

They parted, none too hastily, at Emma's appearance. "I suppose you'll both be happy to learn," she announced, "that Fulton and I will probably never speak to each other again."

Chloe looked up at Big John for a moment, then stepped away from him to approach Emma. "You're not to be a Whitneyville Whitney, then?"

Emma thought of all she might have had, if only she'd loved Fulton, if only he hadn't turned out to be such a rounder. Sacrificing the fine clothes, mansion, and trips to Europe—that part wasn't difficult, for she lived fairly well with Chloe. It was the invitations to afternoon teas she mourned, and a place of honor in the church choir. And the warm smiles as she passed other young wives on the sidewalk or encountered them in the mercantile.

Chloe read the pain in her face and took her hands. "Sweetheart, I'm sorry," she said.

Emma recalled the episode with Fulton in the dark hallway of the hotel. "I couldn't have borne to have him touch me," she confided, forgetting for a moment that Big John was in the room.

Chloe kissed her forehead lightly. "Just go to bed and put the whole night out of your mind."

Emma's gaze drifted to Big John, who watched her with a father's fondness, then she went to him and kissed him, too. "Good night."

In her room Emma stripped off her clothes and put on a wrapper. Then, taking a fresh nightgown from her bureau, she went down the rear stairway and made her way along the hall to the bathroom. A long soak in a hot tub would make her feel better.

After carefully bolting the bathroom door, Emma filled the tub with steaming water and added some of the perfumed salts Chloe had given her at Christmas. The air was redolent with the scent of wildflowers.

Emma wound her braid into a coronet and stepped into the tub to sink slowly, luxuriously, into the water. Memories of Steven making love to her in that field of flowers filled her mind. She remembered how she'd responded, and her cheeks flushed. She closed her eyes and let her mind drift back to that tiny, crowded flat in Chicago, where she and Caroline and Lily had lived with their mother, Kathleen.

She could see Kathleen as clearly as if she were standing in front of her now, her dark hair a-tumble, her brown eyes dancing. Oh, but she'd been beautiful—when she wasn't drinking, that was. And the men had gathered around her, willing to buy baubles and bottles, anything she wanted.

Emma and her sisters had tried to keep out of the way when there was a man in the flat, but the quarters were close—there weren't many places to go. Kathleen's bed had been separated from the one the girls shared by only a canvas curtain, and practically every night there had been shadows melding and coming apart against the cloth.

The men usually left before the sun rose. Some of them were kind enough to build up the coal fire before they left, and there was always money on the table. For a few days, things would be good. Kathleen would buy fresh fruit and maybe a piece of corned beef for Caroline to cook with cabbage, and sometimes they all four went and watched a revue, with dancers and jugglers and men who ate fire.

But then, inevitably, Kathleen would be overtaken by that odd despair that always dogged her from a little distance, and she would spend the last of the money for brandy, drinking until she couldn't even get off the bed. During those times, Caroline had to take care of their mother as if she were a baby.

When the soldier came, everything seemed to change. Kathleen said she was in love, and she was going to marry Matthew Harrington. Life was going to be different for all of them.

Well, Emma reflected with a sigh, Kathleen had surely been right about that. With the coming of Matthew Harrington, in his handsome blue uniform, came great changes.

Kathleen didn't want to do anything but drink and lie behind the curtain with Matthew. Caroline took to swiping money from the pockets of his trousers, just so they could have food to eat.

"He wants to touch me," Emma remembered telling Caroline one bleak winter day, as they walked along the sidewalk, Lily a few feet ahead, kicking a tin can.

*"Matthew?"* Caroline had asked, her brown eyes filled with concern. She was only eight years old, but now that Gramma was dead, she had the concerns and responsibilities of a grown woman. "What did he say?"

"He tries to get me to sit on his lap when Mama's not around."

Caroline became angry. "Don't you go near him," she warned.

As it turned out, they hadn't had to worry, because the next day, when the shopkeepers were hanging Christmas wreaths in the windows, Kathleen announced her decision. Matthew wanted the girls to go west on something called an orphan train, his theory being that they would be better off in the wide open spaces than the city, and Kathleen thought the idea was a good one.

Emma closed her eyes, remembering how little Lily, only six, had cried and begged their mother not to send them away. She'd promised to be a good girl always, and to polish Matthew's boots for him, if only Kathleen would let them stay.

Tears burned on Emma's lashes. Where was Lily now? Was she happy? Was she searching for her sisters, as Emma was? Was her hair still that lovely silver-gold? Was she even alive?

Emma dried her eyes with the back of her hand, and turned her thoughts to her older sister, Caroline. She felt certain that Caroline had survived, because she'd been the strongest and the most resolute of the three. She was searching, too; Emma knew that in her bones.

One day, Emma thought, they would find each other again, and all their questions would be answered.

Marshal Woodridge was getting old. He admitted as much to himself as he sat behind his desk in the jailhouse and scratched the stubborn itch beneath the band of his hat.

He was just glad there hadn't been any problems at the dance tonight. Sometimes a few of the boys got riled up over some pretty bit of ruffle and started in to fighting. He wasn't up to dealing with no trouble, 'specially if it involved young fellers that were handy with a gun.

To distract himself from the disturbing thoughts that followed, the marshal opened his desk drawer. It was stuffed with letters and wanted posters he'd never gotten around to reading. He was going to have to go through that stuff, one of these days.

Resolutely, he took out the wanted posters, carried them over to the stove and stuffed them inside. He was about to do the same with the letters when guilt stopped him. There was one in a pretty blue envelope, with neat handwriting on the front. It wasn't too old, either. Just a week or two.

Curiosity overcoming laziness, Marshal Woodridge opened the envelope with a fingernail and pulled out a single page.

*To the marshal of Whitneyville, Idaho Territory*, it read,

in tidy loopy letters. *I am seeking to learn the whereabouts of my sisters, Emma and Caroline Chalmers, who were separated from me thirteen years ago . . .*

The marshal folded the letter and scratched his chin. Emma Chalmers . . . That was the little redheaded gal Chloe Reese had raised, if he wasn't mistaken. He stuffed the page back into its envelope, thinking he ought to walk on over to Chloe's place and deliver it.

He'd spent most of his pay, but his mouth was dry. Some of that whiskey he had tucked away in his room over at Miss Higgins' place would taste mighty good.

Being a firm believer that a man should never do today what he could put off until tomorrow, Woodridge poked the envelope back into his desk drawer.


The old buckboard jogged and jostled over the dark country road. Joellen Lenahan sat as close to Steven as she could. "I feel safe with you, since you're wearing that Colt," she said, linking her arm through Steven's.

Suppressing a grin, Steven brought the reins down on the horses' backs, making the aging buckboard move a little faster through the star-spattered, moonlit night. "How old are you, Joellen?" he asked, knowing full well that she was sixteen. He wanted to make her think about the difference in their ages, without actually pointing it out.

"I'll be seventeen in six and a half months," she said.

Steven chuckled, but made no comment.

"That makes me just three years younger than Emma Chalmers," Joellen reasoned.

Again, Steven said nothing.

"Do you think she's prettier than I am?"

Steven sighed. "I think she's prettier than any woman alive," he answered.

Joellen disengaged herself from his arm and slid over to the far side of the seat. Steven figured she was pouting, but he didn't look to see. "You in love with her?"

"Maybe."

"Well, you can't marry her because she's spoken for."

Steven didn't bother to tell Joellen the facts of the case. It was none of her business anyway.

Joellen scooted back. "I know you think I'm young," she said, "but I—well—I understand things. How it should be between a man and a woman, and such as that."

The conversation was intriguing, though Steven doubted that Big John would approve of the turn it had taken. "Oh?" he said, with a smile in his voice.

"I'm experienced," Joellen confided.

"That's a real shame," Steven answered. "A beautiful girl like you ought to save herself for one special man."

Joellen subsided, staying quiet for over a half a mile. Then she went on. "Well, I'm not exactly *experienced*. But I have been kissed."

Steven smiled in the darkness. "I see."

"Do you really think there'll be a man for me someday?"

"I'd bet my bankroll on it."

"Maybe I've already found him," Joellen purred.

Steven could see the lights of the ranch looming in the distance, and he longed to reach Joellen's front door and deposit her there, just as Big John had asked him to do. He urged the team to a slightly faster pace. "That so?"

Her arm slipped through his again, and she rested her head against his shoulder. "I'll be scared, staying in that big house all alone. My daddy's going to be at Miss Chloe's till morning, you know. Why, one of the ranch hands could sneak in and rape me!"

Steven didn't like the turn her thoughts had taken. "Big John must have thought you'd be all right," he said. "You can lock the doors, after all."

"I want you to sleep inside the house," Joellen insisted. "That way, nobody'll be able to—"

"I'll be sleeping in my own bed tonight, Joellen."

"I want you to protect me."

Steven let out a long sigh. "No."

"I could stay with you—in your cabin."

164

"Big John would be after me with a horsewhip come morning, and I wouldn't blame him."

Joellen sighed as the surrey rolled through the open gateway that arched over the road leading to the sprawling ranch house. "I never figured you for a coward, Mr. Fairfax."

Steven's patience had been taxed to the limits. He'd never in his life laid a hand on a female in anger, but he was sorely tempted to haul this one off to the woodshed and blister her backside. Gratefully, he drew the rig to a stop in front of Big John's house, set the brake lever, and got down to walk around and help Joellen. And in all that time he didn't say a single word.

He winced at the protest in his ribs as he set the girl on her feet.

Lights streamed from the lower windows of the house, and the door opened. The housekeeper appeared, a silhouette in the doorway, holding the edges of her apron in both hands and babbling in rapid Spanish. It was clear she wanted Joellen to waste no time getting inside the house and away from the gunslinger who'd brought her home.

Joellen stood on tiptoe and kissed Steven's cheek. "Good night, Mr. Fairfax. And thank you for a wonderful evening."

Steven rolled his eyes and the housekeeper came waddling down the walk, still carrying on like a hen trying to gather in chicks from a rainstorm.

No renegade Indian or drunken cowhand was going to wander into that house and rape Joellen Lenahan, not if he was in his right mind.

Because his ribs were still hurting, Steven climbed back into the surrey cautiously and drove it toward the barn. When he'd tended to the horses, he walked slowly back to his small house. There were lights burning in the bunkhouse when he went past, but he didn't stop to join in the card game that was probably going on.

He needed his sleep.

Inside his own quarters, he struck a match to light a lantern and then hung up his hat. There was a pot of coffee on the stove, but it was cold and strong, and the thought of how it would taste made him grimace.

He stripped off his suitcoat and shirt and washed up in the tepid water he poured from a kettle on the stove into a chipped enamel basin with a red rim. He went to the door to throw the water out, a toothbrush jutting out of his mouth, and his eyes were drawn to an upstairs window in the big house. It was the only one with light, and there was a shapely, slender form moving against the shade.

Being fully human, Steven watched the little drama for a few seconds. Joellen was taking off her clothes, and she had a damned good idea he was watching.

With a half-grin, Steven shook his head, tossed his wash water into the yard, and went back inside. His groin was uncomfortably tight, but it wasn't Joellen he was thinking about. It was Miss Emma Chalmers, lying naked with her hair catching fire in the sun.

He bolted the door, blew out the lantern, and after laying his .45 within easy reach on the night table, unbuckled his holster. Tossing that aside, he kicked off his boots, peeled away his trousers, and slid into bed.

He couldn't help thinking what it would be like to have Emma lying there beside him, all sleek and soft and willing. The result was a pain he couldn't relieve.

Steven cupped his hands behind his head and gazed up at the ceiling while he imagined how it would be if everything was all right in New Orleans, if he could take Emma to Fairhaven and make a life with her there. He even went so far as to think about the children she might bear him, to picture them playing on the green lawns and sliding in their stocking feet on the slick floor of the ballroom.

He sighed heavily in the lonely darkness. He couldn't expect Emma to spend her life moving from one town to another, seeing her man draw his gun at every unexpected sound or sudden movement. She deserved a home and a family. She deserved peace.

Louisiana called to him in a whispery, seductive voice, but Steven had no intention of heeding it. With or without Emma, he'd hang within thirty days after setting foot over the border.

# Chapter
## ❧ 12 ❧

$T$he bawling of disgruntled cattle mingled in the first light of dawn with the curses of cowboys and the nickering of horses. Tobacco and wood-smoke tinged the air, along with food smells from the cookshack, manure, and the sour sweat of unwashed cowboys. Steven felt a certain excitement leap inside him at the prospect of the drive, even though he would have preferred to stay near Whitneyville, and Emma.

At the sound of his name, he reined his horse around and saw Big John Lenahan striding toward him. The rancher was still wearing his party clothes, so it was a good bet he'd spent the night in town.

Steven swung his right leg over the saddlehorn and slipped deftly to the ground. The resulting stab of pain in his ribs made him grimace.

"About ready to start?" Lenahan asked good-naturedly.

Steven's first impulse was to say "Yes, sir!" but he overrode it and nodded instead. The day he'd left General Lee's army he'd sworn to himself he'd never address any man that way again, with one exception: his grandfather, Cyrus Fairfax. "We'll be heading out at sunrise."

John surveyed the horde of restless cattle with a look of proud approval. "Don't mind telling you, Fairfax—I wish I could go make this trip. Somewhere along the line, when I wasn't looking, I turned into an old man."

Out of habit rather than forethought, Steven took his pistol from its holster, checked the chamber, and put it away again. "You could still ramrod a drive if you needed to," he answered, with a total lack of sympathy. His hands rested lightly on his hips.

Big John took a pouch of tobacco and a packet of cigarette papers from the pocket of his fancy coat and adroitly rolled a smoke between his fingers. He and Steven walked, without speaking, over to the board fence, where they stood watching the sun rise over the tops of distant evergreen trees.

Finally, Big John blew a stream of smoke into the misty air. "We both know why I don't head up drives anymore. Hell, I'm rich."

Steven chuckled. "That's reason enough not to do it," he agreed.

Lenahan studied him pensively with shrewd blue eyes. "When I look at you, Fairfax, I get the feeling I'm just seeing what you want me to see. You're one hell of a foreman, but you weren't born to this kind of life, were you?"

Steven took leather gloves from the hip pocket of his denim trousers and pulled them on. "I guess most people aren't exactly who they represent themselves to be," he said, avoiding Big John's gaze.

The rancher went on smoking, and his attention was trained on the agitated cattle about to be driven west to Spokane. "I've had a lot of experience at reading folks," he said easily. "I've seen you glance back over your shoulder many a time, and that Colt of yours is always at the ready. What kind of trouble are you in, and how can I help you?"

"You gave me a job. That's help enough."

"A job wasn't what you needed," John contended. "You've got access to money—lots of it, I'd say."

Steven sighed. If there was anybody on earth he would have been willing to tell the whole truth to, besides Emma, it would have been Big John Lenahan. But he was leaving on a cattle drive within a few minutes, and there wasn't time to explain. Even though he was unwilling to call Big John "sir," he respected him. Lenahan's opinion was important to Steven. "When I get back," he said, "we'll talk."

The two men shook hands and Steven remounted. With a hoarse shout, he gathered the cowboys, and with a word, silenced their grumbling. He assigned them each a place in relation to the herd, and spoke briefly to the drivers of the two wagons. Frank Deva, a little man with a black handlebar mustache, a dirty buckskin jacket, and tobacco-stained teeth, would serve as scout, since he knew the terrain between Whitneyville and Spokane.

There was much shouting and cursing, and even a few shots fired, and then the herd was moving. Dust rolled up from the hooves of two hundred complaining cattle and, even though he was mounted, Steven could feel the jarring of the earth in every bone and muscle of his body. He rode midway back, on the lefthand side of the herd, and well away, where he could keep an eye on both the beasts and the men driving them. The two wagons lumbered along behind.

The drive would bypass Whitneyville, but only by a quarter of a mile or so. Steven wondered whether Emma was lying awake in bed, listening to the incessant bellowing of the cattle and the thunder of eight hundred hooves, not counting the horses and the mules pulling the wagons.

Deva interrupted his thoughts. "I figure we can reach the Snake River by nightfall, if we push," the scout said, shouting to be heard over the noise of the drive.

The din was distracting now, but Steven knew from experience that in a few days he wouldn't be bothered by it. "Then we'll push," he called back. "The sooner these lop-eared sons of bitches are the army's problem, instead of mine, the happier I'm going to be."

Deva grinned at that, then touched the brim of his hopelessly battered hat in a motion of farewell. A moment later he and his little paint pony were galloping well ahead of the herd.

With a shrill whistle and a slap of his hat against his thigh, Steven drove half a dozen strays back into the herd. The sun wasn't even high yet, and already his shirt clung to his chest and felt clammy underneath his arms. The dust was enough to blind a man, as well as choke him.

Steven grinned. The drive had begun in earnest.

Emma lay in her bed near dawn, the covers pulled up to her chin, listening to the distant thunder of a passing herd, hearing the mournful cries of the poor beasts as they protested being driven from their winter pastures.

Steven was leaving, and it was very possible that he wouldn't be back. He might just keep on riding, and put Miss Emma Chalmers right out of his mind forever.

Pure despair filled Emma as she contemplated a lifetime without Steven Fairfax. A lump formed in her throat and tears gathered in her eyes.

She swallowed hard and refused to cry. If she never saw Mr. Steven Fairfax again, she'd be better off, she told herself firmly. Being pleasured in a field of daisies was no way for a good Christian woman to behave anyhow.

*He'll be back,* Emma reflected sadly. But she wasn't at all sure of that. Sure, Steven had taken her virginity, and he'd given her no small amount of gratification in the process, but he hadn't made any real promises.

She sat up and reached for the small photograph of herself, Lily, and Caroline, which always stood on her bedside table. With the tip of her finger she touched Lily's image, then Caroline's, wondering where they were and whether they were loved.

The Lily she remembered was delicate, but full of

determination. She'd need a man who knew when to pamper her and when to stand back and let her have her own way. Caroline was headstrong and independent, and probably didn't need a man at all. Emma suspected her older sister would be hot-blooded, too, and while she wouldn't have the needs of a weaker woman, she probably wanted someone to hold her and provide a channel for her passion.

Setting the photograph aside, Emma blushed. If Caroline and Lily knew how readily she'd succumbed to Steven Fairfax's lovemaking, they'd be disappointed in her. They'd think she was just like Kathleen, wild and wanton and totally lacking in self-control.

She lay back down on her feather pillows and tried to think about her mother and sisters, but it was no use. There was no room left in her mind, for Steven filled it to the bursting point. Steven and his brazen skill at driving Emma outside herself, then back in again.

Presently, though, Emma drifted back into an uneasy sleep and began to dream that she wasn't alone . . .

Her nightgown had worked its way up around her waist, and Emma didn't straighten it. Steven stretched out in the bed beside her, naked and strong, and he grinned as he rolled onto his side and kissed her lightly.

Her body was flooded with the same sensations she'd felt when he'd bared her on the island. Her legs parted, and heat surged through her as Steven touched her.

She whimpered, knowing she was dreaming but unable to rise to consciousness, and a soft moan escaped her throat. Steven pulled her nightgown up and off and tossed it aside, exposing her breasts and belly to the light and air.

Emma ordered herself to wake up and get dressed, but to no avail. Another part of her was in charge—the part that governed dreams of both the waking and sleeping varieties. Soon her back arched and she cried out, Steven's face buried in her neck as he carressed her, and then her senses settled into a tenuous peace. Her cheeks throbbed and she awakened with a shock, stunned to find that Steven wasn't there at all. In those moments, the loss of him was so poignant that her throat constricted and her eyes stung with tears.

When her breathing had returned to normal and her heart had slowed to its regular pace, Emma got out of bed, put on slippers and a wrapper, and hurried downstairs. It was a long way to go, but she hated using a chamber pot.

She encountered neither Daisy nor Chloe in her travels, which was a good thing. They were both discerning women, and they knew Emma better than did anyone else on earth. One look at her and they would have known exactly what she'd been dreaming about.

Back in her room Emma dressed quickly in a cotton dress with small pink flowers printed on it, then swiftly braided her hair and pinned it up in a coronet suitable for Sunday. Even though she didn't intend to go to church, Emma was religious in her own way, and she wanted the Lord to know she'd gone to the trouble of dressing up before coming to Him for consolation.

Once she was presentable, Emma slipped down the main stairway and out the front door, knowing Daisy would be in the kitchen by now, making fresh coffee for Chloe.

It was a lovely spring day, splashed with sunshine, filled with the scent of budding lilacs. A bed of bright yellow jonquils bloomed audaciously by the front gate, and a breeze whispered in the tops of the maple trees lining the street. In the distance Emma heard the slow, mellow *dong-dong-dong* of the church bells.

For a moment, sadness possessed her. What a joy it would have been to be a real member of that church, to sit with the choir and sing the old, beloved hymns with all the strength that was in her. But Emma Chalmers wasn't welcome where Emma *Whitney* would have been. She turned toward the lake when she reached the corner, and made her way down a tree-lined path to the rocky shore.

The water sparkled crystal blue in the sunshine, while robins and wrens chirped in the trees. The island rose up in the middle of the lake, green with life and as majestic as a cathedral. Emma kicked off her slippers and waded into the cold water. There, in that private and beautiful place, she felt close to God.

She talked to one of her sisters, as she sometimes did when she was especially discouraged, wriggling her toes against the polished pebbles that moved beneath the soles of her feet. "It's a wretched thing when a man can follow you into your dreams and make love to you there," she said, speaking to Caroline because she was the eldest of the three. She paused to gather her thoughts, then continued. "I hope you don't think I've done the wrong thing, falling in love with a stranger. It's just that he's so handsome, and when I get to thinking about Mr. Fairfax, I've got no sense at all. He can wrap me around his little finger as smoothly as he draws that awful forty-five of his. And you know what he said would happen when he gets back, Caroline."

Emma plodded back to the shore and took a seat on a fallen, bleached-out log. "In case I didn't mention it," she went on, "he said he was going to make love to me wherever he happened to find me. Well, you can bet he'll do exactly that. It might be anywhere. And that isn't even the worst part: I don't think I'm going to be able to say no to him." Despondent, she propped her elbow on one knee and dropped her chin into her palm. The water made a dazzling show before her eyes. "In fact, I *know* I won't be able to refuse him." Unexpected tears blurred the sparkling vision of water and sunlight in front of her. "Tarnation, Caroline, I wish he were here right now."

The birds continued to sing, and the lakewater lapped quietly at the shore. In the sights and sounds around her, Emma saw and heard the voice of a loving God. A quiet sense of destiny and assurance filled her.

She sat for a long time on the fallen log, thinking and dreaming and hoping. Then Emma put her slippers back on her sandy feet and started toward home. Daisy would be cooking breakfast by now, and she was hungry.

The herd reached the Snake River at four o'clock that afternoon. After consulting with Frank Deva, Steven decided to make the crossing before they stopped for the night.

Steven had sensed hard feelings among the men from the first; now he saw them reflected clearly in their eyes. He understood their position—after all, he'd come out of nowhere and been hired as foreman, while many of them had worked for Big John a decade or longer. He had no intention of explaining his qualifications for the job, however; he was head of the outfit and that was all that mattered.

He gave the order to drive the cattle across the river, and one of the men rode forward and spat on the ground.

"We ain't crossin' here," he said. He was a tall, slim man with fair hair and hard eyes. "Two, three miles downriver the water's shallower."

Steven swung out of the saddle to stand on the ground, and the dissenter did the same. The other men watched in silence as the two faced each other.

"We're crossing right here," Steven said quietly.

The drover shook his head stubbornly. "No, sir. I can't swim. I ain't takin' the chance."

Steven was calm. "Then you'd better ride on back to the ranch and pick up your pay. Taking chances is part of the job."

The cowboy's weathered face contorted with quiet, slow-burning hatred. "I ain't no coward, if that's what you're hintin' at. No, sir, Lem Johnson ain't no yellow-bellied coward."

Exasperated, Steven scanned the weary, dust-coated faces of the other riders. There were ominous black clouds forming in the distant sky, and the air was muggy, electric with the portent of the coming storm. "Any of the rest of you have any trouble following my orders?" he asked.

No one responded, but out of the corner of his eye, Steven saw Johnson coming at him.

He waited until the last moment, then caught the cowboy square in the belly with his right fist. Johnson expelled the air in his lungs and then swung on Steven, who blocked the first punch and caught the second, an uppercut to his chin.

Johnson might have been scared of deep water, but he was no weak sister. The blow was only slightly less jarring than the kick of a mule, and Steven figured a couple of his teeth were probably loose.

That made him mad, and he lunged at Johnson, gripping the cowboy's ears like the handles of a jug as they went down.

Heedless of the pain in his ribs, Steven proceeded to beat the hell out of Johnson. It didn't bother him a bit that he had to take a battering in the process.

When he got to his feet, Johnson stayed down. He lay writhing on the ground, muttering. "Goddam Reb— fights dirty—"

Steven found his smashed hat, slapped it against his thigh, causing dust to fly, and put it back on his head. "Any of the rest of you Yankees afraid of the water?" he demanded.

No one answered. The men simply turned and went back to their work, while Johnson scrambled to his feet, dusted himself off, and mounted his horse. "We'll see what Big John has to say about you firin' ol' Lem Johnson," he threatened. "We'll just see."

The crossing was not easy for Steven to orchestrate, with two hundred cattle, two wagons with teams, and eleven cowboys on horseback to think about, but it was accomplished and the men set up camp on the other side.

Wood was gathered and a big fire was built. The Chinese cook promptly set about making supper.

The mood among the men was easier now, and a little friendlier. All the same, Steven kept his eyes open. Experience—both during the war and after it—had taught him to expect the unexpected.

The cook dished out beans and biscuits just as the sun was setting, and he had plenty of takers. While half the men were eating, the other half were out riding herd. Steven ate with the second group, returned his plate to the chuck wagon, and rounded the far wagon, intending to relieve himself.

He was in the process when he heard, quite distinctly, a sneeze from inside the wagon. Frowning, he finished his business and rebuttoned his trousers. By his best guess, all the men were either out with the herd, or finishing up their food.

Tossing back the flap at the rear of the wagon, he peered inside. It was dark, though the light from the fire flickered and glowed against the canvas.

"Who's there?" he asked impatiently. If there was one thing he didn't have time for, it was a greenhorn with the grippe or some equally asinine malady.

Another sneeze was the reply, and he saw a hesitant shadow move against the canvas.

Instinctively, Steven drew his pistol and cocked it. "You'd better state your name and your business," he warned.

"Don't shoot!" cried a feminine voice.

Steven adjusted the pistol and sheathed it in his holster. He would have known that wheedling voice anywhere. "Joellen? What the hell are you doing here?"

She fumbled her way to the rear of the wagon. Although Steven couldn't see her face, he knew she was crying. It was obvious, too, that she was shivering with cold and fear. "I wanted to be with you," she said, as Steven lifted her down to the ground, setting his teeth against the protest in his rib cage. "I knew if you just spent some time with me, you'd find out I'm the perfect woman for you."

He swore, and would have turned away except that she was crying. "Didn't you even bring a coat?" he asked, running his eyes over her smudged white blouse and soggy black riding skirt.

Joellen shook her head miserably and sniffled. "I

didn't think I'd need one—after all, it's almost summer. But then, when we were crossing the river, water poured into the wagon and I got wet."

Steven swore again and jammed one hand through his hair. It was too late to take Joellen back across the river; she'd probably get pneumonia if he tried it. And he didn't know whether he could trust the men if he left her alone with them. "Are you hungry?" he demanded.

"Yes," she whimpered.

Steven caught her hand roughly and dragged her back to the fire. The eyes of the men who were taking the second watch sliced to her and then to each other. Although nobody dared make a comment with Steven present, the air seemed charged. Joellen's presence was a dangerous distraction.

To make matters worse, the wind was up and there was thunder booming in the night air, making the cattle nervous. The storm Steven had hoped would pass them by was about to break.

He settled Joellen down on an upturned barrel near the fire and went to the chuckwagon for beans and a biscuit. He shoved the blue enamel plate at her and swept the circle of men with his eyes, daring any one of them to comment.

"Eat!" he barked, and when Joellen lifted her spoon to her mouth with a trembling hand, he took the blanket from his bedroll and laid it over her shoulders.

It was Frank Deva who first dared to speak. "Her daddy's going to be spitting nails when he finds out she's gone."

Steven could well picture Big John's reaction. He only had to imagine having a daughter of his own to bring all the dangerous emotions to mind. He wondered which, if any, of the men he could trust to take Joellen back to the ranch in the morning, while the herd went on.

A couple of the boys chuckled in anticipation of Big John's wrath, rightly figuring that it would be directed at Steven Fairfax.

Steven glowered at the girl, who sat trembling in front

of the fire. Although he'd never touched a woman in anger, including the one he was accused of killing with his bare hands, he felt a powerful urge to turn her over his knee.

He walked away from both the girl and the urge, and prevailed on the cook to lend him a set of clothes. Sing Cho was the only man in camp whose gear might fit Joellen.

When she'd finished, she went meekly back to the wagon where she'd been hiding all day and changed into the black silk shirt and trousers. While she was gone, Steven reassessed the men in camp and decided not to leave Joellen unattended. His reasoning was simple: it was what he'd want the foreman to do if he had a daughter in this predicament.

Joellen kept her head down when she returned to face Steven, and he had a feeling that, if he lifted her chin, he'd see triumph in her eyes. Because he didn't want to end up blistering her shapely little bottom, he didn't look at her face.

A light rain began to fall, clattering on the canvas tops of the wagons and sizzling in the fire. Steven dragged Joellen along with him when he went to fetch his long canvas coat from his gear. He put it around her and helped her into the saddle before swinging up behind.

"Are you taking me back?" she asked, speaking loudly to be heard over the rising storm and the cries of spooked cattle.

"Not tonight," Steven answered, his voice barely civil. He would have given anything he owned to have Emma sitting in front of him like that, but Joellen was nothing but trouble.

"Then where are we going?"

"In case you haven't noticed, Miss Lenahan, we've got a herd of cattle here. And they don't cotton much to thunder and lightning."

The rain fell harder, soaking Steven's hair and shirt, and the legs of his trousers. He begrudged Joellen his canvas coat and, at the same time, resigned himself to the loss of it. Nothing in his upbringing had prepared him to let a lady—especially when that lady was little more than a child—suffer the cold while he was covered warmly.

After that, Joellen huddled silently in front of him, still shivering. Steven suspected she was crying, and although he couldn't do anything about it at the time, he felt sorry for her. She was a kid, needing to be spanked and sent to bed.

When lightning cracked the sky, Steven's horse reared and some of the cattle started running blindly into the darkness, terrified by the brilliance.

Steven rode after them, grateful that Joellen knew enough about riding to keep herself in the saddle. He had no help, since the other men on watch had their hands full with panicked strays of their own.

For an hour or more the storm grew continually worse. When a lightning bolt struck not fifteen yards away, Steven's horse went berserk. Regaining control was difficult with Joellen in the way, and when the gelding took the bit into his teeth, there was no stopping him.

He ran until he was exhausted, coming to a stop in a stand of towering pine trees. Steven dismounted, cursing furiously, and crouched to check the animal's legs and hooves. Since it was stone-dark that night, he had to do all this by touch, rather than sight.

The animal seemed to be all right, though he was lathered, his sides heaving with the effort to breathe. Steven dragged Joellen roughly from the saddle and set her down in the relative shelter of the trees.

"Stay there," he rasped, "or I swear to God, you'll still have the imprint of my hand on your ass when you're ninety!"

Joellen was understandably subdued.

Steven calmed the horse as best he could, then, using wooden matches from the pocket of the canvas coat Joellen was wearing, he made a small, hesitant fire under the trees.

He and Joellen both crouched close to its warmth.

"Where are we?" Joellen finally worked up the courage to ask.

Steven's horse was winded, the rain was beating down all around them, and the herd was probably miles away. He was so mad it was a full minute before he trusted himself to answer. "The middle of nowhere."

In the distance, a coyote howled. Steven could smell his horse's wet hide, as well as his own and Joellen's.

"Wolves," Joellen whispered, and he saw her eyes go wide in the light of the fire.

Steven didn't bother to lend comfort; he was too furious at the situation. He tethered the horse to a fallen log and added what wood he could find to the sickly little blaze he'd built. When he straightened from that task, Joellen was standing there, holding out the canvas coat.

"Here," she said. "It isn't right for you to be cold. It's my fault we're out here."

Steven wasn't about to deny that, but he shook his head, refusing the coat.

Joellen draped the garment over his shoulders, then pulled it close around them both. "Kiss me," she said.

Steven glared down at her, but he made no move to back away, because they both needed the other's body heat. Without it, they'd catch their deaths. "There isn't a chance in hell I'm going to do that," he replied, his voice rough as gravel in the bottom of a rusty can.

She laid her cheek to his chest and yawned expansively, and he remembered that she was a child. Some of his fury abated, displaced by a protective, fatherly mood.

"I'm so tired," she said.

Steven was worn out, too. In fact, he could hardly see straight. Without answering, he lowered Joellen to the ground, next to the fire, and the two of them lay there, snuggled together, wrapped in the canvas coat.

Joellen gave a contented little sigh and wriggled her pelvis against Steven's. "Miss Emma Chalmers will have a cat fit when she hears about this," she said.

The news was bound to get back to Emma, all right. Cowboys were gossipy as old ladies, and the foreman and the boss's daughter spending the night together on the range would be too good to pass up. Steven closed his eyes and prayed that Emma loved him enough to believe the truth.

Throughout the night he lay inside the coat with Joellen, except when he had to add wood to the fire. Once he dozed off and dreamed that he and Emma were married and living at Fairhaven, without fear of the law. He awakened to find himself lying beside another woman, and an oppressive loneliness settled over him.

He pulled away and stared glumly into the fire until morning came.

# Chapter
## ❧ 13 ❧

Steven and Joellen rode into the main camp just as the Chinese cook was dishing out breakfast. Some of the men stared openly, while others made a visible effort to be subtle. Joellen acted as perky as a new bride just risen from a featherbed, but Steven ached in every bone and muscle of his body. Between his mending ribs, the fight with Johnson the day before, and a night spent on the cold, hard ground, he was a little the worse for wear.

Joellen got down from the horse without waiting for help from Steven and made her way over to the fire. "That bacon smells wonderful," she exclaimed.

None of the cowboys actually spoke to her, but one got up so she could sit on an upturned soap crate. A plate of eggs and bacon appeared in her hands, and she ate happily.

Steven had no appetite at all. After sweeping the men gathered around the fire with one quelling look, he got a mug from the chuck wagon and helped himself to coffee. The stuff was awful, but it braced him up a little.

"Don't you want anything to eat, Steven?" Joellen

chimed, her voice as intimate as a wife's. She was still wearing the canvas coat, and she looked back at him over one shoulder.

Instead of answering, Steven glared at her briefly, tossed his coffee onto the muddy ground, and then pretended she wasn't there. "This is a trail drive, not a box social," he said. "Let's get those cattle moving."

"I'll ride with you," Joellen informed him, still chewing the last of her breakfast.

"You'll ride with the cook," Steven replied.

For just a moment, Joellen's full lower lip jutted out, but then she brightened. "All right, darling," she said, in a voice as clear as a chime in the desert.

The men scrambled to finish their food and mount their horses, but the commotion didn't fool Steven. They were hanging on every word that passed between him and the boss's daughter.

He caught her hard by the arm when she tried to climb up into the box of Sing Cho's wagon. "Tell them nothing happened."

Joellen batted her thick eyelashes at him. "All right, Steven," she said, in a dulcet tone that nonetheless reached every corner of the camp. "If you want me to, I will."

Steven glanced uneasily at the men and saw that most of them were watching. "Nothing happened," he snapped.

He saw disbelief and amusement in their eyes, along with the occasional glint of envy. After all, Joellen was a pretty girl, even after a night spent on the ground, huddled inside an old canvas coat.

Spitting swear words, Steven remounted his horse and reined it toward the herd. They were moving due north now that they'd crossed the river, and Spokane was still five or six days away.

Frank Deva's paint pony came abreast of Steven's gelding. "Mr. Fairfax?"

Steven's expression clearly showed that he was waiting to hear what the scout had to say.

"We'll be coming within a few miles of a town long about four this afternoon. It ain't much, but there's a telegraph office."

For the first time since he'd found Joellen hiding in the supply wagon, Steven smiled. He would wire Big John as soon as he reached the place, and install the young lady in a hotel room to wait for her daddy. "Thanks," he said, touching the brim of his bedraggled hat.

Deva grinned and rode on ahead.

The day was long and grueling. It had rained hard during the night, and the trail was muddy. Twice the supply wagon got stuck and had to be dragged out of the muck, and at noon a half dozen Sioux warriors appeared on top of a ridge. They kept their distance, but they made the men nervous, since there might have been a hundred more of them riding just out of sight.

"What do you make of the escort?" Frank Deva asked, when he came back to ride alongside Steven again.

"Could be they want a few head of cattle," he replied.

"Or the girl," Deva said.

Steven drew the Colt from his holster and checked the chamber, even though he'd already done so half a dozen times. "Maybe I'd better go up and have a word with them."

Deva's eyes widened in his weathered face, and his handlebar mustache twitched just a little. "Alone?"

"I was counting on you to go with me, Frank," Steven answered, hiding a grin.

The scout hawked and spat. "I'm still a young man, Mr. Fairfax," he said. "I ain't through sowin' my wild oats. And you want me to ride up to a pack o' Sioux, just like that?"

Steven was still watching the Indians. "I think there's going to be trouble if we wait for them to come to us," he answered. And with that, he reined the gelding toward the incline leading up the ridge, leaving the choice of whether to come along or not to Deva.

He wasn't surprised to hear Deva's pony scrambling up the rocky hillside behind him.

Three of the six warriors rode forward to meet them. They were wearing paint and carrying spears, and Steven knew a moment of fear—but not because he might be run through or scalped. It was the thought of never seeing Emma again that scared him.

The leader of the little band broke away from his escorts, his black eyes bright with a strange mingling of hatred and hope. His rib cage looked like a washboard, and his stomach was concave. It was soon apparent that he spoke missionary English. "Want cattle," he said.

Steven sighed and rested one arm on the pommel of his saddle. With his free hand, he pushed his hat to the back of his head. Despite this display of good-natured indolence, his Colt was ready to leap into his fingers at any moment. "We'll give you five head," he said reasonably.

The Sioux was caught off-guard. He glanced back at his companions who looked, one and all, as if they were ready to lift some hair.

The Indian got greedy. "Want woman."

With a slow smile, Steven shook his head. "Can't let you take her," he said. "She belongs to a powerful chief. Besides, you'd have to beat her twice a day for a year before she'd be any good to you at all."

"What chief?" the Indian wanted to know. He kept squinting toward the cook wagon, down in the gorge. Joellen's yellow-gold hair was probably the major attraction.

"His name's Big John Lenahan."

The black eyes narrowed slightly. A suspicious silence fell, and the red man clearly thought he was calling a bluff.

"You'll find his brand on every one of those cattle down there," Steven said cordially. "Deva, show him the mark on that horse you're riding."

Behind him, Steven heard the clatter of hooves on rocks as Deva maneuvered his pony, ostensibly to display the intertwined J and L burned into its flank.

The Indian was satisfied, and he eyed the cattle

186

hungrily. If his condition was any indication, the rest of the tribe must have barely survived the winter. "Ten cattle," he said, falling back on bravado.

Steven knew then that half the Sioux nation wasn't lurking beyond the ridge, and he was relieved. His smile didn't falter. "Six," he countered.

The Sioux held up the fingers of both hands, tucking his thumbs against his palms.

"Six," Steven repeated with a shake of his head. "And we'll bring them to you. If you try riding toward that herd down there, there's going to be some bloodshed." The tone of his voice altered only slightly when he spoke to Deva. "I don't suppose I need to tell you, Frank, that you'll probably lose those silken tresses of yours if you take the hillside at a dead gallop. Get down there and have the boys cut out half a dozen of the best heifers."

He heard Deva turn and ride slowly down the hill. A new admiration for the scout was born in Steven in that moment, because it took a brave man to not panic and plunge his spurs into his horse's sides.

The Indian was gazing speculatively toward Joellen and the cook wagon again. "She is bad woman?"

Steven suppressed an urge to turn and look at the girl himself. Knowing her, she was probably standing on the wagon seat, stark naked and waving both arms. "Bad woman," he confirmed.

The cattle had been cut out of the herd; Steven could hear them lumbering up the hill, Deva whistling and shouting behind them.

When the prime heifers had been turned over to the Sioux, Steven offered a hand to the Indian leader, holding it upright the way he'd seen trappers and scouts do. Their palms touched, and their thumbs interlocked briefly.

"Nice doing business with you," Steven said when the handclasp was broken. With a touch to the brim of his hat, he turned and rode down the hill with Deva.

The herd was still moving, but four cowboys had

stayed behind to keep an eye on the proceedings. When Steven reached them, he saw a grudging respect in their eyes.

"Don't you boys have anything to do?" he asked.

With sheepish grins and shakes of their heads, the cowhands spurred their horses to catch up with the herd. The supply wagon trundled along just ahead, and Joellen was peering out through the flap at the back.

Deva glanced over one shoulder at the retreating Indians and gave a low whistle. "It's been a while since I met up with a bunch like that. You suppose we'll see 'em again?"

Steven brought a bandanna out of his hip pocket and dried his neck. Until then he hadn't realized he was sweating. "They'll be busy celebrating for a day or two, if we're lucky. All the same, keep an eye peeled. They might develop a taste for beef."

With that, the two men spurred their horses to a run, closing the gap between them and the herd.

Joellen's eyes were round as cow pies when Steven came up alongside the cook wagon. She'd clambered back onto the seat at the front by then.

"You saved my life," she said dreamily.

"I begged them to take you," Steven replied. Then he forgot the girl and rode on ahead. He didn't return until several hours later, when Frank Deva told him the town of Rileyton was just beyond a little rise.

Joellen's face lit up when he lifted her from the wagon box onto his horse. She rode sidesaddle in front of him.

"You missed me, didn't you?" she asked, smiling in a loony, unfocused sort of way.

Steven was chewing on a matchstick. "About as much as I missed those Sioux after they lit out with six head of your daddy's cattle," he responded, spurring the patient gelding toward the tree-lined rise.

Joellen looked up at him with an affronted expression. "But you're just *pining* for Miss Emma, I suppose."

He maneuvered the match to the other side of his mouth and held back a grin. "I suppose I am."

"Well, she's probably spooning with Mr. Fulton Whitney at this very moment!"

"Probably," he agreed.

Joellen finally noticed that they were going one way and the herd was going another. "Where are you taking me?"

"To town. I'm going to wire your daddy and get you a hotel room."

Her blue eyes filled with silvery stars. "You want to wire Daddy so you can ask for my hand," she crooned. "You're going to marry me."

"I was thinking more in terms of murder," Steven replied.

Joellen's cheeks reddened. "Well, you *have* to marry me, Steven Fairfax—you've compromised my good name!"

"I'm going to compromise your bottom if you don't stop talking as if I had my way with you out there. I never touched you, except to share a coat, and you know it."

"Daddy doesn't," Joellen said, with a cat-that-ate-the-canary smile. "And neither do all those cowboys, or Mr. Deva, or Sing Cho. They're my witnesses that you've spoiled me for any other man."

Steven sighed and kept his silence. They reached the top of the rise and started down the other side. A rutted road wound along at the base of the hill, toward a small town in the distance. Steven's spirits lifted at the sight of telegraph poles and chimney smoke.

Rileyton's telegraph office was located in the general store, according to a boy driving sheep at the edge of town, and Steven headed straight for it.

While he was carefully composing his message to Big John, Joellen happily went through a rack of dresses with her grubby hands.

Doing his best to ignore her, Steven turned back to the counter and the attentive spinster behind it. Her hair was pulled back tight as the skin of an onion, and her two front teeth overlapped. "There is a hotel in Rileyton, isn't there?"

Color rose in her cheeks, as though Steven had asked her to dance naked on the ribbon counter. "Sort of. My mama takes in boarders."

Steven was developing a headache. Besides that, he was hungry and his muscles throbbed. "Where might I find your mama," he asked patiently, "and what's her name?"

By the time he'd garnered enough details to put in the wire to Big John, Joellen had selected a frothy white dress with lots of lace and ruffles.

"I could wear this to our wedding," she said, beaming at him from behind a layer of dirt.

The spinster winced when she saw those dirty fingers grasping that snow-white dress.

"There isn't going to be any wedding, dammit," Steven bit out.

Huge tears blossomed in her eyes. "He's such a rounder," she told the old maid. "Dragging me off into the countryside, making me cry out again and again with passion—then saying he won't marry me."

The clerk gave a little gasp and laid one hand to her flat bosom. Her eyes swung wildly to Steven's face.

He shook a finger at Joellen. "One more word, you little hellcat. Just *one more word.*"

Joellen shrank back, still clutching the dress, and Steven turned to his message to Big John. In the end he simply said Joellen was all right and staying in the only boarding house in Rileyton. He made a point of adding that he was going on with the herd.

"Just charge this to my daddy," Joellen said brightly, laying the white dress on the counter top. "His name is Big John Lenahan."

Steven ignored her and shoved the telegraph message toward the clerk, along with the coins to pay for it. "I'll be obliged if you'll see that Miss Lenahan gets to the boardinghouse safely."

The spinster swallowed and nodded.

"Don't you leave me after what you did to me out

there in the dark!" Joellen cried, when Steven walked toward the door.

He froze for a moment, then turned to stare at her in amazement. Two portly matrons gathered behind her like an armed guard. Then he smiled and spoke in a soft voice. "All right, sweetheart," he said, holding out one hand. "Come along, and we'll be married."

Joellen tossed the dress onto the counter and dashed toward him. He took hold of her hand, paying no mind to the spinster and the old women, and dragged her outside.

"There's one thing you'll have to learn, if you're going to be my wife," he said. "I'm the boss, and I give the orders."

She blinked vapidly and sighed. "Yes, dear."

There was a bench nearby, sitting back against the wall of the land office, and Steven edged toward it. "Did you see the fight yesterday, when Lem Johnson didn't want to cross the river?"

Joellen nodded. "I was hiding in the supply wagon, and I watched the whole thing. You were masterful."

"If you saw what happened, you know nobody defies my orders and gets away with it. And I don't let people tell lies about me, either."

Joellen swallowed, but she still looked besotted. Steven was about to cure her of that.

He sat down on the bench, clasped Joellen by the wrist, and flung her down across his lap. She was so startled that, for a moment, she just lay there with her fanny upended.

But when she looked back over her shoulder, she saw Steven's hand descending and yelped in anticipation of the pain.

His palm made a satisfying *thwack*, so Steven gave her another swat. Joellen squirmed and shrieked, more in anger than suffering, but he kept her legs scissored between his thighs and went right on spanking her.

In the street, wagons rolled past, their occupants staring at Joellen and Steven, but he didn't give a damn.

In fact, he gave Joellen five more solid swats before letting her up.

He felt guilty looking at the tear streaks on her dirty cheeks, but only a little.

"Monster! Fiend! I wouldn't marry you if you could buy and sell my daddy five times over!" Joellen screamed, her hands knotted into fists at her sides. In a few years, when she was of age, she was going to make somebody a fine and spirited wife.

Steven rose from the bench and sighed as he pulled his gloves back on. "Good-bye, Joellen," he said. Taking his wallet from the inside pocket of his leather vest, he pulled out a twenty-dollar bill. "This will keep you until Big John gets here."

For a moment, she looked as if she was going to spit in his face. But then, at the last second, Joellen snatched the money from his hand. "I hate you!" she cried.

Steven grinned as he walked away. In six months Joellen Lenahan not only wouldn't hate him, she wouldn't remember his name.

Wearily, Emma walked along between the two shelves of books the library boasted, plucking out a volume here and there. It had been a surprisingly busy day, and she was eager to get home. Her feet burned; she wanted to pull off her shoes and stockings and wade in the lake.

She was returning to the desk for another armful of books when she noticed old Marshal Woodridge hesitating outside the library window. He peered in at her in a befuddled way and scratched the back of his head.

With a smile, Emma went to the door and opened it, even though the library was closed for the day. "Hello, Marshal. Did you want to borrow a book?"

"Seems like there was somethin' I wanted to tell you," he answered, with a shake of his head. "Things slip my mind somethin' fierce these days."

Emma sincerely hoped there wouldn't be a major crime in Whitneyville before the marshal's upcoming retirement. She shrugged and turned away to close the door again, and as she walked toward the desk, it occurred to her that the old man might have seen a wanted poster with Steven's name on it. Or even a sketch of his face.

She swallowed and glanced nervously toward the street, but Marshal Woodridge was gone.

Resolutely, Emma hoisted another stack of books into her arms and went back to the shelves.

A thrill passed over her when she heard the library door open again, because she'd been thinking about Steven. She couldn't help remembering his vow to make love to her wherever she happened to be when he came back.

But it was much too soon for Steven to be home. And she knew she was right when she rounded one of the shelves and practically collided with Fulton.

"I'll have you know I've spent the last three days in bed," he informed her, straightening his fashionable waistcoat, "with ice packs on my—with ice packs on."

Emma lowered her eyes and bit down hard on her lower lip for a moment, so he wouldn't see her trying not to smile. "I'm sorry you were injured, Fulton," she said, when she could trust herself, "but you shouldn't have behaved so badly."

She went on filing books away, with Fulton moving along behind her.

"It will be all your fault if we don't have any children," he continued somewhat huffily.

Emma glanced at him as she put another book in its place. "We won't have children, anyway," she reminded him. "We're not going to be married."

"I think you're being hasty about this, Emma."

She went on putting books away, averting her eyes this time. "Why do you want me, Fulton, when you know about Steven?"

"As I said before, Fairfax is nothing but a drifter. He'll break your heart if you give him the chance, Emma."

Out of books to file, she turned to him, her hands resting on her hips. "Fulton, you haven't been listening. I gave myself to him. Steven and I made love."

Fulton closed his eyes tightly for a moment. "Don't say that."

"It's true," Emma insisted softly, and she couldn't help touching Fulton's arm because he looked so crushed. "I'm sorry," she added, "but it is."

"I don't care," Fulton insisted. His eyes were too bright and he was talking too quickly. "I can make you forget him. If you'll just let me hold you, let me kiss you, let me do the things he did—"

Emma retreated a step, but there was a wall of books at her back. She flinched when Fulton gripped her shoulders, remembering how frightened she'd been when he'd tried to take advantage of her the night before.

"I wouldn't hurt you for anything," he said brokenly.

"Please," Emma whispered.

Reluctantly, he let her go, but he was still standing too close. He drew a deep breath and let it out again. "Are you almost through here? I'll walk you home. It'll be like old times, before he came along—you'll see."

"I don't think that would be a very good idea," Emma said, turning to walk away.

Fulton caught her by the arm and wrenched her around. "Maybe you want me to play rough," he drawled. "Is that how it is, Emma? Does the cowboy take what he wants, instead of asking for it like a gentleman?"

Emma felt color surge into her face. She shrugged free of Fulton's grasp and managed only by the greatest effort not to slap him across the face. "I don't think we have anything more to discuss," she said tightly. "Please leave before I summon the marshal."

Fulton laughed at that. "Come on, Emma. Can't you come up with a better threat than old man Woodridge?"

She backed away. "You're scaring me."

Instantly, Fulton's face changed. He was all tenderness and indulgence. "I would never hurt you. I love you.

Now, get your things and lock this place up. I want to walk you home."

Being outside where there were other people seemed safer to Emma than staying in the library. "All right," she said, and when she turned away this time, he let her go.

She fetched her handbag and shawl from underneath the desk, along with a book that had come in with a new shipment on that morning's train. As usual, Emma had been there with her posters, and as usual, there was no word of Caroline or Lily.

She was feeling a little discouraged as she and Fulton left the library. He stood by patiently while she locked the door and tucked the key into her handbag.

"We could have supper at the hotel," Fulton suggested.

Emma shook her head.

"Then at least take my arm," he said, bending his elbow.

She pretended not to hear. "Have you heard from your mother?" she asked, to keep the discussion on safe ground.

Fulton sighed. "She's not entirely well, I'm afraid," he answered. "She and Father have decided to delay their trip home from Europe."

They walked in silence for a while, and Fulton paused at Chloe's gate, after opening it for Emma and stepping aside so she could sweep past him.

She smiled gratefully at Daisy, who was on the step, shaking out a rug. The housekeeper gave Fulton an ominous look as Emma ducked inside the house. There, Emma dashed up the front stairs to her room and threw down her shawl, book, and handbag. After changing into an old calico dress, she went down to the kitchen and left the house by the back way.

The sun was still shining brightly, though it was fairly late in the day, and Emma's feet burned more than ever. In the shade of the trees that sheltered Chloe's part of the lake shore from the street, she sat down on the grass and unlaced her shoes. Once she'd pulled them off and tossed them aside, she rolled down her stockings and disposed of them, too.

She was about to head for the water when it occurred to her that the rest of her body was as warm as her feet. On impulse she took off her dress, too, and waded into the water in her drawers and camisole.

The sound of a man clearing his throat made her whirl around, her hands crossed over her breasts, which showed through the thin muslin. He was a stranger, a wiry, well-dressed man with dark hair. There was something very familiar about his brown eyes.

"Miss Emma Chalmers, I presume," he said easily, tugging at the creases on his trousers as he sat down on Emma's favorite fallen log.

Emma could only nod slightly, her face bright with embarrassment. She was afraid, too, but not just for herself. In this man she sensed an all-encompassing threat of a kind she'd never faced before.

The stranger took a cheroot from his suit pocket and lit it with a wooden match. A dazzling diamond ring glinted on the small finger of his left hand, catching the afternoon light. "I've been told you might be able to help me find the man I'm looking for. His name is Steven Fairfax."

# Chapter
## ❧ 14 ❧

$E$mma was growing numb with cold, standing there in her underthings. Purposefully—she ignored the stranger as best she could—she made for her calico dress, which was spread out on a blackberry bush, and pulled it on over her head.

She was bolder, now that she was decently covered. And with narrowed eyes she studied the man who'd come upon her so unexpectedly. He might be a U.S. Marshal, or a bounty hunter, come to find Steven and see him hanged. Or he might mean to do the killing himself.

"Who are you?" she asked.

He looked amused, and when he spoke she noticed a slight Southern drawl. "I've already told you. I'm just a poor wayfarer, looking for a lost friend."

Emma didn't believe a word of it. There was nothing poor about this man, and Steven wasn't his friend. Since she would have had to walk right up to him to get her shoes and stockings, she remained barefoot. "What gives you the idea that I know Mr. Fairfax?"

He smiled indulgently and tossed her shoes and stockings to her. "There's a lot of talk around town about the two of you."

Emma's cheeks burned when she sat down on a good-sized rock to wipe sand from the bottom of one foot before putting on a stocking. "He's gone," she said. "I believe he was headed east, in fact. Toward Chicago." Emma was a lamentably bad liar, and saw immediately that the stranger didn't believe her.

All the same, his smile was friendly. "I've taken a room over at the hotel," he said, throwing down his smoldering cheroot and grinding it out with the toe of his boot. "If you hear anything more about Steven, it would be smart to tell me."

Emma bristled. "Who are you?" she demanded again. "And what do you want?"

He sighed, his compact frame dappled with sunlight and shadow. "My name is Macon Fairfax," he answered reluctantly. "And I'm looking for Steven because he killed my son. The state of Louisiana wants a word with him, too—about the murder of a young woman named Mary McCall."

All the starch went out of Emma. She sagged back against the rock. "Murder? I don't believe it!"

"I don't give a damn what you believe, Miss Chalmers," Macon Fairfax said cordially. "All I want is to see justice done and, if you're wise, you'll assist me." With that, he turned and climbed the bank, making no more noise than he had when he'd approached.

A myriad of emotions raced through Emma's system. She remembered Steven's deftness with that Colt .45 of his and shuddered. Could he really have killed two people?

Emma decided it wasn't possible. Steven was a hard, determined man, but no murderer could have ignited the tender fire that had flared in her when they made love. The embers of it smoldered still.

Catching her skirts up in her hands, Emma quickly climbed the bank and ran toward the back of the house.

After tying her shoelaces and neatening her hair, she hastened to the marshal's office. He was out, but Emma stepped through the little gate in the railing surrounding his desk and oak file cabinet anyway.

There was a potbellied stove in one corner, and from where she stood, she could see the bars of the single jail cell Whitneyville boasted. No prisoner had been confined there in the whole of Emma's memory.

She stepped behind the desk to look at the posters pinned haphazardly to the wall. They were yellowed and old, their edges curling. Butch Cassidy. Black Jack Ketchum. Billy the Kid. But no mention of Steven Fairfax, and no sketch of the face she knew so well.

Emma was not reassured, since she knew these posters had been around a long time. She glanced out through the window to see if anyone was approaching, then opened Marshal Woodridge's desk drawer.

There was a blue envelope—addressed anonymously to the marshal of Whitneyville—which she carefully put back, and a stack of wanted posters. Forgetting that she was trespassing, Emma sank into the marshal's chair and read every one of the posters. Still, she found nothing she could link to Steven.

Emma returned the posters to the drawer and closed it neatly. Steven was in real danger, and she had to do something to help him. But what?

The moment he was alone in his hotel room, Macon Fairfax closed and locked the door and collapsed on the edge of the lumpy bed, his head bent, his hands in his hair. The hatred and bitterness chewed on his gut like rats. Steven had taken his pleasure with that beautiful redheaded woman, he'd seen it in her eyes, and the thought made Macon want to vomit. Dirk and Mary were moldering in their graves, while Cyrus Fairfax's bastard grandson lived on, enjoying such tender delicacies as Miss Emma Chalmers.

Macon comforted himself as he always did—he pictured his half-brother swinging at the end of a rope, that handsome face blue and swollen. God, how he wanted Steven dead.

He drew a deep breath and rose to his feet. He was in his forties now; too old to be chasing all over the countryside after a criminal. No, sir, he should be at home, rolling in the sheets with his mistress, or even his wife, Lucy.

He was desperate for a drink, and the silver flask he carried in his inside pocket was empty. Thinking of Emma Chalmers, and how she'd lied to him, he smiled and unlocked his door.

A few minutes later Macon stepped through the doors of the Stardust Saloon for the second time that day. On the first visit, he'd learned of Miss Chalmers' association with Steven from a good-natured whore named Callie Visco. He'd paid extra for those few words of pillow talk after she'd turned him inside out.

The saloon was doing a brisk business. It was a classy place with wooden floors and signs that said "No Spitting." The tables had green felt tops, and there were some garish but intriguing paintings on the walls. A piano tinkled busily in the background, and the air was tinged with the smell of tobacco smoke.

Scanning the place, Macon spotted a tall fair-haired man sitting by a window, a half-filled bottle of whiskey on the table before him. The fellow looked as if he might be feeling sorry for himself, and Macon had long since learned that self-pity could loosen a man's tongue. He made his way over to the table and smiled down at the man, extending a hand. "Macon Fairfax," he said.

"Fairfax?" The name seemed to taste bad to the dandy, and Macon congratulated himself on his good luck.

"May I?" he asked, already drawing back a chair.

"Sure," the drinker responded glumly, pouring himself another whiskey. He was wearing a bowler hat with his pin-striped suit, and it looked mighty silly, perched on the back of his head like that.

"Your name?"

"Fulton Whitney."

Macon signalled for another bottle and laid a gold coin on the table, to let Whitney know he was no tinhorn just passing through. "You look like an unhappy man, Mr. Whitney."

Whitney sighed melodramatically. He was obviously drunk, but he poured himself another glassful of liquor and tossed it back. "She's the prettiest little piece of baggage in town, and I lost her."

A whore in a short purple dress brought Macon's whiskey and a glass, and when he paid her no attention, she flounced off, pouting. "Who is she?" Macon asked.

Whitney belched unceremoniously. "You wouldn't know her, being a stranger in town. She's the librarian— Miss Emma Chalmers." He looked at Macon again, making a visible attempt to focus his eyes. "Did you say your name is Fairfax?"

Macon nodded. Emma, the saucy little chit he'd heard about from Callie Visco and followed down to the lake. He smiled at the memory of watching her take off her dress and wade into the water. "Yes," he answered belatedly. "Macon Fairfax. I'm from Louisiana, and I'm looking for my brother, Steven." He saw Whitney's face change at the mention of that name. "He's wanted for two murders, you see. I'd like to try to reason with him—and persuade him to come home."

Whitney slammed a fist down onto the tabletop, making both bottles jump and clink together. "I knew it. I *told* Emma he was a good-for-nothing outlaw, but she wouldn't believe me."

"My half brother has a way with the ladies," Macon admitted regretfully. "He's probably cuckolded half the husbands in New Orleans."

Whitney belched again. "Of course, if you found him, you'd take him back to Louisiana."

"Dead or alive," Macon agreed, sitting back in his chair and catching his thumbs in his vest pockets. "Miss

Emma would probably come around to your way of thinking, once he was gone. A woman like that needs a man in her bed."

Color flushed Whitney's cheeks, and, just for a moment, his eyes focused clearly. "Yes," he said, but he was speaking to some vision in his mind, not to Macon. "Yes."

Macon would have bet Fairhaven that Whitney had a hard-on. Sure enough, he wheeled to his feet and the evidence was clearly visible against the front of his pants.

"Gotta go upstairs," he blathered.

Macon smiled. "Before you do, friend, just tell me one thing, so we can both get what we want. Where do I find my brother?"

"He hired on with Big John Lenahan, as a foreman. He's driving a herd north to Spokane."

"Thanks," Macon replied, pouring himself another drink. He watched as Whitney spun toward the stairway. Some whore, he figured, was about to have the town dandy pass out on top of her. And he'd probably be wearing all his clothes.

At his leisure, Macon finished his drink. Inside his head, he was seeing a few visions of his own. Such as Miss Chalmers standing in the lake, with nothing on but her camisole and those little lace-trimmed knickers that came just to her knees. He'd seen the shadow of her womanhood, at the junction of her thighs, and the hint of nipples pressed against muslin.

Something other than the desire for revenge moved inside Macon Fairfax in those moments—lust. He shifted uncomfortably in his chair, thinking of how it would have been to lay the saucy little redhead out in the cool green grass and have her. She'd be one of those that came, long and hard and with lots of noise, whether they'd wanted the taking or not.

Macon's groin tightened painfully. God, what a sweet triumph it would be to have Emma and make damned sure Steven heard every detail.

He sighed. He was going to have to be patient, that was

all. Once he caught Steven—and he wasn't fool enough to think he could do that on his own; he had half a dozen men camped outside of town—he could turn his attention to the little hellcat he suspected his brother loved.

There was one redheaded whore in the place, seated on top of the piano with her bare legs dangling, and Macon crooked a finger at her. She smiled and wriggled down from her perch, then sidled toward him.

Emma paced her room, full of fear and confusion. She had to find Steven, had to know if he'd really killed his own nephew, and some woman named Mary McCall. And she had to warn him.

She took a divided riding skirt from her armoire, together with a long-sleeved blouse made of lightweight flannel, and changed her clothes. She pulled on tall boots and bound her braid up in a coronet to keep it out of her way. Then she took thirty dollars from the secret drawer in the bottom of her jewelry box and crept down the back stairs.

She didn't go into the kitchen until she was sure Daisy wasn't there. When she did, she stayed only long enough to collect an apple and a thick slice of bread. She chewed on the bread as she progressed to the mud porch, where an old coat that belonged to the gardener hung on a peg. Come nightfall, it would be chilly out. Tucking the apple into the pocket, Emma put on the coat and hurried down the back steps.

It was beginning to get dark by then, but she tried not to attract attention as she walked toward the main part of town. Reaching the livery stable, she hastily rented a pinto mare and a saddle from an addlepated stablehand named Henry.

Emma was not an experienced rider, and it was a measure of her desperation that she was willing to let Henry hoist her up into the saddle.

"I hope you ain't goin' out of town, Miss Emma," the middle-aged man said. He had a big belly and thick, uneven features. "There's Injuns and outlaws out there."

Emma suppressed a shudder. She couldn't think about the dangers; Steven's life probably depended on her reaching him in time. "Just see that you don't tell anyone I've been here, Henry. No one, do you hear me?"

Henry nodded reluctantly. "Yes, ma'am, but I think—"

A thought occurred to her. "I'll need a gun. Do you have one?"

"Just a little pistol for shootin' rabbits," Henry answered. "But you don't want to handle no gun—"

"Yes, I do," Emma insisted, ferreting in her coat pocket for the money she'd brought along. She held out a five-dollar bill. "Here, Henry. That's what I'll give you for the use of your pistol and a handful of bullets. And I'll return the gun to you when I get back."

Henry's small, colorless eyes widened at the proposition. "And I'd get to keep the five dollars?"

Emma nodded. "Every cent. What do you say, Henry?"

He couldn't seem to look away from the money. Five dollars was a lot to him, probably more than he earned in a week. "Miss Chloe wouldn't like this none," he fretted.

"Miss Chloe doesn't have to know," Emma said. She felt guilty hiding things from her guardian and best friend, but it was plain in her mind that Chloe would never allow her to go chasing after Steven if she had any idea that was what Emma meant to do.

Overcome by temptation, Henry turned and hurried back into the stable. A few minutes later he returned, carrying the pistol in a holster. It was smaller than the gun Steven carried, with a shorter barrel.

Emma handed over the five dollars and strapped on the gunbelt, just as she'd seen Steven do. Then she rode out, taking care to go the long way and avoid the central part of town.

The trail was well marked, for two hundred cattle don't pass by without a trace, and by nightfall Emma was well on her way.

She had to stop when she could no longer see, and she

and the pinto mare took refuge in a copse of cottonwood trees. She didn't build a fire, and had only the apple she'd brought along for supper. She shared that with the horse and spent a miserable night sitting bolt upright, waiting for the sun to rise.

The moment it did, Emma was up and mounted. When she reached a small creek, she stopped to wash her face and hands and water the horse. By the time she reached the Snake River, she was ravenous, but there was nothing to do but go on.

She hoped Chloe and Daisy weren't too worried about her—in her hurry, she'd failed to leave a note behind—and prayed she wasn't being watched, even then, by Indians or outlaws.

Crossing the river was terrifying for both Emma and the horse, but they made it to the other side and rode on. In the late afternoon, she spotted the smoke of a town full of chimneys. She spurred the tired horse to move faster.

Rileyton was a bustling little place with a general store and a small restaurant. Emma took the horse to the livery stable and left it there to munch happily on fresh oats. Then she smoothed her hair, which had long since fallen from its coronet but was still loosely braided, and walked into the restaurant.

Delightful smells assailed her, causing her stomach to grumble. A hefty dark-haired woman in a gingham dress and an apron eyed her suspiciously.

"You won't get nothin' to eat in here unless you pay first," was her cordial welcome.

Emma was too hungry to quibble. "I've got money," she said, taking out another five-dollar bill to prove it.

Instantly, the woman smiled, revealing big, snowy-white teeth. "Well, you just sit right down, Missy. What'll you have?"

Emma ordered the fried chicken special, and she consumed every bite on her plate. When it was gone, she ate a piece of cherry pie and drank a cup of coffee with lots of sugar and cream. Walking out the door, she almost collided with none other than Joellen Lenahan.

"What are you doing here?" Emma demanded.

Joellen looked fresh as a spring wild flower in her white, gauzy dress. "I might ask the same question of you," she said stiffly.

Emma sighed and looked ruefully down at her dirty blouse and skirt, and the old coat. She was glad Steven wasn't there to see the contrast. "I'm in town on business," she said.

"You're chasing Steven Fairfax," Joellen corrected her smugly, folding her milky white arms across near-perfect breasts. "It won't do you any good. Once Daddy gets here, I'm going to tell him Steven and I spent the night together. He'll horsewhip Mr. Fairfax plumb to death when he finds out."

Emma swallowed, telling herself to remain calm. "You spent the night with Steven?" For all her efforts, the words came out squeaky.

Joellen nodded triumphantly. "It was very romantic. Just the two of us, all alone, wrapped in a canvas coat. Of course, the inevitable happened." She paused to sigh. "In the end it all went wrong, though. Steven Fairfax is a brute, and you're welcome to him."

Emma wasn't sure whether she believed Joellen's story or not, and for all practical purposes, it didn't really matter. She could think of nothing now but finding Steven and warning him that his half brother meant to take him back to New Orleans, dead or alive. Everything else was secondary to that. "Thank you," she said, making her way toward the livery stable.

"Wait!" Joellen called after her. "You didn't tell me what you're doing here."

Emma didn't look back. "Good-bye, Joellen," she replied.

The rancher's daughter ran up beside her. "You mustn't leave, Emma," she pleaded. "Daddy can't get here for a few days because he's branding and the boardinghouse is an awful place, dreadfully boring—"

Emma shook her head. "I don't have time to stay and keep you company, Joellen. I'm sorry."

"I lied," Joellen spouted, still shuffling alongside Emma. "Steven didn't make love to me. In fact, yesterday he spanked me, right on the main street, in front of everybody."

Hiding a smile, Emma stopped and faced Joellen. "What do you want from me?" she asked reasonably.

"I want you to stay here until Daddy comes and gets me."

Incredibly, it was hard to refuse Joellen. She was a brat, but she was also very much a child, despite her womanly face and figure. "I can't," Emma said quietly. "It's really important that I go on."

Joellen drew herself up, obviously incensed that someone had dared to turn down one of her requests, and turned to march regally away. Emma hoped the girl would be safe at the boardinghouse, if bored, and continued on to the livery stable.

The little pinto horse, whom Henry had told her was named Smiley, was rested and ready to go. After buying more apples at the general store, along with a box of matches and a blanket that she rolled up and tied behind her saddle, Emma set out on the trail of the herd again.

Emma and Smiley rode hard, but by sunset there was still no sign of the drive. Emma was sorely dreading the prospect of another night on the cold ground, with nothing but apples for supper, when she spotted smoke wending from a chimney off to the west.

Hoping to find friendly settlers, she turned Smiley in the direction of the smoke.

After a half an hour or so, she found the homestead. It was a tiny log cabin, but there were chickens in the yard and a good-sized barn towered out back. Two little girls in pigtails and calico pinafores ran to greet Emma.

"You a man or a woman?" the smallest one asked. Her nose needed to be wiped, and her face was covered with dirt and freckles.

"She's a woman, silly," said the older child. She was almost an exact replica of the other little girl, only taller. "Look at her braid."

"She could be an Indian," was the staunch argument.

"I ain't never seen a redheaded Indian, and neither have you," came the reply.

Emma smiled. "My name is Emma Chalmers."

"I'm Tessie," said the bigger child, "and this is my sister, Sallie Lee."

Wearily, Emma got down from the saddle. There was still no sign of an adult, and she began to wonder if the little girls were alone. "Is your mama around?"

"We don't have no mama," said Tessie. "We got a pa, though. He's out huntin' rabbits."

Emma felt uneasy. "When will he be back?"

"When he gets a rabbit," replied Sallie Lee.

"Do you think I could water my horse?"

"Sure," said Tessie generously. It was plain that she was delighted to have company. "There's a creek back behind the barn, and we got a privy, too, if you need it."

Emma smiled. "Thank you." She took two apples from her pockets and extended them.

The little girls didn't look as if they'd suffered privation, but their eyes lighted up when they saw those shiny red apples. They accepted them eagerly, with loud thank yous, and polished the fruit on their pinafores. They were chomping happily when Emma led the pinto away toward the creek.

While Smiley was drinking at the crystal-clear brook, which was down a slight hill and hidden by trees, Emma heard a gunshot in the distance and smiled. Sallie Lee and Tessie's pa had just caught up with a rabbit, she guessed.

She went back to the cabin to wait.

Not long afterward, a man of medium height and build appeared in the clearing, carrying a rifle in one hand and a rabbit in the other. He was wearing rough-spun trousers, a shirt that had probably been white once, scuffed boots and a floppy leather hat.

"Pa, this is Emma," Tessie ran to tell him.

"She gave us apples," Sallie Lee shouted.

He looked at Emma from beneath the brim of his battered hat and smiled. When he got closer, Emma could see that he had friendly blue eyes and an abundance of brown hair. "Jeb Meyers," he said, by way of introduction. "I'd offer my hand but—"

Emma looked at the rabbit and the rifle and smiled back, even though the sight of a dead animal made her slightly sick. "Emma Chalmers," she said. "I was wondering if I could spend the night in your barn."

"You'll spend the night in the house," he said, striding on toward the cabin. "*I'll* sleep in the barn."

Liking Jeb Meyers as much as she liked his children, Emma followed him back toward the cabin. He put his rifle away, then went down to the creek to skin and clean the rabbit.

When he returned, Emma was sitting in the tall grass with Sallie Lee and Tessie, showing them how to weave a daisy chain. Since there weren't any daisies, they were using butter-gold dandelions.

"Is your wife away?" Emma asked pleasantly, when Jeb crouched beside her to have a look at the chain of yellow, spiky blossoms. She hadn't wanted to question the girls, thinking that would be slightly unfair.

"Bethie died last January," Jeb answered hoarsely, averting his eyes for a moment.

"I'm sorry," Emma replied.

Jeb watched her for a few seconds, then said, "Thanks. Now, I'd better get that rabbit on the fire, if we're going to have supper around here."

"I could help," Emma volunteered.

"Do you know how to cook?"

Emma sighed. "No," she confessed.

Jeb Meyers laughed at that. "Well, then," he replied, "you'd better go right on with what you were doing." He walked away toward the cabin.

Sallie Lee put a ring of dandelions on top of her head and thrust back her shoulders. "I'm the queen of Montana," she said.

"You ain't queen and this ain't Montana," Tessie pointed out.

Emma laughed and hugged them both, but a corner of her heart was bruised for these children, their affable father, and their lost mother. She wondered what Bethie Meyers had been like.

Later that evening, when the two excited little girls had eaten and gone to bed in the loft, Emma helped Jeb with the dishes. "It must be lonely out here," she said.

He looked at her with concern. "It is. And dangerous, too. What the devil are you doing, riding through the countryside all alone?"

Emma sighed. "I'm trying to catch up with a trail drive," she answered. She didn't want to say more, and Jeb didn't press.

"You can sleep over there," he said, pointing to a double bed pushed close to the wall. "There's no need to worry—I'll stay in the barn where I belong—but I want you to bolt the door all the same. For your own peace of mind."

Emma was struck by a strange, bittersweet feeling that, under other circumstances, she might have made a life with this man. "Thank you," she said.

His eyes caressed her face for a moment, as though he might be having similar thoughts. "Good night," he said, and then he was gone, and Emma bolted the door behind him, as instructed. But for the prospect of wandering Indians and outlaws, she wouldn't have bothered. She knew she had nothing to fear from Jeb Meyers.

Emma was up early the next morning, before the children were awake. She and Jeb talked quietly in the barn while he saddled Smiley, and after thanking her host for supper and a warm bed, Emma rode on.

At midday, sweaty and tired and very hungry, Emma mounted a tree-covered rise and saw the herd. Her heart leaped into her throat when she spotted Steven in the distance, whistling and shouting at the cattle like the other men. She was just about to ride down and announce herself when a horse materialized beside hers and a strong arm curved around her neck.

The cold barrel of a pistol was pressed to her throat. "Just be glad I'm so anxious to see my bastard of a brother," growled a familiar voice. "If I weren't, pretty Miss Emma, I'd be spreading you out in the soft spring grass and having my way with you."

# *Chapter*
## ⇘ 15 ⇚

*F*rank Deva gave a shrill whistle to get Steven's attention, and when he had it, he gestured toward the country stretching out behind them. Steven wheeled his horse around and felt his heart stop beating for a moment, then start again with a painful lurch.

Emma was riding toward him, clad in an old coat and a riding skirt. Her hair was coming loose from its braid, and it made a coppery halo around her pale face. Behind her, mounted on the same horse, was Macon.

All the world went still in that moment. Steven couldn't hear the cattle bawling, the whistles and shouts of the cowboys, the nickering of their horses. Everything he knew and everything he was, every sense he possessed, was focused on Emma's face.

He reached automatically for his gun, moving it in and out of his holster to make sure it wouldn't hang up if he drew.

When they were within a dozen yards of each other, Steven could see that Emma's hands were bound, and

Macon had a pistol barrel pressed to the underside of her jaw.

Macon smiled, showing the straight white teeth that were standard equipment in the Fairfax family. "Hello, Steven," he said. "It's been a long time."

Steven's gaze was fixed on Emma's face. She was wan and wide-eyed, but she looked unhurt. "If you've done anything to her," he told his brother, "I'll kill you."

"I haven't done anything to her," Macon replied smoothly. "I'm saving that for when you're dangling at the end of a rope."

Emma turned in the saddle to glance back at Macon, but an instant later, she was staring at Steven again, questioningly. It made him ache to know she was wondering if she'd given her body to a killer.

"Let her go, Macon," he said quietly.

Macon laughed and drew back the hammer on his pistol. "You're in no position to give orders, Steven. I've got a warrant for your arrest in my pocket, signed by a federal judge. All I have to do is ride to the nearest town and tell the marshal about you and you'll be on your way back to Louisiana in chains. But I'm keeping the little lady here as insurance, so I don't run into any accidents."

Steven glanced back over his shoulder and saw Deva and three of the cowboys there, pistols in hand, ready to defend him. "Put the guns away," he said with resignation.

"Speaking of that," Macon put in, "why don't you drop yours? Right now."

Macon's pistol was still pressed to Emma's flesh; any sudden action could get the top of her head blown off. "Take it easy," Steven breathed, unbuckling his gunbelt and letting it fall to the ground. He held his hands at shoulder height, palms out.

After indulging in a moment of pure spite, Macon lowered his pistol from Emma's neck and shoved it back into the holster. She closed her eyes briefly in relief.

Steven longed to tell her everything would be all right,

that he was innocent of any crime, that he wasn't about to let anyone hurt her, gun or no gun. But he was too afraid Macon would feel called upon to prove him wrong.

It was almost more than Steven had dared to hope for, but Macon became cocky, overconfident. He swung down from the saddle to face his half-brother.

Behind him, her hands still bound together, Emma slipped to the ground, her eyes fixed on Steven. Still, she didn't speak.

Steven would have given his soul to take her into his arms and reassure her, but he couldn't afford the luxury. "So you found me," he said to his half-brother. "It took you long enough."

Macon grinned bitterly. "You killed my son. I would have dogged you to your grave."

Sweat trickled through the trail dust covering Steven's face in a gritty coating. He raised one arm to wipe his brow, and the action created just the right degree of distraction. He backhanded Macon as hard as he could, sending him sprawling into the dirt.

Before his brother could draw, Steven had recovered the Colt, which he trained on Macon's midsection. Emma ran to Steven, and he put an arm around her, pulling her close for a moment, then letting her go. Her hands were still bound behind her, and she stumbled a little.

"Toss the pistol aside," Steven told his brother.

Now it was Macon who was sweating. Gingerly, he drew his gun with two fingers and flung it into the dust. Steven kicked it well out of reach, then handed his Colt to one of the men behind him. Frank Deva was cutting away the rope that bound Emma's wrists.

Macon scrambled to his feet when he saw that Steven was facing him unarmed. It was a moment both of them had longed for, ever since the day Steven first set foot on Fairhaven.

"Steven, no!" Emma croaked.

He ignored her, speaking to his men without looking at

them. "Nobody interfere—no matter what." After that, he circled Macon like a panther closing in on its prey.

Macon lifted his fists and jutted out his chin. Steven's hands remained loose at his sides, but they ached to close around Macon's throat.

For a long time, the two men just stared at each other, each waiting for the other to throw the first punch. Macon weakened first, and landed a solid blow in Steven's middle.

The pain shot through his rib cage in razor-sharp streaks, but Steven smiled. He'd just been granted the license he needed. He caught Macon in a hard right cross and sent him sprawling backwards onto the ground.

Macon lurched back to his feet, his eyes glittering with hatred, and now there was a small, sharp knife in his hand. The blade glinted in the bright sunshine.

Steven smiled. "I always said you were a sneaky son-of-a-bitch," he said, circling Macon again, making him turn like a top. Their gazes were locked together, but Steven knew precisely where the knife was at any given moment.

Macon finally tired of the game and lunged at Steven, making a slashing motion with the blade. It caught Steven in the upper arm just before he sent it flying with a blow from his foot, and he felt blood saturating his shirt sleeve.

If there was pain, Steven wasn't aware of it. He dragged Macon close by his lapels and kneed him hard in the groin.

Macon cried out and sank to his knees, his head down, his hands sheltering his wounded genitals. Steven reclaimed his Colt and jammed the barrel into his brother's jugular vein. "How does it feel?" he rasped.

If Emma hadn't been looking on, Steven would have done considerably more damage to his brother. As it was, he gave him a dose of the fear Emma must have felt, then just left him kneeling there in the dirt while he recovered his gunbelt and strapped it on. Deva collected Macon's pistol and bloody knife without comment.

Emma rushed to Steven, her eyes wide with horror and fear, her throat working convulsively. "You're hurt—"

Steven felt the pain then, and it braced him up, like a stiff drink. He entangled the fingers of one hand in Emma's hair. "I'll be all right," he said hoarsely.

"You need a doctor!"

He shook his head. "The cook'll sew me up, if I need it," he said.

The color drained from Emma's face, and she let her smudged forehead fall against his shoulder. "What's happening, Steven? Is it true what your brother says? Did you really kill two people?"

Steven couldn't have answered any of those questions with a simple yes or no, so he didn't reply to them at all. He was looking at Macon, although his arm was around Emma, holding her close. "Get up," he said.

Macon clambered awkwardly to his feet. The hatred was still there in his face, and so, despite the pain he must have been feeling, was the smugness. "You can't win, Steven," he breathed, wiping blood from the corner of his mouth. "You can't stop me from riding for the nearest lawman unless you kill me. And you wouldn't do that, not in front of so many witnesses."

Steven felt Emma's eyes on his face, pleading. "Later," he told her. "I'll explain later."

Emma hung on to Steven, certain she would collapse if she let go. Looking up at his face, she saw a grim resignation that frightened her.

"I've got to turn these cattle over to the army in Spokane. Once I do that, I'll come back to New Orleans and stand trial."

Emma felt as though the very earth beneath her feet had suddenly caved in upon itself. She held on to Steven's dirty vest with both hands and willed him to say he was innocent, but he didn't speak up for himself.

"What about the woman, boss?" one of the cowboys asked. "We can't take her all the way to Spokane with us."

Steven glanced at Emma, then at Macon. "I'm sure as hell not going to trust my brother with her. Emma stays with me."

While Emma was a little affronted that Steven would make such a decision without even consulting her, she saw the sense in it. She couldn't very well go riding through the countryside with Macon Fairfax on the loose.

Macon spat furiously. "You don't expect me to trust you, do you? The minute I turn my back, you'll be on the run again."

Slowly, sadly, Steven shook his head. "I'm all through running," he said, tightening his good arm around Emma's waist. "All through."

Macon watched him warily. "I've got a half dozen men with me," he said. "I'll be trailing you."

"Fine," Steven answered, and he turned his back on Macon, taking Emma with him, and helped her onto his horse. He swung up behind her, and she felt him wince. She knew his rib cage was probably hurting, as well as the knife wound he'd sustained in the fight, and she longed to comfort him.

All the same, other emotions churned inside her, too. She needed to hear Steven say he was innocent, that he'd never murdered anyone. And so far, he hadn't said anything of the sort.

The herd was moving ahead, and Steven spurred the gelding forward. The cowboys who'd come to his aid flanked him like an armed guard.

When they caught up with the chuck wagon, Steven spoke to Sing Cho, and he brought his team of mules to an immediate halt. While the others went on ahead, Steven and Emma stopped.

Emma glanced back and saw Macon riding away, his horse's hooves making dingy clouds in the dust. She thought about the little pinto mare she'd rented in Whitneyville and held onto the forlorn hope that Macon and his men would return it.

The Chinese cook chattered in his own language when

he cut away the sleeve of Steven's shirt and saw the wound beneath. It was long and wide, and Emma had to turn from the sight of it for a moment and swallow a mouthful of bile.

Sing Cho pointed toward a stand of trees in the distance. "Go there. Need to make fire."

Steven nodded glumly and got back onto his horse, pulling Emma up behind him. She wrapped her arms around his middle and laid her cheek against the hard, muscular expanse of his back. She felt like crying, but the tears wouldn't come.

When they reached the trees, Sing Cho secured the wagon and handed Emma a battered enamel basin. Pointing toward the creek flowing nearby, he said, "Bring water."

Emma was eager to obey. Squatting by the creek, she saw fat brown trout wriggle by, and plain rocks glittered like jewels under the crystal-clear water. She filled the basin and hurried back.

The cook had already started a fire, and Steven was sitting on an upended crate, watching while the Chinese tied a tourniquet around his arm to staunch the bleeding.

The small man with the long queue trailing down his back nodded toward the fire. "Put in kettle and get more."

Unquestioningly, Emma poured the cold water into a pot sitting near the fire and went back to the creek.

When she returned, the kettle was suspended over the flames on a spit, and Steven was drinking whiskey straight from the bottle.

"Where is he?" Emma whispered.

Steven grinned. He was filthy from head to foot, and that made Emma think of the time she'd helped him bathe, back at Chloe's house. "Sing Cho? He's getting out his sewing kit."

"How can you be so calm?" Emma asked. She was trembling at the very prospect of needle meeting flesh.

He shrugged. "If carrying on would make it stop

218

bleeding and knit together, I'd do it," he replied. "Are you all right, Emma?"

She thought for a moment, then nodded.

"You should have stayed in Whitneyville, where you belong," he reasoned quietly, as the Chinese returned with a needle and a length of catgut.

Emma stepped back and put her hands on her hips. "Here it comes," she cried. "The lecture. I was trying to warn you, Steven."

"Mr. Fairfax," he corrected, with a smile lighting his eyes.

Emma wanted to strangle him. "Mr. Fairfax," she complied, but grudgingly.

Sing Cho appeared to be deaf to the conversation. He was busy cleaning Steven's wound with water from the kettle and a soft cloth.

"I probably saved your life or something," Emma went on.

"My life wouldn't be worth a damn without you," Steven replied, just before he downed another gulp of whiskey from the bottle. "And you could have run into a pack of Sioux warriors we met up with the other day. *Or* outlaws. As it was, you're damned lucky Macon didn't rape you. He's not a man of delicate sensibilities, in case you didn't notice."

Sing Cho thoughtfully threaded the catgut and peered at the long, gaping cut on Steven's upper arm.

"I don't believe this," Emma said, temper flaring. "I came all this way to help you and you're *scolding* me like a child!"

"I've got half a mind to take you over my knee and paddle you." He took another swallow of the whiskey and made a lusty sound of satisfaction as it went down.

"You wouldn't dare."

Steven flinched as the needle made its first pass through his skin. "Ask Joellen Lenahan about that."

Emma didn't look at the wound again because she

knew she'd throw up if she did. All she could do to help was distract Steven, and if that meant a screaming fight, then so be it.

"I'm not a sixteen-year-old child," Emma pointed out. "And by the way, I didn't appreciate learning that you'd spent the night with Joellen."

Steven flinched again and muttered a curse as Sing Cho continued his work. "Like you said, Miss Emma— she's a child. I didn't touch her, and you damned well know it."

Emma did know, but she was still jealous. Joellen had lain with Steven, probably huddled close and sheltered in his arms, and that was a privilege Emma reserved for herself. Feeling overheated all of a sudden, she jerked off the cumbersome wool coat and flung it down on the ground. "Did you kiss her?"

Steven managed to grin and grimace at the same time. "What if I did?"

"I'll scratch your eyes out, that's what," Emma vowed fiercely. Her hands were on her hips and she paced back and forth. Her riding skirt and blouse were rumpled and stained, her face was grimy, her braid was coming loose around her face. And she didn't give a damn about any of that.

Steven laughed even as he groaned with pain. He was very pale under his mask of sweat and dirt, and a small cut at the corner of his eye was seeping blood. His clothes were in need of mending and washing. "After the day I've had," he answered, "it wouldn't surprise me if you did."

Emma's heart twisted. She wanted to send the cook away, to take Steven in her arms, to comfort him and tend to his injuries herself. But she knew she'd probably faint if she had to stitch torn flesh together. Her eyes filled with tears and she turned her head away to hide them.

"Talk to me, Emma," Steven said quietly. "I need something to think about besides this needle going in and out of my arm."

Emma glanced nervously at Sing Cho. "Is it true—what Macon said? Did you kill two people?"

Steven looked incomprehensibly weary. "Is that what he said?"

"Yes," Emma sniffled. She was tired and sad and she needed a bath. She wanted to go home, and take Steven with her. "He said you killed his son. And a woman."

"Do you believe him?"

Emma swallowed. "You didn't deny it."

Steven bit down on his lower lip and closed his eyes as Sing Cho tied off the last stitch. In the next instant, the Chinese grabbed the bottle of liquor from Steven's hand and sloshed the wound generously.

Steven drew in a hissing breath and shot to his feet, then let out a stream of curses. Sing Cho leaped backwards, but his face was impassive as he met Steven's glare with a steady and unperturbed gaze.

"Now we make bandage," he said.

"The hell you will," Steven rasped. "Stay away from me."

Emma felt called upon to take Sing Cho's part. She gripped Steven's uninjured arm and said quickly, "He had to put alcohol on the cut—to prevent infection."

Steven let out a long sigh and sat down on the apple crate again.

While Sing Cho was sorting through his big carpet bag for the makings of a bandage, Emma washed her hands in what remained of the water she'd carried from the creek. She splashed her face, too, and the cold made her breath catch.

"I'll do that," she said, when Sing Cho started to wrap Steven's arm.

Steven nodded at him. "Go ahead and catch up with the herd. We'll be right behind you."

Sing Cho bowed, and sparing not so much as a glance for Emma, turned and trotted back to his wagon, taking his carpet bag with him.

"You could at least have thanked him," Emma scolded as she bent to wrap Steven's wound.

"Look at me," he said hoarsely.

Emma brought her eyes to his face and swallowed hard. It was so good to be close to him again, in spite of everything, that she wanted to weep.

"What are you doing here?"

"I told you," she said with some effort, gently knotting the bandage to make it stay. "I wanted to warn you about your brother."

He stood and led her around behind a stand of trees and brush, where he took a seat on a birch stump. Then he pulled her downward, so that she was sitting astraddle of his lap. "You took some big chances, Miss Emma. I want to know why."

Emma lowered her eyes. "Because I love you, Mr. Fairfax," she replied in a soft, broken voice.

Steven was silent for such a long time that Emma feared he was going to send her away. When she finally brought herself to meet his gaze, she was amazed to see that he was smiling. "You love me?"

"Yes, God help me," Emma sighed. Her arms went around his neck. "I love you so much, it hurts."

"Even though you're not sure whether I'm a killer or not?"

Emma nodded sadly.

He laughed, and it was a joyful, raucous sound. His hands interlocked at the small of Emma's back, he planted a noisy kiss on her mouth. "If I didn't know those cowboys up there would tell the story around the campfire for years to come, I'd take you right now."

She would have responded wholeheartedly, but she fancied she could hide the knowledge from Steven.

He put his hand under her chin and lifted. "I love you," he said firmly.

Emma had feared never to hear those words from him, and relief made her sigh and rest her forehead against his. She tensed, though, when she felt his hand unfasten the row of big buttons in the placket at the front of her skirt.

"Steven," she complained. "You just said—the cow-boys—"

He put his hand down inside the skirt, and slid it deftly beneath her knickers. "They can't see through the trees," he whispered against her mouth.

Emma gave a soft moan because it felt so good to have him touch her in that warm, moist place between her legs.

"Open your blouse," he went on, as he continued to caress her with a gentle rhythm that was making her soul spin wildly within her.

Emma could barely breathe. "Dear God, Steven—"

"Do as I tell you, Emma," Steven said, tracing the circumference of her lips with the tip of his tongue. Emma's mouth opened for him, just as another part of her body was doing.

She reached up with fumbling fingers and began unbuttoning her blouse.

"Lift your camisole," Steven ordered, when she was through.

"Steven—"

"Do it."

She bared her breasts and leaned back with a moan. Steven took one of her nipples into his mouth and sucked even as he flicked at it with his tongue.

Emma whimpered helplessly and let her head fall farther back. His fingers glided in and out of her while his thumb worked that taut, tingling nubbin of flesh hidden in her delta. At the same time, he drew greedily on her breast.

Her body began to buck wildly as she rode his hand. "Steven," she whispered desperately. "Oh, *Steven*—"

He moved to her other breast and took nourishment there, all the while continuing the ruthless, skillful motion of his fingers.

Emma's legs stiffened and moved wide of her body when the delicious contractions began, deep inside her. She cried out loudly and arched her back, surrendering without reservation to Steven's hand and his mouth.

When it was over, she let her forehead rest on his shoulder, gasping for breath. He gave her a lengthy caress, meant to assure that she would want him again, very soon, then withdrew his hand. Conscientiously, he rebuttoned her skirt, pulled her camisole down over pebble-hard nipples that were still moist from his mouth, and closed her blouse.

Emma doubted that she'd even be able to stand when he entangled his fingers in her hair and pressed her mouth to his. His kiss was as compelling and masterful, in its own way, as the delightful paces he'd just put her through.

"Why did you do that?" she demanded, when it was over.

"Why did I kiss you, or why did I make you ride my hand?"

Emma's cheeks burned. "Both."

"The days ahead are likely to be rough ones." He spoke gently, and his voice was hoarse with emotion. "I want you to remember, whatever happens, that you loved me and that things were very, very good between us."

Emma searched his face with worried, bewildered eyes. "Steven, please tell me Macon was lying."

"We'll talk about that later, when there's more time. Right now, we've got to catch up with the herd."

Emma's heart fell. It was plain that Steven was keeping something from her, and she knew only too well what it was. "Steven, please," she begged.

He set her on her feet and stood. Sing Cho had poured water onto the fire before he left, and there was nothing left of it but several chunks of blackened wood.

Steven walked down to the edge of the creek and squatted beside the water, and when he came back, his face and hands were clean. He still had the beginnings of a beard, however, and his hair was rumpled where Emma had run her fingers through it.

"Let's go," he said, coming to stand beside the gelding and extending a hand to Emma.

She let him help her up into the saddle, and closed her

eyes for a moment as her tender femininity made contact with the hard leather. Mounted behind her, Steven put his hands briefly on her breasts again, as if to stake a claim on them. His breath was warm and soft as it passed her ear.

"I told you I'd have you wherever I found you," he reminded her. "That was the best I could do."

Emma was still trembling with pleasant aftershocks. "Some folks would say you aren't a gentleman," she said.

"I don't give a damn," he answered, spurring the horse toward the cloud of dust that marked the passing of the herd. They had to ride hard to catch up, and Emma felt as if every pore in her body was clogged with trail dirt by the time they did. She could feel it even between her teeth.

Steven maneuvered the horse among the cattle that strayed from the herd as easily as if Emma hadn't been mounted in front of him, whistling and waving his hat at times. In calmer moments, he told Emma about Fairhaven, his home in Louisiana. He told her how many children they were going to have, and exactly where each one would be conceived. When they got to Spokane, he promised, he was going to take a hotel room and keep her tossing on the mattress for a full day and night.

Emma was warm with arousal and frustration by the time they stopped to make camp that night, next to a broad stream.

Cattle lowed in the twilight, and the cowboys talked self-consciously among themselves, trying not to stare at Emma yet unable to help stealing glimpses. The cook built a roaring fire and began to prepare biscuits, stew, and coffee.

Emma offered to help with the food, but Sing Cho shook his head and shuffled her off with a shooing motion of his apron. Steven was busy going over the next day's travel with the scout, and he didn't spare as much as a glance for her.

A feeling of abject loneliness came over Emma as she looked up at the first stars glimmering distantly in the sky. She'd given her heart to Steven Fairfax, and he hadn't even tried to deny the charges against him.

She might have become Mrs. Fulton Whitney, with practically all of the Idaho Territory at her feet. Now she was an outlaw's woman, shamelessly baring herself to his every whim.

Steven was planning to go back to Louisiana and stand trial, and Emma meant to go with him. Whatever happened, she would be at his side. She swallowed hard. Suppose Macon was right? Suppose she had to watch the man she loved taken to the gallows and hanged?

There were tears in her eyes when she felt Steven's hands grip her shoulders. "It's time we talked," he said softly, escorting her away from camp and into the privacy of the gathering night.

They walked upstream, parallel with the wide creek, until they were out of sight of the others, and Steven seated Emma on a boulder near the water. He leaned against a tree and folded his arms, gazing down at her.

"I love you," he said again.

The landscape around them glowed with the silvery light of the moon. "I know," Emma answered softly, looking up into his face. She'd been working up her courage for hours, and the question wasn't easy to ask. For all that, she needed desperately to hear the answer. "Did you kill your nephew and that girl, Steven?"

He was silent for a long time. Then he replied hoarsely, "In a roundabout way, yes."

# Chapter
## ≈ 16 ≈

*E*mma was still as the stone she sat upon, her hands folded in her lap, her eyes fixed on Steven's leaf-shadowed face. Despite the picture of serenity she presented, her insides were churning.

Steven leaned against the trunk of a towering birch and folded his arms. His gaze met hers with a reassuring steadiness, but he didn't speak. He seemed to be memorizing her features, as though he thought he might never see her again.

Emma could bear it no longer. "Tell me why, Steven," she whispered brokenly. "Tell me how you could—could kill your own nephew—"

"I fired the shot that ended Dirk's life," Steven broke in hoarsely, tilting his head back to study the star-speckled sky for a moment. "At least, indirectly."

Emma didn't speak, but her eyes pleaded with him.

Steven sighed and met her eyes again, then laid a gentle hand on her shoulder. "Illegitimate sons seem to run in the Fairfax family," he said, and the words did nothing to reassure Emma. "Macon was only about sixteen when he fathered Dirk by one of the delicate young ladies in his social circle. The girl died in childbirth, and her family brought the baby to Fairhaven, making it clear that Dirk would end up in a foundling home if Macon's people rejected him.

"Macon was a kid himself, and he wanted to let Dirk go to the orphanage. My father agreed, but my grandfather—Cyrus—wouldn't hear of a Fairfax being turned away from his rightful home. He insisted the baby be raised at Fairhaven and his word was law. Still is.

"Anyway, Dirk grew up as a full-fledged member of the family. By the time I came along, after my father's death, he and Macon were pretty close. And Dirk was in love with a young woman in town named Mary McCall."

Steven paused to study the sky again. He seemed to take courage from the drapery of stars spread out overhead. "Mary had a fancy for me, as it turned out. I was involved with someone else at the time and didn't pay any real attention to her. I just thought she was a flirt, like a lot of girls her age."

Emma found herself wondering about the woman he'd been "involved with." She wanted to know her name, and whether or not Steven had loved her, but she kept her peace. There would be time for those kinds of questions later.

He sighed and rubbed his eyes with a thumb and forefinger. Even in the half-darkness, Emma could see that his bandage needed to be changed. "Evidently, Mary was more serious than any of us guessed. She told Dirk some pretty creative lies—that she and I had been meeting secretly, that we'd been intimate, that we were planning to run away together.

"I wasn't exactly a welcome addition to Fairhaven as it was, and Mary's stories made the situation impossible."

Listening, Emma felt sorry for Steven, and in a strange way for Mary, too. Knowing what it was to love him, she felt pain even in imagining how badly she would be hurt if he spurned her. She laid her hand over his, where it still rested on her shoulder, and encouraged him to go on with a nod.

"Dirk was bitter. Whenever we ran into each other, be it at home or in town, he either glared at me or tried to pick a fight. I ignored him as long as I could.

"Finally, though, his animosity reached into every corner of my life.

"I could have left, but New Orleans was home. Besides, I liked Fairhaven and I loved my grandfather." He paused and rubbed his beard-stubbled chin, and Emma saw the anguish in his eyes.

"One night, in a club, Dirk challenged me to a duel. I could have refused, of course, but I couldn't make myself do it. So Dirk and I agreed on a time and meeting place and, early the next morning, we both showed up with the customary seconds. He brought my grandfather's dueling pistols.

"While I'd been fighting in the war, Dirk was in England, going to school. I knew he didn't have a chance against me in a real duel, and even though we certainly weren't close, I didn't want to kill him." Steven sighed. "We went through all the motions, though, and it was plain from Dirk's face that he'd like nothing better than to kill me. I let him fire the first shot, in fact, and he missed by six yards, just as I figured he would. He was like a crazy man—he screamed curses and dared me to shoot him.

"I didn't give a damn about my honor, but I knew he'd hate me even more if I made him walk away a loser, so I shot him." At the sudden tensing of Emma's face, Steven cupped his hand under her chin and shook his head. "I didn't kill him, not then. I hit him just above his left elbow—I figured that would do the least damage."

Emma ran the tip of her tongue nervously over her lips. "What happened then?"

"There was a doctor on hand, and he went to look after Dirk. I walked away, with my second. Dirk bellowed insults until I was out of earshot."

"Did he die?"

Steven sighed heavily and shook his head. "Not then. But an infection set in, and eventually his arm had to be amputated just beneath the shoulder. If Dirk had hated me before, he wanted to unravel my insides by then.

"He told me once that it would have been more merciful if I'd killed him on 'the field of honor,' as he called it." Steven's expression was one of profound contempt. "He started drinking even more than he normally did, and then he discovered opium. By that time, Mary wouldn't give him the time of day. One night, after a loud argument with Cyrus, he went to the opera, stood up in the middle of an aria, and blew his brains all over the walls with a thirty-eight."

Emma was instantly on her feet, and her arms moved gently around Steven's middle. "My God," she whispered.

He let his forehead rest against hers for a moment, his breathing unsteady, his eyes closed. "Macon already saw me as an outsider, since I was the son of his father's mistress. Dirk's death gave him an even better reason to hate me."

Emma kissed him lightly on the lips and continued to hold him close. "And Mary?"

Steven gave a ragged sigh and trembled slightly in Emma's arms as a cool breeze flowed upward from the creek. "She decided to propose to me, since Dirk was out of the way. She walked up to me at a ball a few months later and asked me to marry her.

"I didn't want to embarrass her, so I told her as gently as I could that she was going to have to look elsewhere for a husband.

"She was furious, and there was a scene. She screamed that I had to marry her because I'd compromised her. As I've told you, I'd never touched her, except to dance with her occasionally. I figured she was probably carrying Dirk's baby, and I felt sorry for her." He shoved one hand through his hair. "After all, if I hadn't come back to

Fairhaven after the war, none of it would have happened. She and Dirk probably would have married and had a houseful of kids.

"I wanted to protect her from any further scandal, so I made my apologies to the hostess and offered to take Mary home.

"She was all smiles, thinking I was going to give in and put a ring on her finger. Instead, while we were riding back to her place in the carriage, I told her that I couldn't marry her because I didn't love her. I offered to see that she and the baby were both taken care of, if she was carrying my nephew's child.

"She started to cry and said her life was ruined, and no decent man would want her.

"I didn't know how to comfort her, since I couldn't give her the one thing she really wanted, so I left her off at her father's house and went on to the club to play cards and have a few drinks.

"The next day Mary was found strangled in her room. The general opinion was that I had murdered her to keep her from telling the world she was going to have my baby. I got out of New Orleans about five minutes before I was to be arrested."

Emma put her arms around his neck. "Surely someone would have believed you—your grandfather, for instance. Your friends."

"I found out I had fewer friends than I'd thought," Steven answered, his lips moving against Emma's forehead, "and even though Cyrus is ten times meaner than Macon and me put together, he couldn't have stood against the whole of Orleans parish."

Emma believed Steven's story, though she had her doubts whether it was because it had the ring of truth or because she loved him so desperately. "I want to go back with you, Steven," she said. "I'll stand by you, no matter what happens."

To her surprise and hurt, Steven shook his head. "No. You're going to Whitneyville, not Louisiana. Until I've cleared my name, I won't have anything to offer you. Besides, what if I'm convicted, and I'm not there to protect you from Macon?"

A chill travelled down Emma's spine, for she knew Steven could just as easily hang as be acquitted, given the fact that his adversary was Macon, a determined man bent on revenge. "If you don't take me with you," she said, "I will follow you to New Orleans, and if you don't believe me, just wait and see. I won't be left behind, Steven."

A muscle in his jaw bunched in suppressed anger; Steven knew Emma meant what she said. "All right, then, we'll compromise. We'll be married when we get to Spokane. That'll give you some protection against Macon, but remember this, Emma—if they hang me, don't wait around for the funeral. Macon wasn't bluffing—the minute the life goes out of me, he'll take you to bed, whether you want to go or not."

Emma was bruised inside. She was in love, really and truly in love, for the first time in her life. And her marriage might last no longer than a murder trial. Her eyes filled with tears. She embraced Steven even more tightly and looked up into his face. "There'll be no funeral, Mr. Fairfax," she said fiercely. "At least, not for forty or fifty years."

He kissed her forehead. "Promise me you'll leave New Orleans the same day, if the verdict goes against us. I have to know that you won't even go back to Fairhaven for your things, Emma. Do I have your word?"

She nodded, albeit grudgingly. "We're going to win," she insisted.

"I'm staking everything on that," Steven replied. And then he kissed Emma thoroughly, and she wanted him to make love to her, right there where they stood. She needed to be as close to him as possible, needed to be totally absorbed in her passion for him, so she wouldn't have to think about the very real possibility that they would soon be parted forever.

She began unbuttoning his torn, dirty shirt, and his

eyes twinkled in the light of the moon. He pretended to be shocked. "Miss Emma!"

She spread the front of his shirt and laid her palms against the gritty, down-covered expanse of his chest, her fingers splayed. "I want you to love me, Steven. I want your baby growing inside me."

He moaned and closed his eyes for a moment when she found his nipples and began stroking them lightly with the pads of her thumbs. "Emma, I've been on the trail for three days—"

She laid the tip of her tongue to one of the taut brown buttons, tasting dust and sweat and Steven, and not caring. He was delicious to her. "Make love to me," she said again. "Right here and now."

Steven's eyes seemed to blaze as he looked at her, and behind him, the stream sparkled and glimmered in the light of the moon and stars, like a wide ribbon touched by magic. He eased her blouse out from under the waistband of her skirt and began undoing the buttons. Reaching her camisole, he pulled the delicate fabric upwards until her breasts were bared.

Emma whimpered in pleasure as his thumbs passed lightly over the nipples, preparing them. Her fingers were already grappling with the buttons of her skirt; in another moment she was stepping out of it. She kicked off her boots, one by one.

"You'd be more comfortable on the ground," Steven murmured, his lips dangerously close to her breast by then, his breath fanning warm over the distended peak.

"I don't want to be comfortable," Emma gasped, as his mouth closed over her and he began to suck with a slow, soft hunger. "I want to be taken, not seduced."

"So be it," he said, and grasping the waistband of her drawers, he ripped them asunder and tossed them aside to lie like a fallen bird on the moonlit grass. He took off his gunbelt and then opened his trousers.

Emma felt the bark of the tree press its imprint onto her back as he plunged into her, catching her cry of shocked welcome in his mouth. All the while he was kissing her, Steven's hips executed a steady rhythm against hers, and his manhood stroked her furthest depths.

When Steven could no longer contain himself, he broke away from her mouth, his head back, his eyes closed. His hands gripped the trunk of the tree and the sweet friction his rod generated grew more intense with every passing moment.

Emma was panting, unable to catch her breath. Her whole being, her every sense was fixed on the act. She and Steven might have made love before, but on that night they mated, not just for life, but for all eternity.

The bargain was sealed in a heated fusion, invisible to the eye but blindingly bright to the spirit. Steven nibbled at Emma's lower lip as she poured out a long, low cry of final surrender, her body buckling against his. He buried his face in the quivering flesh of her neck and moaned as he gave up his seed.

They had both forgotten the cowboys and even the herd. After a few moments Steven righted his trousers, lifted Emma into his arms, and carried her down to the side of the stream. There he laid her on the soft, mossy bank, and gently washed her with the clean, cold water. This experience had a sensuality all its own, and Emma lay dazed when Steven went back to find her skirt and boots.

He brought them to the creek bank and dressed her tenderly. When she kissed him, she put a hand on his upper arm and felt the blood seeping through his bandage.

Her eyes went wide with alarm, and Steven smiled and kissed her again, in no particular hurry to have the wound attended.

But Emma could think of nothing else. She hastily buttoned her blouse, tucked it back into her skirt, and grappled to her feet. Holding Steven by the hand, she half-led, half-dragged him back to the camp.

She paid no attention to the cowboys lounging around the fire eating their dinner, but pressed Steven to sit in the back of the cook wagon, his feet dangling. She left him there to find Sing Cho and ask for hot water and another bandage.

Steven sat quietly while she worked—by the light of a kerosene lantern—to stop the bleeding, then bathed and inspected the injury.

"Some of the stitches have come out," she fussed to Sing Cho, who was squinting in the darkness and giving his handiwork a solemn inspection.

"Should not ride," Sing Cho scolded. "Should not herd cattle." He trotted away to fetch his satchel from the supply wagon.

"Should not make babies," Steven whispered, bending toward a worried Emma and kissing her on the tip of her nose.

Emma was blushing, remembering how wanton she'd been—she the seducer, and Steven the seduced. It was probably her fault that his sutures had come open. "Be quiet!" she said, out of guilt and impatience.

He grinned. "I hope I put a child inside you tonight," he said in a voice that was just a tone too loud for Emma's comfort.

She lowered her eyes, hoping the same thing, and more. She wanted the baby, but she needed for Steven to be with her all the while it was growing up, too. She had borne so much loss in her life: Grammie, her mother, Lily, Caroline. She could not lose Steven, too; the thought was incomprehensible.

"We can't go to New Orleans," she whispered. "We have to run—make a new start somewhere else—"

He laid an index finger to her lips just as Sing Cho returned with the dreaded needle and spool of catgut. "I want my birthright, Emma," he said with quiet sternness. "I want my share of Fairhaven."

"Enough to die for it?" Emma said in a strangled voice, as Sing Cho edged her aside to sew up the place where Steven's wound had split.

This time there was no whiskey to deaden the pain, and he grimaced as the needle bit into already tender, inflamed flesh. "I'm through running," he insisted. "It's time I fought for what's mine."

Emma turned away, unable to bear his suffering anymore, covering her eyes against the terrible images that flashed through her mind.

Ignoring the cowboys as best she could, she helped herself to one of the biscuits Sing Cho had made for supper and glumly bit into it. She didn't feel the least bit hungry, but when she got weepy and overemotional, it was a sure sign that she needed something to eat.

Half the men were lying on bedrolls on the ground while the other half took the first watch, keeping an eye on the cattle. Emma wondered where she was going to sleep, and whether she'd be safe if Steven rode out of camp with the second watch.

She took another biscuit and wandered back to where Sing Cho was just tying off the last stitch. Steven looked wan in the light of the lantern, but he smiled when he saw Emma. That distracted him from the fact that Sing Cho was opening a large brown bottle.

Just when Sing Cho doused the long cut with alcohol, Emma stuffed the biscuit into Steven's mouth and stifled what she was sure was a string of shouted curses.

His eyes narrowed, and his jaw moved angrily as he chewed and swallowed. "Damn it, woman," he rasped, "when something hurts as bad as that, a man has a right to cuss."

"You did enough cussing the first time," Emma replied, watching as Sing Cho wrapped a fresh bandage around his arm. When the Chinaman was gone again, she dared to ask the question that was uppermost on her mind. "Where am I going to sleep?"

"Under the supply wagon, with me," Steven answered. "We'd better turn in right now, because I want that herd moving at sunrise."

Emma's sense of propriety was a little belated, but it was strong nonetheless. "What will the men think?" she asked, her voice barely audible.

Steven grinned as he pulled blankets from the back of the wagon and tossed them at her. "I'm sorry to disillusion you, Miss Emma, but they've probably already figured out that you and I weren't picking gooseberries down by the creek tonight."

Once again Emma made the disturbing discovery that her hindsight was much clearer than her foresight had been. "Oh," she said.

Steven got down from the wagon to stand beside her, his eyes dancing even though they reflected pain and a deep, long-standing weariness. "If you've got any business to take care of, you'd better do it now," he told her in a companionable whisper.

Emma bit her lower lip. Tonight she could go in the bushes, but what would she do tomorrow, in the full light of day, when she was riding with a dozen men and a full herd of cattle?

"I'll stand guard," Steven offered generously, ushering her toward a cluster of bushes some distance from the camp. She only hoped they weren't the kind with brambles.

Self-consciously, but nonetheless compelled by nature, Emma went into the bushes, undid her skirt, and squatted. Her face went red with embarrassment when a pattering sound filled the night air.

"What do cowboys do in a situation like this?" she called out cheerfully, in an effort to drown out the noise.

"Think about it, Emma," Steven replied, with good-natured impatience.

Emma thought, and she felt envious. If there were no women around, they wouldn't even have to get off their horses, let alone find a bush to hide behind. It wasn't fair.

She dried herself with a clump of leaves, stood, and righted her skirt. When she came out of the bushes, Steven was just buttoning his trousers.

They walked back to camp in silence, and Emma was touched to find a basin of hot water and a rough towel waiting on the tailgate of the wagon. She knew Sing Cho

237

had left it for her, and gratefully washed her hands and face.

Steven, in the meantime, was spreading the blankets out on the soft, verdant ground under the wagon. When she'd tossed her wash water into the grass, Emma dropped to her knees and crawled beneath the wagon's floorboards to join him.

"How's your arm?" she asked, to hide the fact that she was feeling suddenly and inexplicably shy. It was as though she hadn't given her body to this man beside a creek only a short time before, or relieved herself within his hearing.

"It hurts like hell," he answered, but there was suppressed amusement in his voice. He drew her close, his uninjured arm beneath her, and gave her bottom a brazen squeeze. "Oh, for a bath and a bed, Miss Emma. If I could have those things, I'd keep you busy comforting me until the sun came up."

Emma arranged the blankets with one arm, her head resting on his chest. She could hear his heart beating strong and steady beneath her ear, and she didn't let herself think that it would ever be stilled by a hangman's rope. "You've had about all the comforting you can stand for one day," she answered.

He chuckled, and it was a homey, cozy sound. Emma could almost imagine that they were lying in a featherbed at Fairhaven, with their children sleeping down the hall and all their worries behind them.

She laid splayed fingers on his chest, letting his heart thump against her palm. *If You must take a life,* she told God in silence, *let it be mine and not his. It's selfish and weak of me, I know, but I couldn't bear to live without him.*

"I love you, Steven," she said.

He raised her hand to his mouth and kissed it. "And I love you, tigress. Good night."

Emma closed her eyes, certain she wouldn't be able to sleep, and immediately lapsed into a dream she didn't remember when Steven awakened her with a kiss hours later. He pressed the butt of a pistol into her hand—the one she'd borrowed from Henry back in Whitneyville.

"I'm going to ride second watch," he told her. "If anybody bothers you, shoot them."

That brought Emma wide awake. "What?"

Steven laid his fingers over her mouth. "You heard me," he answered.

Emma didn't want him to go. Without him there, she was conscious of the hardness of the ground, the chill of the night, and the strange, scary sounds that seemed to come from every direction. "But your arm—"

"My arm is fine," he replied. He was lying half on top of her then, and he put one hand boldly between her legs. Even through her skirt—her knickers were still in the bushes beside the creek—she felt the warmth of his hand and responded to it with a soft involuntary moan.

He gave her an insolent little squeeze and bent his head to kiss her, first sipping at her lips, then letting his tongue sweep the inside of her mouth.

Just when Emma thought she could forget there were other people around, just when she longed to take Steven into her body and make him one with her, he withdrew and crawled out from under the wagon.

Emma curled up in the blankets, the pistol lying a few inches away on the dewy grass, and tried to ignore the sweet ache he'd stirred in her body and then refused to satisfy.

Presently she drifted back to sleep and dreamed that she and Lily and Caroline were all together again. Only she was an adult, and her sisters were still children. She awakened at sunrise with a feeling of sadness wrapped around her heart.

For the first time it came to her that to follow Steven to New Orleans, she would have to give up practically all hope of finding Lily and Caroline. Putting the thought out of her head, she crawled from beneath the wagon, washed as best she could in the water Sing Cho had once again brought for her, and followed the scent of frying pork, coffee, and potatoes to the camp fire.

Steven was there, laughing with some of the men while they ate. He was wearing a clean shirt. Emma felt a pang, wondering if she was the subject of their amusement.

But when Steven looked in her direction, she saw gladness in his eyes. He nodded, and even though he didn't approach her or even speak, something intangible and reassuring passed between them.

Emma helped herself to a tin plate and a hearty breakfast, which she ate quickly because it was nearly time to move on again. She was folding the blankets she and Steven had shared during the night when he rode up beside her, his hat pulled down low over his eyes so she couldn't read his expression.

She tossed the blankets into the back of the supply wagon, and when Steven moved his foot out of the stirrup and offered his hand, she swung up into the saddle behind him.

"Hold on," was the only thing he said to her before he gave a shrill whistle and spurred the agile gelding into motion.

Emma gripped his middle for dear life and pressed her cheek against his shoulder blade. It was going to be a long day.

Throughout the morning Emma breathed dust and bounced ignobly on the back of Steven's horse. Her arms ached from holding on, and when her bladder was painfully full, there wasn't a bush in sight. She had plenty of time to consider how worried Chloe must be, too, since Emma had forgotten to send a wire from Rileyton.

At midday the scout rode back from up ahead to tell Steven there were Indians to the east. He immediately got off the horse and then mounted again, behind Emma.

She looked back at him in question, and he kissed her lightly on the mouth. "If anybody takes an arrow in the back," he said, "it isn't going to be you."

Emma was frightened, but she also felt protected and valued, and there was a certain contentment in that. If she could be close to Steven, she could face anything.

Uneasily, she thought of Macon and the others, riding

somewhere behind the herd. She was wildly afraid, but then she leaned back against Steven's chest, felt his strength and substance. For now she would live only in the moment, cherishing the hardships as well as the pleasures.

The future could damned well take care of itself.

# Chapter
## ≈ 17 ≈

*E*mma lay huddled beneath the supply wagon, her muscles aching from unaccustomed long hours on the back of a horse, too exhausted to join the others at the campfire for supper. Images of Steven's body spinning slowly at the end of a rope tormented her, and she hadn't the strength to hold them at bay.

Turning onto her stomach, she began to cry with soft, despondent snuffles. The sound was covered by the bawling of cattle, the talk of the men, the distant howling of a coyote or wolf.

Emma tensed when she felt a small hand come to rest on her back and turned to see Sing Cho squatting beside the wagon, holding a plate of fried potatoes and meat.

"Missy eat," he said kindly. His thin black queue rested over his shoulder.

Since there was plenty of room to sit up beneath the wagon, Emma did so, dragging one sleeve across her eyes to dry them. Her hands trembled when she took the plate. "Thank you," she sniffled.

The Chinese smiled, nodded slightly, and started to rise.

Emma stopped him by reaching out and taking hold of his thin arm. "Where is Mr. Fairfax?" she asked. She hadn't seen Steven since they'd made camp.

Sing Cho looked reluctant for a moment in the flickering light of the large bonfire and the kerosene lanterns set in strategic places around the camp. "He go back, talk to men who follow."

Emma nearly choked on a mouthful of potatoes. Macon. Steven had gone to his half-brother, the man who wanted more than anything to see him dead. "The fool," she sputtered, setting the plate down and starting to scramble out from underneath the wagon. "Did he go alone?"

"Missy sit down and finish supper," Sing Cho said. "Mr. Fairfax not alone. He take Mr. Deva."

She knew she needed all her strength, so Emma sat down and ate dutifully. She was still worried, though, and the food lay like rain-soaked newspaper in the pit of her stomach.

Sing Cho went back to his work.

Steven and Mr. Deva returned a half hour later, the latter leading the little pinto mare Emma had rented in Whitneyville. Flinging her plate down, forgetting her aching thighs and back and bottom, she raced to meet Steven, fury replacing her anxiety.

She watched him swing down from his gelding's back and hand the reins to Mr. Deva, who led both horses away toward the improvised corral on the far side of the camp.

Angry as she was, Emma remembered the rule Steven had imposed. "You're an idiot, Mr. Fairfax," she said clearly.

He was, though it seemed impossible, even dirtier than she was. His grin made a striking contrast against the dust-caked tan of his face. He took her by the elbow and hustled her around the side of the supply wagon, where they had a semblance of privacy.

"If you have further complaints about my intelligence, Miss Emma," he said with biting cordiality, "I'd appreciate it if you didn't voice them in front of men who work for me. It undercuts my authority."

"You could have been killed," Emma spat, too miserable to care what effect her words might have had.

"Macon isn't going to kill me," Steven assured her, his voice gentler now, his hands resting lightly on her upper arms. "That would be too easy and too quick. He wants to watch me suffer, Emma, and see me humiliated before the whole city of New Orleans."

Emma felt ill. She covered her face with both hands, but the torturous images were there, behind her eyelids.

Steven put his arms around her. "I've been having a lot of second thoughts about your coming to Louisiana with me, Emma. It's not just the trial. There's an epidemic of yellow fever sweeping the South." He paused and sighed, then went on. "We'll still be married, if that's what you want, but I think you should stay in Whitneyville, with Chloe, until the trial is over."

Her head flew back from his shoulder in her haste to look up at his face. "No."

Steven sighed. "I'll come back for you when I can," he promised.

"I'm going with you," Emma insisted feverishly. "I won't get sick and I couldn't stand being apart from you, waiting day after day to hear the verdict—"

He laid his gloved fingers to her mouth. "I don't think you understand what it will be like in New Orleans," he said. "I'll probably be arrested as soon as I step down from the train. Don't you see, we'll be separated for a while anyway?"

"I'm going with you," Emma repeated, her voice muffled by the front of his shirt, and she clung to him as though prison guards were even then trying to pull him away. "If you leave me here, I'll only follow you."

She felt Steven's chest move as he sighed. "You'd have been better off if you'd never met me," he said sadly, and then he freed himself from Emma's embrace and walked away.

She was too proud to go after him, so she went back to the wagon and crawled underneath, still wearing her boots and the big coat that kept her warm when the night air turned chilly. Stretching out on the blankets, Emma curled up into a ball and waited.

The epidemic seemed far away, unreal.

After an hour Steven joined her, smelling of sweat and dust and whiskey. He pulled her close and kissed her lightly on the temple.

She laid her hand on his upper arm and felt the bandage there. Sing Cho had checked the wound regularly; it was healing, and there was no sign of infection. All the same, she withdrew her hand quickly.

He gave her a nibbling kiss on the mouth, then lay down and closed his eyes.

Emma burned for his touch, for the peculiar comforts only he could give. "Make love to me, Steven," she whispered.

He chuckled. "We're not alone, remember?"

"I can be quiet, I promise."

"Well, I don't know if I can. Go to sleep, Emma."

"I can't. My whole body aches, and I want you." She laid her hand on him, took satisfaction in his effort to stifle the resulting groan and in the leaping hardness pressing against her fingers.

He rolled onto his side and began laying her bare beneath the blanket. "You know," he said with gruff resignation, "a few months in prison would probably do me good. I could catch up on my rest."

Emma gasped with pleasure when his cool fingers found her warm, plump breast and closed over it possessively. She laid her hands beside her head and bit down hard on her lower lip.

When Steven's lips replaced his hand, Emma was lost. Her groan of delighted acquiescence would have been heard all over the camp if Steven hadn't covered her mouth with his palm. When a fine mist of perspiration covered her body, and she felt she would die if Steven didn't satisfy her, he displaced her skirt with one hand and mounted her.

She arched against him, trying to take him inside her, but he only teased her with brief samplings of himself. His mouth moved close to her ear.

"This is going to be hard and fast," he warned huskily. "But don't get used to it. When I have you, I like it to be at my leisure. I like taking everything you have to give."

Emma trembled, her thighs widening as she felt him prodding her with his heat and power. She arched her back when she felt him enter her in a long, slow stroke.

He covered her mouth with his, while clasping her hands in his own and pressing them into the rough fabric of the blanket. He swallowed every moan and cry she gave as his body moved relentlessly upon hers.

She longed to writhe in her passion, but his possession permitted her to do nothing more than receive him. The sensations built until she couldn't sort herself into mind, spirit, and body, until she was not one woman, but all women. With every stroke he wound her tighter and tighter, like the spring of a watch. Then in a glorious, silent explosion, the spring spiraled outward in a spinning dash toward freedom.

Steven kissed Emma until she'd stopped bucking beneath him, until she was absolutely still, except for her trembling. She watched, dazed, as he bared his teeth, flung his head back and stiffened violently.

He fell to her, his breathing ragged, and she entangled her fingers in the hair at the nape of his neck, consoling him in his tremulous joy.

"I love you," he ground out when he was able to speak.

Emma moved to close her blouse, but Steven grasped her hands and stopped her. Pulling her onto her side, he slid downward until he could take a nipple into his mouth, and he sucked until exhaustion claimed him.

When Emma awakened in the dark hours just before dawn, Steven was gone. Buttoning her bodice, thinking that her whole life might one day consist of this same aching feeling of aloneness, Emma steeled herself against a fresh flow of tears and went back to sleep.

The coming days were much like that one. Riding the

pinto mare Steven had recovered for her, Emma did her best to keep up with the men. Although there were many times when she felt sure she would fall out of the saddle and just lie there on the ground, never to get up again, she persisted.

Hygiene was a problem, since she had no fresh clothes and no real opportunity to bathe. If they stopped near water, she always crept away and got herself as clean as she could, but these efforts were haphazard at best.

Late in the afternoon of the sixth day they came to the rim of a giant basin and saw the bustling little community of Spokane below, nestled in the curve of a narrow river. Dreaming of hot baths, of hours of sleep in a real bed and food that hadn't been cooked over an open fire, Emma drew strength from the sight.

Driving the caterwauling cattle along ahead of them, the cowboys whooped and whistled at the prospect of money, whiskey, and women.

The herd filled the main street of the city, spooking horses and sending ladies scurrying for the safety of shops and restaurants. Emma gazed with longing at a black sateen skirt and lacy white bodice displayed in one of the windows.

Steven, whose horse was close beside hers, gave her a nudge with his elbow. "Here," he said, handing her a sizable bill. "Buy whatever you need and check into that hotel we saw when we rode in. I'll be with you as soon as I've turned the herd over to the army."

Emma hesitated only for a moment before handing the money back. She wasn't comfortable taking funds from Steven, since he wasn't yet her husband, and she still had over twenty dollars of her own. She was returning his glare and preparing to turn and make her way through the sea of cattle, when she saw a tall, well-built man in an impeccable blue uniform step out of a building and stride toward them. He had gold epaulets on his broad shoulders and wide yellow stripes down the outside of his trouser legs. All in all, he was a most splendid sight.

Some curiosity made Emma linger. "What's his rank?" she asked Steven.

Steven's jaw was set, and his eyes had narrowed slightly in his dirty face. "He's a major," he replied, with a trace of bitterness in his voice.

"You the trail boss?" the major asked. At Steven's nod, he took off his campaign hat and dragged one sleeve across his forehead. Emma saw that he was fair-haired, with beautiful amber eyes, good skin, and teeth as strikingly white as Steven's. He had a tense look about him, though, as if something continually chewed at him.

Steven swung down off his horse and walked up to him, offering a recalcitrant greeting. "Hello, Yank," he said, and Emma closed her eyes. Leave it to Steven to start the war up again, just when everybody else was beginning to forget about it.

The major grinned. "Hello, Johnny," he responded easily.

"His name is Steven," Emma called out impulsively, standing in her stirrups. "Steven Fairfax."

For her trouble, she was rewarded with an over-the-shoulder glare from Steven and a laugh from the major.

"I know somebody like you," the handsome soldier said.

Steven's demeanor had softened a little, but he pointed at Emma nonetheless, and the narrowing of his eyes warned her to be about her business and leave him to his. "You have things to do," he reminded her.

Irate, but still eager for a bath and food and clean clothes, Emma dismounted and tethered her horse to a hitching post. After giving the major a broad smile, not for his benefit but for Steven's, she walked into the dress shop where she'd seen the skirt and blouse she wanted.

"Caleb Halliday, Mr. Fairfax," the Yankee said, offering a gloved hand.

Steven hesitated for a moment, then shook the major's hand.

His soldiers were already taking over the herd from Big John's cowhands. It made Steven nervous to see so many blue uniforms around all at once. He was anxious to get the papers signed, collect the bank draft, pay off the men, and turn his full attention to Emma. Nobody knew better than he did how precious their time together really was.

Halliday inspected a few of the cattle in a knowledgeable offhand way that commanded respect. Then he and Steven went into a saloon together and sat down.

Steven had taken refreshment in the presence of Yankees before, of course, but never one in uniform. Still edgy, he tossed back the first drink and promptly poured himself a second.

"How's Big John?" the major asked, and Steven saw real interest in his whiskey-colored eyes, along with a certain weariness.

Steven would have been willing to bet he had woman trouble. "Ornery as ever," he replied, scanning the papers Halliday had taken from the inside pocket of his gold-trimmed blue coat. "He would have made the trip himself, but he was busy with the branding."

The major nodded, still nursing his first drink. He was a pleasant sort, and Steven found it hard to dislike him.

They completed the rest of their business in record time, then Steven asked, "Where can a man get a hot bath around here?"

Halliday grinned, obviously remembering Emma. "There's a bathhouse just down the street, behind Finnegan's Saloon. Twenty-five cents for fresh water, five for somebody else's."

Steven nodded and stood, extending his hand to the major. "Thanks," he said.

Halliday shook his hand and then tucked his copy of the signed contract into his inside pocket. He acknowledged Steven's thanks with a nod and added, "Give my regards to Big John."

It wasn't hard to find the boys; they were lined up at

the bar, spending whatever they had left of last month's wages.

The herd was on its way to Fort Deveraux, under the care of the army, but the dust of their passing still roiled in the air.

Steven took the draft to the nearest bank, drew enough cash to pay the cowhands, then had the clerk write up a check made out to Big John. When he returned to the saloon to pay the men, the major was gone.

After giving each of the men their agreed salary for the drive, he left the saloon and headed for Sing Cho's supply wagon. He got clean clothes from the back and handed the Chinese his money.

The response was a polite bow of thanks.

Steven left Sing Cho and followed the major's directions to the bathhouse. At the door he paid a quarter, and a short man with grizzled hair and a tobacco-stained beard pointed to a row of cubicles curtained off with canvas. "Last one on the left," he said. "I'll have the hot water for you in a jiffy. You want a cigar and some whiskey? It's fifteen cents extry."

Steven nodded, and five minutes later, he was up to his chin in a tubful of clean, hot water, a glass of whiskey in one hand, a lighted cigar clamped between his teeth. He listened with amusement as men splashed and sang in the cubicles all around him.

When he'd finished the cigar and the whiskey, he set about scouring off the dirt and sweat of a week on the trail. When his hair was clean and his skin was back to its normal color, he climbed out of the water, dried himself with the coarse, frayed towel provided, and put on fresh clothes.

The old ones were so bad that, after retrieving his money, Big John's bank draft, and his copy of the contract with the army, he kicked them into the corner and left them for trash.

He was eager to get to Emma, but he forced himself to take the time to step into a barber shop. He had a close shave and got his hair trimmed, then went on to the hotel.

Emma might have spent the rest of her life in the deliciously hot, clean water the maids carried to her room, but she was hungry and tired, and she knew Steven would be back sooner or later. She wanted to be ready for him.

So, reluctantly, she got out of the tub and dried herself off. Wearing only the new camisole and knickers she'd bought at the dress shop, she combed out her wet, tangled hair and patiently plaited it into its customary braid. When that was done, she sat on the edge of the bed and waited for her dinner to arrive.

A maid brought it on a tray, and Emma hid behind the changing screen until she was gone because she didn't have a wrapper to cover herself.

The moment she heard the door close, she dashed out and attacked the pork chops, boiled corn, mashed potatoes and gravy she'd ordered earlier. When she'd eaten the last scrap, an incredible weariness came over her.

She put the dinner tray on the bureau, pulled back the covers on the crisply made bed, and crawled between the starched sheets. The moment she closed her eyes, she was asleep.

She awakened sometime later to the caress of a cool breeze and opened her eyes to see Steven bending over her with a mischievous grin. He'd tossed back the covers and his eyes moved boldly over Emma's lush figure.

"I'd almost forgotten there was a woman under all that dirt," he said.

Emma stretched like a cat, pointing her toes, reaching high above her head with her arms. Steven was clean-shaven, and his brown hair was neatly trimmed. His chest was bare, and Emma realized he'd already taken off most of his clothes.

A delicious sense of the inevitable swept over her, and she started to lower her hands only to have Steven grasp her at the wrists and prevent the motion. With his free hand he undid the pretty ribbon ties that held her camisole together, and Emma trembled with anticipation when he laid the thin fabric aside.

"Today," he said hoarsely, "I'm taking my time. Be prepared to put in a very long afternoon, Miss Emma."

Then he released her and sat down to pull off his boots.

Emma traced the muscles in his bare back with a lazy finger. "When are we getting married?" she asked.

"As soon as we're through with our honeymoon," he replied with a grin, standing up to unfasten his trousers. The Colt .45, Emma saw out of the corner of one eye, was resting within reach on the bedside table, as always.

Presently Steven stretched out beside her, his hand deftly working the ties on her drawers. He smoothed them away as skillfully as usual and then maneuvered Emma so that she was kneeling astraddle of his hips, the weight of her torso resting on her elbows.

Then he slid beneath her until he could take a nipple into his mouth.

Emma moaned without restraint as he sucked, yearning to feel him inside her. As he'd promised, however, Steven took his time.

When he'd had his fill of both her breasts, he caught hold of Emma's waist and slid even further downward, until she was fully vulnerable to him. He parted the moist curtain of silk and teased her with his tongue until she was half delirious, her palms sweating where she gripped the metal railings of the headboard, her neck arched.

A fevered litany fell from her lips as she submitted, and the headboard rattled as she rode a fiery steed toward a vision of light and fire. His hands clasped her tensing buttocks as the blazes enveloped her.

Emma's climax had been a violent one, fierce and seemingly endless, and she collapsed when it ended, her cheek pressed to the pillow, her breath coming in gasps. Surely, she thought, Steven would let her rest before he asked any more of her.

She felt his hand move beneath her. He found the hard, pulsing scrap of flesh he'd just mastered with his tongue and plied it between his fingers.

Emma moaned. "Steven—oh, please—just a few minutes—"

He kissed her bare shoulder and intensified his efforts, and soon Emma's knees were spread wide to receive him. She clutched at the headboard again, keeping her head turned away from Steven.

"Look at me," he ordered as several of his fingers went inside her.

Emma could no more disobey him than she could stem the searing passion that was about to set her to pitching wildly on the mattress. She turned her head toward him and he watched, rapt, as her face mirrored the breathtaking sensations he created in her.

Finally, with a little cry, she gave up the struggle. Color suffused her face and her eyes glazed with ecstasy as she convulsed, her moisture dampening his hand.

She turned onto her back when it was over, in a daze of need. No matter how many times Steven brought her to the pinnacle, her satisfaction would never be complete until he took her beneath him and made her unquestionably his own.

His control was monumental, and he was far from the point of taking her. That knowledge gave Emma the strength to shift to her knees, facing him, the boldness to meet his eyes even as she clasped his shaft in her hand.

He gave a strangled moan as her thumb caressed the tip, and he plunged his fingers into her hair when she lowered her mouth to him. During the next minute or so she repaid him in spades for all the times he'd made her dance at the end of a string.

At last, with a rasp of desperation, he caught her shoulders in his hands, forced her backwards onto the mattress and came into her with the grace of a diver plunging into a glistening lake.

His hands clasping her bottom, lifting her for his driving strokes, he covered her face with fevered kisses, then her neck and her breasts. He let loose a moaning shout of triumph when his seed was wrung from him, and Emma joined him only a split second later.

They fell asleep, their arms and legs still entwined, with the cool spring air swirling in from the open window to surround and soothe them.

The judge was a nervous, florid-faced little man with a snow-white mustache and no hair at all on top of his head. He wore a striped suit, and his watchchain seemed stretched to the breaking point across his belly.

"You're sure you want to do this now?" he had asked, chewing on a cigar as he perused the marriage license Emma and Steven had purchased only minutes before. "A weddin' is serious business. I don't want one or the other of you back in here in a week's time, wanting out of the contract."

"We're sure," Steven said, as Emma lowered her eyes and blushed. She and Steven had been tossing on that hotel room bed on and off for twenty-four hours. If they didn't get married—and soon—God was probably going to strike them both with lightning.

"What about you, young lady?" the judge demanded.

"I'm sure, too," she said timidly.

At that, the old man fetched a book from his desk drawer, wet a fingertip on his tongue, and began flipping through the thin pages. Finally, he came to the place he wanted and cleared his throat ceremoniously.

Frank Deva and the judge's old-maid sister stood by as witnesses and, when it came time for the exchange of rings, Steven surprised Emma by producing a wide gold band and slipping it onto her finger.

The marriage took less than five minutes, by Emma's reckoning. She signed the license with a trembling hand and took a moment to admire her new name.

Steven looked as happy as she felt when he scrawled his signature with a flourish.

Frank and the judge's sister congratulated them both, then they left. Steven was to drive the supply wagon back to Big John's ranch, his horse and Emma's tethered to the rear of it, while Sing Cho drove the chuckwagon.

Macon rode up beside them just when Steven was releasing the brake lever, the reins clasped in his hands. "I hear congratulations are in order, little brother," he said, and his tone and smile gave the words a tinge of acid. His eyes roved brazenly over Emma. "It'll be a pleasure to console your widow."

Steven's fingers flexed, and Emma knew he longed to close them over the butt of his pistol. "I can still kill you, here and now," he said evenly. "We could be in Canada before you were cold."

Macon's face tightened with hatred, but he said no more. He simply wheeled his horse around and spurred it hard.

Throughout the day Emma was horribly aware of the little band of men traveling just a few hundred yards behind them.

That night, and for the five nights following, when she and Steven and Sing Cho camped, they could see Macon's fire almost as clearly as their own. The specter of Steven's trial hovered over them constantly, even when they were alone in their makeshift bed in the supply wagon, locked in the sweet combat that is passion.

Six days had passed when they reached Whitneyville.

Chloe and Daisy both came running down the walk, Chloe smiling and chattering, Daisy scolding. They both embraced Emma when Steven lifted her down from the wagon.

"I'll be back as soon as I've talked to Big John," Steven told her, planting a light kiss on her forehead.

Emma nodded and watched as he drove away.

"There's a letter for you," Chloe said, her arm around Emma's waist as she hurried her toward the house. "Did I tell you how much we missed you around here, and how mad we were that you just took off without a word?"

"I'm sorry," Emma said, but she didn't explain because the situation was too complicated. She showed Chloe and Daisy the wide gold band on her finger and told them she was Emma Fairfax now, and that she'd be off to New Orleans within the week.

Chloe hugged her, her eyes brimming with happy tears, and produced the letter she'd spoken of.

Emma's heart all but stopped beating when she opened it. It was a brief note, written in a vaguely familiar hand, and it was signed Kathleen Harrington. Emma had to read the whole thing over twice before she comprehended that her mother had found her, after all these years, and written a letter begging her to come to her in Chicago. She'd included a seven-hundred-and-fifty-dollar bank draft, specifying that Emma was to use it for any purpose she chose.

Sitting there in the parlor rocking chair, her eyes closed against years of pain, confusion, and anger, Emma tried to make sense of a tangle of conflicting emotions.

# Chapter
## ❧ 18 ❧

*E*mma watched as Steven read the letter from Kathleen and set it aside on the table in Chloe's parlor. "You realize, of course," he said gently, "that if she's found you, she might have located Caroline and Lily too."

"Yes," Emma said softly, stubbornly. She'd had the same thought, but had been almost afraid to hope, due to the many disappointments she'd suffered in the past.

"Your mother deserves a chance to explain herself," he said. His tone was eminently reasonable and insistent. "She might be very different now from the woman you remember."

Emma shook her head. "A person like that doesn't change, and kindly don't refer to her as my mother. That was a role Chloe filled. I want nothing from Kathleen Harrington."

"Not even to know the whereabouts of your sisters? After all these years, when you're on the brink of finding Lily and Caroline, you're just going to give up?"

"Of course not!" Emma pushed herself out of her chair

because she couldn't let it contain her any longer. She stood with her back to Steven, staring sightlessly at the fireplace, her hands clasped together with such force that the knuckles showed white. "I'm going to write to her and ask her about them."

"You could go back to Chicago now," Steven reasoned, standing just behind her. His hands gripped her shoulders lightly, and she drew a certain strength from his nearness. "It would give you something to think about while I'm—while I'm settling things in New Orleans."

Emma turned in his embrace, her color high with the heat of her conviction. "I love my sisters, and I want desperately to find them." She paused and sighed, her blue eyes searching his face. "I never thought anything or anybody could be more important to me than they are," she went on. "But that was before I met you. We'll go to Chicago together, Steven, when the trial is over."

He drew her into his arms and held her in silence, knowing she'd made her decision and nothing would sway her from it.

Chloe's yard was decorated with streamers and colorful paper lanterns, and a little band of musicians played pleasant tunes on a platform at one end of the lawn. Tables laden with food drew women in gauzy organdy dresses and men in Sunday suits, and little children zigzagged throughout, chasing each other and laughing with glee.

Dressed in an ivory silk dress with a low, ruffled bodice, fitted waist, and full skirt, Emma watched the townspeople enjoying Chloe's picnic. The phenomenon was nothing new, really. "None of them would speak to her on the street," she said to Steven, who stood beside her, wearing a suit and holding a cup of punch in one hand. "But when Chloe gives a party, they trip over themselves to show up."

She felt Steven's finger curve under her chin and turned to look into his face. "You're going to miss Chloe a lot, aren't you?" he asked softly.

Emma swallowed, even though she had yet to lift her cup to her mouth, and nodded. "I don't know that I could have survived without her. She was always there when I needed her."

Steven set her punch and his own back on the refreshment table, took her hand, and led her toward the quickly assembled wooden platform that served as a dance floor. As the music started up again he pulled Emma into his arms, and they were both oblivious to the couples spinning around them.

For a few moments Emma was able to put her worries out of her mind. This was something she could manage only when Steven was making love to her, or when she was gazing directly into his face, as she was now. She was a creature of sunshine, living only in the moment, and Steven whirled her around and around the floor until she was breathless.

When the music stopped, she was laughing, but the sound died in her throat when Fulton walked boldly up to them and said to Emma, "May I have this dance?"

After a glance at Steven, Emma nodded, and Fulton waltzed her away.

"Surprised that Chloe invited me?" he asked.

Emma executed a slight shrug. "Not really. It looks to me like she's invited everybody in the county."

Fulton favored her with an awkward, halfhearted grin. "I was quite stunned when I heard you'd actually married," he ventured to say. "And now you're planning to travel all the way to New Orleans with him."

She was annoyed, but only mildly. After all, it was understandable that Fulton would be surprised, and besides, once the train left on Monday morning, she'd probably never see him again. "Mr. Fairfax is my husband," she answered.

Fulton looked exasperated. "There is talk, Emma. People are saying Fairfax is going to hang. Where will that leave you?"

Emma stiffened, then told herself she shouldn't have been shocked. Macon had probably regaled everyone who was willing to listen with stories of Steven's sins. "I believe he's innocent."

Her dance partner gave an indulgent little smile. "Let's hope the jury agrees with you."

The party was, for all practical purposes, Emma's wedding reception, and she resented having it spoiled with cruel reminders of what might lie ahead. She and Steven were trying hard to live in the moment, but it seemed that no one else wanted to let them.

She deliberately changed the subject. "There's Joellen Lenahan," she said, as the now-subdued girl arrived with her father. According to Chloe, Joellen would be leaving for boarding school in Boston within the week, with Big John's spinster sister Martha escorting her on the train ride.

Fulton took no notice of the Lenahans. His face was slightly red and he cleared his throat. "About the other night—when I—when I was not a gentleman. I'm sorry for that, Emma."

Emma was not one to bear grudges, excepting the one she had against Kathleen, of course. "It's forgotten," she said.

When the dance ended and Fulton had walked away, she sensed someone standing directly behind her and made an eager turn, expecting to see Steven. Instead, Emma found herself looking straight into the eyes of Macon Fairfax. Before she could flee, or even speak, he pulled her into a dance.

"What are you doing here?" she sputtered angrily. She tried to push away, but he was strong and her efforts were ineffectual.

Macon arched one eyebrow. He resembled Steven in the way a caricature might, and while he was handsome, there was a rough-edged coldness in his manner that made him unappealing. "I can't believe you're startled, Miss Emma," he said. "My men and I have never been more than a stone's throw away since the day I caught up to Steven on the trail drive."

Emma blushed furiously, wondering what private

things he might have heard or seen, if any. Then anger took over, as she remembered how he'd kidnapped her and held a gun to her neck. "Steven didn't kill your son," she said quietly. "Or that poor Mary McCall."

"My half-brother is a persuasive man," Macon answered smoothly, but his brown eyes snapped with controlled hatred. "I see he's used his considerable charms to convince you that his heart is pure as the driven snow."

Again Emma tried to pull away, but her hand was grasped tightly in his and his fingers were digging into the small of her back. Her eyes swept over the other dancers and the picnickers, searching for some sign of Steven. He was talking with Frank Deva when she spotted him, and he seemed to feel her gaze, for he immediately looked in her direction.

He'd obviously thought she was still dancing with Fulton, and when he recognized Macon, he strode toward them.

Macon pulled Emma very close, so that her forehead touched his and her breasts were crushed against his chest, and his words washed over her face, warm and foul with abhorrence. "When you get to New Orleans, and my dear brother is out of the way, I'll have to teach you not to spread your legs for killers," he said. And then he turned and hurried away.

When Steven passed her, Emma reached out and caught his arm. "Let him go," she whispered brokenly. "Just let him go."

Steven hesitated for a long moment, then turned his back on Macon's retreating figure and took Emma gently by the hand. "Let's go and have some of that cake Daisy baked for us," he said quietly.

After the cake, photographs were taken. Emma wondered, as she posed in Chloe's parlor, standing solemnly behind Steven's chair with one hand resting on his shoulder, whether she would look at the pictures in later years and see signs of the strain she was feeling now.

She was grateful when the photographer had finished,

and so blinded by the exploding flash powder that Steven had to lead her out of the room.

"What did he say to you?" he demanded, when they were alone in Chloe's study, with the doors closed.

Emma rubbed her eyes. "Who?" she replied, stalling.

Steven only looked at her, his expression wry, his jawline tight.

A headache pounded at the base of her skull and she sighed, wishing she could go to her room and lie down with a cold cloth on her head. They both knew Steven was talking about Macon, but Emma didn't dare admit the man had threatened her again. Steven would get furious, maybe violent, and he might insist on leaving her in Whitneyville until the trial was over, or sending her to Chicago.

"He only wanted to dance," she said, avoiding her husband's eyes.

Steven caught her chin in a rough but painless grasp. "Once and for all, Emma," he breathed, "don't lie to me. I won't tolerate it, not even from you."

Tears gathered in Emma's lashes. "He said—he said he'd have to teach me n-not to spread my l-legs for killers, once you were gone."

Steven's face contorted with rage, and he whirled away from Emma and stormed toward the door. She ran after him and caught hold of his arm. "One murder trial is enough," she cried. "Please, Steven—let it pass!"

She watched as a variety of ferocious emotions moved across his face. Finally, Steven shoved the splayed fingers of his right hand through his hair and said, "I want to kill him." He folded that same hand into a fist and slammed it against the wall. *"I want to kill him."*

"I know," Emma said gently. "But it wouldn't be worth sacrificing all the years ahead, Steven."

He drew her close and held her, and his lips moved in her hair. "When I'm acquitted of killing Mary, the first thing I'm going to do is make love to you. The second thing is beat the hell out of Macon."

Emma smiled up at him. "When I get through with

you," she promised, full of bravado and hope, "you won't have the strength to beat the hell out of anybody."

Steven chuckled hoarsely. "Is that so?" he retorted. "Well, maybe I'd better take you upstairs right now, Mrs. Fairfax, and find out if you're bluffing."

"You'll just have to wait until evening, Mr. Fairfax," Emma responded airily. "I intend to enjoy our wedding party."

"That was exactly what I had in mind." Steven grinned.

Emma laughed and shook her head, her fears lost again, at least temporarily, in the boundless love she bore this man.

Joellen Lenahan glanced distastefully around Marshal Woodridge's dirty, cluttered little office. She was afraid she'd spoil her new organdy dress and was anxious to get back to the party. God knew, once she got to Boston, good times would be few and far between.

"I don't know why that silly old man had to pick today to retire," she fussed, as her father systematically went through the wanted posters pinned to the wall, throwing most of them away.

"Be quiet, Joellen," Big John said impatiently. "Clean out the desk or something."

Joellen gave a longsuffering sigh. "The party isn't even over," she complained, as she pulled open the middle drawer in the marshal's desk and glared down at the mess of papers and letters inside. "You could have let me stay at Chloe's while you did this."

"One more word, Joellen . . ." her father warned, without turning around. "Just one more word."

Lower lip jutting out, she scooped the contents of the drawer out onto the top of the desk and began to look through them. There were more posters, most of them old, and a few letters and telegrams from marshals in other towns.

Casually, Joellen dropped them all into the trash.

One small blue envelope intrigued her, perhaps because the handwriting looked feminine. With a saucy little smile, Joellen prepared for the discovery that toothless old Marshal Woodridge had been carrying on a romance with some widow lady in—she checked the return address—the Washington Territory.

Deftly, for Joellen had had a great deal of practice at snooping without her father finding out, she opened the envelope and unfolded the single page inside.

At first, because the missive obviously wasn't a love letter, Joellen was disappointed. Then with an indrawn breath, she realized that the sender had been none other than Miss Lily Chalmers, one of the lost sisters that snooty Emma Fairfax had been searching for all these years.

Thinking of how she'd lost Steven to Emma, of how their passion was plain to see whenever anybody bothered to look, Joellen saw her chance for revenge, and she took it. She stuffed the letter into her handbag and spoke in a sunny voice to her father, who was just turning to look at her.

"Anything interesting there?" he asked.

Joellen shook her head. "Just a lot of wanted posters for outlaws who've been dead or in prison since before I was born."

Big John sighed and hooked his thumbs through his belt loops. "I must have been crazy when I agreed to be mayor of this town." He was frowning thoughtfully. "Maybe I could get Frank Deva to sign on as marshal. He'd do a good job, but I'd hate to lose him—"

Joellen couldn't have cared less who became marshal of Whitneyville. She just wanted to go back to the party and dance and flirt, all the time knowing she had the letter from Emma's sister tucked away in her handbag. "Don't you think I'm old enough to wear my hair up now?" she asked, wanting to change the subject to a more interesting topic, like herself.

Big John scowled. "After running off through Indian country like you did, you're lucky you *have* any hair."

Her most recent exploit was a topic Joellen had no

desire to pursue. "May we go back to the party now? Please?"

The rancher shoved a hand through his thinning white hair and nodded. "I want to talk with Deva anyway."

Although she wouldn't have dared say so, Joellen figured it was Chloe Reese her daddy wanted to see, and talking was probably the last thing on his mind.

Steven felt restless as he sat in the Stardust Saloon that evening, wanting to go back to Chloe's house, lead Emma upstairs to her bedroom, and make sound love to her. But she and Chloe were engaged in some kind of heartfelt talk, and he wanted them to have their time together.

He was relieved when Big John Lenahan entered the saloon, scanned the faces at the bar and tables, then approached Steven with a smile.

"Mind if I join you?"

"Sit down," Steven said, signalling for another glass. When it came, and Big John was seated across from him, he poured a drink from the bottle he'd ordered earlier.

"You get run out of the house, too?" the rancher asked good-naturedly, after he'd tossed back his first drink and poured another. "Damn if that isn't an improvement over strawberry punch," he said.

Steven grinned. "Right on both counts," he answered.

"We're going to miss you around here, Fairfax," Big John remarked. "You were a good foreman, and you would have made a fine marshal, too."

The idea made Steven smile again. After all, he was wanted for murder in Louisiana. He would have been an ironic choice to serve as a United States marshal. "I've got some things to tend to down home," he said.

Big John nodded, sipping his second drink, and Steven looked around him at the dancing girls in their bright, flimsy dresses and at the lewd paintings on the walls.

"I'm still a little shy of saloons," he admitted. "After what happened to me in the Yellow Belly that day."

Big John guffawed at that, but his expression was

serious when he said, "There'll always be work for you on my ranch, if you ever decide to head back up this way."

Steven acknowledged the offer with a nod. "I'm glad there aren't any hard feelings about Joellen."

Lenahan chuckled. "She's a wildcat," he said fondly, "but I reckon she'll grow out of it. Thanks for looking after her when she ran off, and for not taking advantage of her. A lot of men would have, you know."

"Joellen was going to tell you I'd compromised her. Frankly, I was a little surprised when you didn't even ask me about it."

John laughed again. "Oh, she told me that, all right. I just didn't believe her, is all. Heard about the spanking, too. Fact is, I was grateful, since it saved me the trouble of tanning her hide myself."

The two men drank in companionable silence after that, watching the dancing girls and listening to their bawdy songs, accompanied by the tinkling chimes of a tinny piano.

When Chloe came in, dressed in her usual finery, and approached the table, both Steven and Big John stood up.

Chloe smiled, pleased by the small courtesy. "You can go home to your wife now, Mr. Fairfax," she said to Steven. "Emma and I have had our little talk. As for you, Big John Lenahan," she went on, and her voice changed subtly, becoming lower and huskier, "I'd like a word with you. In private."

Big John actually blushed, to Steven's profound amusement, but he nodded, and when Chloe started toward the stairs, the towering rancher followed eagerly.

Steven was grinning as he laid a coin on the table to pay for his whiskey and walked out of the noisy, smoke-filled saloon.

The moment he stepped outside, Macon materialized out of the darkness, as quickly as if he'd been a part of it.

"Just making sure you don't decide to take to your

heels again," Steven's half-brother remarked as they walked along the wooden sidewalk.

"I'm not going to do that and you know it," Steven responded, never looking at Macon. "You just want to make me as miserable as you possibly can."

"You don't know the meaning of the word misery," Macon answered blithely. "But you will when you're behind bars and I'm bedding that luscious little wife of yours. She'll claim not to like it at first, probably, but I've dealt with her kind before. They tell you they're not interested, but when you throw them down on a mattress, they're breathing hard and spreading their thighs for you in a minute. And how they carry on when they come."

Steven lost the battle to control his rage and gripped Macon by the lapels of his coat, flinging him hard against the outside wall of the newspaper office. He followed that with a solid punch to Macon's solar plexus.

Macon made a sound that was half gasp and half laughter, clutching his middle and struggling to catch his breath. "Your mother was just like her," he choked out. "She was a hot little whore who liked playing games with rich men."

Steven's hand knotted into a fist again, but this time he held himself in check, realizing that Macon *wanted* to be struck. He got some kind of perverse pleasure out of it.

Filled with contempt, Steven turned to walk away.

"You'll be swinging at the end of a rope by this time next month," Macon called after him. "And nine months after that Emma will be sweating in childbirth, bearing the first of my bastards!"

Steven's hand flexed over the butt of his pistol, but he didn't draw. He just kept walking, pretending he hadn't heard.

But Macon had left lurid images in his mind. His stomach churned, and bile scalded the back of his throat.

As always, the thought of Emma was his salvation as well as his damnation. He saw her in his mind's eye, laughing as she stuffed wedding cake into his mouth, and quickened his pace. By the time he caught sight of Chloe's house, a glow in the darkness, he was almost running.

It struck him, as he rushed toward the woman he loved, that he'd been reckless with his life, not much caring whether he kept it or lost it. Now, because of Emma, every breath and heartbeat was precious to him.

Reaching the gate, he made up his mind to leave her behind, to spare her the dangers and horrors like yellow fever awaiting them in New Orleans. By the time he'd gained the porch, however, he knew there was no way she'd allow him to go without her.

He was going to have to trust his granddaddy and the good Lord to take care of her. He had every confidence in Cyrus, though in his experience the Lord was a little on the undependable side.

Emma stood before the full-length mirror in her room, wearing the frothy white nightgown Chloe had given her as a special gift, and thinking about the long talk she and her guardian had had.

Squeezing Emma's hand, Chloe had sighed and told her, "I've always been sorry I didn't follow after that damnable train and make them give me Lily. At least the two of you could have been raised together. But the truth is I was pretty overwhelmed at having just one daughter."

She'd told Chloe she understood, and it was true.

There was a brief tap at the bedroom door, then it opened and Steven came in.

"I was beginning to think you might be one of those husbands who spend more time in the saloons than at home," Emma remarked.

Steven's eyes moved over her, leaving her feeling as though warm, sweet oil had just been massaged into her skin. "Believe me," he said, his voice low, "in the next forty or fifty years, you're going to find out I'm another kind of husband entirely."

She felt deliciously vulnerable, standing close to him in a gossamer nightgown that revealed hints of her secrets, and when Steven tossed his coat and hat into a chair and took her in his arms, she was breathless with excitement.

She loosened the string tie at his throat and then let her hands rest on his shoulders. "I'm so glad you got blown up in the Yellow Belly Saloon that day," she said. "If you hadn't, I might never have met you."

His grin was slow and his eyes danced. His hands, in the meantime, were smoothing the cloud-soft fabric away from her shoulders. "I would have preferred to make your acquaintance at a dance, Miss Emma. Or maybe in the library."

Emma gazed at him steadily as the nightgown fell to her waist, revealing her full breasts to Steven's lazy inspection. He circled each nipple with the tip of one finger, then bent his head to kiss her mouth.

At first the contact was tenuous and soft, but it changed subtly, until Emma's arms were around Steven's neck and his tongue was mating with hers. She gave a little whimper when she felt the gown fall in a pool around her bare feet.

She pulled Steven's shirt from beneath his belt, and her fingers were resting lightly, urgently on top of his as he unbuckled his gunbelt. It disappeared from Emma's awareness, along with his boots and shirt and trousers.

They were both still standing when Steven laid his hand at the junction of Emma's thighs and parted her. She drew in a harsh breath when she felt his thumb begin caressing her, moaned softly when he put his fingers inside her.

"Steven," she whispered.

He kissed her on the mouth again, nibbled at her lower lip as she pleaded with him in senseless words.

Presently Steven withdrew his hand and positioned Emma on the edge of the bed. He soothed and coaxed her into the position he wanted, then entered her womanhood slowly from behind.

His hands stroked her thighs and stomach and breasts as he began to move inside her.

She felt the familiar friction, and it was heightened by the novelty of being taken in such a primitive way.

Steven paused, just when Emma was shuddering on the brink of fulfillment, to kiss her shoulder blades and spine. He was breathing as hard as Emma was.

Angry, she gasped out, "Why did you stop?"

"I want it to last," he answered and then, blessedly, his hips began their slow, steady thrusts again.

Emma clutched the bedspread in her fingers when pleasure finally overtook her. Her eyes widened as one wave after another rolled over her, causing her bottom and abdomen to contract repeatedly in violent response. A low, continuous moan rolled from her throat, and Steven held her breasts the whole time, rolling the pulsing nipples between his fingers.

Moments after Emma had fallen silent, so sated that she would have collapsed onto the bed if Steven hadn't taken a firm grasp on her hips, she felt him moving, rapidly and fiercely, within her. To her surprise, her body buckled in a second, unexpected response while Steven groaned and filled her with warmth.

She fell onto her back when he freed her, staring sightlessly up at the ceiling, her chest rising and falling rapidly as she struggled to catch her breath. Unexpected tears stung her eyes when Steven stretched out beside her.

He wiped them away with his thumb. "Don't," he said.

"We have too much," Emma whispered brokenly. "They'll never allow us to have so much—"

"Shh," Steven said, kissing her eyelids and then her mouth. But secretly he feared she was right, and Emma knew it.

# Chapter
## ❧ 19 ❧

*E*mma twisted a lace-trimmed handkerchief in her lap as the steam whistle blew and the passenger train rattled into motion. Seated beside her, Steven reached out and covered her hand with his own. She shifted her gaze to his face.

"Is this the first time you've ridden a train since you came west from Chicago?" he asked gently.

Emma nodded. Heaven knew, she'd come to the depot nearly every single week for the past seven years, passing out posters and searching for the women Lily and Caroline might have grown up to be. Somehow, though, actual travel on board the "iron horse" brought back a welter of painful memories.

"Tell me about it," Steven said, lifting her hand briefly to his mouth and brushing the knuckles with a soft kiss.

People usually didn't want to listen to Emma's account of that long ago train trip. They said things like, "But everything turned out all right, and you've had a good life, haven't you?" and, "Don't think about it. Put the past behind you." Even Fulton, who might have become

Emma's husband if Steven hadn't come along, had discouraged her from talking about her separation from her sisters. She stared at Steven in mute surprise.

*I'm listening,* his expression said.

Emma cleared her throat and began. "We lived in Chicago. Mama was a very pretty woman, and I'm sure she meant well, but she was weak. And she liked men." She paused to bite her lower lip for a moment. "Lily and Caroline and I all went by the name Chalmers, but I don't remember a father, and I'm pretty sure none of us had the same one . . ."

Steven heard her out patiently, and they were well away from Whitneyville by the time she'd told him the entire story, plus a little about the years she'd spent with Chloe.

"Tell me about you," she finished, struck by how little she really knew about this man she'd married.

He sighed and settled back against the coarsely upholstered seat. "There isn't much to tell. My mother was a rich man's mistress, and she had me. I lived with her until I was six or seven, then I was sent to live at St. Matthew's, a school for boys. Maman died when I was fourteen, and I was feeling pretty alone in the world. When her lover—my father—died, I went to the cemetery and stood outside the gate, watching the ceremony.

"My granddaddy saw me there and came over to talk. Cyrus told me I belonged at Fairhaven, with the rest of the family. I had my doubts about that, and I still do, but I liked the idea of belonging somewhere, so I went.

"Things were pretty damn difficult, but I developed a real affection for Cyrus, and I got along all right with Macon's wife, Lucy.

"The war was on, and the Yankees sailed right in and took over New Orleans—and Fairhaven. I stole a uniform off the clothesline and wore it past the sentries posted on the roads, pretending to be a messenger. As soon as I was safe, I threw the clothes away and joined up on the Confederate side.

"After General Lee's surrender, I came back to New Orleans, and for a while it looked like I'd finally made a place for myself. Then the incident with Dirk happened, and Mary's murder. I ran that night, and I haven't been back since."

Emma let her temple rest against Steven's shoulder and squeezed his hand in hers. They'd each been lonely, both as children and as adults, and it gave a bittersweet dimension to their love. "Maybe we should go to Chicago, Steven, and forget all about New Orleans."

"I wouldn't recommend it," put in a third voice.

Steven closed his eyes for a moment, but Emma turned her head to see Macon standing behind their seats, an obnoxious smile on his face.

For the rest of the trip, which took a full five days, Macon was always nearby, making a point of sitting across the aisle, or just behind or in front of them. When they went to the dining car, he followed and chose a table within sight of theirs, and when they retired to their sleeping compartment, he invariably rapped at the door and called out a companionable, "Good night."

Steven and Emma slept little over the course of their journey; because they knew they might soon be separated forever, they made love well into the early hours of the morning.

The air was hot and muggy when they reached New Orleans, even though it was still early in the day, and Emma had little interest in the strange and beautiful surroundings. She could think only of losing Steven.

With much fanfare, the train whistled and steamed and rattled to a stop at the depot. Steven pulled Emma close and gave her a long, searching kiss before standing up and offering his hand.

"Welcome home," Macon said, appearing in the aisle behind them. "I've arranged for a little party in your honor."

A muscle in Steven's cheek bunched, but he didn't

respond to Macon's remark. He just put his arm around Emma and held her close for a moment while he gathered his courage.

As Emma had half-expected, there were two U.S. marshals waiting on the platform. The moment Steven stepped down from the train, they moved in to block his way.

"Steven Fairfax?"

Emma's heart had stopped beating, and she held on tightly to her husband's arm as he nodded.

"You're under arrest for the murder of Mary Davis McCall," the elder of the two men said solemnly, pushing back his suitcoat to unhook a pair of handcuffs from his belt.

Emma looked wildly about for help, even though she knew there would be none. Her husband was being dragged off to jail, and she was alone in a strange city where a plague was raging.

Steven's hands were bound behind his back. He didn't say a word to the marshals, nor did he resist them in any way. He simply looked at Emma, his eyes begging her to understand. Then his gaze shifted to Macon.

"Touch her," he vowed in a low voice, "and I'll feed you to the gators, piece by piece."

Macon grinned as a white-haired man with pale, bushy eyebrows approached. He was wearing a light-colored suit, like most of the men around him, and there was a black string tie at his throat. His blue eyes were gentle as they moved from Steven's face to Emma's, and he extended a hand to her.

"Hello, Emma," he said simply.

Emma's gaze shifted to Steven as he was led away roughly, and tears gathered on her lashes, blinding her. She wanted to scream that he was innocent, but she knew that would only make bad matters worse.

While a smug Macon watched Steven disappear, the old man smiled at Emma and offered her his handkerchief. "Since my grandson hasn't troubled himself to introduce us," he said, with a sour glance at Macon, "I'll do the honors. I'm Cyrus Fairfax, and now that you've joined the family I consider myself your granddaddy."

Emma dried her eyes and squared her shoulders. She would be no use to Steven if she crumpled into a heap of self-pity and despair. "I'm Emma," she said, even though she realized he already knew that. "And my husband didn't kill anyone."

"I tend to agree with you," Cyrus replied, laying his hand lightly on the small of Emma's back and steering her toward the steps of the platform. "While we're waiting for the rest of the world to come around to our way of thinking, we'll get to know each other."

Emma's gratitude was almost as overwhelming as her despondency. If it hadn't been for Cyrus's appearance at the station, she would have been left alone with Macon. And that was a prospect she certainly didn't relish.

Linking her arm through Cyrus's, she blinked away the last of her tears and smiled up at him. He led her to a waiting carriage and helped her inside, then joined her. Since the rig rolled into motion the instant Cyrus was seated, it was plain they weren't going to wait for Macon.

Emma sank back in relief.

Fairhaven was north of the city, it turned out, and the first sight of it jarred Emma out of her difficult reveries. It was a massive, pillared white house with sloping green lawns. Lovely magnolia trees with pink and lilac and white blossoms lined the long driveway, the slight breeze stirring their lush fragrance.

Although Emma had known that Steven was not poor, she had never once guessed the extent of his family's wealth, and she turned questioning eyes to Cyrus.

"Didn't he tell you?" the old man asked, his weary eyes twinkling just a little.

Emma shook her head. It seemed ironic to her now that she hadn't wanted to marry Steven when she'd first fallen in love with him because she thought he couldn't offer her the same position and respectability Fulton would have.

The carriage stopped in front of the house and a small blonde woman came running out. She was dressed all in black, and Emma found herself wondering if someone had died. Perhaps the fever had already visited this grand place.

"That's Lucy," Cyrus confided, as he waited for the driver to open the carriage door for them. "She's Macon's wife."

Watching the woman approach, an eager expression on her china-doll face, Emma felt pity for her. "Did someone pass away?"

"Lucy is mourning her dreams," Cyrus said sadly, and then the door swung open.

"Did you bring her?" Lucy demanded. "Is she here?"

Cyrus chuckled and reached up to help Emma down from the carriage. As he did so, she felt an alarming cramp shoot across her lower abdomen, and bit her lip to keep from crying out.

Lucy's eyes were large, their color a rich brown, and her skin was as flawless as the finest English porcelain. Eagerly, she took Emma's hand. "It'll be so good to have another woman around," she said in a gentle drawl. "I don't mind telling you that I've been feeling positively outnumbered ever since I came here."

She must have read the look of bafflement in Emma's eyes, for she laughed and added, "You're wondering how we knew you were coming, aren't you? Well, it was easy—Steven sent us a wire. He didn't want you left to Macon's mercy, you know."

Emma was awed that Lucy could speak so blithely of her husband's skulduggery, then saddened: Lucy was used to Macon's cruelty—so used to it that she seemed to assign it the same importance as his boot size or the date of his baptism. "I'm glad to meet you," Emma said, realizing she hadn't acknowledged the woman's greeting.

"Look at her, the poor dear," Lucy clucked, putting an arm around Emma and shuffling her toward the gaping door. "Here she's been on that awful train for nearly a week, with hardly any rest and probably nothing decent to eat, and I'm keeping her out on the step like a peddler."

The cramps in Emma's middle intensified, and she thought she felt a warm moistness between her legs. She knew long before she reached the sunny room allotted to her that the baby she'd hoped and prayed for didn't exist. All the signs of her monthly period were here.

"You probably want a bath and some tea," Lucy said, smiling at Emma.

Emma nodded glumly.

"There's a tub right in there," she said, pointing to an arched doorway on the far side of the room. "Jesse— that's our manservant—will bring up your baggage as soon as it arrives from the station. In the meantime I can lend you a wrapper if you'd like."

"You're very kind," Emma said sincerely.

When Lucy was gone, Emma ventured through the doorway her sister-in-law had indicated and found, as promised, a tub. It was long and deep, with claw feet painted gold.

Emma put the plug in place and turned on the spigots. As soon as she was sure the sound of running water would drown out the sound, she lowered her face to her hands and sobbed.

By the time her bath was over and a maid had brought in Lucy's wrapper, Emma was feeling a little better. She assured herself that she and Steven would have the opportunity not only to make babies, but to raise them together. He needed her to be strong now, and she was determined not to let him down.

She asked a shy young maid for clean rags and when the tea arrived, brought by a smiling Lucy, she was relatively composed.

Macon's delicate wife set the tray on a table near the window and Emma sat down across from her in the fading afternoon light. Lucy's black dress looked hot and uncomfortable. Once again Emma heard Cyrus's words echo in her mind: *Lucy is mourning her dreams.*

"It's kind of you to make me so welcome," Emma ventured.

"I don't suppose Steven told you much about us," Lucy said, waving away Emma's remark with a flick of one pale and slender hand. "Macon despises him, as you probably know, but Cyrus and Nathaniel and I consider him part of the family."

"Nathaniel?" Emma inquired as Lucy poured tea into a bone china cup decorated with tiny pink flowers and held it out to her. Steven had never mentioned the name.

"This family is so complicated," Lucy sighed, filling her own cup. "Nathaniel is really a cousin to Macon and Steven. We took him in after his daddy died in the War of Northern Aggression, you know." Her brown eyes lit up at some pleasant memory. "He was hardly more than a baby then. I looked after him as if he were my very own."

Thinking of her own disappointment, Emma asked, "Do you and Macon have children?"

The words seemed to go through Lucy like a lance. She stiffened in her chair and her face contorted, just for the briefest moment, in a spasm of pain. "The dear Lord never blessed us with a child," she said in a soft voice edged with confusion and a sense of betrayal. "It was remiss of Him, don't you think?"

Emma nodded, sorry she'd brought the subject up. She certainly hadn't meant to hurt the only female friend she had in the whole of Louisiana. "Forgive me," she said gently.

Lucy patted her hand, beaming again. For the first time Emma noticed that there was something frenetic about that smile. "Never you mind. We're going to get on famously, you and I. Steven will be exonerated, and the two of you will *fill* Fairhaven with babies."

"I hope you're right," Emma said distractedly, gazing sightlessly out on a garden brimming with flowers. It was as though the blossoms had become transparent; through them she saw Steven, his hands bound behind his back, being led up the steps to a gallows.

* * *

Emma slept, albeit fitfully, until Lucy came and gently awakened her.

"It's time for dinner," her sister-in-law said.

Emma sat up, confused for a moment, wondering where she was. Expecting to find Steven lying beside her.

"You're at Fairhaven," Lucy told her quietly.

Calling upon all her strength of character, Emma refused to cry. "Have my clothes arrived?" She noticed Lucy had not changed from her grim black dress.

Lucy nodded. "Jubal has put them all away for you," she said. "You'll need new things, you know. Yours just aren't fitting for New Orleans."

"Jubal?" The last thing Emma cared about was the state of her wardrobe. She got up and found a simple blue cotton dress in the armoire, then took fresh underthings from the drawers in one of the two bureaus.

"She's your maid, darlin'," Lucy said in a good-natured, scolding tone. "Her mama was a slave, you understand. But of course, Jubal is a free person."

Emma thought freedom must be a little baffling, when a people had been enslaved so long. Without commenting on Jubal's status in the scheme of things, Emma went behind the ornamentally carved folding screen in the far corner of the room and dressed.

Dinner was served in a massive dining room downstairs, boasting no less than three chandeliers and a long, shiny wooden table lined with chairs.

Emma thought it was a miracle that such gracious items had survived an occupation by the enemy, and Cyrus must have read the reaction in her eyes, because he smiled as he stood up in honor of her and Lucy's appearance and said, "We were fortunate that our conquerors were gentlemen."

Macon, who had not bothered to rise, flipped open his table napkin and made a barely audible sound of contempt. "Gentlemen," he spat.

As Cyrus drew back her chair, Emma deliberately pretended Macon wasn't there and shifted her gaze to the thin, gawky boy seated across the table from her. He had a shock of rich brown hair and large gray eyes, and he seemed about as glad to see her as Macon would have been to see a battalion of Yankees.

"You must be Nathaniel," she said pleasantly.

For a moment, he glared at her. Then after tossing a defiant look at Cyrus, he announced, "They'll hang Steven, and he deserves it."

"Leave the table," Cyrus said flatly, without even looking in the boy's direction.

Nathaniel shoved back his chair and stormed out of the room.

"Are you going to send me away from the table, as well?" Macon inquired of his grandfather, his voice cool.

"If I have to," Cyrus responded.

Macon fell silent, and Lucy tried to distract everyone with chatter. Even for Emma, who liked the woman wholeheartedly, it was draining to listen to her.

She was grateful when Cyrus turned the conversation to the family business. "We're in cotton, primarily," he told her, "though we have timber interests, too. As well as gold."

"Federal gold," Macon elaborated bitterly.

Cyrus ignored him. "Fortunately, we transferred most of our investments to Europe at the first rumblings of war. All we suffered was a little inconvenience."

Lucy broke into the conversation again. "Emma will need new clothes," she announced, embarrassing her sister-in-law, who was made to feel like a shabby found-ling. "None of her things are at all suitable."

"I suppose yours are?" Macon remarked, giving his wife's somber attire a contemptuous once-over.

Lucy paled slightly and patted the glistening blonde chignon at the back of her head. Her eyes never quite linked with Macon's. "Her requirements are quite different from mine," she said tightly.

"Emma shall have whatever she needs," Cyrus broke in, and his tone effectively put an end to the exchange between Macon and Lucy. They went back to ignoring each other.

Dinner was a lengthy affair, but it finally ended, to Emma's enormous relief. She wanted to be alone to think about Steven and the trying times ahead, and perhaps to write a letter to Kathleen in Chicago.

She was seated at the desk in the room she and Steven would, she hoped, share soon, trying to compose the letter, and at the same time, endure the painful menstrual cramps that had dashed one of her most cherished dreams, when the doorknob jiggled. Knowing that Cyrus, Jubal, or Lucy would have knocked, Emma sat up very straight in her chair and held her breath.

She had absolutely no doubt that the visitor was Macon, and she couldn't be sure he didn't have a key. After all, he'd probably lived in this house all his life.

The knob turned again, and there was a light, cautious knock. "Emma," a voice called. It was male, but too young and uncertain-sounding to be Macon's.

She crept to the door. "Nathaniel?"

"Yes," came the answer.

After only a moment's hesitation—Nathaniel hadn't exactly bent over backwards to make her feel welcome—she unlocked the door and opened it a crack.

The youth was standing in the hallway, looking disarmingly like a very young version of Steven. Her own sons, should she be fortunate enough to bear any, would probably look much like Nathaniel when they reached this age.

"I didn't mean what I said about Steven," he said miserably.

Emma stepped back to admit him, even though she was wearing her wrapper and her hair was falling free. She'd brushed the fiery tresses, but hadn't gotten around to braiding them again. "Still," she said shrewdly, "you're very angry with him for some reason. What is it?"

Nathaniel swallowed, Adam's apple bobbing in his throat. "He shouldn't have run off like that—after Mary turned up dead and all. Now everybody thinks he's guilty."

"Not everybody," Emma said, folding her arms. "I don't, and neither does Cyrus. Or Lucy."

"Lucy!" Nathaniel huffed disrespectfully. "She's just a crazy woman. What does it matter what she thinks?"

"You," Emma told him directly, "are a very rude young man. I'm not sure I like you."

Surprisingly, Nathaniel looked injured. "Nobody would take Lucy's word for anything," he said, softening his argument this time. "She's got that room with the cradle inside and everything, and there's no baby. Everybody knows she's loony."

"What room?" Emma asked, startled.

"Down the hall," Nathaniel answered, gesturing. "I'd show you, but she keeps it locked most of the time. There's a cradle in there, and she rocks it and sings and stuff like that." He paused to shiver. "It's peculiar."

Emma was filled with pity and concern. She made up her mind to be a loyal friend to Lucy, no matter what. "Life can't be easy for her, being married to Macon Fairfax."

Nathaniel ran his tongue nervously over his lips. "Soon as you see Steven," he said hastily, glancing once toward the door, "you tell him I kept all his things for him. I took good care of them."

Emma nodded, and once Nathaniel had left the room, she closed the door and locked it again, then went back to her letter. She would send it out as soon as possible, and deposit the seven hundred and fifty dollar bank draft in an emergency account.

If Steven was convicted, she would need the money to escape New Orleans.

The jail was a dismal place filled with the smell of sweat and rotting souls, and Emma hung on to Cyrus's arm as they waited to be admitted to a visiting room. If she hadn't been so determined not to let Steven see her cry, she would have given way to a torrent of tears. She kept a handkerchief over her nose and mouth, at Lucy's suggestion.

Steven was still wearing yesterday's clothes when she

saw him again, although, typically, he'd shed the suitcoat and string tie. His hair was rumpled from running his hands through it, and his eyes had already taken on a hunted look.

At the sight of Emma, though, he smiled and leaned across the table to kiss her. She didn't tell him there was no baby growing inside her, sensing that that was something he was clinging to in order to get through those dark days.

"Are you all right?" he asked.

"Never mind me," Emma scolded briskly. "What about you? Have they hurt you?"

Steven shook his head, but Emma wasn't comforted. He sat down on the other side of the long, scratched table that separated visitors from prisoners. Emma and Cyrus followed suit.

"I'm doing everything I can to get you out of here, boy," Cyrus assured his grandson. "The fact that you ran away once before doesn't make it easy."

Steven's hands were gripping Emma's on the table top, and he was obviously reluctant to look away from her even long enough to acknowledge his grandfather. "If I'm convicted, Granddaddy," he said, "I want Emma put on the first train north. Is that understood?"

Emma sat up straight in her chair. "You're not going to be convicted, Mr. Fairfax," she said firmly. The habit of addressing Steven formally when they were in the presence of anyone else had long since taken hold. "You're innocent."

"That doesn't always matter," Steven argued, gripping her hands a little tighter. His eyes searched her face. "Emma, are you sure you're well? You look pale."

"Of course she's pale," Cyrus pointed out gruffly. "The man she loves is locked up in the hoosegow."

Smiling for the first time since she'd arrived in New Orleans, Emma said, "I have a message from Nathaniel. He says he's kept your things for you."

Steven allowed himself a slight, sad grin. "He's forgiven me, then?"

Cyrus interrupted with a *harumph*. "Forgiven you?

He's a Fairfax. My guess is, he won't do any forgiving until he's come after you with a bullwhip and you've tanned his hide for him."

Emma winced, and Steven gave her hands another squeeze. "I can still handle Nathaniel," he reminded her.

A guard came to stand behind Steven's chair, and although he gave Cyrus a deferential look, he spoke roughly to the prisoner. "Visit's over, Fairfax."

Slowly, Steven stood. He held Emma's hands, running his thumbs over the knuckles, then turned and walked away.

Emma's heart, broken for the first time on an orphan train years before, cracked in all the mended places. Gently, Cyrus took her arm and led her away.

"I can't bear it," she sobbed in the privacy of the carriage.

Cyrus pressed her head to his shoulder and patted her back. "Now, now, Emma, darlin'. You *will* bear it, because you have to. Your husband is depending on you."

Emma nodded, but she couldn't stop crying.

"I was real proud of you in there," Cyrus comforted. "You did just fine for a Yankee."

Emma reared back to look into his face and laughed, despite everything, at the mischief she saw in his wise, gentle eyes.

"Does it bother you that your grandson married a northerner?" she asked, when she'd recovered herself a little and her sobs had subsided to sniffles.

Cyrus smiled. "If you can get used to a bunch of Rebels, we can get used to you. Now, it seems to me that Miss Lucy was right. You're pretty as a magnolia blossom, but you need some new clothes."

With that announcement, Cyrus rapped at the back of the carriage wall and the elegant vehicle came to a stop.

"Yes, sir, Mr. Fairfax?" the driver asked, getting down from the box to peer in through the window.

"We want to go to that fancy shop where Miss Lucy used to have her things made," Cyrus told him.

The driver nodded, and then the carriage was moving again.

Soon Emma was being measured for dresses and skirts, ballgowns and blouses, all of the highest quality and latest style. It was ironic, she thought, since she would gladly wear burlap if she could just be with Steven.

# Chapter

## ❧ 20 ❧

$G$arrick Wright had been Steven's best friend at St. Matthew's throughout the war and during his days as a prodigal. Now Garrick was his lawyer. Despite his reputation and eloquence, it took him a solid week to effect his client's release on bail.

"I was finally able to convince Judge Willoughby that if you were willing to come back here and risk your life to clear your name you weren't likely to light out if he set bail," Garrick told him as they walked out into the fresh air, a blue sky arched above them. "He did, and Cyrus paid it."

Steven rotated his shoulders once, feeling as though he'd spent the last seven days standing in a dark, narrow closet. He smiled when he saw his grandfather step down from a carriage waiting in the street, his hand extended.

"Where's Emma?" was his first question.

"She's at home," Cyrus answered immediately. "I didn't want to get her hopes up until after bail was set."

Steven ached to touch her, to lie beside her, to hold her and be held by her. He couldn't get back to Fairhaven fast enough. He climbed into the carriage, leaving Cyrus and Garrick to follow after him.

Garrick, who was tall, with slicked-down fair hair parted in the middle, and mirrorlike gray eyes, settled in the seat across from Steven's, beside Cyrus. "Who else could have killed Mary?" the young attorney asked, speaking as much to himself as to his companions.

Steven glanced in his grandfather's direction, cleared his throat, and said, "Macon might have done it. God knows, he wouldn't hesitate to frame me."

Cyrus shifted uncomfortably on the seat, without offering a comment. Even though there was no love lost between him and his eldest grandson, the old man had a deep regard for kinship. He clearly didn't like thinking Macon might be guilty not only of murder, but of bearing false witness.

"Did he have another motive? Murder is a big risk to take, just because you want to set someone else up." Garrick's reasoning was sound, as always.

"That's what we need to find out," Steven answered grimly. He was having a hard time keeping his mind on the conversation, crucial though it was. Not a minute had passed during the last week that he hadn't thought about Emma and yearned for the sweet consolations of her presence. "I didn't come back here to hang," he added after a long time. "I want to make a life for myself, and for Emma."

"You must," Garrick sighed, "to take a chance like this. Frankly, I wouldn't have advised you to return. We might have been able to settle things with you at a safe distance."

When they reached Fairhaven, Steven deliberately hesitated to leave the carriage, detaining Garrick with a look. When Cyrus had gone inside and they were alone, he said, "Find out if Macon had any ties to Mary, beyond her dalliance with Dirk."

Garrick nodded, and a cautious grin curved his lips when he glanced toward the elegant house. "Is that Emma?" he asked.

Steven turned to see her standing in the doorway, clad in a gold silk dress. "Yes," he said, breathing the word because he didn't have the strength to say it. He stepped out of the carriage and stood beside it, just looking at her. Memorizing every curve and line of her face and her body, storing away the image of the sunshine catching in her glorious coppery-blonde hair.

A myriad of emotions moved across her face before she flung herself down the marble steps and into his arms.

Steven held her very close and closed his eyes for a moment, just to savor her nearness. "I love you," he said, his lips moving lightly against her temple, and she trembled in his embrace, then looked up at him fearfully, as though she didn't believe he was really there.

"There's no baby," she whispered brokenly, blurting the words as if the knowledge had been a burden too heavy to bear.

He was eager to console Emma, to touch and hold her freely. "It's all right," he said gently, and it was. After a moment, they went into the house.

Neither of them spoke again until they'd reached the privacy of their room, with its massive four-poster bed, lace curtains, and gracious view of the garden.

After locking the door, Steven turned to Emma and drew her into his arms again.

He felt so solid and so strong. Emma spread her hands out against his chest and tilted her head back for his kiss.

It was full of hungry restraint. He shaped her lips with his own, then sought entry with his tongue, and Emma granted it willingly, a little moan of surrender sounding in her throat.

His hand rose to the outer rounding of her breast, his thumb stroking the nipple that pulsed beneath the low-cut bodice of her new silk dress. "You were all I thought about," he breathed, his lips moving against hers. "Oh, God, Emma—I need you so much."

She smoothed away his jacket, reached for his belt

buckle, and unfastened it with awkward hands. He cupped his hands around her bottom and pressed her to him while she opened his shirt. She felt his hard power against her, trembled at the knowledge that it would soon be deep inside her.

Pushing aside the front of his shirt, she spread her hands over the hairy expanse of his chest and felt his nipples harden against her palms. She whispered his name in an anguish of need.

He released her bottom to deal with the buttons at the back of her dress. When he'd undone them all, he pulled down the soft bodice. She was wearing no camisole, since the gown was revealingly cut, and he drew in an audible breath at the sight of her swollen pink-tipped breasts.

Emma felt his trembling, knew he was struggling with the need to take her swiftly, fiercely, without any of the intimate preparations he usually made. And Emma wanted to be taken, like the woman of a primitive warrior.

He pushed her dress down over her slim, rounded hips, only to find a starched petticoat beneath.

He smiled at that and dispensed with the ruffled, ribbon-trimmed garment, leaving Emma standing before him in a pool of white satin and gold silk, wearing only her taffeta drawers and black velvet slippers.

The drawers had pink ribbons for ties, but Steven didn't move to touch them. Instead he whispered gruffly, "Take them off."

Quickly, Emma untied the ribbons and pushed the taffeta knickers downward, stepping out of them. A soft breeze from the windows caressed her satiny skin as she stood there before him, utterly naked, and her nipples peaked to a tautness that was almost painful. Instinctively she folded her arms across her chest.

Steven took hold of her wrists, however, and made her show herself. His gaze was warm, making her feel as though she were bared to direct sunshine.

"So beautiful," he said.

He led her to a chaise longue beneath the billowing lace curtains at the windows and spread her there, legs apart, feet touching the soft Persian rug. His eyes never left her as he stripped off his shirt and tossed it aside, then kicked off his boots and removed his trousers and stockings.

Gilded in sunlight, he seemed perfectly formed to Emma, like a man from a Greek myth. His rod stood high and hard and proud, and Emma's eyes were drawn to it, though she blushed at the sight.

"Give me your baby," she whispered.

He came and sat astraddle of the chaise, his knees touching Emma's. His eyes burned into hers, vaguely troubled now, as he laid both hands to her breasts, fondling them until she whimpered and arched her back slightly.

Steven chuckled at her fiery submission, his hands moving down over the sides of her waist, along her hips. His thumbs met on her abdomen, making small, interlocking circles just above the silken nest where her womanhood throbbed.

Presently he lifted Emma's right knee so that her foot rested on his thigh. He did the same with her other knee, and she tensed and closed her eyes when she felt him part the curtain that had hidden her from him.

His three middle fingers slid inside her, while his thumb caressed the hard, moist nubbin so completely vulnerable to him.

"Steven," she pleaded.

"Shh," he said, and bent to take slow suckle at one of her breasts, all the while continuing his brazen mastery of her body.

"Take me," she whispered. "Please—oh, *Steven*—make me yours—"

He went to the other breast, and was greedy in his enjoyment.

Emma's knees went wide of each other and then tried to close—the pleasure was too intense to be borne—but Steven blocked them with his shoulders. Leaving her breast, he kissed his way down the inside of her right thigh, making the flesh quiver beneath his warm, moist lips. Then gripping Emma's ankles in both hands, he slid downward.

Gruffly, he gave an order, and with trembling, hasty hands, Emma parted herself for the most brazen of pleasuring.

He set her to moaning by giving her several long, slow laps with his tongue. Then he sucked her, as voraciously as he had feasted at her nipple, and Emma's hips writhed in surrender.

Finally, in the throes of a passion so keen that it left no room for decorum or restraint, Emma climaxed, her body buckling beneath Steven's ruthless attentions.

But when he had satisfied her fully, he turned away. After long moments of standing silently with his back to her, he wrenched on his clothes and left the room without a word.

Despite the sweet hum in her body, Emma was wounded. Perhaps Steven was already growing tired of her, wishing he hadn't married with such haste. Perhaps he didn't love her anymore.

She curled up in a quiet part of her soul, too shaken and confused to weep, and went to sleep.

Holding a ball at Fairhaven was Cyrus's idea. He wanted to show the entire parish, he said at dinner one night soon after Steven's release, that the Fairfaxes were presenting a united front, irrespective of the epidemic. That they would stand together in asserting Steven's innocence. Emma was surprised to hear Macon would be there.

On the night of the ball, she avoided him carefully, lifting the skirts of her embroidered blue organdy dress as she mounted the stairs in search of Steven.

In the hallway outside their room, she encountered Lucy. To Emma's disappointment, her sister-in-law was dressed in black, as always.

Emma smiled at her and swallowed a suggestion that

Lucy borrow something of hers to wear to the ball. Lucy gazed at her with red-rimmed eyes, looking for all the world like a mourner fresh from a funeral.

"Is everything all right?" Emma asked, reaching out to touch Lucy's arm.

Lucy nodded a little frantically, and while Emma knew the gesture for an unspoken lie, there was nothing she could do about it.

Reluctantly, Emma left her sister-in-law in the hallway and entered the bedroom she shared with her husband. Although the strain of his impending trial showed in the lines of his shoulders and the distracted look in his eyes, and he had taken to sleeping in another room, Steven was bearing up well. He and Garrick met every day to discuss strategy, and sometimes they went out together for hours at a time.

"Nervous?" Emma asked, standing behind Steven as he scowled into the mirror, battling his tie.

"No," he lied, and Emma stepped in front of him and took over the recalcitrant tie.

"It's important that you seem confident," Emma reminded him softly, her hands resting on his lapels now. Because she loved Steven so much, she was trying hard to put aside her own questions and fears for his sake. "Some of those people downstairs will probably serve on your jury."

"How many times do I have to be tried?" he rasped impatiently. "Emma, it could be *months* before my case comes to trial—"

She stood on tiptoe to kiss him gently on the lips. "Don't try to deal with the whole thing all at once," she scolded. "You've got to take one day, one hour, one moment at a time. We all do."

Steven sighed. "You're right," he conceded, laying his hands gently on the sides of her waist and letting his forehead rest against hers. And then he changed the subject. "Did you ever write to your mother in Chicago?"

"Yes," Emma said. "Naturally, I haven't heard back

yet—it's much too soon. I wrote to Chloe, too, of course, to let her know we got here safely."

He kissed her forehead, then stepped away. There was mischief mingled with the weariness and strain in his eyes when he went to the armoire, opened the carved mahogany doors, and took a sizable box from the shelf.

Emma was seated on the bed by this time, and he brought the box to her and laid it in her lap. She looked at it in confusion. "What—"

"My mother's jewels," Steven explained, and though his voice was hoarse, his manner was almost offhand. "They're about all she had to show for her years with my father, except for me, of course. They were hidden in the wine cellar during the occupation."

"I don't understand," Emma said, staring at him.

"They're yours now," he replied, with a gesture meant to convey that if she didn't want to wear the jewelry, he'd understand.

Emma lifted the lid slowly, and her eyes were met by a dazzling diamond choker set with dozens of stones. Beneath it were pearls with a milky glow to them, and an amethyst ring that would reach from knuckle to joint. There were bracelets of emeralds and rubies, and topaz earrings encircled with diamonds.

Emma was so overwhelmed that she slammed the box closed and stared at Steven with wide eyes.

He took it gently from her hands, opened it, and lifted out the diamond choker. Then he put the magnificent piece around her neck and fastened it.

Emma blinked as he pulled her to her feet.

"Don't you like them?" Steven asked, his voice low and gruff, his eyes searching hers.

"Of course I like them," Emma whispered, her fingers rising to touch the band of perfect stones at her throat. "It's just that—well—I never expected to have anything like this—"

His hazel eyes danced as he looked down into her face. "Not even as a Whitneyville Whitney?" he teased.

Emma gave a strangled little laugh and socked him

ineffectually in the shoulder. "No. Not even as a Whitney."

Steven's finger curved under her chin. "Someday our daughter will wear them."

His words reassured her slightly, even though they reminded her of all that was at stake. Happy, productive years together. Children who might never be born. Laughter and tears that might never be shared. Her throat constricted, for the boxful of jewels paled by comparison to all she would lose if they were to find Steven guilty and hanged him.

"Now, now," Steven reproached her huskily, reading her thoughts in her eyes. "Who was it who just told me to live in the moment, and let the future take care of itself?"

Emma drew a deep breath, let it out again, and nodded. She was ready to face the people who had been arriving at Fairhaven for the past hour. Steven put the jewel box back into the armoire and offered his arm to Emma, and she took it.

They descended the stairs arm in arm, their smiles bright and confident, betraying no hint of what they both feared. He put his arms around her for the first dance of the evening. When that ended, Cyrus took Emma from group to group, proudly introducing her as his new granddaughter, while Steven renewed his acquaintances with still other guests.

Although she had hoped to, Emma wasn't able to evade Macon, and ended up waltzing around the ballroom in his arms. Remembering Cyrus's wish for the family at least to *seem* unified, she smiled up at him woodenly and tried to endure the enforced contact.

Obviously enjoying her dilemma, Macon made a point of reiterating his plan to make Emma his paramour. "We'll begin the evening of his funeral, I think," he said, grinning as furious color rose in Emma's face. "You'll need consoling."

Emma was fairly quaking with rage, but she kept her smile in place and replied, "I'd sooner be a swamp rat's mistress than yours!"

Macon threw back his head and laughed at that, and it made Emma fume to realize the people around them probably thought the exchange was an affectionate one. "Your spirit only makes you more appealing," he said presently. "I'll break it, I assure you, if Steven's hanging doesn't do it first."

Saliva gathered in Emma's mouth, but she didn't quite have the nerve to spit in Macon's face. "It might not be Steven who hangs," she blurted out on some wild and ill-advised instinct. "Perhaps the real murderer will be brought to justice."

Catching her implication, Macon went pale with fury and lapsed into a stony silence.

When the dance ended she offered a silent prayer of thanks and turned to flee. Flushed and angry, she fairly collided with an outraged Steven, who took her none too gently by the arm and dragged her out of the ballroom and into the garden. He didn't release her until they were standing beside a moonlit marble fountain. It was covered with moss, and the flow of the water made an eerie sound.

"What the hell are you trying to prove?" Steven bit out.

Emma wrenched her arm free. "I don't know what you're talking about," she retorted, and although she sounded indignant, what she actually felt was hurt.

"You were dancing with Macon," Steven pointed out, practically spitting out the words like watermelon seeds.

Emma bridled, her hands on her hips. "Yes, I was. And I told *him* a thing or two."

Steven was suddenly still. Ominously still. "Like what?"

"I let it be known that he isn't above suspicion where Mary McCall's murder is concerned," Emma said proudly.

Steven sputtered a string of swear words as he released Emma and turned away to shove a hand through his hair in frustration.

"What's wrong?" Emma asked, rounding him and looking up into his eyes.

"Garrick has been investigating Macon," Steven told her. "There was reason to believe he was involved with Mary somehow. Now that he knows he's under suspicion, he'll probably cover his tracks."

Emma calculated the cost of her rash words and was devastated. She lifted one hand to her mouth. "I was only trying to help—"

"From now on," Steven interrupted harshly, "keep your help to yourself."

Stunned, she turned and fled, not into the house where everyone could see her crying, but into the darkness.

"Emma!" Steven called after her, but she ignored him.

She took refuge in the gazebo, where she crumpled onto a dusty bench, covered her face with both hands, and sobbed. She cried for a long time, giving way to all the emotions she'd been holding in check.

She was startled when she felt a hand come to rest on her back, and whirled on the bench, expecting to see Macon or Steven, either of whom she would have slapped soundly across the face.

But it was Cyrus who sat beside her. Wordlessly, he took Emma into his arms and held her. She relaxed against his chest, trusting him utterly. He didn't ask what had upset her, because he knew.

"What will you do if Steven's convicted?" was his question.

At first, Emma couldn't face the thought. Then she allowed the nightmare to take root in her mind and answered. "I'd go away—maybe to Chicago or New York—and try to make a life for myself."

"You wouldn't stay at Fairhaven?" Cyrus asked and, for all of it, he sounded surprised. Even a little wounded.

She told him about Macon's repeated threats and felt his arm stiffen around her shoulders.

"I'd protect you," he said after a long time. Then with a sigh he added, "But, of course, I'm an old man."

Emma caught one of his hands in both of hers and squeezed it. "I can't tell you how much your kindness has meant to me. You've been so good to Steven——many men would have refused to acknowledge him, let alone take his side in a murder case."

Cyrus smiled sadly. "He's got my blood flowing in his veins."

Emma frowned. "Why does Macon hate Steven so much?"

He sighed. "Because he knows Steven's a better man than he is. And that makes Macon damn dangerous."

Emma gazed up at the summer moon riding above the tops of the magnolia trees. "Sometimes I'm so afraid," she confided in a small voice, "that I don't think I can get out of bed and face another day."

Cyrus's arm tightened around her. "This'll all be over soon. Then you'll be worrying about something else. Now, you go and find Steven, and you tell him he'd better straighten up or his granddaddy's going to take a buggy whip to him. Hear?"

Emma nodded, feeling better just for having told someone what she was thinking and feeling. "Thank you," she said, kissing Cyrus's cheek before she stood up and walked bravely back toward the French doors leading into the ballroom.

She had barely stepped over the threshold when seventeen-year-old Nathaniel came up to her. He had the beginnings of a mustache, Emma noticed for the first time, and he looked nervous. "I was hoping——er——thinking——" He went crimson from his neck to his hairline. "Would you dance with me, Miss Emma?"

She smiled and offered her hand. "I'd like that very much," she said, hoping her face didn't show the ravages of her earlier crying fit.

Nathaniel cleared his throat and marshalled Emma awkwardly into a waltz. It seemed strange that, only three years before, she'd been his age.

"If Steven or Macon is mean to you," he ventured

boldly, "you just come and tell me. I'll give 'em what-for."

Resisting an urge to kiss his cheek, because she knew it would embarrass him too much, Emma nodded solemnly. "I'll do that," she promised, both amused and touched that Nathaniel was willing to do battle with such formidable opponents for her sake.

Nathaniel's handsome young face was dark with conviction and his palm was moist against Emma's. "I know you think I'm just a kid, but I'm strong, Miss Emma. I won't let anybody hurt you."

"Thank you," Emma said, and she meant it.

After that the conversation became less earnest and Emma began to steal subtle glances around the ballroom, searching for Steven. She wanted to find him and make things right between them; their time together was too precious for fighting.

"Have you seen Steven?" she asked Nathaniel, just as the waltz ended.

He shook his head. "I'll find him for you if you'd like," he offered eagerly.

"No," Emma said in a gentle voice, seeing a look of challenge in Nathaniel's face that might just get him into trouble with his impatient cousin. "I'll look for him myself."

Using her fan because the house was hot and crowded, Emma wove her way through the crowd of finely dressed guests. She smiled confidently as she passed, to let them know she didn't consider her husband capable of murder.

Climbing the stairs, holding her whispering skirts with one hand, Emma frowned as a strange sound came to her ears. It was muffled and distant, barely discernible for the music and laughter downstairs, and that made it all the more troubling.

Reaching the upper landing, Emma strained to hear the noise, and decided it was coming from the master suite at the front of the house. Knowing that was Macon and Lucy's room, Emma hesitated to investigate. After all, if someone came rushing to the rescue every time odd sounds came from her and Steven's chambers, the results would be disastrous.

Some instinct told Emma that what she was hearing was not ecstasy. She hurried along the hallway, and as she neared the luxurious rooms, Lucy's voice reached her in a strangled sob of rage and pain.

Her heart beating faster, Emma raised her hand to knock, only to find the door was open when she reached it.

Lucy was half-sitting and half-lying on the floor, her back to a heavy, ornately carved bureau. For all her cowering position, her brown eyes snapped with hatred as she glared at Macon, who stood over her with one fist still doubled up.

A slow trickle of blood came from the corner of Lucy's mouth.

"You've humiliated me for the last time," Macon rasped, his shoulders tense beneath his evening coat as he glared down at his wife. He gestured wildly toward the door, though neither he nor Lucy seemed aware that Emma was there. "Do you know what they're saying down there? That you're insane, that you ought to be put away. And I'm beginning to think they're right!"

Lucy levered herself tremulously up from the floor, and it was all Emma could do not to rush forward and help her sister-in-law to stand. "I don't give a damn what they think," she spat. "And you can go straight to hell, Macon Fairfax." She gave a bitter laugh that alarmed Emma and waggled her finger at her furious husband. "You had to bring Steven back," she taunted. "You were so sure it would be he who hanged. Well, it won't be—Mammy Judkins told me so. You've consigned your own soul to perdition, and I'll laugh while you burn!"

Macon advanced on Lucy again, then he raised his hand, and Emma was forced to interfere.

"No!" she screamed, starting into the room, but before

she could step through the double doorway, Steven pushed past her, gripped Macon by the lapels of his fancy coat, and flung him against the armoire.

"Come on, you courageous bastard," Steven wheedled, beckoning with both hands. "Let's see how you do against somebody who can give you a fight."

Macon, who'd had the breath knocked out of him, threw his half-brother a look of sheer hatred as he squared his shoulders and straightened his coat. "She's a madwoman," he muttered, gesturing toward his wife, who had lost her glorious bravado now and was huddled against Emma, watching the scene with wide eyes. "Always talking about that old swamp witch and her spells. Wearing those damned black dresses—"

"I don't care if she's sticking pins in dolls and praying to the moon," Steven broke in, his voice level and yet dangerous. "The next time you lay a hand on her—or any other woman—in anger, I'll see that you hurt like you've never hurt before. Is that clear?"

Macon didn't reply. He just glared at Lucy for a long moment, then walked slowly out of the room.

Steven went to Lucy and took both her hands in his. "Are you all right?" he asked hoarsely.

Lucy shook her head, her eyes full of distraction and pain. "We're damned," she whispered. "All of us."

# Chapter
## ❧ 21 ❧

*I*n those hot, muggy days preceding the start of Steven's trial, Emma was torn between two conflicting needs: to be with him every moment of every day, and to separate herself from him, emotionally and physically, so the pain would be lessened.

Her love for Steven would not allow her to take the latter course, and the former was impossible. As soon as the sun peeked over the horizon, he was up. Before Emma was fully conscious, he had left the house, and he generally didn't return until ten or ten-thirty at night, by which time he was numb with frustration and fatigue. He never made love to her, and Emma had a poignant sense of the distance growing between them.

One morning late in June, when Emma came downstairs to the dining room, dressed in yet another of her seemingly endless supply of new gowns—this one made of yellow printed lawn—she found Lucy lingering over breakfast.

As usual, Lucy was dressed in black, and that day there were deep purple smudges beneath her eyes.

Anger flared in Emma's bosom, for she thought, at first, that the marks were bruises. Reaching Lucy's side, she realized they had been caused by fatigue instead.

After filling a plate at the sideboard and pouring coffee for herself, she sat down next to Lucy and spread her napkin in her lap. In all this time, Macon's wife had not so much as glanced in her direction.

"Lucy?"

The small, doll-like woman looked startled to find she wasn't alone. A distracted smile came to her lips. "Oh. Hello, Emma. Are you well this morning?" Ironically, considering her own situation, Lucy was always solicitous of Emma.

Emma nodded. "You look very tired," she commented cautiously, after a sip of coffee. "Have you been resting well?"

Lucy arched her pale, perfect eyebrows in apparent surprise. "Why would you ask such a question?"

Emma cleared her throat. "Well, there was that incident the night of the ball, when Macon struck you. I was just wondering if perhaps—"

Lucy interrupted Emma's words with a dismissive gesture of one hand and a shake of her head. "He's not like that all the time," she said. "He'd just had a little too much to drink that night."

"You shouldn't excuse his behavior," Emma dared to say. She'd learned her frankness from Chloe, and it was a trait that didn't always endear her to others. "It was wrong of him to strike you."

Lucy sighed sadly, distantly. "I know," she said in a soft and miserable voice. She sounded utterly without hope.

Emma lifted her fork and pushed the eggs around on her plate. She'd come to the table with a voracious appetite, but now it was gone. "How long have you and Macon been married?" she asked, trying to make her tone bright and conversational.

Lucy's forehead puckered into a pretty frown as she

calculated. "We were wed the year Macon's daddy died, and Steven came to us. That was about—seventeen years ago, I guess. Nathaniel's folks passed away when we'd been married just a few months—I was like a mother to him."

Although she was a bit jolted by the disjointed quality of Lucy's remarks, Emma forced a smile to her lips. "I knew Macon was older than Steven, of course," she said, "but I didn't realize the gap between them was quite that wide."

"Oh, yes. It's a good thing Steven was almost full-grown when he came to Fairhaven. If he'd been little and helpless, like Nathaniel was, I'm fairly certain Macon would have killed him." After delivering this opinion in a sunny tone, Lucy smiled and stirred more sugar into her tea.

Emma choked on the bite of fried sausage she'd tried to swallow and dabbed at her lips with a table napkin. Suddenly, she just couldn't face the prospect of spending another long, pampered, dreary day in that house, doing nothing but waiting. Once she'd recovered herself, she asked, "How well did you know Mary McCall?"

At the mention of Steven's alleged victim, Lucy pursed her lips for a moment. Immediately afterward, however, her vaguely hysterical smile returned, dazzling in its brightness. "Not well, of course," she said cheerfully, flouting protocol by resting her elbows on the table, her tea cup between her palms. "Mary was much—younger. She was Dirk's friend, and Steven's."

"Did she leave any family? Friends?"

"Her father, Jessup. But he died two years ago of a heart ailment." Her brow creased again as she thought hard. "Oh, and there was her aunt, Astoria." Lucy paused to make a face. "Dried up old prune. She probably hasn't so much as stepped outside her front door in twenty years."

"She lived in the same house as Mary, though?" Emma pressed, feeling a strange excitement building within her.

Lucy nodded and gave her sister-in-law a surprised look. "Why are you so interested in Astoria McCall? I promise you, she's dull as cold dishwater."

"I want to talk to her about Mary's murder," Emma said, pushing her food away virtually untouched and shoving back her chair. "I'm going into town," she announced. "And I'd like you to come with me if you would."

Lucy still looked baffled, but she put her napkin on the table and stood. She clasped her hands together automatically in a pathetic wringing motion. "Well, I guess I could—" she looked down at her black dress and smoothed the shiny sateen skirts with nervous hands, then touched the back of her chignon. "Do you think I look all right? Astoria might not get out much, but she's a dreadful gossip."

Emma gave her sister-in-law a reassuring smile. "You're the most beautiful woman in Orleans parish," she said, thinking her words might be true if only Lucy would wear becoming colors and get out more often. "Anything Astoria might say about you would surely be grounded in pure jealousy."

Twenty minutes later Emma and Lucy were settled in one of the Fairfaxes' several carriages, passing beneath the fragrant blossoms of the magnolia trees. Half an hour after that, they drew up in front of a brick house that must once have been elegant but now had cracked walls and an overgrown garden.

Emma shuddered at the sight of it. "The murder happened here?" she asked in a very small voice.

Lucy looked out the carriage window and made a tsk-tsk sound as she straightened her gloves. "Yes, but it was a grand place then. Fit for receiving guests."

"The family must have had money once," Emma observed, her tone hushed as the driver opened the door and helped her down. "What happened?"

Lucy sighed as she joined Emma on the buckled sidewalk, where grass sprang up between the cracks. The metal fence had rusted through in places, and the gate creaked as the carriage driver opened it. "Old Jessup was never the same after Mary died. He adored the little scamp, you know. He became careless, according to Macon, and one day all the money was just—gone." She threw up her small gloved hands to emphasize this last word.

"Astoria never married?" Emma asked, feeling sad for this broken family, and reluctant to stir the ashes by presenting herself as Mrs. Steven Fairfax.

When they'd climbed the steps and approached the front door, Lucy reached out and turned the bell-knob.

Emma flipped open the ivory-handled fan Cyrus had given her as a gift and began waving it in front of her face. She was never going to get used to the heavy heat of New Orleans, she reflected, as she waited.

A small black woman with very large white teeth and a kerchief tied over her many tiny braids answered their call. She peered at Lucy, then at Emma, as though her eyesight weren't quite what it should be. "Yes'm?"

"Please tell Miss McCall that Mrs. Macon Fairfax and Mrs. Steven Fairfax have come to pay a visit," Lucy said in a business-like tone that belied her odd ways. "And kindly don't leave us standing out here in the midday sun while you dillydally."

The woman hurried away, and Lucy turned to Emma and confided, "You must be firm with people of color. After being told what to do for so long, they can't always be trusted to reason for themselves."

Emma held back a sharp retort. This was not the moment to antagonize the unpredictable Lucy.

A moment later the maid returned to admit them. Her large eyes darted fearfully from Lucy's face to Emma's, and she seemed almost to cringe away from them.

They were led through a dark but well-maintained foyer, and into a parlor to the right. Here heavy velvet draperies were drawn against the light, and the room had a musty smell. Emma had to squint to make out the shapes of chairs and tables and of the woman seated in a rocking chair beside the ivory fireplace.

"Hello, Astoria," Lucy said warmly, as though theirs were an ordinary, everyday sort of call, in a normal kind of house.

Miss McCall was portly, and she was dressed in black, like Lucy, except for the white lace bonnet that covered most of her hair. Her hands were large and weighted with jewels, and even in the dim light, Emma could see the blue veins standing out on them, beneath pale transparent flesh. "Lucille," Astoria greeted her caller, somewhat grudgingly. Her eyes shifted to Emma. "Who's this?"

"Why, it's Emma," Lucy replied, displacing a large gray and white cat to sink into a Queen Anne chair upholstered in shabby velvet. "Steven's wife."

Following Lucy's lead, Emma sat down in the chair next to hers.

Astoria leaned forward, assessing Emma in a disturbingly thorough way. "Steven's wife?" she echoed. "They should have hanged that murdering scoundrel after he strangled our Mary. Told his lawyer that just the other day."

A sudden attack of dizziness made Emma grip the arms of her chair. Before she could jump to Steven's defense, however, Lucy reached out and silenced her with a light touch to her hand.

"There hasn't been a trial, yet, Astoria," Lucy assured the woman who had probably been her friend once, in a congenial tone of voice. "Steven is innocent until proven guilty, remember."

"Innocent!" Astoria cried. "If you'd seen the way Mary wept that night, after he'd tossed her aside—"

"Did you see him?" Emma broke in quietly. "Did he come inside the house?"

Astoria inspected Emma thoroughly, clearly reassessing her. "I didn't actually see him, but I know he was here. He and Mary were having a lovers' spat. He must have followed her in—"

Emma was forced to interrupt again, but she did so quietly, and in a moderate tone of voice. "Did you see anyone else, Miss McCall?"

Astoria settled back in her chair, and the gray and white cat leaped up into her lap, startling both Lucy and Emma. "No."

"You're absolutely sure? After all, this is a sizable house," Emma pressed. "It seems to me that one or more persons could venture inside without being seen."

Astoria nodded. "That's true. And it was Steven Fairfax who came in and went right to Mary's room."

"How can you be sure of that?"

"I heard her screaming his name," she said, her voice faraway now and harsh with emotion. "At first I thought I was just having a nightmare. By the time I realized it was really happening, he'd gotten away and poor Mary was lying in the middle of her bedroom floor—dead."

"But you might have dreamed that she was screaming his name," Emma reasoned. She knew she sounded a little desperate, but she couldn't help herself.

"He was the one," Astoria insisted. "Oh, those Fairfax boys were always trouble. I told Mary to have no truck with them, but she wouldn't listen. Liked their quick smiles, she did, and the fancy presents they gave."

Realizing she was going to get nowhere with Astoria, Emma was already shifting her attention to the maid. "That woman who answered the door—what's her name?"

"You certainly are full of questions, dear," Lucy scolded, reaching out and patting Emma's hand again, this time so firmly that it stung a little. "That was Maisie Lee, and she's been here for years, hasn't she, Astoria?"

Astoria's gaze was fixed on Emma and was openly hostile now, when she replied, "She came to us before the Late Unpleasantness."

Emma was made to feel responsible for the entire civil conflict in those few moments, and she withdrew a little while Astoria and Lucy chatted on about remembered balls and cotillions. When she could bear it no longer, Emma interrupted. "Does Maisie Lee live here at the house with you?"

Astoria leaned forward in her chair, studying Emma

again in that daunting way of hers, but she finally answered. "She lives down by the docks with her man. He loads and unloads ships." She sniffed once. "He's right uppity, too, and contentious. If I were you, Mrs. Steven Fairfax, I wouldn't go meddling in *his* household."

"If I could just speak to Maisie Lee here, then," Emma reflected, and before anyone could say yea or nay, she was out of her chair and walking purposefully toward the foyer.

"Emma!" Lucy cried in surprise and anger.

"Maisie Lee!" Emma called, proceeding in the general direction of the kitchen. Like the one at Fairhaven, it turned out to be separate from the main house, and Emma was walking along the path toward it, her skirts in her hands, when Lucy caught up with her.

"What on earth are you doing?" Macon's wife demanded. It occurred to Emma that Lucy might feel the need to protect her husband, even if he was cruel to her.

"I've got to talk to that housemaid," Emma answered, not even slowing her pace.

Lucy reached out and caught hold of her arm, and it struck Emma that she was surprisingly strong, considering her diminutive size. "She's going to be afraid to talk to you," Lucy said, so furious that Emma stopped to look her square in the eyes.

"Why?"

"Because you're rich and you're white. Don't you see, Emma, that if you go blundering about in Maisie Lee's affairs, you might just find out something you don't want to know?"

The color drained from Emma's face, and her heart missed a beat. "You think Steven is guilty," she breathed.

Lucy drew a deep breath, let it out again. "He *was* with Mary that night. There was a dreadful scene at the ball—"

"He didn't kill anyone," Emma said tightly. Then she broke away from Lucy and marched on toward the kitchen.

Although there was smoke twisting lazily from the chimney and two pans of bread dough had been set out on a table to rise, Maisie Lee was nowhere to be seen.

Determined, Emma called her name.

"She won't come," Lucy said softly from the doorway. "She's too afraid."

"I'll give you money, Maisie Lee," Emma went on, ignoring her sister-in-law. She opened her purse and took out the generous allowance Steven had given her just the night before. Holding it up, she added, on a hunch, "You could buy things for your children—fruit and clothes and new shoes."

The door of what was probably the pantry creaked open and Maisie Lee stepped out, her beautiful eyes huge in her brown, glistening face. She didn't once look away from the hundred-dollar bill Emma was holding out.

"Tell me if you saw Steven Fairfax here the night Mary McCall was murdered," Emma said, her hand remaining steady.

Maisie Lee swallowed hard. Her desire for the money was plainly visible; she was almost trembling as she stood there, willing herself not to reach for it. Her eyes darted once to Lucy's face, widened momentarily, then came back to Emma. "I done tole that lawyer man, Mr. Fairfax brought Miss Mary home from the ball. She was screamin' and cryin' somethin' fierce."

"And Mr. Fairfax? What was he doing?"

"He was tryin' to help her, much as I could see. He kept sayin', 'Don't cry, Miss Mary. Please don't cry.'"

Emma closed her eyes tightly for a moment, seeing the image as clearly as if she'd been standing by the McCalls' high iron fence on that very night, watching the two of them go up the walk.

"Did he follow Mary inside?" Lucy demanded, startling both Emma and Maisie Lee.

Maisie Lee swallowed again. "No, ma'am, I didn't see him do that."

"Did you see anyone else?"

Maisie Lee shook her head. Sweat moistened the front

of her tight cotton dress, and she ran floury hands down the sides of the skirt, leaving dry white trails. "Nobody else, ma'am."

Emma handed Maisie Lee the money, even though she sensed there was more the woman wasn't telling her. Something she was terrified to say.

"Thank you, ma'am," Maisie Lee blurted out, ducking her head.

Emma stood still, even though the kitchen was hot and close and she desperately needed air. "Do you love your husband?" she asked.

The black woman looked at her in surprise. "Love Jethro?" She laid a hand to her bodice, where she'd tucked the hundred-dollar bill away, as though to hide it from his eyes. "Sure I do. He my man. We got babies together."

"I love my Steven, too," Emma said clearly, "and we haven't had any babies yet. He might hang for something he didn't do, before we get a chance to start our family."

"I don't know nothin' else!" Maisie Lee wailed, obviously at the end of her endurance.

Emma studied her for a long moment, then turned away and followed Lucy down the path and around the side of the crumbling McCall house. Climbing roses, wild and unkempt and buzzing with bees, snagged at their dresses as they passed.

"You shouldn't have given her all that money," Lucy fussed, walking very fast ahead of Emma. "Jethro will just beat her senseless for trying to hide it from him, then drink every penny 'til it's gone."

"She knows something," Emma mused, ignoring Lucy's diatribe. "Something important, that she's afraid to tell."

The carriage was waiting in the street, and Lucy surprised Emma by gripping her by the arm and propelling her toward it. Her other hand was raised to her forehead, her thumb and forefinger each pressing against a temple. "I do have the most *dreadful* headache," she complained. "I wish we'd never come here. We should be home, like proper ladies, having a mint julep in the gazebo and working at our needlepoint!"

Emma rolled her eyes. But she liked Lucy and had sympathy for her. When they arrived at Fairhaven, she escorted her sister-in-law to the master suite and then fetched a headache powder for her, mixing it into a glass of cold water.

When she returned to Macon and Lucy's room, Lucy was curled up on the bed like a child, wearing nothing but a chemise. She accepted the water gratefully, drank it all down, and rolled over with a moan. "Oh, my, but my head hurts."

"Rest," Emma answered gently, slipping out of the room and closing the door behind her.

Needing some time alone to think about Maisie Lee and the strange sensation she'd had that the woman was telling a lot less than she knew, Emma retired to her own room, rather than go downstairs.

She always hoped that Steven would be there when she opened the door, and sometimes he was, but that day she was unlucky. His clothes were in the armoire, the book he'd been reading lay open on the table near the window, the air was redolent with his distinctive scent. But the room was empty.

With a sigh Emma closed the door and walked over to the table where she often sat looking out at the magnolia trees and wondering. Most often, of course, she wondered whether she and Steven would be allowed to have a life together, but she thought of Lily, too, and of Caroline. Not a day went by that she didn't ask God where and how to find them.

When she saw the letter lying on the table, she lifted one hand to her breast. The envelope was of fine white vellum, with the faintest gray stripes, and the return address was Chicago. Kathleen. The letter was from Kathleen.

Fingers trembling, her lips moving in a prayer that had

no words, Emma ripped open the envelope and pulled out the letter. She dropped it, in her anxiety, and bit down hard on her lip in an effort to restrain her curiosity.

The date and salutation were written in a neat but unfamiliar hand. *As Mrs. Harrington's attorney and closest advisor, the duty of reporting her death falls to me . . .*

The duty of reporting her death.

Emma sagged backwards in her chair, unable to trust her muscles to support her. The room seemed to spin crazily for a moment, and she closed her eyes and drew a deep breath.

She was still sitting in the same chair, holding the letter and staring out at the lengthening shadows slowly stealing the color from the trees, when the door opened behind her and she heard Steven's voice.

"Emma?" His hands came to rest on her shoulders, and she pressed her cheek to the back of one. "What is it?"

"She's dead," Emma whispered, as Steven pulled up a chair close to hers and sat down.

Gently he took the letter from her hand and read it. "I'm sorry," he said, and the gentleness of his tone made her want to cry.

"The attorney didn't mention Lily and Caroline. That means Mama probably didn't know where they were."

"It means he didn't mention them," Steven corrected her quietly, touching her chin, turning her head so that she looked at him.

"I expressly asked for news of my sisters," Emma said, her lower lip wobbling.

"Write to him again. Better yet, send him a wire."

Emma was gazing at the gathering twilight again, remembering the Kathleen she'd known. Although her mother had had a drinking problem, she'd been merry when she was sober, full of laughter and music. "I wonder if she died alone."

Steven drew her out of the chair and onto his lap,

where he held her, pressing her head down against his shoulder. His arms felt so good around her that Emma began to cry at last; she'd found this man only to lose him.

Thinking Emma was crying for Kathleen—and maybe, somewhere deep inside herself, she was—Steven held her tightly and waited for the emotional storm to pass. When it did he carried her to the bedroom, undressed her to her chemise, and laid her down like a child, pulling the slippers from her feet, laying the covers over her.

She reached out for his hand. "You're leaving." It wasn't a question, but a statement.

He shook his head. "I'll be right downstairs, Emma. With Garrick."

She struggled past the shock of Kathleen's death long enough to ask, "Did you find out anything new?"

He bent and kissed her forehead. "We will," he assured her.

Emma wanted to tell him that she'd talked with the McCalls' servant, Maisie Lee, and that she suspected the woman knew something vital, but she couldn't rally the strength. She tightened her hand around Steven's, just momentarily, then drifted off into a fitful sleep.

The next day, when Emma awakened, Steven was gone again.

Feeling inexpressibly lonely, Emma got out of bed and went through her ablutions by rote. When she was dressed, she went down to the dining room for breakfast, only to find that she couldn't eat. She sent one of the maids to have the carriage brought around.

Emma's first stop was the nearest telegraph office, where she sent a wire to the attorney who had notified her of Kathleen's death, asking if he had any knowledge of her sisters, Lily and Caroline. An answer could take hours or even days, the clerk informed her. Any response would be delivered to Fairhaven immediately upon receipt.

Unable to face going home to wait, Emma instructed

the driver to take her to Garrick Wright's office. She wanted, *needed* to know what progress the lawyer was making on Steven's case.

But Garrick wasn't in, and his clerk didn't know when he would return.

In despair, Emma went home, only to be told by one of the maids that "Mr. Steven" was waiting in the study to see her.

She hurried there and found Steven pacing, looking more agitated than she'd ever seen him. She knew there had been a new development in his case, and that it wasn't a good one.

"What's happened?" Emma whispered, grasping the back of a chair.

"Miss Astoria McCall has come forward to testify that I was in her house the night of the murder. She claims she heard Mary screaming my name."

Emma was certain she would faint. She gripped the back of a chair in both hands and waited, knowing instinctively there was more.

Steven poured himself a drink and took a sip, his eyes blazing as he looked at his wife. "According to her, this memory only came back to her after you and Lucy called on her yesterday."

Emma stumbled around the chair and fell into it. "You're blaming me?"

"Of course not," he said brusquely. "But the whole thing brought me to my senses. We've made a mistake, Emma. I want you to go back to Chloe's and forget you ever knew me."

One of Emma's hands rose to her mouth to hold back a cry that never came. "You don't mean that," she said after a moment of struggle. "You're only trying to protect me."

He stared at her for a long moment, and she saw a stranger looking out of his eyes. "I'm not protecting you," he said. "I'm trying to get rid of you. Damn it, do I have to come right out and say I shouldn't have married you?"

Emma rose from her chair with dignity. "You're a liar, Steven Fairfax. And I won't leave you. Nothing but death itself could make me do that!"

Steven turned his back to her and went to stand at the window, gazing out. "I don't love you," he told her.

"You're a liar!" Emma said again, and this time her voice held a note of hysteria. "You've given up, and you think you can spare me by sending me away! Well, I won't go, do you hear me? *I won't go!*"

He whirled and glared at her, and she wished for death at the look she saw in his eyes. "If you won't go, then I will," he spat. And he stormed past her.

She followed him into the hallway, watched in numb disbelief as the only man she would ever love, no matter how long she lived, took the stairs two at a time.

Sometime later, when Emma finally worked up the courage to follow, she went to the bedroom they'd shared so briefly. He was in the next room, packing.

Emma sat down on the edge of the bed, holding the little photograph of her and Lily and Caroline and running one finger slowly, repeatedly, around its oval frame, as if to conjure her sisters like some magician in a storybook.

# Chapter
## ❧ 22 ❧

*C*yrus Fairfax was so angry that his face went florid and his white mustache quivered. He tossed back his brandy and slammed the glass down hard on the surface of his desk. "By God, if I were twenty years younger," he thundered, "I'd drag you outside and horsewhip you!"

Steven would have laughed if the situation hadn't been so grave. But as it was, he was going to lose both his life and Emma, and one was as precious as the other.

"I never should have brought her here in the first place," he said quietly, staring down into his own glass of whiskey. The drink had left a sour taste in his mouth, and he set it aside. "I took Emma away from the people and places she knew, so she could live with strangers—one of whom delights in telling her he's going to make her his mistress as soon as I'm gone."

Cyrus glared at his grandson. "So you've given up," he said. "I thought you were better than that."

Steven turned away to stand looking out over the sloping lawn where he'd hoped to see his children play. And perhaps even his grandchildren. "Garrick and I

316

have questioned everybody we could find, and we've come up with exactly nothing," he reflected, ignoring his grandfather's jibe. "My trial is scheduled to start on Monday morning, and all we've got is my statement that I'm innocent and the fact that I came back to face the charges." He turned just far enough to look back at Cyrus over one shoulder. "If I hang, I'll do it knowing that Macon plans to make Emma's life a living hell."

Cyrus sat down heavily in the leather chair behind his desk. "You can count on me to look after Emma if things go wrong. You know that."

Steven went to stand facing his grandfather, his hands clasping the edge of the desk, his gaze level. "I want you to swear to me by all that's holy that you'll get Emma out of here the minute I'm sentenced."

The old man took a cigar from the box at his elbow and offered it to Steven. When his grandson refused with a shake of the head, Cyrus slipped off the paper band and tossed it into the trash basket. Then he bit off the end of the cigar, spat it away, and lit a match. "Seems to me you're living in the future, boy," he commented at last. "You haven't even been tried and you're already climbing the gallows steps." Puffs of blue smoke encircled his head as he drew on the cigar.

"Do I have your word?" Steven demanded.

"You know you do," Cyrus replied. "Macon won't lay a hand on her. What did she say when you told her you didn't want to be her husband anymore?"

Steven shoved a hand through his hair, ashamed of the memory. "She said she didn't believe me—called me a liar."

Cyrus chuckled ruefully. "Then you started moving your things out of the house. You're a fool if I've ever seen one, Steven Fairfax. Now you go find that brave little wife of yours and you make up to her, or you'll have me to answer to."

Steven sighed, then turned and walked out of his grandfather's study, leaving the door open behind him.

His spirit hungered for Emma as voraciously as his

body did, and he knew he could no longer keep himself from going to her. Even the fear of siring a child who would grow up without a father failed to hold him back.

He took the stairs two at a time, desperate to hold Emma and to take back the cruel words he'd said, even though he still believed it would have been better if she'd left him.

He knocked at the door of the room they'd shared and, receiving no answer, tried the knob. It gave, and he stepped inside.

There was no sign of Emma, and for several terrible moments Steven thought she'd actually taken him at his word and left Fairhaven forever. The pain that idea caused him was beyond anything he'd imagined.

He went to the huge armoire and opened it. Her gowns were still there, and her jewel box was on the shelf, but these things offered no comfort. Emma's pride would have made her leave them behind.

Steven turned and crossed the room to their bed, wrenched open the drawer in the nightstand, and closed his hand around a small, oval-shaped object. He gave an audible sigh of relief as he lifted out the framed photograph of Emma, Lily, and Caroline. She hadn't left him; she wouldn't go without taking the picture.

He put the photograph in plain view on the nightstand and strode out of the room. Concern was beginning to replace relief. He felt compelled to find Emma, to see that she was all right, to apologize to her.

But he'd been away so much, working on his case with Garrick, that he had no idea where or how she spent her time. He made his way down the hallway to Lucy's door.

A cheerful "Come in," was the response to his knock.

"Have you seen Emma?" he asked of his sister-in-law, who was sitting in a chair beside the window with a baby doll lying in her lap.

Lucy didn't look at him. She was smiling down at the doll as she gently entangled one finger in the golden curl at its forehead. Her voice had an odd, childlike quality. "She's gone to town in the carriage," she answered.

Knowing he'd learn nothing more from Lucy, feeling sick on some deep level of his soul, Steven walked out of the room and closed the door behind him.

Thoughtful, he made his way down the stairs and out through one of the rear doors. Reaching the stables, he chose a horse and began to saddle it.

The carriage rattled briskly over the road, and Emma sat fanning herself inside. She felt vaguely nauseated, but she attributed that to the situation with Steven, and the heat. She was too emotionally drained to cry, although her eyes stung with unshed tears and her throat ached.

The first stop, just as Emma had ordered, was at Astoria McCall's run-down house. She rang the bell, and Miss Astoria herself answered the door.

Seeing her jeweled fingers, it struck Emma that Astoria McCall might not be so poor after all. Perhaps she was just bitter, and too despondent to care about such things as keeping up her property and socializing with her friends and neighbors.

"You," Miss Astoria said coldly.

Emma squared her shoulders. "I'm looking for Maisie Lee."

"Well, she isn't here," grumbled the aging spinster. "She's home with that drunken husband of hers." Miss McCall started to close the door, but Emma blocked the effort with her shoulder.

"Where does Maisie Lee live?" she insisted politely.

"Heavens," barked Miss McCall. "I don't know! Down by the harbor somewhere, in one of those back-street hovels."

"You must have an address in your records somewhere," Emma pressed, refusing to budge an inch.

Astoria glowered at her, but Emma wasn't intimidated. No one could possibly hurt her as badly as Steven had by telling her he no longer loved her; she could wander the world without fear.

"Oh, *all right,*" the older woman snapped, turning and disappearing into that shadowy, musty house.

Emma stepped inside the foyer to wait, looking around her and seeing cobwebs in the corners of the ceiling. The place ought to be swept down, she thought, and all the windows thrown open to the fresh air and the light.

Presently Astoria McCall returned with a scrap of paper clutched in one hand. "Here," she snapped. "And it'll be on your conscience if Jethro beats the poor girl half-senseless for meddling in matters that are none of her affair."

Emma had no desire to get Maisie Lee into trouble. She only wanted to find out what the frightened woman knew and was keeping to herself. "Thank you," Emma said, as though she and Astoria had just passed an enjoyable time together. "And good day."

The carriage driver frowned when Emma handed the address up to him, but he must have seen how determined she was because he gave her no argument.

In the part of town where Maisie Lee lived, which was near the waterfront, the houses were close together and seemingly filled to the rafters with people. Mahogany-skinned children ran barefoot over broken cobblestones, and the smells of fish, horse dung, garbage, and urine made the thick air nearly unbreathable.

When the carriage came to a stop, Emma got down on her own before the driver could help her.

"Miss Emma," he began nervously, "Mr. Steven wouldn't like my bringing you here, 'specially with the sickness everywhere like it is."

"I won't be long," Emma answered, her eyes already scanning the walls of the brick buildings for numbers. There were none, so she approached a trio of little boys playing marbles. Reaching into her handbag, she produced a coin for each of them. When she had their undivided attention she asked, "Where does Maisie Lee Simpson live?"

One of the boys pointed, wide-eyed, toward the end of the street. "Down there, where the flowerpot is."

Emma nodded her thanks and proceeded toward the

house in question. The driver followed along beside her in the carriage, and she could feel his puzzled gaze as she walked.

The chipped clay flowerpot contained a single, drooping red geranium badly in need of water. Emma felt sorry for it as she knocked at the rickety door of Maisie Lee's house.

She pulled it just far enough open to peer out at Emma, and her eyes went wide when she saw who the visitor was.

"Are you alone?" Emma asked.

Maisie Lee nodded, almost wildly, but she made no move to admit her caller.

"Then may I come in, please?" Emma pressed.

Reluctantly, Maisie Lee stepped back, and Emma entered a room that was crowded but quite clean. Several small children played on the floor, and laundry had been strung between two walls.

Maisie Lee's huge eyes kept darting toward the door, as though she expected Satan himself to burst through it and drag her off to hell. "What you want, Missus?" she pleaded.

"You know something about the night Mary McCall was murdered—something you haven't told anyone. I want to know what it is."

The black woman retreated a step, hoisting one of the children onto her hip when it began to cry. "I don't know nothin'," Maisie Lee protested, sounding a bit desperate.

"You do, and my husband is going to hang if you don't tell me. Who was there that night, Maisie Lee? Was it Macon Fairfax?"

Maisie Lee's eyes went wider still. "No, ma'am, I didn't see Mr. Macon. I swear to God I didn't."

"But you saw someone, and it wasn't Steven. Whom did you see?"

Maisie Lee looked at the door again. "My man'll be home soon," she fretted. "He don't like me to have company."

Emma sighed, then pleaded, "You've got to help me."

Great tears welled in Maisie Lee's eyes and glistened there. One made a crooked path down her cheek when she shook her head. "I can't, missus," she said. "I don't know nothin'. I swear—"

Emma's discouragement went soul-deep. "All right," she said with a sigh. "If you decide to tell the truth, Maisie Lee, send word to Fairhaven."

Maisie Lee swallowed hard but didn't speak again. She held the now-squalling child a little closer as Emma opened the door to leave.

On the threshold she encountered one of the largest men she had ever seen. He was obviously Maisie Lee's man, and he didn't look pleased to see company. He fairly seethed with hatred as Emma eased past him and hurried down the walk, where the agitated driver was waiting with the carriage door open.

Just as Emma was settling herself in the tufted leather seat, she heard a scream from inside the house and closed her eyes briefly against the images that crowded her mind. Maisie Lee's man stepped outside just long enough to kick the geranium pot onto the sidewalk, where it splintered, sending dry dirt everywhere and revealing the plant's naked roots. Then he went back in again and slammed the door.

"Hyah!" the anxious driver yelled to the horses, just when Emma was ready to go back and try to protect Maisie Lee.

Sadly, she looked down at her hands. She probably wouldn't have been much help anyway. In fact, just as Astoria had said, it was her fault Jethro was angry with Maisie Lee, and if the woman suffered, that would be because of Emma, too.

She was completely discouraged by the time she reached Fairhaven's front door.

The driver tried to help Emma down, but he found himself elbowed aside by a tight-jawed Steven.

"Where the hell have you been?" Emma's husband demanded, grasping her shoulders in his hands.

Emma met his eyes steadily. "What do you care?" she countered.

His hands came to rest on her cheeks. "I care," he answered.

Emma pulled away from him and started to walk into the house, but he caught hold of her hand and pulled her back.

"We're going to talk," he announced, and then he dragged her around the front of the house, through the complex and well-tended garden, where Lucy liked to spend time when she was having a good day. He didn't stop until they'd reached the screened summerhouse, which was practically overgrown with wisteria.

Opening the door, Steven pulled Emma inside, and she was amazed to see that the place was relatively clean. There were narrow beds with mattresses on them, and several wicker chairs with worn cushions.

"I used to sleep out here sometimes when I first came to Fairhaven," Steven said.

Emma's lower lip was caught between her teeth. She prayed Steven wasn't going to hurt her anymore, because she wouldn't be able to bear it. "Do you still want to send me away?" she dared to ask.

"Yes," Steven answered forthrightly. "I'd still rather see you safe in Whitneyville, with Chloe to look after you."

Emma was wounded, but she held her head up nonetheless and kept her shoulders straight. "I see."

He curved one hand under her chin. "I don't think you do, Emma," he said huskily. "I lied before—I've never loved you more than I do right now, this minute. You were right in the first place—I wanted you to leave Fairhaven so Macon couldn't hurt you, so you wouldn't have to see—"

Emma's heart pounded with relief, and she slipped her arms around Steven's middle and rested her cheek against his chest. "Thank God," she whispered.

He held her very close. "Where were you today, Emma? What were you doing?"

Emma didn't dare admit she'd gone to see Maisie Lee; Steven had been furious the last time she'd meddled in his case. "Does that matter?" she hedged.

He chuckled ruefully and kissed her forehead. "No, I guess it doesn't." He lifted her chin again, and his eyes searched hers. "I'm sorry, Emma. For everything."

The tears she hadn't been able to shed filled Emma's eyes. "Hold me," she said, her arms slipping around his neck. "Tell me everything is going to be all right."

His embrace tightened, but he didn't speak, and Emma knew it was because he couldn't make himself say the words.

Need of a kind she'd never experienced before was born in Emma's tired, trembling body. She pulled Steven's head down for a kiss that said everything.

With a groan, he broke away. He started to lift Emma into his arms, and she knew he meant to carry her inside the house and upstairs to their bedroom.

"No," Emma whispered, touching his lips with her finger. "Here, where I can smell the flowers and hear the bees. Right here, Steven."

For a long moment he stared at her as though mesmerized, but then he kissed her so thoroughly that Emma's knees weakened. While she was still leaning against him, struggling to recover, he began unfastening the row of buttons at the back of her dress.

When he'd finished, he tugged the bodice downward, revealing Emma's breasts. She pulled her arms from the sleeves and then stepped completely out of the dress, standing before Steven in nothing but her drawers and petticoats.

He stripped her of the petticoats, leaving just her drawers, and lifted her by the waist, so that she was forced to wrap her legs around his hips and feel the possession that awaited her. His mouth took the nipple of her bare breast, and he drew on it greedily.

Emma clung to him, her head tilted slightly back, a little whimper escaping her as he shifted his hips, teasing her with the elemental power he held over her.

He went to her other breast and feasted there, and Emma's hand moved feverishly in his hair, pressing him closer. "Tell me what you want," he muttered, when he'd drained her of the intangible nectar he so craved.

"You," Emma moaned fitfully. "I want you. Oh, Steven, please—don't make me wait—not this time—it's been so long and I need you so much—"

He put one of his hands between her legs and gripped her boldly where her knickers were damp, and Emma groaned loudly, riding up on him, seeking to take him in.

Steven reached inside her drawers to find the hidden nubbin and tease it with his fingers. She grew moister still, and all the more frantic. "Oh, no," he whispered, "I'm not going to make it easy. I want everything you have to give, Emma—everything."

She whimpered, because she knew what that meant—a long, slow session of lovemaking, with Steven coaxing her to release after release before he finally entered her and provided the final satisfaction. "Please," she begged.

But he went back to her breast, even as he continued to tease and manipulate the most vulnerable part of her body. Emma was like a wild creature, clawing at his shoulders and back with her hands, trying to close her legs around him.

Presently he took away her drawers, laid her on one of the old mattresses and knelt between her legs, gripping her by the ankles and setting her feet wide apart. Emma cried out when he fell to her, writhing as he consumed her without hesitation or mercy.

Her head tossed from side to side as she felt her senses escalating toward an explosion powerful enough to tear her asunder. She sobbed Steven's name as her body convulsed in frantic surrender and her thighs pressed close against his head.

He did not leave her until she was lying still again, quivering with satisfaction and that peculiar, sweet fury that comes of being totally mastered. He kissed her lightly on the belly while she berated him in gasped, husky words, and he punished the insurrection by having a second helping, although this time he made Emma stand over him, utterly vulnerable.

When it was over, she sank to her knees on the floor, astraddle of his lap, too dazed and breathless to speak. She made a grateful sound, low in her throat, when she felt his rod spring to freedom and begin probing her lightly.

Emma could bear no more teasing. She caught Steven in a velvety trap and took him as forcefully as he'd ever taken her, and his groan of submission was sweet music to her ears.

She lowered her mouth to his and nibbled at his lips while she rose and fell slowly along his length, subjecting him to the same leisurely ecstasy she'd had to endure. She tasted his neck, his earlobes, and finally his nipples, and his hands roved up and down her bare back in desperation.

When Emma sheathed him in earnest, he moaned and laid his head back against the edge of the mattress, his eyes closed. She began to ride him, faster and faster, glorying in the expressions that crossed his magnificent face as she made love to him.

Then with a powerful upward thrust and a cry, he spilled himself into Emma and she began to climax when she felt his warmth, leaning toward him and brushing her nipple back and forth across his mouth. He sucked hard while she trembled on his rod, her body contorting all around it.

When Emma came back to herself and realized that she was naked in the summerhouse, with her hair falling down around her shoulders and her husband still inside her, she flushed and averted her eyes.

Steven caught hold of her chin and made her meet his eyes again. "I love you," he said clearly.

Emma let her forehead rest against his. "Steven," she whispered, tears in her voice. "Let's run away as soon as it's dark. We'll start over somewhere else—"

His hands cupped her bottom, as if to squeeze the last

drop of response from her. "No, Emma. No more running."

Fury shot through her, and she would have left him, but he held her by her hips and made her stay where she was. "Do you want to die?" she pleaded desperately. "Is that it?"

"Of course I don't," he said, and she felt him growing hard inside her. He began to guide her idly along his length and she was already responding, despite everything. "But I'm not going to run. I was finished with that the day I met you."

Emma didn't want to make love; she wanted to fight. But he was raising and lowering her, and her nipples were brushing against his rocklike, hairy chest, growing hard and pointed. She tried to argue, but the only sound that came from her throat was a strangled groan of defenseless pleasure.

He lifted his hands to her breasts and caressed them, the thumbs working her nipples mercilessly.

"There's a baby inside you right now," he said, leaning forward to trace her collarbone with kisses as Emma gave in and let her hips move of their own accord. "And as soon as you're over having this one, I'm going to put another in you, Emma. And then another. I'm going to have you morning, noon, and night—"

"Ooooh," Emma groaned helplessly, as he cut off his own words by closing his mouth over one of her nipples. He was deep inside her now, and as hard and insistent as before. He grazed her just lightly with his teeth and Emma's body went wild.

Moments later she watched through hooded, sultry eyes as Steven's release appeared to blind him momentarily, then wrung a long, low groan from his throat. All the while his powerful body arched taut and lean beneath her.

Presently Emma rose from him and began putting her clothes back on. Steven finished dressing first and was ready to fasten the back of Emma's dress when she turned to him for that purpose.

"Do you think there's really a baby?" she whispered.

"Yes," he told her, turning her to face him. He worked her hair free of its bedraggled braid and combed it gently with his fingers.

She pressed her forehead to his shoulder and clung to him, both arms around his middle. *Don't leave me*, she pleaded in miserable silence. *Oh, Steven, please don't leave me. Not now or ever.*

When they'd both composed themselves, he led her out of the summerhouse and through the noisy summer evening. Emma was surprised to see that the day had slipped away without her noticing.

They entered the house by a rear door and took the back stairs to the second floor, and Emma felt relief when they reached their room. She'd been afraid of encountering someone in her disheveled state; anyone who saw them would guess what they'd been doing.

"Hungry?" Steven asked, as she stood in front of the bureau mirror, brushing her hair.

Emma thought for a moment, then nodded. "But I don't want to eat with the others," she said.

Steven nodded his understanding as she braided her hair and then pinned it up in a coronet at the crown of her head. She was just sinking into a tubful of hot, scented water when she heard his voice again. She couldn't help smiling to think that, with all he was facing, Steven was humming.

He stuck his head around the door of the bathroom and his eyes widened when he saw her there, soaking away the evidence of their lovemaking. "I—er—brought your supper up," he told her distractedly.

Emma smiled sleepily, then stretched her arms above her head and yawned.

Steven swore softly. "Don't do that," he scolded.

Emma nestled back into the water, too contented to move, even though she was hungry. Her eyes closed languidly as she relaxed, popped open again when she felt Steven's hand touch one of her breasts.

He grinned and took a strawberry from a small bowl in

his left hand, outlining Emma's lips with it before slipping it into her mouth.

"Ummm," she said, feeling wonderfully decadent.

Steven gave her another berry in the same way, then set the bowl aside. Emma started to rise out of the water, but he put a strong hand to her thigh and held her where she was. Then he placed a particularly ripe berry on her breast and bent his head to take it from her with his mouth.

Ferocious pleasure shot through Emma's system when she felt his lips encompass not only the berry, but her nipple as well. He consumed both before lifting his head.

Emma laughed shakily at the mischievous grin she saw on his face. "Don't tell me you're going to make love to me again," she protested, as he lifted her out of the water and began toweling her well-pleasured body dry.

"All right," he answered, still grinning. "I won't tell you."

He lifted her up and carried her to the bed, spreading her gently on the silk counterpane. His eyes caressed her creamy flesh as he removed his clothes and poised himself over her on the bed.

Emma stretched, even though common sense told her to curl up in a ball, and when she did, Steven caught her hands together above her head and kissed her lightly between her breasts. She whimpered and pushed her legs apart to accommodate him, even though she was sure she had nothing more to give.

"No waiting this time," he promised, then he rolled his tongue around Emma's nipple until it stood up for him, ready to nourish.

She received him with a low cry of welcome, not expecting to be aroused, certain that her body had given all it could. But soon her thighs were thrashing on the mattress, and Steven was kissing her, and swallowing her exclamations and pleas.

When it was over, and they'd regained some of their strength, they sat cross-legged in the middle of the bed, facing each other, eating from the same plate. After that they lay together beneath the covers, Emma's head resting on Steven's shoulder while he read aloud from a book of sonnets.

Presently Emma fell asleep and dreamed that she and Steven were old, and the happy laughter of their children's children flowed in through the windows to touch her ears.

# Chapter
## ❧ 23 ❧

*T*he courtroom was crowded, the epidemic notwithstanding, and the mood was oppressive. Emma sat stiffly beside Cyrus, her ivory-handled fan clasped unopened in one hand, her eyes scanning the jury members. All twelve faces were masculine, and all twelve were impassive—impossible to read.

Emma shifted her gaze to Steven, sitting just ahead of her at a table, Garrick Wright beside him. As though sensing her perusal, Steven shifted in his chair to look back at her, and to her utter amazement, he winked.

She pursed her lips, amazed that he could take so serious a proceeding so lightly. He mimicked her dour expression, then turned to face the front of the courtroom again.

The Louisiana state flag stood behind the judge's massive desk, along with the Stars and Stripes. There was a pitcher of water at hand for His Honor, along with a glass, and Emma's mouth felt dry looking at it.

A bailiff entered the room to stand in front of the towering desk. "The Honorable Judge J.B. Beeman presiding," he thundered, obviously taking his job seriously. "All rise."

Emma suffered a wave of dizziness when she stood with the others, and teetered for a moment. Cyrus quickly took her arm and supported her with surprising strength.

Judge Beeman, a large, balding man with a fringe of red hair around his pate and with snapping blue eyes, took his seat and lowered the gavel. Everyone sat down again.

"Are you all right?" Cyrus asked, leaning close to speak into Emma's ear.

Emma nodded, though the motion was a lie, and focused her mind on the proceedings that would determine her future as well as Steven's. The hot, stuffy air smelled of sweaty bodies pressed too close together, and a fly buzzed loudly around the head of the prosecuting attorney, causing him to swipe at it fruitlessly with one hand.

The first witness called to the stand was a man who had attended the ball the night of Mary McCall's murder. He was the first of a virtual multitude to testify that Miss McCall and Mr. Steven Fairfax had indulged in a public display of rancor before half the city of New Orleans.

Garrick didn't cross-examine even one of these witnesses, which Emma thought was a gross oversight on his part, but of course no one asked her opinion.

As the morning passed, the room got hotter, the smells and sounds more odious to bear, and the frantic motions of Emma's fan provided no relief at all. The room started to go black around her, and in sudden panic, she shot to her feet and attempted to flee toward fresh air.

The strange thing was that she could still hear clearly, though she couldn't see at all. There was a murmur from the crowd of onlookers, then the scraping of chairs against the varnished wooden floors.

"Emma." She heard Steven speaking her name and struggled through the dense blackness surrounding her to reach him. A horrid, piercing ammonia smell made her eyes fly open in surprise and alarm.

Steven smiled down at her, and after handing a vial of smelling salts back to a woman hovering nearby, he tenderly smoothed tendrils of coppery hair back from her face.

She was mortified to find herself lying prone in the aisle, to realize she'd made a scene that probably seemed calculated to the jury. She tried to stammer out an apology, but Steven laid his fingers to her lips and shook his head, then helped her back to her feet.

Cyrus was immediately at her side, his arm around her slender waist, supporting her. "I'll see she gets home safely," he assured Steven in an undertone.

Emma started to protest, but Steven shook his head and Cyrus escorted her firmly down the aisle to the door. As they passed, Emma felt curious, pitying eyes touch her, and lifted her chin a notch. For all her fierce dignity, she would not have made it through the lobby of the courthouse and down the marble steps outside if it hadn't been for Cyrus.

At a signal from him, one of the Fairhaven coaches pulled up to the curb. Gently, Cyrus helped Emma inside. "The minute you get back home," he ordered kindly, "I want you to lie down and put your feet up."

Emma clutched his hand for a moment, glad Cyrus meant to stay and lend his staunch support. "I'll come back tomorrow," she said, wanting desperately to believe those words.

Cyrus nodded and she saw sympathy in his face. He spoke to the driver and the carriage lurched away from the curb.

Emma sat inside, gripping the edges of the leather seat and praying she wouldn't be violently ill. Her stomach was roiling, her head pounded, and the inky darkness that had consumed her before gathered at the edge of her vision, ready to close in.

When they reached Fairhaven, Jubal rushed out to collect her. "I knew you shouldn't have gone to that ole trial, Miss Emma," fussed Jubal. "I tried to tell Mr. Steven that. You's makin' a baby, you can't go gallivantin' all over the parish—"

Emma might have smiled if her husband hadn't been accused of a murder he didn't commit. As it was, she just let Jubal prattle.

She was settled on the bed, wearing only her knickers and camisole, her feet propped on pillows and a cool cloth resting on her head, when she drifted off to sleep.

She awakened with a start to find Macon standing at the foot of the bed, watching her with a grin stretched across his face. His finger and thumb still lingered on her big toe.

Stunned, she scooted toward the headboard, as if it could lend her some protection, her eyes wide. Steven's .45 was in the drawer of the nightstand on his side of the bed. She inched in that direction. "What are you doing here?" she croaked.

Macon dragged his eyes over her lush figure, her sleep-rumpled underthings made of the thinnest lawn, and smiled. "You might say I've come to admire the spoils. It won't be long now, Emma, dear. Things are going very badly for Steven. Soon you'll be giving me fine, redheaded sons. Of course, I won't be able to keep you here at Fairhaven—that would be indiscreet. We'll have to get you a place in town."

Emma tried to shield her breasts with one arm as she moved nearer and nearer the side of the bed. "You're vile, Macon Fairfax, and I'd sooner die than let you touch me. Now, get out of here before I scream!"

"You can scream all you want," he chuckled, spreading his hands wide of his lithe body. "There's nobody here but the servants, and they wouldn't dream of interfering, believe me."

Emma swallowed hard. She couldn't be sure whether he was bluffing; after all, this was Macon's house as well as Cyrus's. If he gave instructions, they were probably obeyed. "Get out," she said again. Her hand was on the knob of the nightstand drawer, but she knew she wasn't going to have time to get the pistol out and aim it before Macon was on her. He was too close, and his eyes showed that he knew exactly what she meant to do.

"It won't be so bad, Emma," he coaxed, his voice a syrupy croon by then. "I know how to make you happy, and you're in just the right place for me to prove it."

"Don't touch me," Emma breathed, shrinking back against the headboard, her eyes wide with horror. "Steven will kill you if you touch me!"

"You wouldn't tell him." Macon was standing over her by then, looking down into her face. She could see a vein pulsing at his right temple as he set his jaw for a moment. "You'd keep it to yourself because he wouldn't have a chance in hell of winning this case if he assaulted me in a fit of rage—would he?"

Emma's heart was thundering against her ribs and she was sure she was going to throw up. She tried to move away from Macon, but he reached out and grasped her hard by the hair.

"Please," she whispered.

He indulged in a small, tight smile. "Don't humiliate yourself by begging, darling. It won't save you. Keep your pleas for those last delicious moments before pleasure overtakes you."

Bile rushed into the back of Emma's throat. "Let me go."

He pressed her flat against the mattress, his hand still entangled in her hair. She gazed up at him in terror, unable to speak at all.

The crash of the door against the inside wall startled them both.

Emma's eyes swung to the doorway, and so did Macon's. Nathaniel was standing there, still dressed in the suit he'd worn to Steven's trial, his tie loose, his Fairfax eyes riveted on his cousin's face. In his shaking hand was a derringer, aimed directly at Macon's middle.

"Let her go," he said furiously.

Macon released Emma, but only to shrug out of his coat and hang it casually over the bedpost. "Get out of here, Nathaniel," he said, sounding as unconcerned as if he were about to open a book or pour himself a drink. "This is business for a man, not a boy."

Emma was breathing hard, her eyes fixed on Nathaniel, pleading with him. With everything in her, she longed to dive for the other side of the bed and run for her life, but she knew she wouldn't escape Macon. Not without Nathaniel's help.

"I won't let you hurt her," the boy said with quiet determination. The derringer, wavering before, was steady now.

Macon gave a heavy, rasping sigh and ran one hand through his thick hair. "I'm going to take my quirt to you for this," he told Nathaniel evenly.

Nathaniel ran his tongue nervously over his lips.

"Don't listen to him," Emma said breathlessly. "Cyrus won't let him hurt you—neither will Steven."

Macon's hand delved into her hair again, pulling hard. "Shut up," he breathed.

"I said let her go!" Nathaniel shouted.

Macon sighed again. "I guess I'll just have to take care of you first," he said reasonably. He started toward Nathaniel, and in that awful instant, Emma saw the boy's intent in his frightened eyes.

"No!" she screamed, leaping off the bed. "Nathaniel, don't!"

Macon advanced another step and the derringer went off. Both Emma and the boy, who had fired the shot, watched in horror as Steven's elder brother went down, sinking first to his knees and then sprawling, spread-eagled on the floor. His blood soaked the rug.

"My God," Emma whispered, wrenching on her wrapper and rushing to kneel at Macon's side. In this moment of desperate need, his earlier transgressions were forgotten; nothing mattered but keeping him alive. "Nathaniel, run and get the doctor—quickly."

The boy just stood in the doorway, his face devoid of all color, the derringer still in his hand.

"Nathaniel!" Emma screamed again, just as three of the servants pushed past him to enter the room. His paralysis seemed to be broken then; he dropped the gun to the floor and stumbled a few steps closer.

"Is he dead?"

Emma and Jubal turned Macon over onto his back. He was breathing, but unconscious, and his shirtfront was soaked with so much blood that it was impossible to tell exactly where the wound was.

"No," Emma said briskly. "Go and get the doctor, Nathaniel, right now."

He nodded, turned, and groped his way out of the room.

Emma's fingers were sticky with Macon's blood as she unbuttoned his shirt and searched for the wound. It was high in the right side of his chest, and inch or two below the collarbone.

Macon groaned.

"Let's get him onto the bed," Emma said, and she and Jubal and another woman hoisted him to his feet and half carried, half dragged him back to Emma's bed.

"He's bleedin' like a stuck pig," Jubal fretted.

Emma found the nearest pulse point and pressed on it hard with three fingers, the way she'd seen Chloe do years before, when Emma had stepped on a rusted barrel hoop and cut open her knee. The flow slowed to a seepage. "Get some hot water," Emma called to anyone who might be listening, and she was rewarded with the sound of footsteps thundering down the stairs.

During the coming hour Emma and Jubal managed to stop the bleeding, clean Macon up a little, and bandage his wound. He still hadn't regained consciousness, though.

Another hour had passed before the doctor arrived, and he stared at Emma in amazement when she met him in the hall, her hair trailing, wearing a wrapper stained crimson with blood.

"I'm not hurt," she assured the man, wondering what, if anything, Nathaniel had told him. "It's Macon."

The portly snowy-haired man followed her into the room where Macon lay, still white as the best linen tablecloth in Emma's hope chest. "What happened?" the doctor demanded, snapping open his bag and taking out a stethoscope, which he promptly fitted to his ears.

He was bending over Macon, listening to his heartbeat and to Emma's explanation at the same time. She stumbled over the description of Macon's attempted assault; everything seemed unreal now.

"Didn't know what I was going to find when I got over here," the doctor replied when she'd finished. He stood up straight again. "That boy was about as upset as anybody I've ever seen. He kept saying there'd been a murder."

Emma said nothing while he unwrapped the wound, disinfected it, and bound it again.

"Whoever looked after this wound did a damned good job," the doctor said, turning to face Emma. "Was it you?"

Emma's throat was tight, and she felt a perverse desire to laugh at the irony of it all. She could do nothing to save Steven, the man she loved more than life, but she'd dragged Macon, practically her worst enemy, back from the brink of death. "I had help from Jubal," she said.

He peered at her over the wire rims of his spectacles. "You're Steven's bride, aren't you? I would have thought you'd be at your husband's trial. Of course, Macon always did have a way with the ladies."

Emma felt the bottom fall out of her stomach as she absorbed his implication. Then her cheeks were suffused with sudden color. Despite this, she managed to speak evenly and with cool dignity. "Macon may very well have 'a way with the ladies,' Doctor, but *this* lady loves her husband. I did not encourage my brother-in-law's attentions."

The old man studied her for a moment, then smiled somewhat sheepishly. "I apologize, Mrs. Fairfax," he said. "It just seemed odd to me that you'd be here at Fairhaven, instead of in town, at the courthouse, like practically everybody else in this parish. Even the threat of yellow fever doesn't keep them at home."

Emma wasn't going to explain, feeling she owed this offensive man nothing, but then it occurred to her that he might well be the one to bring her baby into the world, should she be carrying one. "I was overcome by the heat and the foul smell of the air," she confessed, "and I fainted."

The doctor looked her over with astute eyes. "Could be you're carrying a child."

He would never know how devoutly Emma hoped he was right. She averted her eyes, disconcerted at the prospect of discussing so intimate a topic with any man other than Steven. "Perhaps," she said.

He turned to start down the hallway, black bag in hand. "I'll come back and check on Macon around sunset. My guess is by that time he'll be awake and grousing about the pain."

Emma nodded uneasily, already dreading the task of explaining the afternoon's events to Steven. He would want to kill Macon with his bare hands, and the man's near-fatal wound might not deter him.

Jubal appeared with a clean wrapper of pale pink corduroy, probably belonging to Lucy, and gently took Emma's arm. "You need a bath, Miss Emma. Let me help you."

Now that the crisis was over, Emma was feeling weak again, and her knees were like pudding. She leaned on Jubal's arm as the woman led her down the hallway toward Macon and Lucy's quarters. She had to get away from her own rooms.

The scent of Lucy's jasmine perfume filled the air, though the suite was empty. Lucy, like Cyrus, was at Steven's trial.

"You can just bathe right in here," Jubal went on. "I know Miss Lucy wouldn't mind at all."

For her part, Emma was almost as nervous about

Lucy's reaction to the events of the afternoon as she was about Steven's. Telling the truth and still sparing her sister-in-law's feelings would be patently impossible.

The bathroom in the master suite was dazzling. The tub was made of gray marble, streaked with white, and the fixtures looked to be gold-plated. There were thick, fluffy white rugs on the tiled floor, and a row of high lace-curtained windows flooded the chamber with light.

Solicitously, Jubal seated Emma on the lid of the commode before turning to start water running in the tub. "These here rooms belonged to Mr. Macon's mama and daddy when I came here," the black woman said, and Emma found herself wondering how old Jubal was. Her face was unwrinkled, her hair without a trace of gray, but there was a wealth of experience and pain visible in her eyes. "Afore that, it belonged to Mr. Cyrus and Miss Louella. Didn't have running water so long as that, 'course."

Emma didn't comment. She was busy looking back over the afternoon, realizing that she'd nearly been raped, that the man who'd accosted her was lying unconscious in the very bed where he'd meant to force himself on her.

"You all right, Miss Emma?" Jubal asked.

Emma nodded glumly and pushed the splayed fingers of one hand through her hair. It was matted with dried blood, and the smell filled her nostrils. She shivered.

After hesitating a few more moments, Jubal turned and went out.

The moment she was gone, Emma ripped the spoiled wrapper off, only to discover that the garments beneath were stained as well. Gingerly, she peeled them away and stepped into the tub.

She felt better once she'd soaked away every trace of Macon's blood, but the shaky, tremulous feeling in her knees and shoulders remained. When she'd shampooed her hair and scoured herself with lemon-scented soap, she climbed from the tub and began drying off with one of the thick white towels Jubal had laid out for her.

She was using Lucy's comb to work the tangles from her hair when there was a rap at the door and Steven came in, looking grim and pale. "Jubal told me you were here," he said when Emma froze at the sight of him. "She said Nathaniel shot Macon."

Emma nodded, not trusting herself to speak. More than anything in the world, she needed to be taken into Steven's arms and held. She needed reassurance from him, and tenderness.

"Why?" he rasped, though the lethal expression in his eyes told Emma he already knew.

"He—Nathaniel was trying to protect me. Macon meant to—to—rape me."

A curse exploded from Steven's lips, but he stood ominously still. He glared at Emma for a long moment, as though everything were somehow her fault, and in that time she suffered the agony of the damned. Then, however, he gathered her into his arms, wet, tangled hair and all. "Did he hurt you?" he asked hoarsely, his lips moving against her temple.

"No," Emma managed, clinging to him. "But he frightened me. Oh, God, Steven—I've never been so scared—"

"Shh," Steven whispered, and he lifted her easily into his arms. "You need to lie down."

"How did the trial go?" Emma asked anxiously, as he carried her out of Macon and Lucy's sumptuously furnished suite and across the hall to what was probably a guest room.

He set her gently on the four-poster bed, drawing the coverlet up to her shoulders. Then taking the comb she still clutched in one hand, he began to groom her hair for her. The ritual was comforting, but he still hadn't answered her question.

"Steven," she prompted.

"Not well," he answered reluctantly. "The trial is not going well. I sat there listening while everybody in New Orleans came forward and testified that I killed Mary McCall."

Emma closed her eyes for a moment, nearly overwhelmed by panic, but she fought it down. She couldn't afford to fall apart, though sometimes she thought it would be a mercy to retreat into a strange little world all her own, as Lucy did.

One of his hands gripped her bare shoulder. "It's all right, Emma," he reassured her.

"Is—is Lucy home? Someone will need to be with her—"

"Jubal is looking after her, and Cyrus sent somebody for the sheriff."

Emma whirled to look up into Steven's face. "The sheriff? They're not really going to arrest Nathaniel, are they? Oh, Steven, he's only a boy!"

He silenced her by laying an index finger to her lips. "There hasn't been any talk of arresting anybody. But the sheriff has to investigate things such as this, Emma. We can't just say, 'Someone's been shot here at Fairhaven, but don't worry—we'll handle it.'"

Emma would have smiled if she hadn't felt so much like breaking apart.

Steven grinned ruefully. "If I hadn't been at the courthouse, on trial for murder, they probably would have blamed me." He finished combing Emma's hair and sat down on the edge of the bed, facing her.

She put her hands on his shoulders, rested her forehead against his and sighed. She was about to tell him she loved him when she sensed another presence and lifted her head.

Lucy was standing in the doorway of the guest room, her eyes round and wide, her flawless skin pale as milk. "What happened?" she said, staring at Emma, seemingly unaware of Steven's presence. "Jubal said he was with you. He's lying in your bed, half alive. *What happened?*"

Steven got up and went to Lucy, gently escorting her to a chair near the bed.

Emma looked at her husband, feeling devoid of courage. He was standing behind Lucy's chair now, watching her just as his sister-in-law did, and Emma felt curiously alone. "Macon meant to—to force his attentions on me," she managed to say. "Nathaniel interceded. H-he had a gun. Macon didn't t-take him seriously—he said he was going to take his riding quirt to him. He started toward Nathaniel and—and the gun went off."

For a long time Lucy just sat there, her eyes darting nervously between her lap, where her hands were twisted together, and Emma's face. Finally she gave a choking sob and bent forward in her chair, her arms folded across her middle as though to hold herself together.

"I'm so sorry, Lucy," Emma said gently, near tears herself.

Lucy went on wailing, and Steven hurried out of the room, returning a few moments later with a brown bottle and a small glass. He poured some of the amber liquid for Lucy, and she drank it down.

"What is that?" Emma asked, as Lucy's sobs began to subside a little.

"Laudanum," Steven answered. He got Lucy to her feet and helped her as far as the doorway, where a maid was waiting to collect her mistress.

"Does she take a lot of that?" Emma asked, looking at the bottle distastefully.

Steven sighed and set it aside. "She's been using it ever since I've known her," he said, screwing the lid back onto the bottle. "Obviously, being married to my brother is no field of daisies."

His words triggered a sweet memory of the first time he and Emma had truly made love. Steven had taken her in a bed of daisies, and suddenly Emma wanted to be back there, reliving those innocent delights, all her terrible problems yet to be faced. "Hold me," she said.

Steven closed the door, removed his jacket and his boots, and stretched out on the bed beside her. He was wearing suspenders, and Emma gave one of them a playful snap, even though she still felt like dissolving into tears, just as Lucy had.

He smiled and kissed the tip of her nose, one hand

resting lightly on her naked hip. "It's time this old house saw some joy again, don't you think?"

Emma nodded. "Your father and Macon's mother— were they happy?"

Steven shrugged. "All I really remember about my father is that he always gave me rock candy when he visited, and that he adored my mother. It doesn't seem likely that he'd have kept a mistress if he loved the woman he married."

"What about Cyrus and his wife, Louella?"

He grinned. "My guess would be they were happy. Granddaddy gets a certain light in his eyes when he talks about Louella, and he told me once that he'd never been unfaithful to her."

Emma wet her lips with the tip of her tongue, her eyes wide and weary as she looked at her husband. "Would you ever take a mistress?"

He kissed her, his tongue sweeping her lips once, awakening her needs in spite of all that had happened that day. "Never," he said with such quiet certainty that Emma was greatly comforted. "I get everything I need from you."

She nestled against him, slipping her fingers beneath his suspender strap again. She felt him shiver slightly as she tilted her head back to kiss the base of his throat. His hand moved to encompass her small, plump buttock and squeeze it lightly, at the same time pushing her closer.

She slid her hand downward so that her fingertips were reaching just beneath the waistband of his trousers, and he gave a low moan.

"Speaking of what I need," he muttered, capturing her mouth for a kiss that left her breathless, her lips swollen, her indigo eyes dazed.

He rolled over so that he was poised over Emma, still kissing her, and she dragged his suspenders down over both shoulders in a brazen motion of her hands. He raised himself, his mouth still consuming hers, and she unfastened the buttons of his white shirt, then the fastenings on his trousers.

One of her hands was there to greet him when he jutted free of his pants, and he moaned against her mouth as she caught hold of him firmly and ran one thumb over the moist tip of his manhood. His tongue lunged into her mouth, entangled with hers, foretelling another kind of conquering that would take place soon—very soon.

Emma dragged his trousers down over his hips and guided him to her, then spread her hands on his down-covered chest as he took her. This was one of those times when their common need for union was too ferocious to wait, and Emma arched her back as she felt Steven filling her, a little cry of welcome and need tumbling from her lips.

Soon nothing was real to either of them but their own two bodies, locked together in sweet combat.

# Chapter
## ❧ 24 ❧

*C*yrus looked gray as wash water, and his hand trembled slightly as he lifted his customary after-dinner glass of brandy to his lips. "You've got to go and find Nathaniel," he said to Steven, who had followed his grandfather into the study at his request.

Steven wanted to go back upstairs to Emma, to lie beside her and let her drive all the specters of death from his mind and soul, but he did care about his young cousin. He saw in Nathaniel the hurt, confused boy he'd once been himself.

"He won't listen to me," Steven insisted, pouring himself a drink. "He believes I killed Mary, that I ran away because of that."

"I don't give a damn what he believes," Cyrus said. "I just want him safe under this roof, where he belongs."

Because he'd never been able to refuse his grandfather anything, Steven nodded, set down his drink untouched, and left the study without another word.

Nathaniel's favorite horse, a spirited Appaloosa gelding, was not in the stables. Steven selected a bay, saddled it himself, and set out into the moonlit night. Instinct sent him into the swamps well behind the house and stables, rather than onto the road. He'd taken refuge there many times when he'd first come to live at Fairhaven.

Sure enough, he found Nathaniel sitting forlornly under a moss-draped tree, a lantern at his side, his horse tethered nearby.

"Maybe you don't mind being eaten alive by mosquitoes," Steven told him, crouching beside the boy on the soft, loamy ground, "but I'm of a different opinion entirely. Get off your rear end, Nate—we're leaving."

"Go to hell," Nathaniel muttered, never looking at Steven. "You're a coward and a killer, and now I'm no better than you."

Steven gave a raspy sigh. "I'm not a killer, and Macon isn't about to die, so neither are you."

At last Nathaniel looked at him. His adolescent face was draped in shadow, but the pain inside him was clearly visible all the same. "If you didn't kill Mary, why did you run away?"

Steven swatted at a horde of buzzing mosquitoes. "I ran because I knew I wouldn't get a fair trial," he said. "It was wrong, I know, but I didn't want to die. If it hadn't been for Emma, I probably would never have come back."

"I stood up to them," Nathaniel spat. "I stood up to the people who said you murdered Mary—you don't know how many times I had to fight—and then you ran away!" These last words came out as a strangled sob of betrayal and hurt.

Steven grasped Nathaniel by the arm and hauled him to his feet, bending to take up the lantern. "I'm sorry, Nate," he said, squiring his young, shaken cousin toward his horse.

Nathaniel was crying, but Steven could tell he begrudged every sob. "It was terrible—the way Macon looked at me—the way he fell—"

Steven slapped the boy on the back. "He's going to be all right, Nathaniel."

"I only did it because he meant to hurt Emma—"

"I understand that," Steven broke in, as the young man hoisted himself onto his horse and dragged one arm across his wet eyes. "And I'm grateful to you for protecting her."

Nathaniel swallowed, but said nothing more. Steven made a silent vow to spend more time with the boy—if he was to be allowed to live out the rest of his life.

They were leaving the stables, their horses properly attended to, when Nathaniel choked out, "Will I have to go to jail?"

Steven shook his head. "It isn't very likely that Macon will press charges, considering the circumstances. He might be a philanderer, but I guarantee you, he won't want to explain to the whole parish why he was trying to rape his own sister-in-law."

Nathaniel nodded and scratched at a mosquito bite on his neck, and they went into the house together.

Emma stood in the hallway outside the locked doors of Cyrus's study, her ear pressed to the panel. She had a good mind to hammer at it with her fist until they let her in. After all, it wasn't just Steven's fate they were deciding, it was hers as well.

She imagined the scene inside the room, weaving pictures from the words of the men.

Cyrus was seated behind the desk, while Steven stood at the fireplace, one arm propped on the mantel, his back to the doors.

"Garrick thinks I should jump bail and run for my life," he told his grandfather.

A sound at the end of the hallway sent her fleeing back up the stairs to the guest room where she and Steven were staying now, her thoughts reeling. She'd known things were going badly in the trial, but she'd never guessed the situation was so hopeless that Steven's own lawyer wanted him to run away.

Panic seized her. Garrick was right, of course. An outlaw's life would not be an easy one, but anything was better than seeing Steven hanged.

Desperately, she paced, trying to get control of her raging emotions. It had been a truly terrible day, between the trial's starting, her fainting, and Macon attempting to rape her, then getting shot before her very eyes. She drew a deep breath and let it out again.

If it hadn't been for Nathaniel, she might have shot Macon herself, and Steven's .45 would have done a lot more damage than Nathaniel's little derringer.

She shuddered to think of what could have happened.

Steven's voice practically startled her out of her skin. "Get into bed," he said. "You're freezing."

"D-did you find Nathaniel?" Emma asked, obediently climbing between the covers, which were still rumpled from their lovemaking, and stretching out.

Her husband nodded. "He was in the swamp, letting the mosquitoes chew on him." Steven undid his string tie and tossed it aside, then shrugged out of his jacket.

"Is he all right?"

Steven sighed. "He's in shock, like the rest of us. Did you look in on Lucy?"

"Yes," Emma answered, turning onto her side and watching as her husband undressed. She prayed she'd see this same sight every night until she was a hundred and ten. "I'm worried about her, Steven. She's in worse shape than Macon."

He slipped into bed beside her and lay on his back, his hands cupped behind his head. "I know," he said ruefully.

Emma entangled a finger in the lush hair on Steven's chest. "Has she always been so strange—wearing black dresses and playing with dolls?"

"No," Steven said sadly. "When I first knew Lucy, she was full of life, always laughing and always wearing the latest fashion. Whatever her problem is, you can bet Macon is at the root of it."

Emma nodded, wanting to ask Steven, again, if they

could run away, but afraid to reveal that she'd been eavesdropping outside Cyrus's study. She snuggled closer to him, her head resting on his shoulder, and continued her idle exploration of his chest, adding the occasional foray to his taut belly.

"Are you scared?" she finally dared to ask.

"I'd be a damned fool if I weren't," Steven responded, and a little groan escaped him as her fingertips strayed downward. He caught hold of her hand. "You little vixen—wasn't the first time enough for you?"

She shook her head, and he turned to her and kissed her. Soon she was astraddle of him, riding him as though he were a bucking stallion, draining him—and herself— of every response, every moan and sigh and gasp.

When he slept, though, Emma was still wide awake. She lay beside him, enfolding him in her arms. Time was running short, and Steven was determined not to run again, even if that meant his life. She was going to have to find a way to prove he was innocent, and soon.

She suspected Macon of the crime more than ever, now that she'd seen how cruel and ruthless he could really be. But she was still convinced that the key to it all lay with Maisie Lee, who was too frightened of her husband to talk.

Presently Emma fell asleep. Too soon it was morning.

"I want you to stay here," Steven told her as he stood at the bureau, arranging his tie. He'd already bathed, and he was wearing a fresh suit.

Emma sat up in bed, a protest on her lips, but the look in Steven's eyes silenced her. She lay down again, her arms folded. "I'm not sick," she said petulantly, and before she could go on, a wave of nausea swept over her and sent her scrambling for the basin.

Steven held her hair as she vomited, and he brought her a cold cloth and water to rinse her mouth when she was through. While the ever-vigilant Jubal carried the basin out, he put his wife back in bed and bent to kiss her forehead.

"I don't have the plague, Steven," Emma insisted fitfully. "I'm just pregnant, probably. You need me at the trial—"

"I need to know you're all right," Steven corrected, brushing her hair back from her face. "Please, Emma. If you love me, stay here. Don't make me worry about you."

Her eyes filled with tears as she looked up at him. "I love you so much, Steven."

"And I love you," he answered. He kissed her again, and then he was gone.

Although she would have expected to toss and turn, doing nothing but fretting about the progress of the trial, Emma went right back to sleep again. When she awakened, several hours had passed, by her calculations, since the sun seemed high.

She got out of bed, washed her face and cleaned her teeth, then braided her hair. All traces of nausea were gone, and she felt strong and determined as she put on the lovely floral morning dress Jubal had laid out for her. She would visit Maisie Lee Simpson again today, and no matter what she had to do, she would find out what the woman was hiding.

The door to the master suite was open, but there was no sign of Lucy, and she wasn't sitting with Macon or having coffee in the dining room, either. Assuming her sister-in-law had gone to the courthouse with Steven and Cyrus, Emma sat down at the long table and forced herself to consume the toast and weak tea Jubal pressed upon her.

When she'd done that, she sent for a carriage.

"You mustn't go out, Miss Emma," Jubal argued. "Mr. Steven say he don't want you to. He say you stay here, where Jubal can see to you."

Emma didn't like defying the kindly servant, but she had too much at stake to sit in the house and wait for her husband's death sentence to be pronounced. She had to *do* something. She went outside, in back of the house, and sent one of the children who was playing around the kitchen building to ask for a carriage.

The driver, an elderly black man with kindly eyes, came to her with his cap in his hands. "I's sorry, Miss Emma," he said, "but Mr. Steven, he tell me no carriage for you. And no horses, neither."

Thoroughly exasperated, Emma dismissed Ebel and ventured into the kitchen, where Jubal and a half dozen others were already making preparations for supper. She'd set her mind on going to question Maisie Lee again, but she couldn't very well *walk* into the city. It was miles to Miss Astoria McCall's house, where Maisie Lee was probably working.

Feeling like an intruder, Emma wandered out of the kitchen again. When she next saw Mr. Steven Fairfax, she would give him a piece of her mind for leaving her stranded like this, with no way to get into town.

She was crossing the lawn when inspiration hit her. With a loud and dramatic cry, she gripped her stomach and dropped to her knees in the manicured green grass. She only hoped she wouldn't get stains on her skirts.

Instantly she was surrounded by worried children. She felt guilty, scaring them that way, but there was no alternative if she was to carry out her plan. She moaned again as Jubal rushed to her side, summoned by one of the little ones.

The fright in Jubal's trusting face deepened Emma's contrition, but she continued to moan and hold her stomach. "I need the doctor," she murmured.

Jubal snatched at one of the children's cotton shirts. "You go and fetch Ebel," she told the little boy. "Tell him bring the doctor for Miss Emma right now!"

Emma sat up with pretended difficulty, one hand to her forehead. She was grateful Steven wasn't around to witness this performance; he would have seen right through it. "No—I can't wait," she gasped out. "Ebel must take me to him."

And so it was that poor Ebel unknowingly defied Steven's orders by bringing the carriage around and helping Miss Emma into it. When they'd reached the doctor's downtown office, she let the driver help her out, then darted away toward a nearby cab.

While Ebel hurried after her, politely calling for her to *please* come back, the other carriage bore her away.

Luck was with her, it seemed. When she reached Miss Astoria's house, Maisie Lee was there alone. Emma found her in the backyard, hanging up laundry. She gave Emma a fitful look and tried to ignore her, but her hands shook as she pegged a gigantic pair of knickers to the line.

Emma could hear another carriage in the cobbled street, coming to a stop behind the one she'd hired. Ebel had followed her, and there was no telling how far he'd go to comply with "Mr. Steven's" orders. Hurriedly she said, "Maisie Lee, you've got to tell me whom you're protecting, please! Who was here that night?"

Maisie Lee looked at her, but stubbornly. "Go 'way. I ain't gonna say nothin'. Jethro'll thump my head if'n I do."

"You're going to let a man die?" Emma whispered in amazement. "A man you *know* is innocent?"

"I heared Miss Mary screamin' that night," Maisie Lee insisted angrily. "She was sayin' his name—Mr. Steven's name—over and over! She was real scairt, too."

"She was screaming his name," Emma repeated, talking rapidly because she sensed Ebel's approach. "Try to remember, Maisie Lee—please—did she say anything else?"

Maisie Lee squeezed her eyes shut, remembering. "She say, 'It was Steven.' She say that two, three times."

"That means she was addressing somebody else, don't you see?" Emma insisted frantically.

Ebel was beside Emma now. He didn't quite dare take her arm, but she could tell he wasn't going anywhere until she agreed to return to Fairhaven with him.

Maisie Lee's eyes darted to Ebel, then came back to Emma's face. "You go home, missus. You'll find the killer right there in yo' own house!"

Macon. Emma sighed. There was no choice. She was going to have to confront Macon, and she knew even before she tried that it was a hopeless effort.

Subdued, Emma allowed Ebel to lead her patiently around the crumbling McCall house, through the gate, and over the bumpy sidewalk. He handed her gently into the carriage, looking at her with baleful eyes when she offered a silent apology.

During the drive back to Fairhaven, Emma was in despair. She'd find the murderer right in her own house, Maisie Lee had said, but that was useless information. She knew as well as Steven and Garrick did that Macon had strangled Mary McCall, and he would never confess.

When Ebel helped Emma down from the carriage in front of Fairhaven, she walked despondently into the house, feeling like a prisoner, and made her way up the stairs.

Passing the room she'd shared with Steven until the day before, she saw Macon through the open doorway. His eyes were wide, and his face was flattened into a mask of sheer horror. He was making an anxious little sound deep in his throat.

Although she felt little pity for him, Emma could not pass by without finding out what was the matter. She stepped quickly into the room and was aghast to see Lucy approaching the bed with a pillow.

While Emma watched, frozen, Lucy pressed the pillow to Macon's face, using both hands and putting the weight of her small body into the task. "You've shamed me for the last time," she said in a voice that sounded strangely sane. "First all those women, then you actually tried to rape your own brother's wife. But then, I shouldn't be surprised. Your conscience didn't keep you from fornicating with Dirk's intended. And Dirk was your own son, though God knows it wasn't me who bore him for you, was it, Macon?"

Jolted out of her stunned state, Emma found her voice and rushed into the room. "Lucy, no," she pleaded, her voice surprisingly calm and evenly modulated. "He's your husband—"

"He's a viper," Lucy answered, making no move to lift the pillow. Macon struggled lamely beneath it.

Emma tried to pull her away, but Lucy was incredibly strong in her madness. "Lucy, in the name of God, this is murder!"

"He's hurt so many people," Lucy went on, as Emma tried again, in vain, to make her lift the pillow from Macon's face. "All you have to do is look the other way, Emma. Pretend you didn't see anything."

Emma was desperate. "They'll put you in prison," she reasoned. "And prisons are dreadful places."

"I know," Lucy answered in a chillingly distracted way. "Steven will live out his life in one if they don't hang him, and all because of Macon. Don't you see? It's only right for Macon to die."

Emma tried to keep her head, though she wanted to run from the room, screaming for help. "You killed Mary didn't you, Lucy?" she asked quietly, playing a sudden hunch, remembering Maisie Lee's assertion that she would find the killer in her own house, and how frightened the woman had seemed. Now Emma knew it was because she'd seen Lucy leaving Mary's room that awful night.

Macon was still writhing beneath the pillow, but he was so weak, it wouldn't be long before he lapsed into unconsciousness and then death, unless Lucy lifted that pillow.

Lucy looked back at her over one shoulder, frowning. Remembering. "Yes," she said. "I had to. She was going to have a baby—Macon's baby—and I couldn't let her do that. I was never able to give him a child, you see. But it was my right. *My right.*"

*It was Steven,* Mary McCall had screamed that night according to Maisie Lee. *It was Steven.* She felt faint, but nonetheless she laid her hand on Lucy's arm. "Everything will be all right, Lucy," she said softly.

A tear streaked down Lucy's alabaster cheek, and she let go of the pillow, which Emma quickly dragged off Macon's face and tossed away. Her brother-in-law was purple and staring up at her in helpless terror, but Emma felt no obligation to reassure him.

All her concern was for Lucy. She helped her sister-in-law to a chair and eased her into it.

"The baby Mary was carrying was Steven's," Emma guessed, her voice wooden. She could come to no other conclusion, given the circumstances. It seemed remarkable that all along, as desperately as she'd loved him, he'd been lying to her.

But Lucy shook her head. She was strangely lucid, now that she'd made the admission. "She was just saying that, the lying little tramp. It was Macon's baby."

"It was—*Dirk's*—" Macon rasped from the bed.

Emma stared at him, and so did Lucy.

He tried to sit up against his pillows but failed. Emma went to him, her eyes wide, her heart beating painfully fast. Steven's life was safe now, but her trust in him was flickering like a candle on the sill of an open window.

"The baby was—Dirk's—" Macon insisted again, and then he closed his eyes, whether from weariness or swooning, Emma couldn't know.

She turned to Lucy, who was deathly white, her brown eyes enormous in her face. Her trembling fingers, pressed to her mouth, made Emma know Macon had been telling the truth.

Steven wasn't going to die; the whole universe turned on that axis. *Steven wasn't going to die.*

She knelt beside Lucy's chair, taking her hand. "Do you want some of your medicine?" she asked gently, feeling no rancor toward the woman, only compassion. Things might have been so very different for Lucy if she'd been able to bear a child, if she had married a man capable of any compassion.

Lucy shook her head, and a shaky smile formed on her lips. "Perhaps now God will forgive me," she said.

Emma felt tears burn her eyes. "I'm sure God understood all along," she said softly. And then she wept—for joy, for grief, for all this woman and Steven had suffered, and for poor Mary McCall, who had died too soon and for the wrong reason.

Jubal's voice broke the heavy silence that followed.

"Miss Emma? Miss Lucy? Is everything all right?"

Emma turned her head to look at Jubal. "Someone needs to go to town and bring back the sheriff and Cyrus. Right away."

Jubal was obviously afraid. Her gaze strayed questioningly to Macon, who was lying with his eyes closed.

"Mr. Fairfax is all right," Emma assured her quietly. "Please do as I say. I'll look after Miss Lucy in the meantime."

Lucy began to rock in the chair when Jubal was gone. "My baby," she said. "I need my baby."

Emma looked at her in bafflement and agonizing pity. "Baby?"

Lucy started to lift herself out of the chair, and Emma got awkwardly to her feet. She followed, after one anxious glance back at Macon, as Lucy walked steadily out of the room and down the hallway.

Stopping in front of a door next to her own, she produced a key from the pocket of her black skirt and worked the lock. She stepped into the room, and Emma went in behind her.

Sick shock struck Emma with the impact of a fist when she saw that the room was a nursery, outfitted with toys, a cradle, a rocking chair—every sort of item a baby would need. Lucy went, crooning, to the crib, and lifted out a stiff little form wrapped in a lacy blanket.

Emma's tea and toast came to the back of her throat in

a rush, but then she realized Lucy was holding a doll "See?" the woman said, holding the carefully dressed and wrapped "baby" out for Emma to admire. "Isn't she beautiful? Her name is Helen."

A shudder moved through Emma's system, but she managed a slight smile nonetheless. "Yes," she said, her voice hoarse. "She's lovely."

Humming softly to her "baby," Lucy went into the hallway and back to the room where Macon lay. He was awake again now, and Emma felt more sympathy for him than she had before, even though she knew she would despise him for the rest of her life.

While Lucy sat down again and began to rock her doll, Emma poured water into a glass and lifted Macon's head so that he could drink. He took several grateful swallows, then fell back against his pillows, gasping.

Emma could remember Nathaniel mentioning a room Lucy kept locked, and now she understood all too well. "Did you know?" she asked, her eyes locked with Macon's.

He looked at her helplessly for a long time, then nodded. At the same moment, Steven and Cyrus hurried in, accompanied by the sheriff. Macon saw them, but went on. "I knew about the doll," he said, in a gruff, defeated voice, while Lucy continued to hum to it. "But I really thought Steven killed Mary—I swear it."

"You weren't involved with her yourself?"

Macon closed his eyes for a moment, and Emma knew then that he'd wanted to be, but Mary had spurned him.

Emma started to turn away, wanting to run to Steven, but Macon gripped her hand and held her there to the limit of his strength.

"You don't know how it was," he rasped, "living with Lucy—"

"No," Emma replied, pulling free of him. "But I've got a pretty good idea of what it was like living with you."

With that, she went to Steven and laid her cheek to his chest.

"Jubal said—" Cyrus began, but when his eyes fell on Lucy, who was still beaming and rocking her "baby," he went silent.

"It was Lucy who killed Mary," Emma said, raising her head. "She'd learned the girl was pregnant, and she thought the baby was Macon's."

Steven's eyes were filled with horror as he looked at Lucy, but there was a glimmer of hope in their depths when he turned them to Emma's face. He was just realizing that he was a free man, that he and Emma would have all their lives to share.

Soon after, the doctor arrived, and Lucy was taken to her room and sedated. She fell asleep holding her doll close, a contented smile on her face. For her, everything was resolved, and she was at peace.

"For a while, I thought you'd lied to me," Emma confessed when she and Steven were walking in the moonlit garden that night, holding hands. "I thought you really had made a baby with Mary McCall."

Steven reached out and caressed her face. "I've told you the truth about myself and my past," he assured her. "There aren't going to be any ugly surprises jumping out at you. Not now."

Emma put her arms around him, nestling close, resting her head against his shoulder. "What will happen to Lucy? They won't send her to prison, will they?"

"I don't know," Steven replied sadly.

Emma looked up at him and kissed him lightly on the chin. "We'll make up for all the unhappiness," she vowed rashly. "We'll fill Fairhaven with noise and babies."

He held her close. "Judging by what happened this morning, it seems possible that the first one is already on the way."

Emma nodded. "Do you want a boy or a girl?"

"I want a baby," he said, grinning. "I don't give a damn whether it's a son or a daughter."

"I'd like a boy, one who looks just like you," Emma mused, reveling in their closeness, and in the future that lay before them.

"Not a girl, to name Lily or Caroline?" Steven asked gently, and Emma felt the old sadness return. For the first time she realized that there hadn't been a response to the wire she'd sent to her mother's attorney in Chicago.

Despite Steven's freedom, and her great love for him, her happiness was not complete after all.

# Chapter
## ❧ 25 ❧

*S*teven was publicly exonerated of all charges at nine o'clock the next morning, and onlookers, many of them soundly disappointed, were dismissed from the court-room. Steven and Garrick Wright exchanged a hand-shake, and then Steven turned to Emma, who was standing directly behind him.

He offered her his arm and that little half-smile that had both attracted and alarmed her when she'd first met him. "It's over," he said, and somehow she heard his voice over the general uproar.

"No, Mr. Fairfax," Emma answered, smiling up at him with her eyes and laying a hand on his forearm. "It's only beginning."

"What will happen to Lucy?" Steven asked of his grandfather as he sat, later, in Cyrus's study, gratefully accepting a snifter of brandy.

Cyrus glanced at Dr. Mayfield, who was standing by the fireplace, his arms folded. "I guess that will depend on what Paul here has to say."

The doctor cleared his throat. "Prison's no place for Miss Lucy, we're all agreed on that. She's not competent to stand trial in the first place. If I can bring Judge Willoughby or one of the magistrates around to our way of thinking, we should be able to send her to a hospital I know of out in San Francisco."

"I won't send our Lucy to some hellhole," Cyrus warned. "I'd sooner keep her right here and hire nurses."

Dr. Mayfield shook his head. "Crawford Hospital is not a 'hellhole,' Cyrus," he told his old friend impatiently, "and I ought to call you out just for suggesting I'd consider such a place for her. 'Course, I won't, because there's been enough bloodshed around here as it is." He glanced briefly at Steven, then turned his intelligent gaze back to Cyrus. "It wouldn't be good for Lucy—or for any of the rest of you—if she stayed here. She needs fresh new surroundings."

"What if she recovers?" Steven asked. "Will she have to stand trial then?"

Dr. Mayfield sighed ruefully. "The damage runs deep with Lucy. She'll probably live out the rest of her life at Crawford."

Steven and Cyrus exchanged looks as the doctor excused himself, promising to make arrangements with the proper authorities and the hospital, and when he was gone, Steven asked, "Have you talked to Macon about any of this?"

Cyrus made a disgusted sound and plucked a cigar from the box on his desk, biting off the tip with a vengeance. "He wouldn't give a damn if we put her on a raft and set her adrift on the Mississippi," he muttered. He spat away the tip and struck a match, and soon clouds of smoke billowed around his white head. "You might as well know that he's planning to put Fairhaven behind him for good as soon as he's up and around. Said something about Europe."

Steven took another sip of his brandy. His knees were beginning to feel steadier, he thought with a smile. He'd have to see what he could do about making them weak again. "I don't imagine he exactly relishes the idea of my taking an active part in running Fairhaven."

"You'll have to take more than an 'active part,'" Cyrus informed him. "I'm too old and too tired to oversee this place much longer, and Nathaniel's still wet behind the ears, so he won't be much help."

Steven reached out and helped himself to one of his grandfather's cigars. Emma hated the smell they left on his clothes and in his hair, but he knew how to get around her sensibilities. "You'll have to hold on for a while," he told his grandfather. "There's something important I have to do, and it's going to take some time."

"Emma's sisters?" guessed Cyrus, who missed very little, all things considered.

Steven nodded. "She needs to find Lily and Caroline and get to know them."

"And live near them, perhaps?" Cyrus fished, obviously worried that he might be losing his heir so soon after finding him.

"Emma understands that Fairhaven is our home," Steven answered with a shake of his head. "She just wants to be in contact with her sisters, to know they're happy."

Cyrus sighed heavily. "Any leads?"

"Not much to speak of," Steven replied, frowning. "But she does have an address where her mother once lived, back in Chicago, and the name of an attorney."

"So that's where you'll be going? To Chicago?"

Steven nodded. "With any luck we'll find out what we need to know when we get there." Through the large window behind Cyrus's desk, he could see Emma walking across the grass, looking distracted and more than a little lost.

He stood, snuffed out the cigar, and excused himself.

He found her sitting in the summerhouse where they'd made love one day not so long past and probably conceived the baby they both knew was growing inside her. She was sitting on one of the mattresses, a letter in her hands, a forlorn look on her face.

"What is it?" Steven asked, taking a seat beside her.

She turned her head and looked at him with tears glistening in her eyes. "The attorney has retired," she said sadly, "and his successor has no records of any association with a Kathleen Harrington."

He took her hand and squeezed it reassuringly. "We'll go to Chicago anyway, Emma. We'll talk to her neighbors—"

She was shaking her head. "It's just foolishness," she said despairingly. "All of it. I'm not going to go gallivanting around the country when I've got a fine home right here, and a husband who loves me."

"What about Lily and Caroline?" Steven pressed softly.

Emma bit her lower lip for a long moment, the picture of utter misery, before answering. "They're probably perfectly happy without an interfering sister to complicate their lives—if they're alive at all."

Steven gave her a look of gentle sternness. "Emma—"

She shook her head again. "It's over. I'm giving up."

"You're just saying that because you're pregnant and your emotions are pulling you every which way. We'll talk about this again after the baby's born."

Emma wiped away her tears with the back of one hand. "I love you," she whispered.

Steven smiled and started to rise from the mattress, his hand still clasping hers. But she resisted, and he looked back at her in surprise. "What—"

Her lips trembled, but she didn't speak. It was her eyes that told him what she wanted, and he was only too happy to accommodate her.

The first letter from Lucy was like a message sent from boarding school by a homesick child. She didn't like the ocean, or the fog, or the sunshine that burned it away at midday. She wanted to come back to Fairhaven.

Macon scoffed at her letters and said she should have been sent to perdition for all the trouble she'd caused. He packed six trunks full of clothes and other mementoes and left for Europe on the tenth of August, without so much as troubling to drop his wife a note.

Steven and Cyrus were too busy reorganizing the family holdings for such sentimental pursuits as writing letters, and Nathaniel was courting a girl over in St. Charles parish, so he was away most of the time. Thus the task of keeping up a correspondence with Lucy fell to Emma, who derived some comfort from sharing the love she might have given to her sisters.

She composed long discourses, telling Lucy everything that was going on—except, of course, for describing Macon's uncharitable attitude or saying that she was going to have a baby. She wrote about Steven and Cyrus and Nathaniel, and about the servants and the neighbors. She recounted gossip painstakingly, and copied down lines of poetry and occasional Bible verses meant to shore up Lucy's courage.

In November, when Emma was big with child and Steven had business to conduct in San Francisco, she accompanied him and went to visit Lucy at Crawford Hospital.

It was a lovely, quiet place overlooking the stormy gray sea, and Emma found Lucy sitting in a solarium with a view of the shore, her small hands moving over the keys of a grand piano. She played beautifully, and Emma stood listening with a mixture of sadness and joy. She was eager to see Lucy, but a little afraid her obvious pregnancy might upset the woman. After all, Lucy had wanted a baby of her own more than anything else in the world.

"Lucy?"

The trim woman stiffened on the piano bench, then turned to look up with a curious, childlike expression in her eyes. She was wearing a soft ivory blouse and a sateen skirt of a cheery blue, and her brown eyes widened with delight. "Emma!" she burst out, standing up to clasp both her sister-in-law's hands in her own.

The two women embraced—an awkward proposition, considering Emma's large protruding stomach.

Lucy looked down at her in questioning amazement. "Oh, Emma," she whispered, raising her eyes to her sister-in-law's face. "When?"

"January, the doctor thinks," Emma answered softly.

A wide smile spread across Lucy's face even as her doe-like eyes filled with tears. "That's wonderful," she said, and they embraced again.

"I've brought you some books and some new sheet music, and Jubal sent along some of her pecan fudge," Emma told Lucy as they walked arm in arm along the hallway. "It's all waiting for you in your room."

"Where's Steven?" Lucy asked, looking and sounding almost normal.

"He's in the city, tending to business," Emma answered gently, "but he's promised to take us both out for dinner tonight. If you want to go, that is."

They entered the suite of rooms where Lucy stayed, and she immediately opened the box containing Jubal's fudge and helped herself to a piece with a child's mischievous relish. "Would you like one?" she asked, extending the candy to Emma, who ruefully shook her head.

"My waistline is expanding rapidly enough as it is," she protested.

"How is Macon?" Lucy asked, and her voice was eager, as if she'd been in accord with her husband all her married life.

"He's fine," Emma responded evasively. "Busy as always."

Lucy and Emma visited until Steven came to collect them at four o'clock, and they all rode into the city in an elegant carriage. Lucy talked delightedly the whole way there and throughout dinner, and it wasn't until they'd returned to the hospital that she took Steven's hand and said, "Please, Steven—can't I come home?"

Emma appreciated his gentleness as he touched Lucy's cheek and said softly, "Not yet, love. You're not ready for Fairhaven. But we'll come to visit you as often as we can, I promise."

Lucy seemed to be mollified by that, and it came to Emma that, within a few hours, Macon's fragile little wife might not even remember that they'd been to see her. "I'm sorry," she said as Steven and Emma were about to leave. "I know you suffered because of what I did."

Steven kissed Lucy's forehead. "All that is over now," he assured her. "You just concentrate on getting well."

Lucy nodded—maybe even then she knew her situation was hopeless—and there were tears in her eyes when her company finally left her standing in the solarium, beside her piano.

The first legitimate baby to be born in Steven's immediate family in over forty years decided to arrive on a rainy night in January, when the roads were thick with Louisiana mud.

Emma awakened Steven rudely by arching her back and letting out a howl of startled discomfort. He sat bolt upright in bed, shoved one hand through his hair in agitation, and babbled that he was willing to pay five thousand dollars for the piece of land he wanted, and not a cent more.

In spite of her pain, Emma laughed at his incoherency. "I'm in labor, Mr. Fairfax," she told him, as her stomach contorted visibly beneath her nightgown and her face twisted in a grimace. "You'd better get the doctor, fast."

Fully awake now, Steven clambered out of bed, shouting for Cyrus and Nathaniel.

They both appeared posthaste, clad in flannel nightshirts that would have started Emma into laughing again if she hadn't been in so much pain. Steven didn't recall that he was naked until after he'd dispatched Nathaniel to fetch Dr. Mayfield and Cyrus to bring Jubal from the servants' quarters. And when he did, he didn't give a damn.

He struggled into his clothes, swearing under his breath the whole time.

Emma let out a peal of amusement that somehow

transformed itself into a loud moan. Her belly rose up as though it were being pinched between two giant, invisible fingers, and she felt a rush of water between her legs.

"Is it supposed to happen this fast?" she asked Steven, panting out the words in the wake of another hard contraction.

"How the hell should I know?" Steven barked, stumbling around in the darkness until he managed to strike his shin against the chest at the foot of the bed. When that happened he bellowed another curse and demanded, "Where the devil is the doctor?"

"He lives five miles away," Emma reasoned. "Calm down, Mr. Fairfax. Having a baby is a perfectly normal—" At that moment another pain seized her, wringing out a squeaky scream.

Jubal rushed in then, carrying a lamp and shooing Steven aside with impatient motions of one hand. "Get me some clean sheets, Mr. Steven," she ordered. "Right now."

While Steven rushed off on this errand—Emma would have bet he had no idea where the linen closet was— Jubal lighted all the lamps in the room and lifted her mistress's nightgown for a brief examination.

The black woman indulged in a long, low whistle. "This one's mighty anxious to get here," she said, just as one of her helpers rushed in with hot water.

Jubal used the water to wash her hands up to the elbows, then helped a writhing Emma out of bed and into a nearby rocking chair. While Jubal waited for Steven, the other woman stripped down the bed and spread several old blankets over the mattress.

When Steven returned with the sheets, the bed was quickly made up again and he was told in no uncertain terms to stay out of the way.

Jubal and her friend put Emma back on the bed and propped pillows behind her. "You squeeze on my hands," Jubal ordered when Emma shrieked with pain. "You squeeze real hard, so's to push the bones together."

"I never seen one come so fast," prattled Esther, who generally tended the kitchen.

"Oh, God," Steven fretted, pacing at the foot of the bed.

Emma felt another contraction closing in on her and clasped Jubal's hands hard, determined not to scream again.

"She's gonna tear," Esther warned.

At this point, there was a *ker-thump* and Emma decided Steven had probably fainted, though she had neither the time nor the inclination to find out.

After that everything was a blur for Emma. She remembered little beyond blinding pain, hazy, shifting faces, and finally, relief and the furious squall of an infant.

"My baby," she whispered, lying back. "My baby's here."

"It's a fine girl," Dr. Mayfield said. When had he arrived? Emma decided she didn't care, and smiled wearily.

"Steven?"

"He's not feeling too well right now," the doctor explained. "Crumpled to the floor when I had to cut you."

Emma laughed. Steven the outlaw, with his dreaded Colt .45. She'd never let him forget the occasion of his first child's birth. "Let me see her," she said.

The infant lay squirming on Emma's sweat-soaked stomach, her tiny body covered with blood and a powdery substance, her arms and legs waving wildly in the air, her cries furious and indignant.

"Don't worry," she said, wriggling an impossibly tiny toe. "Your daddy will protect you with his forty-five."

"Very funny," said a weary voice at her side, as Steven sat on the edge of the bed, his face ghastly pale in the first light of a rainy dawn. "What's her name?" he asked presently, looking down at his daughter. "Lily or Caroline?"

"Both," Emma answered, and five days later Lily Caroline Fairfax was formally christened and a party was held in her honor.

As January passed into February, Emma thought constantly of her sisters. On the fourteenth a letter arrived from Big John Lenahan, back in Whitneyville. He enclosed a blue envelope addressed to Marshal Woodridge, saying Manuela had found it in Joellen's room. He apologized for his daughter's actions and said he'd have sent the message on sooner, but the housekeeper had found it only a few days before. He offered his own regards, as well as Chloe's, and signed off.

Her heart beating fast, her hands trembling, Emma lifted the flap of the blue envelope. She was sitting in the sumptuous master suite that now belonged to her and Steven, their daughter sleeping peacefully in a cradle at her feet.

She pulled out a single page and unfolded it. *Dear Marshal,* the missive began, in a hand she knew was Lily's even before she looked at the signature. It went on to tell how she was searching for her sisters, Miss Emma and Miss Caroline Chalmers.

Tears were slipping down Emma's face as she kissed the paper, then lowered it to her lap. Lily. She'd been living in Spokane when she wrote the letter—Spokane! Emma had been there, in that very community, and never known her sister was near.

Steven came in an hour later and found Emma nursing his daughter and rereading the letter for perhaps the twentieth time.

"Lily," she said, holding out the paper to indicate that she was talking about her sister, not their infant daughter. "Steven, I've found her. She lives—or lived—in Spokane. She mentions a man named Rupert Sommers."

Smiling gently, Steven kissed Emma's mouth, then the rounding of her bare breast, then the downy top of his daughter's head. "I'll send a wire right away," he said, and left the room again.

When the baby was satisfied and sleeping again, Emma

paced the sitting room, waiting. Through the windows she saw Steven returning, and from the set of his shoulders, she knew there wasn't any news.

"We'll have to wait for a response, Emma," he told her gently, holding her close to reassure her.

"I can't bear to wait," she whispered, but Steven sat down in the very chair where she'd fed little Lily, and pulled Emma after him, settling her on his lap.

"Neither can I," he answered, his fingers nimble as he opened the bodice she'd just closed. "Is it time yet?"

Emma chuckled warmly, for even in her most stressful moments she could find comfort in Steven's lovemaking. "It's time," she replied, and closed her eyes in ecstasy when he took her nipple into his mouth, sucking the breast their child had just nursed from.

The first few days in Chicago exhausted, as well as disappointed, Emma. The old neighborhood where she had lived with Kathleen and her sisters was gone, replaced by smart brick townhouses, and attempts to find her mother's attorney failed.

She took to going around to Kathleen's fancy house—now all closed up—and ringing the bell. There was never any answer, but Emma persisted. Together she and Steven called on all the neighbors, too. They either refused to answer the bell entirely or else made it clear that they hadn't known Kathleen.

One day, when Steven was meeting with some potential business associates, Emma left baby Lily with her Scottish nanny and took a carriage to Kathleen's house. She couldn't have explained the compelling instinct that urged her to go, nor could she have resisted it.

Reaching the house, she once again rang the bell. This time a charwoman answered, her hair tied back in a wispy bun, her dress of shabby calico. "Yes?" she said.

"My name is Emma Fairfax," Emma said quickly, almost overcome at finally finding someone there. "Kathleen Harrington was my mother."

The charwoman nodded, assessing Emma's face and

371

now-trim figure. "The redhaired one," she said. "Well, you might as well come in," she added after a moment. "There isn't much to see since Mr. Harrington's family came and collected most all of it, but you're welcome to look around."

Emma stepped inside. "Can you tell me about Mrs. Harrington?" she asked eagerly. "Did she leave any letters or papers?"

"Like I said," replied the housemaid, "the Harringtons took most everything, 'cepting the piano. I can't tell you anything about her except that she surely did want to find you and make up for everything."

Emma wandered into the parlor and sat down at the piano, her eyes burning with unshed tears. She ran her fingers over the keys, awkwardly at first, then with more finesse as a familiar tune came back to her.

She began to sing.

> *Three flowers bloomed in the meadow,*
> *Heads bent in sweet repose,*
> *The daisy, the lily, and the rose . . .*

The words had barely left her mouth when a cold draft filled the room and Emma's heart caught on a sound, or a feeling, she couldn't be certain which.

She looked up and saw that a lovely woman with fair hair and enormous brown eyes was standing in the parlor doorway, staring at her as though stricken.

Emma's fingers froze on the keys. "Lily," she whispered.

# Fantasy.
# Temptation.
# Adventure.

## Visit PocketAfterDark.com, an all-new website just for Urban Fantasy and Romance Readers!

- Exclusive access to the hottest urban fantasy and romance titles!

- Read and share reviews on the latest books!

- Live chats with your favorite romance authors!

- Vote in online polls!

 www.PocketAfterDark.com

26119